ORCAS
AFTERLIFE

Books by Laura Gayle

The Chameleon Chronicles:
Orcas Intrigue
Orcas Intruder
Orcas Investigation
Orcas Illusion
Orcas Intermission

Tales from the Berry Farm:
Orcas Afterlife

ORCAS AFTERLIFE

Book 1
Tales from the Berry Farm

Laura Gayle

BOOK VIEW CAFE

Orcas Afterlife, by Laura Gayle

Copyright © 2024 by Shannon Page and Mark J. Ferrari

All rights reserved. Any reproduction or distribution of this book, in part or in whole, or transmission in any form, or by any means, electronic, mechanical, photocopying, recording or otherwise, without the written permission of the publisher or authors, is theft.

Any similarity to persons living or dead is purely coincidental.

Cover art and design: Covers by Christian
Interior design by Shannon Page

First Edition

ISBN: 978-1-63632-208-7

www.bookviewcafe.com

*To all the staff at Darvill's Bookstore
who have done so much to support and inspire us.
Thank you for being so excited about Cam's continuing story!*

CHAPTER 1

"Well, I'm off." Jen stood in the bright entryway of Lisa Cannon's house, purse over her shoulder, puffy jacket stuffed under her other arm. "Need anything from town?"

"I can't think what," I said. "We're all done here, and the new place is completely ready."

"More cream? Cat food? Another bag of Brussels sprouts?"

"Jen, there isn't room left for an extra radish in that kitchen."

"What about this one?" She glanced mournfully over at Lisa's huge fridge.

I gave her a sympathetic smile. Losing this five-star kitchen was a lot more painful for a foodie like Jen than it was for a chili-and-cheese fiend like me. "Are you kidding? We've stocked a week's worth of meals in her freezer, and pretty much spring-loaded the pantry. Are you afraid that prison's turned Lisa into a binge eater or something?"

That got a snort of amusement from her, at least. Then her face fell. "Coffee! We've left her hardly any coffee!"

"*Jen*," I said. "We're done. Really. Just go; you'll be late."

"Okay," she said, too fast. "It's just…"

"I know," I said gently. "But we're going to love it there too, you'll see." Then I had a thought. "Actually, there *is* something. Since it's the first night in our new place, maybe pick up a bottle of something festive? Champagne, prosecco?"

Her eyes lit up, and I knew I'd made the right call. Jen Darling needed to feel useful, to feel—well, *needed*. And there was nothing more squarely in her skill set than bartending, though I wasn't going to blame her if she'd gotten a little rusty after three years of pandemic shutdown. "I've just got time to grab it on my way! See you at bubbly o'clock!" Then she breezed out the door.

The Covid-19 pandemic had hit Jen a lot harder than it had me. Very little about my life had changed. Whether styling hair, caretaking estates, or writing plays, I'd always been more of a solo act than she was. But inns, restaurants, bars—nearly every place Jen had worked back then—had all closed overnight, leaving the queen of so many things around Orcas very little left to rule. She'd even lost her dog walking jobs, as all her wealthy clients started working from home, with lots of time to take their own pets walking on the island's gravelly beaches as they reassessed their lives.

That was when she'd moved in here with me. That had been great for both of us in many ways, though if there was one thing Jen liked less than having nowhere to be indispensable, it was feeling dependent. She'd made herself extremely useful, bringing her years of skill and knowledge at hospitality work to everything from our cooking, to household maintenance, to last year's big remodel of the guesthouse we'd be moving into tonight. But no matter how we'd both ignored the fact, I was basically her landlord, still doing my pre-pandemic job, and not needing much more from Jen than her company.

The one job she hadn't lost was her least favorite: the package delivery gig. Her hours there had actually increased as shopping online had become everybody's mainstay. But delivering heavy packages to empty porches all day long was not a great fit for an extrovert like Jen, and with the world finally moving on, she was hoping for some more gratifying work again. Her new job at Darvill's Bookstore was just ten hours a week. But Jen had her fingers crossed that they'd want more hours from her soon.

I finished my coffee and took the cup back up to the kitchen, where morning light slanted across the marble countertops from the giant dining room windows. Though Lisa wasn't actually expected back for two more weeks, Jen and I had decided to move out now so that our transition would be done before Lisa needed our help with hers. And as I rinsed the cup out and stuck it in the bespoke dishwasher, I wondered—not for the first time—how much I was actually going to miss living in her luxurious house overlooking Massacre Bay. While I'd sure enjoyed the past three years here, this had never been anyone's home but Lisa's—and her long-delayed return to it made me anything but sad. Not only would I soon have one of my most treasured friends and mentors back, but with her here I too would finally have meaningful work again.

Lisa had only hired me as her personal assistant a few months before her arrest, and our pre-pandemic plan had been to have me manage her estate here on the island, and run her theater company, Orcas Island Rep, while she was away. But I'd brought precisely two plays to the stage before the shutdown, both of them staid little antique comedies because, even after *Salon Confidential*'s success, I was still leery of trying anything too avant-garde. To my relief, they'd both been well received by the island's distraction-starved community. But after that, with public theater closed and my employer off in prison, there'd been very little work to justify my cushy pay. And then, after serving her eleven-month sentence at Alderson Federal Prison Camp in West Virginia, for trying to cover up a murder committed by an unhinged former employee, the warden had asked her to stay on there for a while longer—as a staff member! Because Lisa was just the kind of person who excelled at everything, even jail time.

As she'd come to see how many of her fellow inmates had also been thrust into trouble by the men they worked for or were married to, and how rarely their own wealth or business success had translated into confidence, security, or self-possession, not even an orange jumpsuit had dented Lisa's commitment to mentoring women who needed a hand up. She'd gotten permission to start a prison drama group that wrote and performed theatrical productions to help them and their captive audiences reimagine their own capability and power.

The program had turned out to be so helpful that after her release, the warden had begged her to stay and keep it going until they found someone to replace her. By then, travel had been nearly shut down anyway, and I'd been here to hold down the fort. But no one had imagined it would take *two years* to find someone who was really equipped for the job, and wanted it. As they say, no good deed goes unpunished.

At Lisa's request, Jen and I had spent the past year overseeing a thorough remodel of the guesthouse. Fortunately, Jen knew a lot about dealing with San Juan County's elusive contractors and amazingly dysfunctional permitting departments—which had made her queen of something again, to both her relief and mine. But navigating such a complex and chaotic project had also been a valuable education for me.

Ironically, our new residence had once been occupied by Sheila Bukowski, Lisa's murderous former head of security, and my former kidnapper. So the remodel had also been a great chance to clean any traces of her mojo from the place. I still had mixed feelings about Sheila as a person—and about the tragedy of her own life story. But knowing she would be safely locked up far away for many, many years sure made it easier for me to sleep at night.

What didn't make my sleep easier was the play I was supposed to have finished writing years ago. Somewhere between Lisa's arrest and the pandemic's arrival, I'd fallen into a bout of writer's block for the record books, and I was willing to bet that Lisa's first question when she got back would be, "How's that play coming, Cam?"

Well, as I'd just told Jen, there was nothing left to do in preparation for tonight's big move, so…maybe I should spend these next two weeks down at my lovely little writing studio doing something about that.

I pulled on my jacket and slipped into my boots, calling to James as I headed for the front door. "Want to come help me find my muse, little man?"

My orange tabby cat blinked over at me from his cushion in the living room where he'd expertly arranged himself to absorb the maximum amount of sunlight from those expansive bay windows. The look he gave me was easy enough to interpret. *You woke me up to ask…what?* He yawned, stretched, and turned his fuzzy belly to the sun before closing his eyes again.

"Lazy bones," I grumbled as I stepped outside—though I wasn't all that sure which of us I was really talking to as I headed off.

After moving into Lisa's house, the old A-frame cottage perched on its cliff top over the bay had become my de facto office, writing retreat, and love nest. My cheeks warmed with the memory of Kip's last visit.

I was every bit as gaga over him as I'd been nearly four years ago when we'd first gotten together. Sadly, he wasn't on the island very often these days. After quitting his job as a sheriff's deputy, Kip had decided to get a graduate degree in social work, wanting to come back and help people in these islands out of trouble instead of just getting them deeper into it.

I'd thought that was a fabulous plan back during the pandemic when all his classes had been on the internet. But with the shutdown over, Kip was now required to be on campus, all the way down in Portland, Oregon. We talked every night by phone, and he came back home as often as he could, but that was never even close to long or often enough for either of us. I was getting more and more impatient for the day when we would finally be free to move forward to wherever we were going. I had dreams, of course—including marriage, maybe even children—but I tried not to think too hard about the future. Life had already taught me plenty about the folly of thinking you can know what's really going to happen.

THE DAY WAS GETTING MORE beautiful by the hour. I moseyed down to the A-frame smiling at the blooming crocus flowers and daffodils along the trail, and running my fingers through the soft, bright green needles tipping every fir bough. It was so tempting to just go for a long, healthy hike instead. *Stop and smell the flowers;* wasn't that what everybody always said?

But I'd been finding "better things" to do for months now—every time I even thought about the play. By now I felt kind of lucky, in a guilty way, that theaters had been closed down all this time. It helped hide my complete failure to come up with the new play Seattle's Emerald City Repertory had commissioned from me on *Salon Confidential*'s opening night. Now theaters were reopening, and I was still flailing through my third attempt at a halfway decent script. I needed to get past this wall of writer's block! I drew a deep breath, closed my eyes, and stretched my arms out in the warm air, inviting inspiration to come find me at last on this gorgeous morning.

A minute later, the A-frame came into view, and my cheerful optimism took a hit. There was a whole pile of giant white plastic bags mounded up against its door—and I knew way too well what was in them. "Oh, Paige, now?" I groaned. "Seriously?" I climbed the porch steps with a sigh and pulled the nearest bag open. Mounds of kale, of course. She'd been gifting me with these deliveries since before the day we'd met. As much as Master Bun, my rabbit, as well as Jen and I loved all that fresh produce—especially since Jen bought an air fryer—these surprises could still be inconvenient.

And *five bags* was easily the biggest load Paige had ever brought me. What had she supposed I would even do with it all—open a produce market? I couldn't even imagine how she'd gotten them all down here. Paige eschewed driving, preferring to walk nearly everywhere she went, all the way from her house high above Massacre Bay. But I could not believe that even a robust old woman like her had carried this much down here. With all our preparations for the move, I hadn't even come to the A-frame for, well, at least a week or two. Had she done this in several trips maybe? But why go on leaving bags of perishable produce when I clearly hadn't found the ones before?

I looked into a second bag and winced at all the muddy, giant bunches of beets inside. Everything still seemed fairly fresh, at least. But where had she thought I'd even put it? She knew how tiny the studio's fridge was.

Well, I had come here to *write*, damn it, not to be waylaid by some truckload of unsolicited vegetables. They'd keep fine outside for a few more hours. I just hauled the bags to one side of the doorway and went inside to get serious about my dang play.

I opened some windows to let a bit of air in, then set up my computer on the cabin's little dining table and put the kettle on for tea. Tea would calm me down. Get me focused. When that was underway, I came back to the laptop and opened the most recent file of my latest failure at a play. According to the time-stamp, it had last been saved in…*February.*

I rolled my eyes, and went back to check the kettle. What business did I have calling *James* a lazy bones?

My first try had been a romantic murder mystery. I'd felt a little tired of comedy after churning out *Salon Confidential*, and given everything I'd just been through, romance and murder had seemed like pretty low-hanging fruit.

But I'd also been warned about avoiding the attention of whoever we'd all just helped send to prison—besides Lisa, that is. I mean the *big fish* that JoJo Brixton and Sheriff Clarke and even FBI Agent Veierra had kept refusing to tell me anything about. And staging a play about the whole thing, at a prominent theater in Seattle, hadn't seemed like a very good way to stay low-profile. So I'd kept trying to make everything different enough from what had actually happened to be "safe," whatever that might mean.

Of course, nothing I invented seemed half as interesting as the real story, and I'd finally just given up and tried to write a romance with no crime in it at all. Sadly, even that idea didn't work. I'd just kept writing scenes that turned out to be about Kip, and I was so absolutely not going to make that mistake a second time.

Then I came up with a brilliantly creative new approach: I would invent the most interesting *character* I could imagine, and see if journaling as that person could inspire some plot that had less to do with my own real life. But guess what? I just kept channeling JoJo—which got me thinking about him missing in action out there somewhere—which just made me too sad to go on writing anything at all. I hadn't heard a single word from him since he'd left to go find himself. Where had he spent the pandemic? Was he okay? Was he even alive? Had he thought about *me* the way I did about him even once in all this time?

Anyway, *that* meltdown had apparently been in February, and now it was nearly May. I had two weeks before Lisa stepped off the ferry and asked how Emerald City was liking my new play…

Suddenly, I couldn't think of anything more callous or ungrateful than letting all those fresh, heavy winter vegetables Paige had carried down here on her ninety-year-old back just rot out in the sunshine on my porch. I slapped my laptop shut and went out to deal with them.

The other three bags were stuffed with spinach, radishes and turnips, as if she'd packed up her whole winter garden. I dragged all the leafy greens inside first, and loaded the spinach into the fridge. That filled both of the little crisper drawers so, before tackling the kale, I cleaned out everything else that didn't really need refrigeration: eggs, mustard, ketchup, bread, tortillas—some of which needed tossing by now anyway. Then I started packing kale onto the lower shelves. That seemed a bit rubbery, which made me wonder how long ago Paige had left these things, and why she hadn't come to the main house to let me know. Or just to say hi, at least.

I was almost to the bottom of the bag when I found an envelope jammed in among the crushed, tattered leaves. Some piece of junk mail that fell in while she was shoveling kale?

But as I pulled it out, I saw *Ms. Camille Tate* on the front in Paige's unmistakable handwriting.

CHAPTER 2

Camille? Paige had never called me anything but Cam. Nor did she write me letters. And why on earth had she left it at the bottom of a giant bag of kale? That seemed bizarre, even for her. What if I'd just thrown the whole thing out?

I slid my fingers under the seal and drew out a thick, folded sheet of expensive-looking paper with quite a lot of writing on it. *My dear Camille.* There she went again. *I must apologize for leaving you so much produce all at once, but I shall be traveling soon, and I just couldn't bear to see any of it go to waste.* My mouth fell open. Traveling? *I'm sure you'll have no trouble finding lots of friends to share it with—along with that deserving little rabbit of yours, of course.* I grimaced. So, she knew? Of course she did.

For some time now, I've been feeling a kind of wanderlust I've not known since I was your age, and can resist its pull no longer. I'm actually quite excited by the prospect of a lengthy journey into unfamiliar territory. That's always been my favorite kind, and I've been gathering such an excellent collection of useful maps for so long now. But plans and maps are no substitute for going there oneself, are they? I'm sure you know what I mean—or will in time. We have much in common, do we not?

I hope you'll excuse me for requesting an even larger favor before leaving. It would please me greatly if you would be kind enough to look after my estate and its residents in my absence.

Despite my growing confusion and concern, I had to grin at this. Her rambling acreage with its huge cluttered house and grounds, outbuildings, animals, and of course gardens, was certainly large and, um, *interesting*, but it was no estate—not by any normal definition of the word. She'd just always liked calling it that.

They are all dear to me, and you have such a way with the animals. You are even coming along with plants, I believe. But it won't take my touch to keep them happy anyway. You have your own touch, dear girl, which should be more than sufficient.

Growing to know you these past few years has been so much more than delightful. You have been a great gift to many people here, but more to me than most, I think. It has been so very satisfying to find someone here, after so many years, with whom I can talk so freely about everything. *You are a treasure, my girl. Do not ever forget it.*

The garlic in the second greenhouse could use thinning in the next few weeks. Clara should be ready to start weaning Nick and Nora in five or six weeks—she, or they, might need some convincing on this issue. Nick will need banding sooner than that; Laurie at Lum Farm can help you manage it. I don't expect I'll get a chance before leaving to rotate the canned peaches in the cold storage; last year's batch is still in front of the previous year's. I was just never down there without my hands full of something else. And Morgan spends most of his days by the fire now, even as the weather improves—when I can coax him inside off the porch at all, that is. I fear he is not long for this plane. But he could have no finer company while I am gone than I know you will be.

Be well, my dear Camille. Remember to let your gifts use you, not the other way around, and know that you have my full confidence, appreciation, and love. I look forward to hearing about all of your adventures someday, and telling you of mine. Until then, thank you for everything.

Your devoted friend, Paige

For a minute, I just stood staring at the letter. I wasn't really sure how old Paige was. She'd never said exactly. But she'd told me she'd come to Orcas in the fifties, so she had to be nearing ninety at the very least. Yes, it was amazing that such an old woman could carry five giant bags of vegetables to my studio; but...running off on some long trip to "unfamiliar territory?" Without any warning? That might be okay for troubled youth like JoJo Brixton. But it didn't sound even a little realistic, or even safe, for a ninety-year-old gardener.

I didn't even want to think it, but...could her aging mind finally be going?

The only thing I knew for sure was that I'd better get up to that *estate* of hers right now and find out what was going on. I shoved her letter into my back pocket, made sure the kettle was off, grabbed my coat, and left my laptop where it was as I headed out the door and almost ran Jen over on the porch.

"There you are," Jen said softly.

"Jen! Why aren't you at work?"

"Cam, I have some… Has anyone told you yet…about Paige?"

Oh no. I'd been right. "I just got a letter from her." I pulled it out. "It was in a bag of kale she left here. It's…pretty weird."

Jen just looked at me, her face revealing nothing.

"Has she done something, um, stranger than usual?" I asked. Underneath her oddness, Paige had always been a very dignified person. I hoped dementia hadn't robbed her of that dignity.

"Oh, hon…" Jen said. "I'm so sorry."

Things went very still inside me. "Sorry…about what?" But Jen's tone and expression had already told me. My hands flew up to my mouth, crumpling the letter as I tried to hold back the sob swelling up.

Jen stepped in to wrap her arms around me. "Porter found her this morning," she murmured against my neck. "Dressed up in one of her frilly shawl things. He says she was lying peacefully underneath that big maple just off her front porch. He just came to tell us—at the bookstore."

"She *knew!*" I wept. "She left that letter to…to tell me…" I couldn't even bring myself to say the word *goodbye*. "She was right here! On this porch! Why didn't she come find me? I could have…I should at least have had a chance to—"

"Let's go inside, okay?" Jen found my hands and pulled me gently toward the door. "I'll make us some tea. Then we can talk about it—or not. Whatever you need, I'm here."

༄

You don't really understand how much a person means to you—until suddenly you do. I was learning that now. About Paige, and about Jen too.

In the years since Paige had helped me accept my ability to chameleon—to vanish when I feel frightened or threatened—she and I had grown very close. The pandemic hadn't stopped her from coming by with her bags of garden treasure, or sachets of homemade herbal tea, or smelly salves she swore would heal everything from bruises to "the croup," as she called any kind of cold or flu. She and Jen and Kip had been my pandemic pod, and as she had said in that letter, there'd been nothing she and I couldn't talk about.

I'd never had that freedom with any other friend. Not even Jen—at least, not about my deepest secrets. Telling people who've been taught all their lives that things like my gift don't, and can't, exist is not like telling them you've had an affair, or you're an addict, or that you've lied to them about your age. It's telling them you're crazy, and can't be trusted to *know* the truth, let alone tell it—as I'd learned the night I'd stupidly tried telling my *very* ex-boyfriend, Kevin. With Paige alone, there'd been no need to worry about any of that.

Paige had never treated anyone as if they might be too fragile to handle. So there'd never been any worry about upsetting or offending her either. She'd just been a force of nature who meant *almost* everybody well, which may have been why her many friends might roll their eyes sometimes, but always loved her back. I won't say she had become a second mother to me. I'd gotten all I could have wished for in that department from my own adoptive mom. But Paige had been midwife to my birth into self-acceptance, and helped me come to terms with the strange "gift" I had been running so hard from before she turned me gently back to face it. She'd helped me learn how to control it and, in time, to set it down. I didn't vanish anymore. I didn't need to.

And even though she'd never done a thing to hide her age, I'd let her fierce presence and bottomless energy convince me she'd just go on being there forever—like the forest or the sky.

Until now.

And Jen?

I had looked up to her back when we'd first met. She'd seemed like all the things I couldn't imagine myself ever becoming: outgoing, confident, fearless. Her unexpected friendship had done as much as anything to help me to fit in here and start becoming who I really was. As I got to know her better, she was still everything she'd first seemed to me, but I also began to see how comically over-dramatic or pushy she could be as well, and that she could feel anxious about approval and recognition from others—even me. After the pandemic took most of her jobs, I'd realized that even the amazingly capable and confident Jen Darling was human after all.

But now I was discovering that maybe I still hadn't taken my closest friend as seriously as she deserved. I'd never guessed until that afternoon how much care, strength, and wisdom she kept hidden behind all that melodrama. I'd have come totally apart if she hadn't known exactly how to give me all the space for grief I needed while holding me firmly together too. I hadn't met this Jen before. I had never needed to.

I didn't go on crying for long after she got us settled back inside the studio. I didn't drink the tea she made me either. My stomach was in no mood for even that. But the warm mug felt comforting between my hands. Jen didn't fill the air with talk, except to ask if I'd like her to make us a fire, or fetch a blanket, or go get James or Master Bun from the main house. Beyond that, she just sat beside me, sipping her tea, gazing through the A-frame's wall of windows. Accompanying me.

I'd gone blank inside by then, my mind trying to absorb the news—and trying not to.

"How did Porter happen to find her?" I finally asked.

"He got a letter from her too."

My face went slack. "When?" How had she... "What did it say?"

"He didn't tell us. He just said that it worried him enough to go check on her." She paused, looking back at me curiously, and I knew she was wondering about my letter. But even if Paige hadn't referred so openly to our gifts, that still felt too painful. "He came looking for me at the store as soon as the deputies were done with him, and asked if I wanted to come tell you, or if he should."

"Thank you," I said, "for doing that."

"What else would I have done?"

Run away? I thought. Let Porter do it, and sneak back to see how I was doing later when the difficult part was over? Lots of other people would have. But not Jen.

I hoped that I'd have been that brave if it had been the other way around.

But, if Paige had written Porter a letter too... "Was she sick?" I asked, still not able to ask the real question. "And just not telling anyone?"

"I don't know. He didn't say. He was...still pretty upset too."

Of course he was.

"Porter did say he might come by to see you later," Jen added. "When you'd had some time."

I wanted that. Talking with him might help as much as anything could right now. "Did he say when?"

"No. I didn't think to ask. Sorry, hon."

"It's fine. But maybe we should go back to the house, then. I don't want him having to come look for me like you did."

"Sounds like a good idea." Jen got up and stretched a hand down to help me up.

※

As we entered Lisa's house, James strolled up to rub his cheek against my legs, and purred as I reached down to pick him up. "Finally finished napping, lazy bones?" I asked him. "That must mean you're hungry, huh?" But when I went to look, his bowl still had food in it, so I carried him to the living room couch, scritching his ears as Jen and I sat down with him on my lap. He lay there kneading my legs through my jeans. Was he aware that something was amiss?

James had loved Paige. He'd leap right onto her lap whenever she visited. The thought made my eyes well up again. Would he wonder where she'd gone?

"Do you want to just stay here after all tonight?" I asked Jen, suddenly realizing I didn't want our first night in the new house tied forever to…all of this.

She looked relieved. "That's a great idea. We'll have one of those frozen dinners we left for Lisa, so we won't even need to cook or clean up."

"You're so smart."

"You're right, though," she said. "This is no time to do anything but take care of yourself."

I nodded, grateful for her understanding. "I need to call Kip."

"Of course you do. Want some privacy?"

"No," I said, pulling out my phone. "I just didn't want to be…rude, I guess."

"You don't need to worry about me right now either, hon."

"Thanks." I made the call, but it just rang and rang before going to voicemail. I hate talking to voicemail even at the best of times, so I just hung up and texted him: *Hi, love. Call me when you get this, okay?* Jen gave me a sympathetic look as I closed the phone and shoved it back into my pocket. "I'll bet he forgot to turn his sound back on after class again," I told her. "I wish he weren't all the way down there."

She nodded, reaching over to take my hand, and we just sat listening to James breathe until Jen let out a little chuckle.

"What is it?" I asked.

"Oh…I'm just remembering how Paige carried on about those intermission snacks at your play. Kale and macadamia nut cookies, remember? The island owes you big time for talking her out of that one."

That made me think of my very first encounter with Paige, back at the Brixtons' caretaker cottage. I hadn't told a lot of people about the "investigation" Paige had gotten me tangled up in that day. That whole thing still touched too many secrets—for all of us. But I saw no reason now not to tell Jen about that first bizarre conversation, when a raggedy old woman had shown up at my kitchen door one night with a giant jar of homemade pickles and an hour-long tirade about old garden club scandals.

"I think we should have a drink," Jen said, when I was done. "The prosecco's in my truck, but this doesn't feel like that kind of occasion anymore."

"No." I dredged up a smile for her.

She started to get up as a quiet knock came at the front door. Jen walked over to answer it; I heard Porter Wendergrast ask her if he'd come too soon.

"No, you're right on time," I called out, getting up to join them as he came inside, a bottle of wine in each hand, and looking doleful.

"Oh, Porter. I'm so sorry." I wrapped the old man in a hug as he handed his bottles to Jen, who took them off into the kitchen. "Jen says it was you who found her?"

He hugged me harder as we both started dripping tears onto each other's shoulders. "I can't believe she's gone," he quavered. "I always thought she'd be the last of us to go."

"I know," was all I could think to say.

"Verna sends her love," he told me as we finally let each other go. "We thought it might be best if I came alone for now. Didn't want to flood you with company before you were ready."

"I'm starting to get better now." I squeezed his hand. "How are you guys doing?"

He shrugged and looked away. "I…have had better days." He struggled again for composure, then said, "You're one of the only people I could ever say this to. But…I can't stop thinking about how…how satisfied I'd have felt once to hear she'd died." His face scrunched up again, and more tears came. "She and I have been closer these past few years than we ever were. And that's all thanks to you, Cam. I'm so very grateful to you. More today than ever. So was Paige. She told me so, many times. She thought the world of you, you know. So do I and Verna."

Now I was struggling not to cry again.

"Would you like to come sit down, Porter?" Jen asked, reappearing just in time.

He nodded. "Should we open one of those bottles?" he asked, wiping at his eyes as we negotiated the three steps down through a blur of tears. "I've got a lot of Paige's favorite Côtes du Rhône in my cellar, and thought you ladies would have the palate to appreciate some of it."

Of course Paige would have arranged somehow for the universe to send us a man with a good French red the minute we'd decided prosecco wasn't called for anymore.

With a wave of her hand, Jen directed our attention to three full glasses already sitting on the coffee table. Maybe her bartending superpowers hadn't grown so rusty after all.

When we were seated with glasses in hand, Porter raised his. "To the ineffable Paige Berry."

"To Paige," Jen and I echoed.

We sipped in silence for a minute, reflecting on the rich, hearty, and complex qualities of our lost friend and her favorite wine.

"So…" I said at last. "How did, um… Jen tells me she looked… peaceful?"

Porter set his glass down without looking at either of us. "She did. Dolled up in her favorite frock, with her arms out as if in welcome, and the hint of a smile, I think. It didn't look like she'd been gone too long when I…happened by." He looked up uncomfortably at me then. "I guess I mentioned her letter to Jen, didn't I. But, if you'll forgive me, Cam, I would rather not… I'm not really feeling ready yet to—"

"No, it's fine," I leapt in to reassure him. "I'm not ready either."

He tilted his head, looking puzzled. "You're not ready for…?"

Oh. "I'm sorry. You wouldn't know. Paige, um, left me a letter too—in a bag of kale I found this morning at my studio."

Porter looked less surprised than thoughtful. "So…you already knew as well."

I shook my head. "Her letter just confused me. None of it made any sense until Jen came home." I couldn't keep myself from asking any longer. "Did she look… What I mean is…had she been hiding some kind of sickness, do you know?"

He gave me a small, sad smile. "But that's *not* what you mean, is it? Forgive me if I'm wrong, but you're wondering if she took her life intentionally." Jen shot me a look as Porter went on before I could come up with a reply. "How could either of us not be wondering that? *Two* letters—if not more. She had so many friends, after all. The question shouts itself. And it will just be worse if no one brings themselves to ask it aloud."

I nodded—afraid to speak for fear of bursting into tears again. Jen glanced between us as if wondering who might lose it worse if Porter's next words were, *Yes, I think she may have.*

But Porter shook his head now. "I wondered too, of course. At first. But I don't think so. Neither do the deputies. We can't know for sure, I guess, until the coroner has examined her, but there were no wounds, and most poisons leave pretty obvious signs, apparently. The deputies listed all of them for me, and assured me there were none on her." He looked away and smiled sadly. "I said she didn't look long gone, but the truth is, she looked…well, like she might just get up, give us all a wink, and go run a marathon." I felt myself starting to unclench as he turned back to me. "Can you really imagine Paige committing suicide, Cam?"

"No. I can't." To my huge relief, the question suddenly seemed completely absurd.

"Neither can I," he said. "And I've not only known her longer than you've been alive, but I've seen her at about her worst, I think." I knew better than most how true that was. "Even back then, Cam, everything inside Paige Berry was the *opposite* of suicide."

I knew he was right, and felt so grateful to him for laying it out so clearly. "But then why did she write those letters? How could she have known she was about to die?"

He gave me a wry look. "Well, I don't know if you ever noticed, but there were always more than a few strange things about that woman."

"Yes, I did notice that." I hoped he just meant her giant vegetables or her knack for showing up at exactly the best or worst possible moments. I didn't think she'd have told even Porter about any of her deeper secrets, much less mine.

"Then I guess we'll just have to chalk this up as one more of them. Though it may not really have been all that strange anyway. You'd have no way of knowing this yet, young lady, but older bodies have a nasty habit of announcing bad news loud and clear. Paige would not have been the first person I've known who seemed aware the time had come. It happens; and if anyone would know how to read such signs, she would have."

I hadn't even thought of that. I nodded again, feeling even more relieved.

"To change the subject," Porter said, "I do think Verna would be interested in joining us if you two feel comfortable with that. May I give her a call?"

Jen looked at me for an answer.

"Of course," I said. "The more the merrier." Irony had always been more JoJo's thing than mine. But this occasion seemed to call for an exception.

Porter pulled his phone out. But the conversation turned out to be longer and more complicated than I'd expected. After a long string of *uh-huh*s and *you don't say*s, Porter said, "Well, I don't know. Hold on a minute." He looked up at us. "Verna's started getting calls from people worried about how I'm doing."

Of course she had. Everyone who'd known that Paige and Porter couldn't stand each other also knew that they'd become the best of friends again. And with the island's grapevine surely on overdrive by now, they probably also knew that he'd been the one who found her this morning.

"She says they're asking if we want company or solitude." Porter looked expectantly at us. But my mind had been a total jumble all day and, from Jen's blank expression, it didn't seem like she had any idea what he was asking either.

"Uh, *do* you guys want company?" I asked, finally.

"No," he said. "Do *you* two want company? You know what Paige was to people. It sounds like we're not the only ones looking for help to process this."

"Oh, I see," said Jen. "You and Verna want to host a wake?"

"Mmmm…possibly," Porter said. "But it's a lot of people, and our house is pretty small." He looked back at me. "So what shall I have Verna tell folks? I'll supply the wine, of course. And others will bring the food; that's how it's done. Everyone will know that."

"Wait, you want to invite people over *here?*" I asked in disbelief.

"Tonight?"

"I bet I know what Paige would say," Jen put in.

And, suddenly, I saw Paige's reproachful smile in my mind almost as clearly as I saw Jen's.

Paige had given me a piece of very important advice one night, years before: *Take the leaps that come. Take them all. Life is too short for hesitation.*

Or for hiding from loss behind a wall of grief.

"You're right," I said. "She'd want us all to have a party. Why not here?"

Jen gave me a thumbs-up. "That's my girl."

Porter put the phone back to his ear. "Sorry to keep you waiting, dear. Yes, give people Lisa Cannon's address and tell them to bring anything they like except for wine. Put the rest of the Côtes du Rhône in the trunk and come on over." He listened for another moment, then said, "I'll tell her. She's doing pretty good. I love you. Drive safely." When he'd put the phone back in his pocket, he turned to me. "Verna says people have also been asking her if she knows how *you're* doing, Cam. I'm clearly not the only one Paige sung your praises to."

I was really moved to hear that, but wondered why people had been calling Verna to find that out. Why not Porter, or me? But that was the way of things, I realized. People edged closer, not wanting to be a burden. Not wanting to intrude.

I could practically hear Paige telling me what a good way this "party" might be to start letting people in. Jen had been right—again—to nudge me into it.

Who'd have guessed she'd be so talented at grief counseling?

But then I thought, *Well, duh—bartender!*

❧

If there'd been any funeral arrangements after my birth mother's murder, no one ever said a word to me about them. Maybe they'd thought I was too young or traumatized to cope with it, I don't know. I hadn't asked, either. She was gone. And the man who'd provided the other half of my DNA was the one who'd killed her—right in front of me. Those were the only parts of it that had mattered to me then, and I've never even cared whether he was still alive somewhere or dead now too.

But I'd still been to a few wakes before Paige's.

My adoptive parents both lost family members while I was still in grade school. Their wakes had been held in community halls or restaurants, and seemed vaguely sad and confusing. The extended members of my new family had still been little more than strangers to me back then. When a girl at my high school was killed in a car wreck, dozens of us went to a gathering at her parents' home after the memorial service. But, honestly, that had been more about teenage theater for most of us than anything like closure. Years later, I'd lost another friend my age in Seattle. "Accidental overdose" was what they called it, though some of us weren't so sure about the "accidental" part. His wake had been at a bar, which I'd thought seemed awfully tone deaf.

The only thing all of those events had in common for me was how strange they'd felt. Parties that *weren't* parties. All that food and drink, even laughter, without any real celebration. People chatting away about all sorts of things except for the death that had brought us there. I'd never felt quite sure why any of us were there.

Paige's wake was completely different, though, in so many ways.

To start with, it felt real. I'd been more of an emotional bystander at such things before, just paying respects, supporting others. But Paige's death had punched a giant hole in the middle of my life, and now I was just going with the current, staying on the surface, trying to keep that hole from swallowing me completely.

As Verna arrived with her trunk load of wine, Porter and Jen went down to bring all of Paige's produce over from the A-frame so that she could cook it up in Lisa's kitchen for the crowd we were expecting. Recalling the assurance in Paige's letter that I'd have no trouble finding friends to share her giant delivery with, I wondered if she'd seen even this coming somehow.

Within minutes, a van full of garden club members showed up bearing a giant bouquet of flowers, of course, along with boxed and bagged ingredients for a feast. On their heels came two carloads of Paige's senior center lady friends with the makings for a whole second feast. Realizing that Lisa's dining table wasn't going to be nearly big enough for what was coming, I went looking for card tables or TV trays—anything to extend the buffet line, and get me away from all the sympathetic attention I was already being showered with. Unfortunately, the senior center ladies all rushed to help me search, clucking about their shock at losing Paige, and how dreadful this must be for me.

I was only rescued from their attentions by the arrival of *more* people and *more food* from all over the island. Half of them were total strangers to me, and before long I was feeling literally beside myself as I struggled to *perform* the role of grieving hostess in some strange play about the very pain I was suppressing in order to play that part.

An hour later, Lisa's sunken living room was filled to bursting with island residents in various degrees of shock, grief, bewilderment, and, in a few cases, tipsiness. This wake was no somber, subdued gathering. It was a shifting roar of voices, tears and laughter. And after years of pandemic isolation, being in a room crowded with people, some in masks, others not, was beyond weird. But it also felt like a giddy, daring affirmation of hope and life. For years, there'd been almost no one to share our lives with; and now, all around me, people were pouring out their stories, not just about Paige, but about themselves and the world in general. And, to my surprise, even people I'd never met kept bringing all those stories to me in particular.

I don't just mean in some casual way. I mean a crazy parade of both acquaintances and strangers who seemed to home in on me, introduce themselves, and launch right into sometimes very personal stories about their relationships with Paige, or their pandemic struggles, some recent family crisis—almost anything. At first, I wondered if it was just because the wake was at "my house," and they were just coming to talk with the hostess out of politeness? But Jen, who was a naturally more engaging person than I was, lived here too, yet I didn't see this happening to her—or to Porter or Verna either, who'd spread more word of this event than anyone else, as far as I knew. Before long, it began to seem…bewildering.

I sure did hear a lot of interesting stories about Paige, though, which I was eager to listen to. A lot of those people had known her for decades—a few of them since not long after she'd come to Orcas. I was not surprised to learn she'd made numerous cottage businesses out of her vegetables and animals when she'd been young, selling everything from produce and preserves to goat cheese and fresh eggs. One old woman told me Paige had spun, felted, and dyed goat and rabbit hair, and woven textiles and clothing out of them for a while. She seemed to think the very idea of goat hair clothing was hilarious for some reason, though I was pretty sure I'd seen Paige in more than one outfit that had probably been made out of exactly that.

Another old couple told me about Paige's "exotic imports shop" back in the seventies when local tourism had really started to boom. They still had a driftwood mobile she'd sold them, hung with a dozen dried puffer fish all blown up like balloons. "She told us it would be just the thing to stimulate conversation in our living room. And she was right!"

I heard about wild parties she'd thrown up at "that big house of hers" when she'd been younger, and comical outbursts at community meetings later in her life.

One of my favorite stories came from a portly, white-haired man who told me about her secret involvement in a "heroic act of public vandalism" many decades earlier when county officials had installed a traffic light at Eastsound's main intersection. "What did we need a stoplight for?" he asked me. "Everyone was outraged! So she helped me and a couple other guys pry that thing right back outta the sidewalk one night, and carry it to a tavern down the street. I cannot tell you which one, of course. But we set it up in a corner there, and got its lights all blinkin' merrily." He nodded with a self-satisfied smile. "Those fools never came back for a second try. Still won't find a stoplight anywhere in this county—not even on San Juan." He was right, I knew. "People still had a voice back then," he said. "And hers was always one of the loudest, I can tell you."

I was fascinated by all these glimpses of a younger Paige I'd never known, and saddened by them too. It brought home how much I'd never know about her now. How much more might I have learned if I'd just thought to ask while she was here?

I kept expecting this tide of storytellers to wind down, but it only seemed to increase. And, as if all that weren't strange enough, it also became clear that Paige had talked quite a bit about me for some reason. "Paige always told me you're quite the talented young woman..." "...sure thought the world of you..." "...quite an asset to our community..." "...heart of gold..." "...a real head on your shoulders..." "...lucky to have known you..." I'd hardly known how to tell her what a difference she'd made in *my* life, but I hadn't been aware of making any big difference at all in hers. We'd become very close, of course, for all the reasons she'd mentioned in her letter. But I had no idea why she'd have mentioned me at all to so many people I'd never even met until this evening, much less with such praise. It was...all so puzzling.

And then, as a woman who'd just thanked me for bringing everyone together here tonight wished me well and moved back into the crowd, I recalled something Paige had said to me the night we'd finally talked directly about our gifts. She'd wondered whether my talent might really be more about blending things in around me rather than just vanishing itself. She'd seemed to think that by fostering "connection and belonging," I'd already changed a lot of lives around me—including hers.

That night was also the first time she'd told me to avoid trying to use my gift, but to let it use me instead. Could that be what was happening now? I wondered. Was my gift…shaping this event somehow? That was a very uncomfortable idea, for all sorts of reasons, which I did my best to push aside as fast as possible.

I turned to go seek out some more private space for a minute, and there was Jen, standing at my shoulder, drink in hand. "What an amazing group, huh? Have you had anything to eat yet…or even sat down?"

So, she'd noticed too. "I'm…just being here." I glanced around. "You guys were right. People clearly needed this."

"You need a breather?"

"You know, I think I do. I'd like to go try calling Kip again, if you—"

"Hey! Cam!"

I turned and saw Colin and Priya weaving toward me through the crowd. They were wearing masks, but clearly smiling underneath them.

"I'm getting you a drink," Jen said, and turned to go.

"It's so good to see you!" Priya gushed, hugging me. "This is just what everybody needed! Thank you so much for doing it."

"Life goes on, right?" I said, doing my best to sound as cheerful as she seemed to be. "So glad you guys could make it!"

A few minutes later, as Colin and Priya went off to have a go at some food, a tap on my shoulder made me turn to find Porter holding out a glass of something gorgeously dark and filled with dancing, ruby red reflections. "Jen said you were thirsty."

"Oh! Thanks." I'd told her no such thing, of course. But I'd never been one to look a gift horse in the mouth. I took the glass and brought it to my nose. "Ooooh! That's amazing!"

His smile widened. "Do you happen to remember a cabernet I poured for you at the cast party for *Salon Confidential?*"

I looked back at the glass in amazement. "This isn't!"

"It is!" he said gleefully. "For you, my dear!"

I took a sip, and Porter's amazing cab washed across my tongue, then slid down my throat in a warm, soft wave of perfect bliss. I closed my eyes and smiled before turning back to him. "*This* is exactly what I needed. You're an angel."

"Oh, not an angel, dear. Just a minor saint at best. I'm happy to see you smile, though. Keep it up. You're doing great."

"At what?"

"At *what*? Look around you!"

But before I could respond, Jen squeezed out of the crowd behind us. "Verna's asking for you in the kitchen, Porter."

Porter looked worried. "Should I don protective padding before going in?"

"She just wants your advice about what to restock the wine counter with."

"Well, that's all right then," he said with exaggerated relief, then gestured at my glass. "Let Jen know if you'd like more."

"I'll just savor this one for a while," I said.

"A sound approach." He nodded, and was gone.

Jen looked down at my wine glass. "Can I taste that?"

I laughed, and handed her the glass.

As she took a sip, her eyes went wide. "I must be much nicer to Porter from now on!"

When she tried to hand it back to me, I waved her off. "Have some more."

"You sure?" she asked, already raising the glass for another taste.

"Totally. You've earned it at least as much as I have."

"Oh, I don't know. You haven't had a moment since this thing—"

"Good grief!" I said, as my phone buzzed in my pocket. "Someone's calling me." I pulled it out and my irritation changed to delight as I saw Kip's name. "There you are! Finally," I said, bringing it to my ear. "Hi, love. Can you hang on a minute?" I turned back to Jen. "I'll take this in another room."

"Okay!" She reached out to return my wine glass, but I shook my head.

"Enjoy it. I'm good, really." As I headed for the hallway, I said to Kip, "I'm going to my bedroom where we won't have to shout over the noise."

"Sounds like you've got people over?" he asked. "Sorry for not calling sooner. I was in classes all afternoon, and then I forgot—"

"—to turn your sound back on, I know. It's fine."

"So…I just found your text now. Is this a bad time? Should I call back when—"

"No no, I am *so glad* to hear your voice." At the bedroom door, I flipped the light switch and walked into the carefully cleaned and made up room I'd never planned to use again. So…if he'd just found my text… "I'm assuming no one's called to tell you about Paige?"

He was silent for a moment. "Uh-oh… Honey, I'm… I wish I'd found your text earlier. What's going on?"

"She… Well, Porter found her dead this morning. At her home."

"Oh, Cam," he groaned. "I'm *so sorry*. I can be there in the morning—or tonight even, if you want. I should be there now. Damn it, I just wish I'd checked my—"

"Hey, don't," I said gently. "You get focused on your studies, and forget about your phone. There's nothing wrong with that. You had no way of knowing anything was different this time, and I'm doing…I'm fine. Jen's been here all day, and Porter, and, well, as you heard, there's a wake going on here now—long story—but I have way more company than I need."

"So…you don't want me to come up then?"

"Of course I do! But I don't *need* you here this minute, and I don't want to screw up your studies. It would be awfully nice to have you here this weekend, though, if you can make that work? I know we didn't plan another visit until—"

"I'll be there Friday," he cut in. "As early as you want."

"Saturday will be fine. You have classes Friday, and I just said, no screwing up your studies, right?"

"Right. Saturday it is, then."

"Thank you."

"I love you, Cam. And I'm still sorry I'm not there."

"I know. I love you too, and it's still okay you're not."

"So…what happened? I mean, if you want to talk about it."

I did want to. And I didn't.

I told him pretty much everything from finding her whole vegetable garden in bags on the A-frame porch to how I'd ended up hosting her wake, omitting only the parts of her letter that touched on our mutual secrets. He listened with clear sympathy and interest, hardly ever interrupting, and it felt good to have him in this with me now, and feel his care and concern—even over the phone. And yet… Listening to myself describe all the loss and grief I was feeling, I couldn't stop wondering if it might seem strange to him that I was this undone over some wacky old neighbor lady sixty years older than me. I wanted to explain it better. To tell him why she'd been so irreplaceable. All she'd really done for me. But, of course, I couldn't. Not even to Kip—for all the same reasons I couldn't tell Jen or anybody else. There'd never be anyone to share that with again, now that Paige was gone. Unless, someday, somehow, I happened to meet one of the "others like us" Paige had mentioned once, and never said more about. Another thing I would have pressed with her, if I'd known to in time.

When Kip and I had finally said all there was to say, he told me again that he loved me, and that he could hardly wait to see me that weekend. I said the same, and wished him a good night's sleep. Then I hung up and sat there on the bed, wishing I could just lie down instead of going back out to face all those people again—sharing and listening to each other's stories about Paige, and about each other.

That, I finally saw now, was the trouble I'd been having ever since this wake had started. We'd invited everyone to come and help each other make it through this painful moment *together*. What I hadn't understood until now was that I wasn't really free to join in.

I was still alone with my grief, and always would be.

CHAPTER 3

I woke up feeling more than a little hung over, though I'd drunk hardly anything at all. By the time our last few guests were gone, Jen and I had been exhausted. And there'd still been a party to clean up. Porter and Verna had stayed to help. But they'd been even more tired than us, and we'd finally sent them home.

For a while, I just lay in bed staring up at a familiar ceiling I had planned to leave behind by now. Then I looked over at the clock, and realized I'd slept way past my usual five-thirty. Jen must be about to leave for work. I crawled out of bed and lumbered to the kitchen to at least say goodbye.

"There she is!" Jen looked almost perky as I walked in, which I tried not to find annoying. She'd even filled James's bowl, though there was no sign of James himself—I hoped he wasn't still outside somewhere hiding from last night's invasion. "Coffee's still hot. Want me to pour you a cup?"

It looked like she was done with hers, and she already had her coat on. This was one of her package delivery days; those started on the early side.

"I can do that," I said. "Hey: thank you again for yesterday, and maybe we can make another stab at moving to the guesthouse when you're back tonight, if you're up for that—and we haven't come down with Covid yet?"

"Yeah," she said with a grim little smile. "I guess there's that to consider. I'll get some home test kits at Ray's after work."

"Seems like a good idea. I sure hope Paige's wake doesn't end up killing off a few more of her elderly friends."

"True that. They're seeing hardly any infections in the islands right now, so maybe we'll get off easy. But let's just see how we feel about the move tonight, okay?"

"All right." I shuffled to the fridge to get some cream, and saw the bottle of prosecco in there, still unopened. "Nobody drank this?"

"I didn't put it out," said Jen. "That's for us, remember?"

"Right..." I pushed it aside. "When it's time to celebrate."

"That can wait until we're ready, of course," she said.

"I can't imagine when that will be."

She shrugged. "Sometime before Lisa's arrival, I hope?"

"Sounds like a plan."

"So, what's on your list for today?" she asked, all cheerful again.

And that's when I remembered that Paige had asked me to look after her menagerie up on There's No Point Road. While she was *away*. Well...that had sure been a *much* bigger favor than I'd realized when I'd first read the letter. I turned around and stared at Jen. "I have to go up and take care of all of Paige's livestock."

"What?" Jen gaped at me. "Why you? There must be someone else who can—"

"She asked *me* to do it," I said wearily. "And I will—until her family shows up. It's their problem after that, god help them."

Jen was staring at me. "She asked you when?"

Damn it. "In the letter." Which I needed to stop bringing up. I turned away and reached back into the fridge for the cream, then went to get my cup.

"Okay," she said. "Well...that sounds like a pretty big job. Do you want some help?"

"Aren't you leaving for work now?"

"Yes. But under these circumstances I'm sure I could call in and—"

"Not a chance," I cut her off. "Thank you. Really. I'd have been lost without you yesterday, but I don't want you losing *all* your jobs just to stay here and keep holding my hand."

"All right. But you'll call me if it turns out you need something, okay? I do have a lunch break. And I'm usually done early in the middle of the week like this."

"Jen. You're a saint. I mean that. But I'm fine."

"Glad to hear it." She picked up her purse and started for the door. "Have a good day, hon. And good luck with those goats of hers. Call if they start eating your tires or something. I won't have any idea how to help, but I know people who will." She turned back with a slightly wicked smile. "I can put you in touch with them."

There was the Jen I'd known all these years. "Thanks. I may take you up on that. Have a good day yourself."

"Will do." As she walked out the door, James came tearing in between her feet and trotted right over to his food bowl. So, that was okay now as well.

As soon as I'd finished breakfast, I pulled on my boots and jacket. There was no sense putting this task off. James had fallen asleep down in his favorite sunny corner of the living room right after gorging himself. I didn't even bother him as I left.

It was a fairly quick walk up to the road, then across and down a bit, then up Paige's steep, winding driveway. I'd made this trip many times. As always, it left me out of breath, yet filled with energy and wonder at the beauty everywhere I turned my eyes.

Paige's "estate" was a sprawling compound covering maybe ten acres. Though the way up passed through thick woods, you arrived into a clearing with lovely views of the water far below and, charmingly, no sight of the road or any other houses. There was a large pond within view of the house's main entrance, and a fair number of outbuildings scattered here and there. I'd always thought it a very beautiful place, but now I avoided even looking at the house. I didn't want to see its dark and empty windows, its chimney without any smoke curling up into the chill spring air. Her animals and gardens I could deal with. They were all still *here*, and very much alive. But the house where Paige had always lived, and should still be puttering around in somewhere now… I'd been wondering if I'd find police tape, or maybe even deputies still at work up here. But when I crested the hill, I saw no sign that anything at all had ever happened.

Deputy Larissa Sherman, of all people, had shown up at the wake when her shift had ended, and assured me that Paige's body had been delivered to the funeral home in Anacortes to await arrangements by her next of kin. I sure looked forward to meeting them, and not just to hand off these responsibilities. If anyone could tell me more about Paige's earlier life, it would be them.

Morgan, Paige's beyond-ancient German shepherd, lay in his usual spot on her front porch. He didn't lift his head, just flicked an ear, and thumped his tail in warm if weary greeting. "Hey, boy," I said, stepping up onto the porch and patting him on his head. He licked my hand, groaned softly, and closed his eyes.

Paige's other two dogs, a mismatched pair of short-haired little mutts named Pep and Jinx, came trotting over from the main goat barn where the nannies lived with their kids. They often took it upon themselves to supervise the goats, who seemed to find their intrusion dubiously amusing. Today, however, I could hear them bleating in protest of something. "Hey guys," I said to the dogs, patting them as well, then called over to the goats: "I know I'm late, just hold onto your tails! I'll get to you!"

They responded with an extra-loud chorus of *Baa-aa-aa*s. Had Paige milked or fed them before…lying down and leaving yesterday? While I could imagine her doing something like that, I was betting she hadn't. No wonder they were upset.

Still careful not to focus on the house, I went around to the back porch where Paige's sturdy metal containers of dog food were kept and filled everyone's bowls with dry kibble. Jinx and Pep, who'd always seemed overly energetic about food of any kind, just looked up at me in silence now, seeming anxious and subdued as I poured out their breakfast. I knew Paige had been generous with her table scraps as well, but they were going to have to settle for this now. After rinsing and refilling their water bowls, I took Morgan his bowl, and went to see about the goats.

They were clearly upset too, bleating at me loudly even as they shied nervously away from my approach. I was deeply grateful that Clara's kids, Nick and Nora, had *not* yet been weaned; that meant Clara wasn't as desperate to be milked, though she did eagerly jump up onto her milking stand and start nosing around for her feed bucket. "Patience, lady," I told her. The other nannies—Ginger, Freddy, and Klinka—weren't currently in milk, so I only had to see to Clara (another reason to be grateful). Paige had taught me how to milk goats, though I was not exactly a natural at it. To put it mildly.

I locked Clara into the stand, gave her some goat-kibble in the feeding tray, then cleaned her teats carefully. Paige had left plenty of cloths and clean milk buckets, and there was a sink in the "milking parlor" section of the goat barn; I got set up and took a deep breath. "Just do it," I told myself. If Clara finished her snack before I finished milking her, she'd get even more restless. And that was a good way to lose a bucket of fresh milk.

So I sat on the stand beside the plump goat and got started.

At first it seemed like nothing was going to happen. I squeezed my fingers in the downward-wrapping motion Paige had taught me, but nothing came out. And then—success! A stream of warm fragrant milk hit the bucket.

Which of course was when I remembered that you're supposed to discard the first squirt of milk.

I got up and put the bucket in the sink, grabbing a new one to bring to the stand. By now, Clara was mostly done with her chow, so I scooped a little more in for her. "You're lucky I'm so incompetent at this," I told her. She didn't even give me a glance, just hoovered up her unexpected windfall.

I sat back down and made quick work of milking her, getting a reasonable supply into the bucket—a quart or more, I thought. Probably I could have gotten more, but I didn't really need the milk, and Nick and Nora would surely take care of the excess.

Paige had an old-fashioned Frigidaire in there to keep the milk in. I poured my haul into a clean bottle and stuck it in alongside three other full bottles. Maybe Jen would know how to make cheese or something out of all this orphaned milk.

By the time I'd refreshed the bedding straw and water in the goat barn, checked the feed hay, and headed back outside, the goats, at least, seemed a good deal calmer. After that came the chickens and ducks, who I let out of their enclosure to roam free during the daytime, though I'd have to come back here every evening to lock them all in again, I realized. This favor Paige had asked of me was a mighty one. I just hoped her family wouldn't drag their feet getting out here.

When I'd gathered all the eggs I could find, I went to check on the rabbits, who, happily, did not roam free. I didn't even want to imagine what it would be like to try rounding up a bunch of free range rabbits every evening. The barn cats saw to their own business, thank goodness; but they showed up anyway to see what I was doing. Though I'd spent enough time up here over the past few years to be familiar to them now, even they seemed skittish of me. Paige had only been gone for a day, but I wondered what they made of her absence. Did these animals already know that she was gone for good this time? She'd died right out here in the yard, apparently. Had they known what was happening? What did animals make of death?

Finally, there was nothing left to do but go into Paige's kitchen to feed Sam and Harry, her indoor-outdoor house cats. The kitchen porch door was unlocked, of course, as were most household doors around the island. But it took a strange amount of energy just to reach out for the handle and open it.

The moment I heard the hollow echo of my steps in that too-still, too-silent room, I was hit by an almost physical wave of grief. *Gone, gone, gone…* Every tap or creak my boots made on the hardwood floor seemed to shout the word. I felt…like a trespasser, though there was literally no one to trespass on here anymore.

As I found the bag of cat food and refilled the food and water bowls, trying not to listen for sounds of movement or activity elsewhere in the house, Sam, a brown tabby, and Harry, all black with bright yellow eyes, appeared in the kitchen's interior doorway, gazing up at me suspiciously. I moved away to stand by the farthest kitchen window as they came cautiously in and attended to their bowls. At least half their attention stayed on me as they ate. They seemed ready to dart away if I should show any sign of trying to approach them. Seeing that we'd all be much more comfortable if I were gone, I went back outside, shutting the door behind me with a deep sense of relief.

My only remaining task was to go check on the garden and greenhouses.

I walked downhill to her vegetable beds first, and found nothing growing there at all, just ragged mounds of dirt. For a second, I thought deer must have gotten through her fences somehow. Then I remembered all those giant bags on my studio porch, and realized that, of course, she really had brought me her entire crop, just as she'd said. Oddly, though, I found nothing growing in her flower beds either except a handful of perennials, budding from old stems and trunks, or rising from the dark spring soil after spending winter hidden in the ground. Some of those beds should have been planted a month or more ago, and been full of shoots and sprouts or even young plants by now. But on closer inspection, the soil didn't seem disturbed by birds or rodents. I saw none of the ragged, chewed-off stumps that slugs leave behind. Just neatly tilled and mulched but empty beds—as if she'd just never planted anything at all there.

With nothing to water or weed here either, I moved on to check the greenhouses, but found the same thing there. Tidy beds of spaded, fertile soil in which nothing seemed to have been planted, with the exception of one small, rangy patch of garlic at the far end of a raised bed in the second greenhouse: what she'd told me might need thinning. But thinking back, I realized there'd been nothing else in her letter about caring for the gardens. Only about looking after the estate's "residents."

Those garlic bulbs would have been there underneath the soil all winter waiting to come up again all on their own. But if she'd planted nothing else—even in these greenhouses... Could she have known even back in March that she wouldn't be here to tend any of it?

And *still* said nothing to any of us?

"Why?" I asked aloud, my face turned up at the glass ceiling, and the sky beyond it. "Why didn't you at least give us a chance to say goodbye?"

No one answered me, of course.

No one ever would now.

I closed the greenhouse door and then sat down on the steps. Across the yard, the chickens pecked and scratched beneath bare fruit trees in Paige's small orchard; Morgan slept on the house's porch, while Jinx and Pep had resumed their supervision of the goats. As if everything were still the same.

I still hadn't called my mom to tell her about Paige. And she would want to know. I pulled out my phone.

"Hello, dear," she answered, sounding pleased and a little bit surprised, the way she always did, no matter how often I called.

"Hi," I said, trying to sound neutral, which never worked.

I heard her quiet intake of breath. "What's wrong?"

"I have some news." She listened as it tumbled out of me. "I'm up here now, actually," I finished. "There's...so much."

"Cam, I am so sorry," she said. "I know how much Paige meant to you. It sounds like keeping busy has been good for you, at least for now."

"Yes." I sniffled. "She was really old, but I never imagined her gone."

"I know. She seemed in the bloom of health the last time I saw her."

"Didn't she? And that was just a few days ago, for me. I guess it was just her time."

"Which will come for all of us, of course," Mom said. "But do you know what I believe?"

"What?"

"She lives on, in your heart, in your memories. In the memories of all those people who came to your house last night. In her land and her animals and her house. The people we love are never truly gone."

"I…I think I believe that too. At least, I want to."

"Then it's true."

I nodded, as if she were there to see. "Well, I should probably finish up here."

"All right. You take care of yourself, my dear," Mom said. "Don't keep so busy that you don't get rest and nourishment. And call me any time you want to talk—I'm here."

"Thank you."

"I love you."

"I love you too."

I stood up, and looked around again at everything Paige had left behind, including so many now unanswerable questions. As I'd been talking with my mom, the nameless barn cats had gathered stealthily again to see what I was doing now. At least, I assumed they were nameless; Paige had never called them anything in my hearing except *you people*. Had they gathered like this around her yesterday? Did they know what had really happened, or why?

"You people knew her pretty well," I said. "Can you help me make sense of any of this?"

One of them, a sleek gray tabby tom with a passing resemblance to Sam, the house cat, twitched his tail; but the rest of the gang just gazed at me impassively, as if to say, *You think this is supposed to make sense?*

෴

After hiking back down the hill, I stopped at the main house just long enough to roust James and convince him to come with me to the studio. Mom was right. Busy was helpful, right now; and another stab at writing seemed like a healthy distraction.

My laptop was still right where I'd left it when everything had fallen in on me yesterday, and I decided to try a play about loss and grief. Why not? Things like that always seemed to win the big awards, didn't they? But, all that really hit me was a nap up on that sweet McRoskey mattress in the little loft.

Lots of people at the wake last night had told me to be gentle with myself, and Mom had echoed their words. So...here I was heeding their advice.

I was awakened not much later by the vibration of my cell phone. By the time I dug it from my pocket, I'd missed the call. I looked at the screen: a local number, but not one I knew. Probably some hacker scam robocall. If it mattered, they'd have left a message; and I'd already talked with way too many strangers last night anyway. I sat up, stretched, then climbed back down the ladder to give my Pulitzer prize-winning play another chance to present itself. *Let your gift use you, Luke!*

I'd hardly sat down at the table, though, before a voicemail popped up. "I am trying to reach Camille Tate," said a woman's crisp voice. "This is Margaret Rosen, attorney-at-law. Please call me back at your earliest convenience."

I pulled the phone away from my ear and stared at the number again—as if that might make anything clearer. Why was a *lawyer* calling *me*?

I called the number back, and gave my name to the receptionist who answered. "Ms. Rosen just called me a few minutes ago?"

"Yes, Ms. Tate. Please hold while I transfer you."

A moment later, that same crisp voice: "Ms. Camille Tate?"

"Yes?" I said, cautiously.

"I represented Ms. Paige Berry, and may I first say that I am so very sorry for your loss." She sounded businesslike but not insincere; only, why on earth would Paige's lawyer be calling to offer *me* condolences? "There are some documents here that require your signature. Are you by any chance available to come to my office in Eastsound today?"

"I..." *Documents?* I could not imagine what they'd be. More instructions on how to care for something up at her estate? Contact information for her family—because I was taking care of her, or rather *their*, house now maybe? But no... She'd said *documents*. "May I ask what this is about?"

After an odd pause, she said, "I'm very sorry; I had assumed you'd know."

"Know what?"

"Ah...I see. Well, I do still think it might be best if we discussed the matter here. How soon might you be available?"

Why wasn't she just telling me? Was I in some kind of trouble again?

"Any time, I guess," I said. My arms were tingling for the first time in years—though, happily, I had full control over all that now.

"Would half an hour work?" she asked.

"Okay," I said. "Should I…bring anything?"

"Your ID, please. Nothing else."

She gave me an address in town, and we hung up, leaving me an awkward span of fifteen minutes or so to…do what? Pace around the A-frame? Call Jen and tell her…what? I still had no idea, but at least she'd know where to send them looking for my body later. And yes, I knew that I was being a little ridiculous. But it had been quite an eventful twenty-four hours, and maybe I was not quite as over all that as I'd told Jen I was that morning.

"Well, James," I sighed at last, "there's nothing for it but to head for the Brown Bear." He just blinked up at me from his patch of sun on the floor.

If I ended up being drugged and dragged out of this mysterious appointment in the back of some unmarked black van, I was going to do it with a chocolate muffin in my belly. "You want to hold the fort down here, or go back to the main house?"

James didn't move.

"Right, well then, I'm closing this place up before I go, so you'll just have to walk through the wall when you're ready to leave." I reached down to scritch him about the ears, and he was kind enough to purr and lean against my hand. "Or you could wait for me to come back—if I ever do."

◊

IN TOWN, AFTER THE BEST Brown Bear chocolate muffin yet, I found the lawyer's office above a shop not half a block away. It seemed just as casual as most island businesses were. The receptionist was in blue jeans and had her long hair pulled back in a pink scrunchie; the furniture looked…vintage, we'll just go with that. All of this, at least, felt right. Paige would never have hired a corporate-style lawyer.

"Right this way, Ms. Tate," the receptionist said, leading me around her counter and down a short hallway into an inner office.

Margaret Rosen, attorney-at-law, stood up and walked around her desk, holding her hand out for me to shake. Which was weird for me too; we'd all traded hand-shaking for elbow-bumping or *Namaste*-ing at each other years ago. I set aside my discomfort and shook her hand. She had a very strong grip.

"Thank you for coming. Please, have a seat." She indicated two chairs before her desk. I took one, and studied her as she went to sit down as well. She was in late middle age with sleek white hair in a no-nonsense, short yet feminine cut; strong features; dark gray slacks and a plain white blouse. Her one nod to color was a large, stylish pair of fuchsia-colored glasses.

"Again, I *am* sorry for your loss," she went on, "and for all of this confusion."

"Thank you," I said, still mystified.

"Death is always a profound insult to our collective delusional agreement that we're immortal beings." She opened a thick file folder on her desk. "It upends the boundaries that define our universe."

Yep, this was just the attorney Paige would have hired. "That, um, sounds about right…I guess?"

She shuffled through the contents of her folder. "Fortunately, the law is here to restore those structures and boundaries. Ah, here we are." She pulled out a document—three or four sheets of paper, stapled together—then glanced at the first page, and leafed quickly through the rest before handing it to me. "I know the movies always show us reading the will aloud, for dramatic effect, but that's not how it's really done."

"The will?" I said, stupidly, looking down at the document, which did indeed say "Last Will and Testament" right across the top. The dense paragraphs of writing below it, however, were impossible to take in at a glance. I looked back up at Ms. Rosen. "This is…Paige's will?"

"Yes, that is her will," she said patiently. "And since it seems Ms. Berry did not see fit to tell you of these arrangements ahead of time—as most people would have done—I have tried my best to give you at least a few moments to absorb the situation, rather than just blurting it out as you walked in—or worse yet, over the phone." She raised her brows behind those glasses and gazed at me expectantly. I said nothing, just waited…for the rest?

"As Paige's heir, that copy goes to you," Ms. Rosen said at last.

And she'd been right. My brain went right into vapor lock.

"I will retain the original here in my offices," she continued, "unless you'd prefer to seek different counsel, in which case—"

"Wait, hold on, stop, *what?*" I blurted, my brain beginning to grind back into gear. "Paige and I aren't even related! I'm just, you know, a friend, her neighbor…"

"And sole heir to Ms. Paige Berry's estate," said Margaret Rosen, unperturbed. "American law recognizes no inherent legal restriction tying inheritance to blood or family relation unless so specified within the terms of a given will or trust. No such condition is specified in this one. Ms. Berry updated her will two and one half years ago, naming you as her sole beneficiary and successor trustee, which fully established your right to inherit. There is a schedule on page four of that document which lists the assets in her trust, including the house and grounds on There's No Point Road, and her banking and investment accounts."

She seemed…so completely unruffled. Did she just not understand how *insane* this was? I guessed people must freak out in front of her pretty frequently. Did lawyers have to take some class on staying calm when everyone around them was losing their minds?

"I had *no idea,*" I said, struggling for enough breath to speak the words.

"That is apparent. And I have no idea why she didn't tell you; but I'm sorry to have been the cause of yet another sudden shock."

Two and a half years ago.

I had been Paige's *heir* for two and a half years! She'd clearly known she was going to die, and she'd known about this too, and she just kept it all a secret because *why, Paige?*

But wait. Were there relatives somewhere that were going to come after me now? "Who was her heir before she changed the will?" I asked.

"The San Juan Preservation Trust."

I gaped at the attorney. "The land trust? Really?"

"Yes, donors leave bequests to the trust quite frequently. That's why we have such ample supplies of well-maintained public land here in the islands. Surely you're aware of that?"

"Well, yes, of course." One of my favorite trails, up Turtleback Mountain, was part of the land trust, but… "But doesn't Paige have family somewhere?"

"If so, she never mentioned them to me, and they are of no legal concern in this matter."

I shook my head again and looked back down at the document, turning pages as my eyes—and brain—went on struggling to take any of this in. Yes, there it was: my full name. *How had Paige learned my middle name?* And that was my P.O. box address all right. So Ms. Rosen hadn't just mistaken me for some *other* Camille Tate.

And there were those impossible two words: *sole beneficiary.*

"Why me?" I asked.

Margaret Rosen raised an elegant white eyebrow. "She did not share her reasons with me, nor did I ask. But some considerable degree of affection or high regard for the beneficiary is usually involved in such bequests. Clearly, you were close."

"Well, yes… She meant a great deal to me. But after…such a long life… How could I have been the best person she had to leave all this to?"

Ms. Rosen leaned back in her chair. "As I said before, I would *normally* expect her to have informed you of this matter, and explained her reasoning then. But I can think of few people around here who'd have described Ms. Berry, or much of anything she ever did, as *normal.* Can you?"

Despite my swimming head, I had to smile slightly. "No."

"I can see that you might need a few more minutes to take this in before we move further forward," said Ms. Rosen. "Can I get you a cup of coffee, or tea?"

"Um, yeah. Tea would be great. Thank you."

She nodded and got up, but paused and asked for the ID I'd brought. "I'll have Cathy make a copy for our files," she said while I dug through my purse to find my driver's license. Then she stepped out of the office, closing the door behind her.

I flipped through the will again, still trying to make any sense of it, and came to the assets schedule on the final page. There was the lot number and description of the structures and acreage up on There's No Point. And right below them was—*oh my.* Bank and investment accounts. Showing balances as of two and a half years ago…

Paige Berry hadn't been as rich as Lisa Cannon, but she clearly hadn't lived so ruggedly because she couldn't afford anything better.

"Oh…my…goodness," I breathed aloud.

Ms. Rosen came back in, holding a steaming cup of something that smelled restorative.

"Thank you," I said softly, as she handed it to me.

"You're welcome. Be careful, it's hot."

I blew on it, a little absently, then set it down on the edge of Ms.

Rosen's desk and went back to staring at the schedule's list of bank accounts.

Ms. Rosen leaned in to see what I was viewing. "Ah, yes. Ms. Berry had little wealth to start with that I am aware of, but, as you can see, she was a shrewd investor." She straightened, and went back to her seat behind the desk. "It's likely that those balances will have changed some since this will was drafted several years ago. You'll want to check with the financial institutions listed there about current balances."

I reached for the teacup and took a tentative sip. Some sort of herbal blend, spicy and soothing at the same time. And yes, hot, but not scorching. Just the sort of tea Paige would have liked. Had she and Ms. Rosen shared their blends with each other?

Tea was such a nice, comforting thing to think about. I understood tea. Hooray for tea.

I took a second sip and set the cup back down on the desk. *Calm…* I thought. *Breathe. Breathing is important.*

"Now. If you're feeling ready," said Ms. Rosen, "there are explanations and instructions I'm required by law to give you. Do you feel sufficiently…caught up yet to go over them?"

"I think so. Yes." I let the pages in my lap fall closed, and looked up at her.

"Then let's get started." She reached up to adjust her glasses as she opened the thick folder on her desk again.

Sometime later, when she'd finished making sure I understood how all of this would work, and had answered all my questions, sometimes more than once, she said, "And now, Ms. Tate, I'll just need you to sign a few documents, mostly confirming that I have apprised you of your rights and responsibilities, and given you your copy of the will. Then you're free to go and read it through at your leisure. But please do reach out if you have any further questions or concerns. My time has already been paid for in this regard."

"I, uh, thank you…"

She shuffled through more papers on her desk, eventually presenting me with a copy of the trust, made out in my name, plus four or five other sheets to sign. I did so with the heavy fountain pen she gave me, which wrote more smoothly and beautifully than any pen I'd ever held.

I could buy myself a hundred fountain pens like this, I thought as I capped the pen and handed it back to Ms. Rosen. *But I won't, of course,*

I rushed to assure myself as she put the signed papers back into their folder. I had no idea what to do with Paige's mind-boggling bequest. But it wouldn't be anything as stupid as a hundred fountain pens.

"All right then; there you are." Ms. Rosen handed me a neat file folder. "As I mentioned, I am available for further consultation on this matter, and also to administer the trust on an ongoing basis should you desire that. If you do decide to change representation, just let me know where to send the files." She stood up and reached across her desk for another handshake. "It's been a pleasure meeting you, Ms. Tate." She gave me a warm, professional smile. "And, if I may proffer one last piece of advice, I would caution you vigorously against making any large decisions right away."

Proving, of course, that Paige had clearly hired *this* lawyer because she could read minds. I got to my feet as well. "I understand. Thank you."

"Give this bequest sufficient time to seem real to you," she went on. "And don't let anyone pressure you into doing what *they* think you should do with it. Well-meaning friends and loved ones are often full of 'good advice' which might not prove either wise or helpful after all—to say nothing of the many *less* well-meaning parasites and scammers that are always out there, waiting to take advantage when we are at our most vulnerable."

"I'll be very careful," I said, nodding.

"I believe you will. Good luck."

༄

"Wow," Jen said. I'd told her everything as soon as she got home from work. "I mean, just… *WOW*."

"Yeah. I'm still trying to get my head around it. I keep thinking I'm there, and then some other new thing occurs to me, and…yeah, wow."

"Have you told Kip yet? Or your parents?"

"Nobody but you, so far. Well, and *this* guy," I said, scritching James between the ears. He was stretched out in my lap—the only way he was allowed on Lisa's fine sofa. "I run all my business past him."

"That's wise," Jen said before taking another sip of her wine. "I guess you'll need to let Lisa know, huh? I mean, this is going to change things quite a bit."

"Why? What do you mean?"

Jen gave me a look. "You own a house and farm now, Cam. You don't think that's going to cut into your schedule here a little?"

"Well, okay, yes; I guess it will at first. I'll have to find new owners for the animals, and—oh *crap!* I have to close the chickens and ducks back in their coops! I've just been in such a daze all afternoon, I forgot!"

"Don't worry, hon," said Jen. "I can pop up and do it."

I started to protest—but some little voice inside me reminded me how much Jen liked being useful. "Thanks. I guess I am a bit wiped out."

"I bet you are. In fact, I'll just start doing it on my way back from work, if you like. It's an extra twenty minutes, and I'm already on the road."

"You're a saint," I said. "There's a lot of things that need doing up there. But I can afford to hire people for that now, till I figure out what I want to do with the place. I'll just get on that, and be as free as ever to do my job here."

Jen looked skeptical. "You're going to *hire* people to work up there so that you can keep working for Lisa?"

"I love my job," I protested. "I love my whole life here, just the way it is. I've never wanted a farm. Plus, Lisa's going to be kind of starting over here, you know, after everything that's happened. She'll need me more than ever now."

"Okay. And soon, then," said Jen. "So you still need to tell her."

"Well, of course." I sighed. "I never said I wouldn't tell her, just that I don't think it's going to change things that much. I mean, I've been Paige's heir for over two years. Do things need to change now just because I know that?"

Jen went on looking at me for a moment. Then she laughed and shook her head. "You're not going to let a little thing like inheriting a fortune change you—because of course you won't." She leaned back against the cushions. "But I guess you're right. That was good advice the lawyer gave you—about not making any big decisions right away."

"Yeah. See? That's all I'm trying to say. There's no reason to start running around with my hair on fire. I'm just going to go on with my life and let this all sink in a little."

We sipped in silence for another minute before Jen said, "I'm sure she didn't mean you shouldn't even *tell* anyone, though."

"Oh, I'll tell everyone, I'm sure. I was bursting to tell you. But Kip's been in class all day, and my mom won't even sleep tonight if I call her about it now. And, besides…she'll be full of that well-meaning advice Rosen warned me about, you know?" I grabbed a grape from the bowl Jen had brought out. "I think I may wait a while before telling Mom, actually. I mean, what's the rush?"

"Okay," Jen said. "But Kip must be out of class by now. And he's already going to be ticked off that I knew before he did."

"No he won't. He doesn't care about that kind of thing." I glanced at the time on my phone. "And, as it happens, he *is* still in a class now."

"It's almost dinner time!" Jen said in disbelief.

"He's taking classes at night now too, to get this degree done as fast as possible so that he can move back home and be with me, if you must know."

"Oh for goodness' sake!" Jen sighed. "Is there any kind of luck you don't have?"

"Me? Jen, I became a murder magnet before I'd been here twenty-four hours, remember? And that was after years of dating *Kevin*. You remember *him*, I take it."

She rolled her eyes. "Yes. The schmuck. But now you're with Kip! And he was the last man worth looking twice at on this whole forsaken island. I know, because I've tried all the others."

Oh, please, I thought. *Let's not do* this *again.* "The pandemic's over, Jen. All sorts of people will be coming here, and since *you* are the most fabulous woman on this forsaken island, you'd better brace yourself for a giant boom in business. I'll be living like a widow soon until Kip is done with school."

Jen laughed and gave me a swat on the arm, hard enough to make James look up in irritation. "You'll be selling me crypto next." Jen took a handful of grapes too, and munched thoughtfully. "I guess this means it's up to us to plan the memorial service. If there's no other family, huh?"

"*Us?*" I asked. "Are you volunteering to help?"

"Well, of course, you ninny; you think I'm just going to leave you alone with all of this? Now?"

I shook my head, but couldn't help smiling. "I just hadn't given any thought to that yet. Or anything else really, for that matter. You know?"

"I do know, and that's why I'm offering to help you." She leaned forward. "Listen, hon, this is all as big a surprise to me as it is to you, but with one major difference: it's not *happening* to me. I'm on the outside, so my brain still functions. No offense."

"None taken. I've been trying to find my brain all afternoon. Oh! Speaking of which, I forgot! There's two chocolate muffins in the car." I'd gone right back to the bakery after my meeting with the lawyer, figuring I could certainly afford two more muffins now.

Jen looked puzzled. "Granted, muffins are fairly large and somewhat head-shaped, but how do they relate to your brain exactly?"

"Seriously? Chocolate is prime brain food, Jen! How can a foodie like you not know a thing like that?"

"Ah. Right. I'd forgotten. Probably not enough chocolate in my diet."

"And you know what else?" I asked. "Why don't we have some prosecco with those? I think this new development is worthy of some celebration, don't you?"

"Oh, now you're talking!" Jen said, already standing up to go get it. "Let the revels begin!"

☙

WHEN WE'D SCARFED DOWN OUR chocolate muffins and prosecco, Jen went up to close the ducks and chickens safely away for the night, and then came home and whipped us up an even healthier and more nutritious meal for, um, dessert. That sobered us up enough to sit down and start thinking about the memorial service I was clearly now responsible for.

"It'll be easy to get word out to all her local friends," Jen said. "But if she had friends off island anywhere, I have no idea how we'll find them?"

"Well, she had one, at least. In the will Paige left instructions to ask someone named Elle Gascaux to preside at the memorial service. There's a New Orleans address, I think, but no phone number. So we'll have to contact her the slow way."

"Well, we'd better do it soon. She may be the only person who can help find any of Paige's other friends."

"If Elle's address is still even any good," I said. "I have no idea how long ago that part of the will was written." I thought again of Paige's one, vague reference to a community of others *like us*, and wondered if this might be my chance to meet some of them. "Paige must have an address book or letters, at least, somewhere in her house." Which would mean going back inside there, of course—and not just for a few steps around. A thing I still so *did not want to do*. That house was mine now, though. Paige had given it to me. So I'd just have to buck up and face it. "I'll look around when I go back up there to feed the animals in the morning."

"I'd be happy to go with you," Jen said. "I mean, if you want me to; or I can also just stay out, it's your house and—"

"Oh Jen!" I cut her off. "That would be so great! Yes, *please* come with me. I'm so completely overwhelmed." This would all be so much easier with Jen there at my side. Why hadn't I thought of that myself? "You work tomorrow, right? At the bookstore?"

"I do," she said. "But because you really are the luckiest person on this island, they've asked me to take the afternoon shift for the rest of this week, and most of next week too. Tracy's gone to see her folks back east—for the first time in three years—so they've got me filling in for her."

"Oh, that's great!" I said. "For Tracy, I mean. Three years; just imagine." Jen could help me with all sorts of things now. "Right after breakfast then?"

"Can't wait," Jen said, and glanced at her phone. "So, is that workaholic boyfriend of yours still in class now?"

Well! Nothing pointed about *that*, was there? "I don't think so." I stood up and started for my bedroom. "I'll go call him now."

"Terrific idea, hon!" Jen said. "Tell him I said hi."

In my room, I kicked my shoes off, got comfortable on the bed, and made the call.

He answered on the second ring. "Hi, you," he said. "Today gone any better?"

"Oh, you won't believe what's happened now. But before we go there, how was *your* day?"

"Okay…" he said. "I hope your news is something nice, at least?"

"Yes. I think so. But really, I'd like to hear about you first. How were your classes?"

"I don't know; informative, I guess. I've got a second quiz on Friday now. For Adolescent Psych."

"Oh, I'm sorry they're piling things on just as I made you come visit."

"Not your problem," he said lightly. "So what are you circling around? I used to be a cop, you know. I can tell when someone's holding out on me."

"All right, I surrender. Are you sitting down?"

"Oh boy," he said. "You can't be pregnant. I haven't been around enough for that. Unless... Who is he?"

"As if!" I scoffed. "I've had Kip Rankin in my arms. Who could possibly compete with that? Who would even try?"

"Brad Pitt?"

I snorted. "Brad Pitt's so yesterday. Now, if *Timothée Chalamet* ever came to Orcas Island, you might want to look out. But once he found out I was dating a former cop, and such a handsome one, he wouldn't have the nerve to try me."

"Who the hell is Timothy Shallot?" he asked, sounding less amused than I had hoped.

"Oh, Kip, you're adorable."

"Well, you don't seem as sad as last night. So I guess your news can't be too bad. But you're making the back of my neck itch. Just spit it out, okay?"

Okay fine. "Paige left me her whole estate, and a small fortune too."

Now he laughed. "Seriously, Cam; just tell me."

"No, that's it! I'm serious. I got a call from Paige's lawyer this morning, and went to her office to sign documents and everything. I have the will right here to prove it."

He was completely silent for so long that I pulled my phone away to look and make sure the call hadn't dropped. "Kip? Are you still there?"

"You're...not joking?" He sounded almost fearful; and I realized that I'd just made the very same mistake with him that Ms. Rosen had tried so hard not to make with me.

"I'm sorry. I shouldn't just have blurted it out like that. I swear I haven't cracked or anything. I had the same reaction when the lawyer told me—and then I spent the whole afternoon practically in a coma. Jen and I have been talking about nothing else since she got home."

"Oh my god, you're serious! I... No, *I'm* sorry, honey! I didn't mean to call you a liar or anything, I just—that's incredible!"

"Isn't it? I still have no idea why, but Paige changed her will over two years ago, and left everything to me instead of to the land trust. And, Kip," I said, my voice dropping, "she had a lot more money than I'd ever have believed."

"Well… Sounds like kind of a game changer. How's that feel? All right?"

"A little overwhelming—okay, more than a little. But I don't plan to change a thing. The lawyer was very nice, really, in a weird, Paige Berry kind of way; and before I left, she suggested I make no big decisions or changes until I'd had time to let this all sink in first. That's exactly what I'm going to do. I'm not even going to tell anyone yet, except for Jen and you and Lisa. Not even my mom."

"That sounds wise." He seemed a little more like his normal, level self again. "But can you really just keep something like this to yourself?"

"Oh, you'd be surprised." *Way more surprised than you might imagine.* "When Lisa hired me, we had a long talk about the importance of discretion. And, if you ask her, I think she'll tell you how well I've kept her business private. Plus, you know what I did for Sheriff Clarke and the Feds."

"I sure do," he said. "And I don't mean to question your strength or discretion, love. Anyone who knows you at all would know better. I just meant… Well, most of the secrets you've had to keep were either someone else's business, like with Lisa, or dark and dangerous stuff. This is more like Christmas Eve, and it can be a lot more tempting to tell *fun* secrets."

"I know. But don't worry. I'll keep it under wraps for now."

"I think your plan's a great one," he said. "Just be prepared for at least a little bit of change once more people find this out. Because we both know it'll happen faster on that island than almost anywhere on earth."

I sighed. "True that."

"As long as you're prepared to hold a steady course even after people know, I think the world is going to be your oyster. And I don't know anyone who deserves that more than you do. Seems Paige was even wiser than I gave her credit for—and I gave her lots of credit. Even before that little brush-up between her and Porter got resolved."

"I love you, so much. Even more than Timothée. You do know that, right?"

"I do," he said. "Whoever he is. And I can't wait to see you. We'll go have a look at your new property on Saturday, and if you need my help with anything up there: moving furniture, clearing greenhouses, shoveling manure—whatever—you just name it, and I'm yours."

I laughed softly. "You *are* mine, aren't you. That makes me so happy."

"Makes me even happier."

I could hear the smile in his voice.

Oh, how I did look forward to the time when he was done with school. "Study hard for those quizzes, and I promise to make all your hard work feel worth it when you get up here this weekend."

"Way to not distract me from my studies," he said with a chuckle. "See you soon, love. Good night."

CHAPTER 4

As Jen and I left Tigress and started toward Paige's house the next morning, Pep and Jinx came tearing over to dance around our ankles. Jen dropped immediately to pat their little heads, burbling and cooing at them like the dog person she was. They wriggled and licked her hands, then went running up onto the porch so they could greet us there all over again.

Morgan lay in his usual place, tail slowly moving in something like a wag. Jen reached down and petted the old shepherd. "You miss her, don't you?" she asked him. He just closed his eyes in apparent pleasure at her touch.

"I feel like I should bring them down the hill with us," I said, feeling guilty about leaving them up here all alone day after day.

Jen straightened up and gave me an appraising look. "No, these goobers are all sweethearts, but they don't seem very well-mannered."

"Yeah, well, whatever they know about manners would have come from Paige."

Jen nodded, smiling. "But the real issue with taking any of these dogs home is that, I know you love animals, hon, but you're just not a dog person." She wasn't wrong; and they clearly knew that too. They'd never been this wiggly and excited with me. "So the kindest thing to do is find them a new person who *is* into dogs."

"Yeah…" We both looked at ancient Morgan. "I'll feel terrible making this guy move. I'm not sure he's been off this porch since…I don't know when."

Jen leaned down to pat him on his grizzled old head again. "Well, they'll be fine here, for a while at least, as long as we come feed them every day."

I loved hearing that *we* from her. I didn't want to keep tangling her up in my affairs this way, but I'd finally just come out and told her during the drive up here how uncomfortable even being near Paige's empty house had made me yesterday, and how grateful I was to have her with me.

"And we don't have to make any decisions about them right now," she went on. "We're here to find an address book." She gave me an encouraging smile. "You ready?"

"Ready as I'll ever be."

She pulled me in for a quick hug. "Just imagine we're jumping in a swimming pool. It's scarier before you do it, and fine a couple minutes later."

"I know you're right." I sighed. "I don't know why being here bothers me so much."

"Because it's full of someone who loved you," she said gently. "And she's gone now. There's nothing wrong with that."

Yes there is, I thought. *She's not coming back. That's as wrong as anything can be.* But I also knew that Jen was right—again. I drew a deep breath, took hold of the doorknob, pulled it open, and…walked inside. No problem, right?

Jen followed me in as I tiptoed forward, looking everywhere except up at the long, broad staircase right in front of us, rising into shadows at the landing. *Gone*, said those shadows. *Gone*, said the silence.

"How about some lights," Jen said behind me. She pressed the two-button switch beside the entrance, and the large brass and milk glass fixture above us lit the foyer and the stairs. The clatter of tiny dog claws on hardwood announced that Pep and Jinx had joined us, as Jen gazed appreciatively at the brass plate switch. "Do you know what these things sell for now on eBay?" She looked back at me. "If that's an original switch, this place must be very old."

"I think it is. Paige told me once that it was abandoned when she found it—sometime back in the fifties, I think."

"She was here that long, huh?" As the dogs moved off to sniff at the baseboards, she looked over at the door to our left. "What's in there?"

"The kitchen."

Jen looked back at me. "Right off the main entrance? That's kind of weird."

"You haven't ever been here?"

"No. I wasn't one of her 'come to lunch' friends like you."

That was a little startling. In my head, my best friends all knew each other just as well as I knew them. But I'd nearly always come up here to visit Paige during the day while Jen had been at work, so their interactions must all have been elsewhere. "I can't believe I never brought you here," I said, joining her as she pushed the door open.

"Holy cow, what a mess!" she said, peering inside.

I smiled. No greater horror for Jen than a messy kitchen. *"Mess* was Paige's primary decorating scheme."

"And why would anyone put a kitchen right here at the front of the house?"

"It's a strange house," I conceded. "But Paige lived here…" Jen gave a little snort of amusement. "She told me this was originally a boardinghouse, and that when she got here, the dining room was through that set of pocket doors behind us. I guess eating was front and center at boardinghouses. There were no bathrooms inside either. She put those in."

"So outdoor privies were too much even for Paige," Jen said. "Good to know there was a line somewhere."

"She seemed to spend most of her time here in the kitchen, though. I think this was the real main room of her house."

"Sure looks like it." Jen shook her head again at all the chaos.

"Sam and Harry's food bowls are in here." I walked over to them; they were empty.

"Who are Sam and Harry?"

"The house cats," I said, getting the food bag out of the cabinet. "And not very friendly."

Jen laughed. "Maybe that's because she gave them cranky-old-man names."

After I refilled their food and water bowls, Jen and I stood gazing around in dismay at all the piles of magazines and mail, stacks of empty plastic nursery pots mixed with cookbooks and utensils, dishes, glassware and canning jars that covered every horizontal surface. Jinx and Pep came in from the foyer, clacking in between our legs to start nosing around the house cats' bowls. "Hey guys," I said, "those aren't for you."

Jinx looked up, snurfled, and put his nose right back into Sam's bowl.

"Leave it," Jen said in a commanding, alpha voice. Not loud, yet

forceful.

To my surprise, both dogs immediately left the bowls and, after a few more appraising glances at us, trotted back out, across the foyer, and disappeared through the front parlor's pocket doorway. We followed, and found them settling on a big soft sofa back in the second parlor, which Paige had used as her living room.

"Should I make them get down from there?" Jen asked.

"No, that's their place." *And Paige's*, I added silently.

"Okay. So, if the kitchen was her main hangout, we might want to start by looking through those piles of paper first. Or we could double our efficiency, if you want to look someplace else while I do the kitchen."

But I hardly heard her. My attention had already fastened on the room in front of us. I'd spent so much time here…always with Paige.

Gone, murmured some voice in my mind.

I half glanced at Jen. "Uh. Sure. I'll join you in a minute."

She gave me a curious look, then started back toward the kitchen.

I went to stand in front of the worn easy chair that had been "mine" whenever we'd had tea here. Then I turned around to look across the low, jumble-covered coffee table at the dogs, sitting still as statues in their places now…to either side of where Paige always sat.

Except she wasn't there between them now.

Gone.

I sank into my chair and wondered where she was now. Both dogs looked at me, as if to say, *I know, right? Where is she, anyway?*

It was not a question I had asked myself before then. I'd still been getting past the basic fact that she was gone at all. But now I recalled all that talk in her letter of journeying to unfamiliar territory, her collection of "useful maps." What had she even meant by that?

"Maps of what?" I asked the dogs, overrun by a sudden, desperate flood of grief from out of nowhere. "Do you guys know?" My eyes blurred with tears as I suddenly imagined wandering through her house from darkened room to darkened room, sobbing *where's she gone? Where's she gone?* It was as vivid as any dream. "Do you know?" I implored the dogs again, reaching up to wipe at the cascade of tears streaming down my cheeks now. "Did she tell any of you out there anything before she went?"

"Did you say something?" Jen called from the kitchen.

The grief, the dream of wandering her house, it all just…shattered—gone as quickly as it had come on. I sat up, feeling addled and alarmed, and glanced toward the doorway, wiping moisture from my face. "No—well, yes," I called back, trying to pull myself together. "I was just talking to the dogs." Who still sat motionless, gazing at me as they'd been doing the whole time. Did they think I'd lost my mind? Or did humans just seem crazy to them all the time? Where had all that even come from?

I'd heard grief came in waves. But this wave now seemed ridiculously large and sudden. For two days, I'd been telling everyone I was okay. But was I?

I heard Jen coming back through the front parlor, and took a last swipe at my cheeks before her head popped through the doorway. I put on a smile, but she just looked back at me strangely.

"Are you okay?" she asked.

I almost laughed. How obvious was it?

Happily, the dogs leapt off the couch and raced up to her for more head-pats and burbling little accolades from the only person here who understood them, and Jen's question was forgotten in their scuffling exchange.

"Did you find anything?" I asked her when their love-fest was over.

"*Oh yes!*" she said dramatically. "*Hundreds* of seed and flower catalogues; at least two dozen recipes for greens and roots of every known kind; and *pounds* of fundraiser junk mail. Did you even know non-profit horticultural organizations existed? Because I didn't." She looked back down at two now extremely attentive dogs. "I know your person loved you boys a lot, but she had a very serious addiction to garden porn, did you know that?" She reached down to ruffle their fur again, to their obvious delight. "You should have gotten her some help! Oh yes, you should have!" She stopped petting them to waggle a finger at their faces instead, and they both froze, staring up at her. "But did you even try?" she asked with mock severity. "No you didn't, you naughty little enablers. You just let her go on filling your food bowls, didn't you?" Jinx barked twice and Pep leapt up to put his forepaws on her leg. But Jen just nudged him down, and shooed them both out of the room before looking back at me. "I also found a washer and dryer out on the kitchen porch. They seem in good condition, though I'm not as sure about the boiler."

"Boiler?"

She nodded. "Yeah, there's a set of stairs just off the porch back there leading down to...I guess it's a root cellar. There's an ancient giant boiler in there, which must be where the central heat comes from."

"I never knew she had central heat," I said, puzzled. "She always just had a fire going on cold days."

"Huh. The registers are right there in every room. But maybe it doesn't work." She shrugged. "Anyway, no address book. Where should we try next?"

I spread my arms at the untidy parlor. There was a writing desk in one corner that looked promising. "We might as well try here."

But it wasn't there either. So we went on searching methodically through each cluttered room in the house—separately, as Jen had suggested. Being in the house no longer bothered me at all now, even alone. I'd once heard a recently divorced friend talk about how she'd "turned a corner" a few months later. Was that what I'd just done in the second parlor? Right now, our search was distracting enough to muffle the question.

I'd never actually had cause to go upstairs in Paige's house, but it was even messier up there, and most of the bedrooms seemed to have become storage lockers for everything from *more* furniture and clothing to framed paintings, photographs and, in one room, even a spinning wheel and a loom—left from her textiles phase, no doubt.

Finally, I entered a bedroom at the very back of the house that was larger than any of the others, and had clearly been inhabited. By Paige. I stopped just inside the door, surveying her small, neatly made double bed, her cluttered but charming Art Deco vanity, a stunningly carved wardrobe, and a worn but elegant maple rocking chair. The room she'd spent her last night in, I presumed, waiting for the grief to come again—the dread of her absence. But it didn't. I was sad, but only that; not whatever I'd just been downstairs. All that had apparently run its course. For now, anyway.

A small door in the far wall just beside her bed stood slightly ajar. I went to check it out, expecting a bathroom, but found a tiny room clearly set up as an office. Underneath its single dormer window was a miniature roll-top desk, open and, amazingly, completely tidy. Its many cubbyholes and drawers were neatly arranged, and its polished desktop was free of any object at all—except for one small reddish leather-bound ledger book. It sat there all by itself at the center of what had to be the house's only cleared and clean horizontal surface, practically shouting *read me*.

I walked up to take a closer look, certain she'd left it there intentionally, where I could not possibly miss it. I reached down to open it, wondering what I'd find. Records of some secret stash of treasure or magic spells listed nowhere on that schedule in the will? Would there be a second note tucked between its pages, full of answers, finally, to all the unanswerable questions her previous letter had left me struggling with?

I lifted its cover, smoothed and worn from use at the edges, and found…

Names and addresses.

This was her address book? She'd used a *ledger*?

But, of course, it turned out to be even stranger than that. Because Paige Berry couldn't even make a normal list.

As near as I could tell, the organizing principle was "sequential." Judging by the faded ink written with a stronger, younger hand on its first few pages, those names and addresses were considerably older than the rest—and among the very first of these was Elle Gascaux! Some entries were crossed out, with arrows pointing right, which I soon figured out meant that the person's address had changed, and she'd updated the information on whatever later page of the book she'd reached by then. Many of the earliest crossed-out names led to subsequent crossed-out names many pages later, which led to later updates pages after that. Following some of those trails eventually led to crossed-out names without any further arrows. People who had died or just fallen out of touch, I presumed. Elle's original listing was attached to several of those arrows which eventually led to an address that I was pretty sure matched the one I had—and no crossed-out name, which was encouraging.

Compiling a mailing list out of this was going to be a real chore. And, of course, there was not a single phone number in it, and certainly no email addresses. If Paige had ever made a phone call, I'd never heard about it. And the thought of her using a computer? Laughable. So we'd have to send all these announcements by regular mail—which would push the memorial off a while.

But at least we knew who to write now! I hurried out of the little office, back through Paige's room, and down the stairs, calling out for Jen as I reached the foyer. "I found it!"

"I'm coming!" Jen called, jogging through the front parlor pocket doorway, and grinned as I held up the ledger. "Where was it?"

"In a little office she'd set up behind her bedroom."

I flipped through it again, showing her Elle's name, and we followed a few more of its Chutes-and-Ladders paths to their destinations.

"Well, mission accomplished, team!" Jen said at last. "Go us!"

"Thank goodness it wasn't buried in a wall somewhere."

"Speaking of walls, I found something tacked up back here that I think you'll want to see. Come on."

She walked me back to the second parlor. As we entered the room, two mobile patches of fur came scurrying out around us and kept running through the front parlor and out into the foyer as if their tails were on fire. After watching them go, Jen turned to me. "Sam and Harry, I presume?"

I nodded. "Maybe they finally just figured out we filled their bowls."

"Or heard Pep and Jinx scarfing down the last of their meal."

I followed her in and across the parlor as she stopped to look down at yet another pile of paper on a side table underneath the window. But then she turned around, looking confused. "I'm sure that's where I left it." She leaned to one side of the table, then the other, looking at the floor, and murmured, "Where *is* she?"

I gave her a sharp look. "Where is who?"

She turned to me. "What?"

"You just said, 'Where is she?'"

"No I didn't. I said, 'Where is *it*?'"

That wasn't what *I* had heard.

"It was an old black and white Polaroid photo of Paige, I think," she mused, turning around to look again. "When she was really young, and so pretty. I set it down right there when I heard you call me, but now it's gone." She sighed, then shrugged. "I blame the cats. I'm sure it'll surface at some point when we're cleaning this place up. We should probably go feed the rest of the animals and get out of here. We've only got two hours before I have to be at work."

"Right," I said, shaking my head. "Let's go then."

We'd just reached the parlor door when Jen stopped and turned to me, looking horrified.

My shoulders tensed, and the skin on my arms prickled. "What is it?"

"We don't have to milk those goats, do we? I did not sign up for milking goats!"

Now I rolled my eyes. "No. *We* don't. *I* do, and Clara's probably good and ready for me by now. The other goats aren't in milk now, and won't be any time soon unless we're dumb enough to march one of them over to Chuck's pen to get knocked up."

"Oh, thank goodness." Jen sighed. "I am *so* not going to put my hands on some goat's boobs. That'll have to go on being your gig, I'm afraid."

Oh, these native islanders, I thought, trying not to smirk. *Such hardy pioneer women.*

༄

I WAS WALKING DOWN A dark hallway, toward a landing barely moonlit. I could not remember where Paige's room was. I'd already looked in lots of other rooms, all dark and filled with sheet-draped piles of furniture. Everyone had left while I was sleeping. Everyone but me. Was Paige gone too?

I tried to call her name, and failed. No matter how I pressed, the words jammed into something soft but solid before reaching my mouth.

I didn't feel alone here, which was frightening. I'd caught glimpses of people flitting in and out of shadows at the corners of my vision, but when I tried to look at them, they disappeared. I didn't want to meet them anyway. That would not be safe. I just wanted to find Paige. Everything would be fine once I found her.

I walked faster, nearly running for the stairs as I remembered, finally, that Paige's room was on the floor above me. The stairs went right up into it! I stepped off of them as if exiting an elevator, and saw her standing silhouetted before a large, round window at the far side of the room, gazing out at the moonlit night. I walked toward her, pushing at my voice harder than ever, and finally got her name out. "Paige!"

She turned, still an inky silhouette, and leaned forward to kiss me. But then I wasn't sure if it was really her, or if—

I opened my eyes with a little gasp, and turned to see Kip pull back in alarm.

"Honey?" he said, gently. "It's just me. Are you okay?" His eyes were wide with concern under that tousled mop of bronze curls.

I rolled toward him. "Did…you just kiss me?"

"You were thrashing around. And making gargling noises, like you were trying to say something. I just meant to wake you up as gently as I could."

Such a sweet, kind man. And so gorgeous like this in the mornings. He'd come late last night after all, ignoring my clear instructions about waiting until today. Was I peeved with him for that? Nope. "It was…a pretty awful dream. Thank you for getting me out of it." I slid closer to him underneath the covers, nuzzled against his shoulder, and put my arm around his silk-smooth torso. "You can wake me up with kisses any time you like."

"You want to talk about it?" he asked gently.

"Kisses?" I asked coquettishly, wanting only to forget the nightmare. "I'd much rather *do* than talk." I leaned in and gave him a much less gentle kiss than he'd just given me. He knew how to take a cue, I'll give him that.

When we were finished, I rolled back to my side of the bed, staring up at the ceiling in complete contentment. "I am *so* not sorry that I dragged you up here from your schoolwork."

"I don't know," he said. "Keep this up, and it might take me years to finish that degree."

"Fly now, pay later." I sighed, turning back to smile at him. "That's my new philosophy."

He levered himself up on one arm to grin at me. "So, I'm getting you don't want to talk about it then."

I looked at him in confusion, then realized he still meant the nightmare. "Oh for heaven's sake," I laughed. "You're like a terrier sometimes. The dream was about Paige, if you must know." My smile slipped away. "What isn't these days?"

"Sorry. I didn't mean to be a killjoy."

"No. You meant to be a caring and concerned boyfriend." I pushed myself up to lean over and give him another little kiss. "Just one of countless things I hate about you." I smiled to make sure he knew it was a joke. It amazed me how slow on the uptake he could be sometimes—about humor, anyway. "We should probably get up." I pulled back the covers and swung my legs out of bed. "We've got a big day ahead of us up on the Berry Farm."

He just sat there for a moment, smiling up at me appreciatively. I struck a little pinup pose for him, then went over to start putting my clothes on. No sense showering yet, just to get all grubby again up the hill—starting with milking Clara.

"The Berry Farm," Kip said, sliding out of bed as well. "That's kind of cute."

Oh yes it is! I thought, watching him walk over to where his own clothes were draped over a chair. "Does she have any berries growing up there?" he asked, pulling his T-shirt over his head.

What a lucky thing you have no idea how beautiful you are, I thought. *I'd be the one with cause to worry if you did.* Unless it just made him too insufferable to be interesting at all, I supposed. "No," I said, "there's not much of anything growing there now, which just seems so weird."

"Weird how?" He sat on the bed again to tie his shoes.

"Her gardens should have been planted months ago. Unless she knew even then—which I guess she must have. I just keep wishing she'd…" I fell silent, knowing I had to stop complaining about this.

As he finished with his shoes, Kip said, quietly, "My father told me he'd be dying soon, almost a year before he did."

I turned to look at him, mouth open in surprise.

"I didn't believe him," Kip said. "I just asked why he'd even say such an awful thing." His gaze fell to the floor. "His first heart attack wasn't six months later. Even Dad's doctor hadn't known there was any trouble before that. The third one killed him, four months after that." Kip sighed, and raised his eyes to me. "If Paige knew too somehow, and chose not to tell anyone, then I'm sure she had her reasons. She was the kind who always did—for better or worse. And, I mean no offense, love, but… If you trusted and respected her as much as I believe you did, maybe it's just time to trust her again now, and let it go. Let *her* go."

My eyes were suddenly brimming. I turned away to finish with my clothes, as if that might hide the fact. "I think you're going to make a very good social worker."

He came to put his arms around me from behind. "I wasn't trying to scold you. That was not a criticism."

"I know." My eyes overflowed. "That's why I'm crying." I turned around to press my wet cheek against his chest. "I know you're right. And I'll do my best; but I also know I'm never going to find another friend like her." *And I wish I could tell you why.*

He just held me for a time and let me cry. Then he said, "None of the people we love are replaceable, Cam. But I don't think someone like you is ever going to run out of them."

"Oh, just stop!" I pushed him half-heartedly away as I wiped at my tears. "You're only going to make me cry harder. You'd think a man as wise as you would see that." I offered him a smile that was hardly forced at all. "I need a warm scone and a mimosa. And a plate of bacon, if we're going to be moving furniture around."

"Well, let's go find them. I'm buying."

☙

SADLY, AS EXCITED AS I was about scones and bacon, there were goats and chickens that needed seeing to before we went looking for our own breakfast. When I'd gone to Lum Farm to find out about caring for goats, a lovely woman named Laurie had told me how important schedules were to them, and how unsettled they probably were already by Paige's disappearance. So I'd been careful to start tending to their needs at regular times every day. This was my life now. When I'd milked and fed everyone at the goat barn, let the chickens and the ducks out, and fed and watered the rabbits, we went into the house to fill Sam and Harry's food and water bowls, and Kip got his first look at Paige's kitchen.

"Oh boy…" He gazed bleakly around at the drifts of assorted junk. "And all the other rooms are like this?"

"Well, this one's more or less the heart of darkness. But basically… yes."

I'd warned him about conditions inside the house, but he clearly hadn't grasped the real magnitude of our task until now. "This is going to take a lot of weekends," he said grimly.

I put my arms around him. "I know, love. But they don't all have to be your weekends. I'm so glad you're here to help us get started, but your studies come first, and Jen and I can carry on just fine, even in your absence."

With the animals taken care of, we headed back to Lisa's place to get Jen, wished James and Master Bun a good day, and went to town at last for brunch.

Brown Bear's line was always miles long on Saturdays, so Jen suggested we try Gertie's, one of the new restaurants that had popped up since the shutdown. It was a project of Jen's friend and former boss at the Barnacle, Katrina; we were soon seated outside on their sunny deck poring over a fabulous menu.

Sadly, they didn't have scones, or even a plate of bacon. But I got a scrumptious salad with warm goat cheese, and they *did* make me a mimosa, so all was not lost. Kip ordered their giant "French toast on steroids" thing covered in custard and dripping with maple syrup. He ate like that all the time, and it all just went into that lovely six-pack, apparently. Men—go figure. Jen opted for Gertie's insane version of a grilled cheese sandwich and tomato soup which, fortunately, she needed help finishing. I rolled my eyes in pleasure from the cheesy oozy deliciousness of it, and felt completely ready for any amount of furniture moving as we paid our bill and moved on.

After slipping our letter to Elle into the post office's mail slot, Jen asked if we could make a brief stop at Ray's Pharmacy. Kip and I glanced at each other, knowing very well what that was likely to mean. She knew everyone, and *everyone* would be at Ray's—especially on a Saturday. Jen had no idea how to just say hi and move along. But it wasn't like we had a ferry to catch.

Ray's Pharmacy was a pharmacy, of course. The only one on Orcas. But it was also the island's only real game and toy store; gift wrap, greeting card, and candy shop; along with the purveyor of large selections of household sundries and electronics, jewelry, socks and underwear, scented candles, reading glasses, and souvenir clothing for the tourists—which was why it was always so busy. We walked in, already dodging other shoppers as I stopped to use the giant pump-bottle of hand sanitizer they kept out on a cart. It wasn't as crowded in there as Paige's wake had been, but I still hadn't gotten used to being indoors with so many people wearing so few masks.

Jen, of course, hardly got past the front counter before she fell into a "quick" conversation with Felicia Santos who worked at the local hair salon.

"Here we go," Kip sighed into my ear.

"I know." I noticed he was eyeing Ray's huge display of Jelly Bellies. "You know what? Can we just wait outside? Maybe she'll be faster if she doesn't think we're shopping too. And…it's sunnier out there."

He took a last longing look at all that candy as we turned and headed out.

Fifteen minutes later, Jen emerged to join us with a small paper bag and a guilty smile. "Sorry. That took longer than I thought. But you'll be thrilled when I tell you why."

"Okay, I'll bite," I said. "Why?"

"I ran into Marliese back in the pharmacy."

I blinked at her, then said, "Oh!" Marliese was the town vet.

"She told me Larry and Henny Taylor had to put their dog down last week," Jen said, "and that Henny wants a new dog real bad. She's going to check with them and get back to us."

"That's awesome!" I said. "Did you tell her about all the other animals?"

"I sure did. She says she'll ask around."

"Oh, good work!" I gave her a hug.

Kip nodded. "So, shall we go up and keep this party moving then?"

*

Half an hour later, our caravan of vehicles was back up at the Berry Farm. After what he'd seen that morning, Kip had thrown our whole supply of big plastic garbage bags into the cab of his truck, and we'd agreed to start by hauling all the obvious trash out of the house so we could even tell what needed doing next.

"We've already seen Paige's unique approach to filing things," Jen said as we stood in the kitchen, "and we can't risk tossing out the deed to a diamond mine or something because it was tucked into a pile of seed catalogues." She gave Kip and me a weary look. "So, just to slow things down even more, I'm afraid we'd better do this a few pieces at a time, and check for old financial documents or legal papers, or whatever other treasures may be buried in it all."

I sighed. "You're right."

"Well, let's get started then," said Kip, looking brave and resolute as he reached down to start pulling thirty-three-gallon garbage bags out of their box for everyone.

After doing the kitchen all together for moral support, we spread out to divide and conquer. While Kip and Jen tackled the downstairs parlors and dining room, I went upstairs to start sorting out the bathroom and bedrooms where there'd seemed to be a lot less paper and trivial junk and a lot more interesting old furniture and memorabilia.

Hardest of all, though also most interesting, I was sure, would be Paige's room. But I was not yet feeling ready to brave whatever emotional weather that might bring on. So I stepped into the corner bathroom just left of the stairwell. Beyond a lot of mismatched and unlabeled homemade lotion and unguent jars, the most interesting—and least disgusting—things I found there were a couple tiny books on top of the toilet tank: *My Little Zoroastrian Companion* and *Wabi Sabi from Attic to Lobby*, which had a lot of very interesting pictures, despite the silly title.

After throwing almost everything else there into one of my garbage bags, I went across to the other side of the stairwell, and entered what I was pretty sure had been a little bedroom once. There might even still have been a bed in there somewhere under the pile. Stacks and stacks of books—mostly moldering paperbacks and fraying clothbound textbooks—barely left space to get the door open and still stand inside. And behind those, a whole pile of picture frames leaned onto one another with their backs toward me like pages of some even bigger book against a tall mahogany dresser whose drawers I was never going to get open until all the rest of this was moved away.

The books were a much bigger project than I was ready to face today. So I leaned carefully past them to lift out the closest of the frames. I wanted to see what, if anything, was actually framed in them. The first few held prints of no real interest. But my persistence was finally rewarded by an old black and white portrait photo of a good-looking young man and a pretty, somewhat tall young woman. They were standing hand in hand before a small maple tree, smiling at each other. You could see enough of the house behind them and the tree's trunk and lower branches to recognize it. The roof and railings of the porch seemed at least partially under construction, but it was, without any doubt, Paige's house. I leaned forward to study the woman's face, and yes, that was almost surely her nose and jaw line. Her eyes were less deeply set, and her face was utterly smooth and unwrinkled. But it was Paige—and she was beautiful.

Through the half-open door, I heard a stair creak under someone's foot, then another, closer creak. Possibly Jen, but more likely Kip, coming up to see what I was doing here while they did all the heavy junk mail lifting in the big rooms below. "Hey, come look at this!" I called over my shoulder.

When I got no answer, I turned and sidled out around the door with my discovery, hurrying to the top of the stairwell to see which of them it was. But there was no one. "Kip?" I called. "Jen?" I started down to the middle landing where the staircase split, and looked around the corner to find Jinx and Pep, standing perfectly still there, looking up at me as if afraid they were about to be punished. "Oh, it's you guys," I said, just as Kip and Jen walked into the foyer well below them.

"You called?" Kip asked.

"Everything all right?" asked Jen.

"Oh, sure. I just heard the dogs coming up the stairs, and thought it was one of you. But come look what I found!"

I held out the photo as Kip followed Jen up toward the dogs, who watched them in surprising silence. Jen looked down at them, and bent to pet their furry heads. "What's wrong with you boys? Huh?" she cooed. "Have you done something naughty? Is that what's going on?" She looked up at me. "Did you scold them or something?"

I gave her an incredulous look. "Why would I have scolded them?"

She smiled and shrugged. "For not being us? I don't know. They just look like dogs in trouble—and believe me, that's a look I know well." She bent down and patted them again. "Whatever it is, we'll find out. And you know what we'll do then." She scratched Pep's back. "That's right. We'll feed you! That's what we'll do!" Jinx issued demanding little barks until she scratched his back too. Then they all continued up the stairs toward me, the dogs all wiggly with excitement and bravado now.

I held the photo up again to Jen, vaguely aware of some half-forming thought, which vanished as she looked at it and cried, "Oh my lord! Is that who I think it is?"

"I think so! It's definitely this house behind them. Can you believe how gorgeous she is? It was in a stack of other pictures in that room. I haven't even seen the rest of them yet."

Kip stepped in for a closer look as the dogs ran up and disappeared onto the landing. "She's a looker, all right."

"And who's this handsome fellow holding her hand?" Jen asked. "Could that be a *boyfriend*, do you think?" She looked up at me. "Can you *imagine?*"

A boyfriend! *Paige?* I couldn't even…

"If she looked like that, I guarantee you she had suitors," Kip said.

"So you're falling for *her* now?" I asked, trying to look scandalized.

"Why not?" He grinned. "You've got your thing for Timmy Shallot."

"Who's Timmy Shallot?" Jen asked, looking back and forth between us in obvious fascination.

We were saved by Jen's ringtone. She pulled her phone out. "Hello? ...Oh! Hi Marliese!" She gave us a thumbs-up. "That's great! When?" Her brows rose. "Well, sure. We're up at Paige's place right now. You gave them the address? ... Perfect. We'll be here! And thank you! ... Okay, bye." Jen hung up and spread her hands. "Larry and Henny will be here in fifteen minutes!"

"Oh, it would be so great to have these guys—" I almost just said *gone*, but caught myself in time. "—in a nice new home."

"Yes," Jen said, smiling down at the dogs, who'd come running back down at the sound of her phone and were looking up at all of us in great excitement now. "So I guess we'd better go get you boys fed and cleaned up some, hadn't we!" She patted her thighs and started back down the stairwell, followed by two barking dogs and Kip.

As I watched them go, I realized what had been tugging at me a minute ago. None of the stairs made any sound as they descended... any more than they'd done while they were coming up.

But, then, a whole flock of dogs and people made all kinds of their own noise. Maybe the bunch of them had just drowned out the creaking stairs. Or, maybe, I thought as I carried my photo down behind them, those were just two very heavy little dogs.

There was a ruckus of excitement coming from the kitchen as I reached the foyer. I set the framed photo on the wide ledge above the wainscoting, leaning back against the wall, and went to see what I could do to help prepare for Jinx and Pep's big audition.

As I came through the door, Jen looked up from her attempt to keep them away from the cats' not quite empty bowls. "Any chance you could find me a stiff brush somewhere? I'd love to make these guys look at least a little bit more civilized before they get here."

"I think so," I said, already turning to head back up to the second-floor bathroom. It made me cringe to think of using anything in there on myself or any other human being. But the bristle brush I'd seen in Paige's tub would be okay for dogs. I blew a little kiss to Paige and her nice-looking friend as I went by on my way up the stairs.

☙

By the time Larry and Henny arrived, Jen had done everything but tie little bows around Jinx and Pep's necks. Even I might have been tempted by these two picture-perfect little doggies now, though I felt a stab of guilt as the Taylors bent down smiling to scuffle with their new furry friends. Were we committing fraud by dressing these little monsters up this way?

The whole meeting lasted less than twenty minutes, and went better than I could have dreamed. To our surprise, the Taylors even asked me how I'd feel about letting them take Morgan too. All three of us looked at each other awkwardly. "Are you sure," Kip asked at last, "after all you've just been through? This is a *very* old dog, and—"

Henny cut him off. "I appreciate your concern, Kip. But of course we understand…" She looked away for a moment, her eyes suddenly red-rimmed. "The thought that this poor creature might just die alone up here some night, on the darkened porch of an empty house…" She reached up to rub her eyes. "That would hurt me so much worse than having him with us when that time comes."

Kip nodded, looking as sad as I had ever seen him.

Larry bent his head, nodding in agreement with his wife.

Jen called Jinx and Pep back over, and their antics soon had all of us at least a little cheered up again. A few minutes later, Larry opened the rear cab doors of his large black truck, and beckoned to the little dogs. They came barking and leaping, though Larry had to lift each of them inside. When that was done, he started toward the porch where Morgan lay, as always, in his place. But before Larry had gone more than a few steps, Morgan astonished us all by climbing slowly to his feet, lumbering down the porch stairs, and coming slowly over to stand beside the truck, looking up at Jinx and Pep, who barked down at him in a frenzy from the cab above.

Then all of us gasped as Morgan suddenly lowered himself onto quaking haunches and leapt up toward the open cab. Larry lunged forward to grab the shepherd's thrashing hindquarters and shove him the rest of the way in, as the two smaller dogs backed away in relative silence. When Morgan had used what looked like his last ounce of strength to turn around and flop onto the seat with his face poking nearly out the door, Larry leaned toward him until their noses almost touched. Very quietly, he said, "That was brave, boy. But next time, you let me lift you too, you understand? No more heroics."

I knew then that Jen had found exactly the right family for Paige's dogs. Unless Paige herself were still orchestrating all of this herself somehow. I would not have put it past her.

Larry turned to look at his wife, and heaved a sigh. Then he looked at us. "Thank you. We'll take good care of them."

"That's clear," said Kip. "Thank you." He turned to Henny. "Thank you *both*."

We waved goodbye as they pulled away toward the long gravel drive, Pep and Jinx still barking out the windows. Then we turned and headed for the house again.

That's when I realized that Jen had been extremely quiet since Morgan's spectacular stunt. I looked over to see her staring at the ground as we walked, and went to take her hand. She turned to me and smiled.

"You'd already bonded with them, hadn't you," I said.

"It's okay. I'll probably be getting paid to walk them again soon anyway. That kind of work should come back now too." I gave her hand a squeeze as we reached the porch. She looked up at the open doorway. "It's sure going to be quiet in there now, though."

"Well, we've still got the cats," I said, trying for grim humor.

As we stepped back into the foyer, the first thing I saw was my new photograph of Paige, lying on the hardwood floor. "Oh no, it fell!" I said, rushing over to pick it up. There was a long, curved crack across the glass now, running right across the young man's face. I sighed and rolled my eyes toward the ceiling in frustration as Jen and Kip came to join me.

"It's okay, hon," Jen said. "The photo doesn't seem damaged any. Neither does the frame, except this tiny gouge here at the corner, and who'll ever notice that?" She gave me a sympathetic grin. "Probably the cats again, speaking of those weirdos."

I'd seen no trace of Harry or Sam since we'd filled their bowls. Had they shown up at last just to knock my photo off that ledge? Maybe Marliese could find *them* some new home next. They hardly seemed to live here now, really.

Kip slid an arm around my waist. "It'll be easy to replace the glass. I'll take care of it."

"No." I sighed, setting the photo back down against the wall—on the floor this time, where I should have put it to begin with. "We've got half a day tomorrow before you go back to Portland. Let's not waste any time on this."

☙

As much as I'd have preferred to spend one last lovely, lazy morning in bed with Kip, the three of us were back up at the Berry Farm by nine a.m. Kip had been lucky enough to get an afternoon ferry reservation back to America—on a *Sunday*—an almost impossible feat now that spring tourists were no longer hiding at home from the pandemic. That meant we had just five more hours of his muscular assistance. And we meant to make the most of it.

After seeing to all the outdoor animals, we walked into Paige's house and found Sam and Harry standing up on the middle landing, gazing down at us with hooded eyes and disapproving expressions.

"Well, look who's here," I said. "Hunting for something else to break?"

They just went on staring at me for a moment, then turned in eerie unison and trotted back upstairs to vanish onto the upper landing.

Having cleaned out so much basic trash and clutter yesterday, we were now finally able to see what had been buried underneath it. A treasure trove of really beautiful, if often mismatched, furniture was scattered with gorgeous old lamps and vases, knickknacks and souvenirs made of bronze, porcelain, or carved meerschaum, baskets of shells, blown glass floats, and all kinds of other pretty or curious objects—from her import dealing days? The giant breakfront in her dining room was stuffed with lovely old china and crystal. The second parlor's built-in shelves were filled with beautiful books, many quite old. Elegantly framed paintings, photos, pressed flowers and even mounted insects hung on the walls; and richly colorful, if somewhat worn, Persian carpets covered many of the floors. *These rooms must have been dazzling once*, I thought. And the piles of treasure filling all those little upstairs rooms looked at least as rich as what we'd found below.

The problem—especially upstairs—was that even the treasure here was still too piled up to sort through, much less rearrange in any helpful way. So today's mission was to carry whatever furnishings we didn't actually want in the house out to the large barn adjacent to the goat shed/milking parlor.

It was amazing how much we got done in the next few hours. Kip could easily lift and carry things that I was pretty sure would've put me on a Life Flight helicopter if I'd tried it myself. Jen's strength seemed almost superhuman too—from years of innkeeping and restaurant work, I was sure, not to mention all those heavy packages she delivered. The two of them moved bookshelf after table after chair or dresser, loom or spinning wheel, writing desk or antique trunk down the stairwell's two steep flights, across the foyer, off the porch, and clear out to the barn—again and again.

My own skills were…a bit more literary. So I stuck to hauling boxes of books, clothing, or bric-a-brac. By the time Kip had to leave, we'd cleared most of the upstairs rooms of everything except for furnishings that looked like they belonged there. Only Paige's room and office were left—which I was still as reluctant to enter as I'd once been about the house in general, for what reason, I wasn't even sure myself. There was just a strange anxiety hovering over any thought of "intruding" there.

After a lingering goodbye kiss at the door of his truck, I stood watching Kip vanish down Paige's sunny driveway, bound for the Orcas ferry landing, then across the water to Anacortes and a five-hour drive to Portland after that. If dinner or traffic didn't hold him up too badly, he might get in by eleven, with classes starting early in the morning. All for love of me. My knight in shining armor. Or okay, maybe dusty, cobweb-covered armor now. But that just made it even more romantic. *Travel safe, my love*, I whispered to him in my mind.

As I stepped back into the house, I sighed loudly enough that Jen must have heard me from upstairs. "I know, hon," she called down. "He's a keeper. And it's hard to let him go." She came down to the landing where the stairway split. "But he needs to get all trained and certified to make a good living too instead of feeling like he's leeching off some heiress he hooked up with." She gave me a little grin. "That's just how it works with keepers."

I tried to think of some snappy comeback, but I could see the sadness she was trying to hide behind that grin, and it was not for me. Jen was a keeper too. *Such* a keeper! Why hadn't someone noticed that and swept her up already? I just could not understand it.

CHAPTER 5

Jen woke up the next morning feeling pretty stiff from hauling all my furniture around, which made me feel more than a little guilty. "There's plenty to keep me busy up there for days now," I assured her. "You've already done so much; why don't you take a breather today, and go take a long, hot bath?"

"That sounds...like a really nice idea," she said. "Thanks."

"For *what?*" I almost laughed. "Letting you stop working on my stuff for a minute? How about I thank *you?*" Which gave me an even better idea. "In fact, I'll buy you a massage at the Healing Arts Center!"

"Oh, don't be ridiculous," she said. "It's just a few stiff muscles."

"A few stiff muscles is what massages are for," I said, pulling out my phone. "Let's see if they have an open slot today."

"No, seriously. Thank you. That's super sweet, but...I have to cover for Tracy again this afternoon at Darvill's." She gazed out the window for a moment. "And we should probably get moved into the guesthouse today, don't you think?"

I shrugged, frowning. She really didn't like being taken care of, did she. After hosting that huge wake, and dealing with everything up at Paige's place—where I would have to go again in just a couple minutes to feed, milk, and water the livestock—I was in no mood to cram yet another project into my life today. Not that it was really all that big a project. We'd just have to make up both our bedrooms again, and the bathroom we'd been sharing, not to mention cleaning and re-provisioning Lisa's kitchen. Which I knew was nothing next to all we had been doing, but I just couldn't find the mental space for another big change—which was the real issue, I realized. *Change!* There'd been way too much of it, literally from day to day this week.

"You know what? I think both of us could use a little rest," I said. "It's been a crazy week. And I haven't even heard from Lisa yet about her actual return plans. So I'm sure we have at least a few days left—probably a week. We can move tomorrow. I've got errands in town today too."

"Fine with me." Jen craned her head to one side, reaching back to rub her neck. "But tomorrow, definitely. She paid a heap for that guest-house remodel. I don't want to look like a flake when she walks in and finds us here still."

"No, you're right. Tomorrow for sure." Jen was clearly hurting. But she'd been pretty clear about that massage, so I didn't ask again. "I'll just go up and do the livestock rounds, then."

"Tell the goats hello for me," she said. "And bring some of that milk home. I've been looking into goat cheese, and it doesn't sound that hard to make."

"Oh, boy, now I'm going to owe you even more." I had really loved that goat cheese salad Saturday morning.

Jen nodded. "Okay. Great. See you when you're back."

"You bet. Have a lovely soak."

As she headed toward the hallway, I went to put some extra food in James's bowl, and gave him a scratch as he came to check my work. Then I went to find my purse and jacket—and the folder with my copies of the will and those other forms. There was another task I'd been both itching to take care of and wanting to put off since practically the minute I'd walked out of Rosen's office. *You'll want to check and see how much those balances have changed.* Well…getting that one off my list would take almost no time at all, and free up a whole lot of mental space, I suspected.

Any real attention to the money Paige had left me still just seemed so fraught. It didn't really feel like mine. That was the real problem. It still felt like someone else's bank accounts I was supposed to go check up on. To see how much of Paige's money I could spend now, and…I'd be just as happy not to know. Which was silly. Right? But it was how I felt.

So, maybe just checking off this last item off of that to-do list would help me set it down and stop thinking about it? Only one way to find out. I didn't even stop up at the farm first. The morning milking and feeding could wait till I got back, especially now that the dogs had been rehomed. I could just see myself getting up there and finding some excuse to delay the bank trip yet again.

Mysteriously, however, it was Brown Bear Bakery I ended up parked across from—not the bank, still blocks away. Fears were so much easier to face after a chocolate muffin. I'd learned that lesson countless times—even just last week, in fact.

So, I got a nice thick slice of their custardy quiche as well: the ham and chive kind. And a perfectly reasonably sized mug of hot chocolate with whipped cream to wash it all down with. Then, feeling much steadier, I dabbed at the corners of my mouth to make sure there wasn't any foam left, and walked off to the bank, ready for anything.

Minutes later I walked back out to the street in something of a daze. The checking account balance listed on my schedule had increased during the past two years. Enormously. I could not see why anyone would have kept that much money in checking. But, then again, there'd been a lot less to spend money on while we'd all been shuttered up in our homes, and maybe Paige had been paying as little attention to financial details during the past few years as she clearly had to housekeeping. *My god*, I thought, wandering back to my car, *if there's anything at all left in those brokerage accounts, I will never need to sell that house.*

After a quick stop at the hardware store on Crow Valley Road for tarps, I drove up to Paige's place—or, um, my place; I'd get that through my head too someday soon now—and walked in to find Sam and Harry pacing around their empty bowls. But as I went to refill them, the cats scrambled off into the foyer in even greater agitation than usual. In general, I had a pretty big soft spot for cats, but those guys were really starting to get to me. I was glad James hadn't ever been exposed to them. I didn't want them teaching him any of their rude behavior.

Outside, the goats seemed weirdly restless too. Chuck hollered and bleated way more than usual from his pen on the other side of the yard, and Clara even kicked at the bucket while I was milking her, though her chow was only half-eaten at that point. Was she mad because I was so late? Were some of the other nannies going into heat? Or were the goats all actually missing the attentions of Pep and Jinx? I quickly dismissed that absurd idea; the goats had seemed to tolerate the little dweebs at best. But I did spend a few extra minutes with each goat, rubbing their rough shaggy heads and telling them that everything was fine. Even stinky old Chuck, whose response was to try to eat my sweater buttons.

The ducks and chickens seemed no more flustered than they ever did, but one of the barn cats actually flattened his ears and hissed at me as I walked by. What was going on? Had some predator come by during the night?

We didn't have many predators on Orcas—raccoons, otters, and a lot of owls, eagles and hawks—but I couldn't see how any of those would have upset the goats. A big raccoon might, I supposed; they were quite fearless. And so-called "river otters" could just go galloping across fields or forests looking for a new body of water if they felt like it. Paige did have a large pond. An otter had actually come bouncing onto Lisa's deck last fall, which was when I had discovered just how much bigger they were than I'd imagined—and how wickedly bad-tempered, too. Not really very cute at all.

But what would an otter or raccoon have wanted with goats? Their feed was untouched, not even any signs of something trying to break into the bins.

Maybe my imagination was just stirring up more nonexistent trouble. All these cranky animals had even my nerves on end now.

After going to sprinkle water on that one sad little patch of garlic in the second greenhouse, I went back to Tigress for the tarps I'd bought, and took them to the barn where we'd stacked up all those extra furnishings yesterday. The structure seemed fairly dry inside. But there was no telling how much that might change the next time we got a good stiff rain. The air out here was going to be damp either way, and who knew how many creatures—large or small—were living up in its raftered ceilings just waiting to poop or pee on all these pretty things?

As I got everything we'd left out there covered, and the tarps weighted down, I realized it might not be a bad idea to go have a closer look at all her other outbuildings, just to see what, of anything, needed more attention there. I'd spent plenty of time in this barn and the goat and fowl enclosures. But I'd hardly even stuck my head inside Paige's carpentry shop, packing shed, or her potting shed, since…well, since visits with her last summer, actually. What a long time ago that seemed now.

If anything, the first two buildings seemed eerily tidy—as if even she hadn't entered them since last summer. I went to the potting shed last because I knew her absence would be waiting for me there. I'd spent more time with Paige in that long, narrow, many-windowed building than anywhere else up here except the house, helping her plant her seeds in plastic trays or little pots each spring, and with other tasks required to maintain her impossible gardens through the fall. I hesitated before even opening its lichen-crusted door.

When I walked in, the too-familiar smell of soil and fertilizers, dried-up leaves and moist, musty wood hit me like a punch. It smelled of her. I drew a shuddering breath, and looked willfully around at everything. It was all still there, but more neatly packed and stowed away now than I'd ever seen it before. She'd certainly taken better care of this place than she had her house—which, knowing Paige, was not all that surprising, I supposed.

I walked along beside the dry, empty workbench running down its center, taking more deep breaths of that smell, hoping to harden myself against the feelings it inspired. But at the bench's farthest end, I discovered half a dozen seed packages spread out like a fan beside a short stack of plastic nursery pots and a well-wiped if rusty spade—as if she'd been here only minutes before to start this year's planting, and just gone off for a bag of potting soil.

And then I saw which seeds they were.

Blue chicory, Siberian wallflower, jellybean poppy, Sonata cosmos, red lobelia, and yellow straw flower: all of *my* favorite flowers from her garden.

Just last summer, she and I had spent a whole morning watching jellybean poppies bloom out by her pond—pushing their little green caps up and off in mere minutes as they swelled and then burst open in the sunshine.

What were these things doing here like this? Had she left them for me to find, imagining that I might want to plant them...in her empty flower beds? Was this some kind of well-intended invitation to take her place somehow—as if I or anybody ever could? I was suddenly filled with a strange surge of grief and irritation. *You are even coming along with plants, I believe. ... You have your own touch, dear girl, which should be more than sufficient...* Had she thought she could leave not just her garden, but her *gardening* to me too?

I was back outside, stalking toward the house almost before I knew I'd moved, and crying. But these weren't sad tears, they were angry ones. I had to keep swiping them away just to see the porch steps; I yanked the front door open and stomped inside. After pacing around the foyer for a while, I sat on the bottom stair and buried my face in a knot of folded arms and knees.

I was so tired of being ambushed every time I thought things might finally be smoothing out. My life had been great! Happier than any life I'd ever dreamed of! Now I was being bombarded by this hail of *gifts* I'd never asked for. Did I even want them? Did I have to take them? What was I supposed to do with any of it? Those seeds weren't going to make me any kind of gardener. I couldn't just step into Paige's shoes. How had she even thought I would be able to? Paige had been too smart for that. Had her mind gone after all?

Things had been so simple—just a week ago. I *loved* simple! I missed simple *so much*.

Almost as much as I missed Paige.

Where was she? Where had she gone? *Why wasn't she here? I wanted her HERE!* And...then I realized that it was happening again—just like with Jinx and Pep that morning in the parlor. Whose thoughts were these? Whose feelings? Not mine. Or...not mine in any normal state of mind, at least... Was this stress? I shook my head. I'd been under much more stress than this, on plenty of occasions during the past few years. So...what was happening to me?

For a time, I just sat there trying to breathe more slowly, letting all that steam drain back out of my pipes—which it did, oddly quickly. It felt almost like waking from a bad, angry dream. I couldn't remember which number anger was in the stages of grief, but I'd had no idea they could be so sudden and dramatic. If that's what this was...

I looked up and around me, really taking in what a huge, strange place this was now that we'd emptied all that garbage out of it. It had so clearly been a boardinghouse. What was I supposed to do with this much house? Just always have a ton of guests? Board half of it off, like some old Gothic mansion whose family had fallen on hard times? I really should sell the place, whether I needed the money or not. Someone else would make something great out of it, I was sure.

These thoughts were interrupted by a yowl of feline outrage from upstairs, followed by a soft thump and scuffle. I stood up in alarm, hearing one or both of the cats racing across the floor above me. Then I rolled my eyes and headed up the stairwell to find out what dear, darling Sam and Harry had broken now. What was wrong with all these animals today? Were we all stuck on the same stage of grief? When I reached the landing, though, I found no trace of them—as usual. I flipped the light switch on, bathing the landing in the golden glow of a central fixture almost as large as the one downstairs, and looked around again. But I saw nothing out of place.

When my phone buzzed, I almost jumped out of my skin. *"Damn you cats,"* I muttered, pulling it from my pocket to see Lisa's name scrolling across the screen, which cheered me up instantly. I touched the "accept" button. "Hi! I've been wondering when you'd call!"

"Oh, I'll bet you have," she said. "This whole trip back from Virginia has been quite an adventure, I'm afraid. The pandemic may be over, but travel seems to be as big a mess as ever."

"Ugh, I'm sorry to hear that. Where are you now?"

"Well, I'm so sorry to be giving you such short notice, but my itinerary has been changed twice in the past three days—not by me—and… well, I'm actually in Seattle."

"Oh my!" I said. "You're nearly here!"

"Yes. And I just booked a four p.m. flight to Eastsound on Kenmore Air, for tomorrow."

"Wow, tomorrow!" I tried not to sound alarmed. "That's great!"

"It was that or wait three more days in the hellhole this city seems to have become—unless I wanted to take a three-hour shuttle bus to Anacortes, which I'd much rather not. And, from what I hear, the ferry is a pretty dicey proposition these days too?"

"It is. You won't believe how awful it's gotten. They run ninety minutes late half the time now, or just get canceled. What time do you land?"

"If all goes well—which would be a first this week—a little before five. But please don't worry if it's not convenient to come pick me up. If you can arrange a ride—"

"Don't be silly!" I exclaimed. "I can't wait to see you. Although…I do have a confession to make. It's been a crazy week here too. Jen and I had planned to be moved into the guesthouse before you came home, but—"

"Oh, Cam," she cut me off in turn, "that doesn't matter… Is my bedroom unoccupied?"

"Of course! We've never even gone in there—except to make sure there weren't cobwebs hanging from the ceiling or dead bugs on your pillows."

"Well, thank you!" She chuckled. "But please don't worry about moving out. In fact, it may take me some time to get used to all that space again. It'll be nice to have some company."

I almost laughed at that. "Believe it or not, I understand. More than you might guess. So, thank you. And I'll be there with Tigress at a quarter to five tomorrow!"

"Tigress. You still call it that?"

"I still call *her* that, yes. And I'm still grateful to you every time I start her engine."

Lisa sighed happily. "It's so nice to know not everything has changed."

"Well...not everything has. Can't wait to catch up in person tomorrow."

"Me too. Thanks so much, for everything. I'll let you go now."

"Okay. Have a restful night."

"Thank heaven for earplugs," she said. "I look forward to being done with hotel rooms too."

When she hung up, I shook my head and groaned, *"Tomorrow?"* Then I started down the stairs, shoving my phone into one pocket as I dug my car keys from the other. There was so much to get done now, even if we weren't moving to the guesthouse.

✥

Back at Lisa's place, I went right to work on the bathrooms. Then I went from room to room tidying up whatever looked rumpled or out of place. I wanted the house to look good, at least. The kitchen would have to wait until after breakfast tomorrow.

As I was finishing up, my phone buzzed, and I pulled it out to find another unfamiliar local number. *Who now?* But it turned out to be the coroner, calling me as Paige Berry's next of kin to discuss her autopsy findings. After expressing his sympathies for my loss, he told me that she'd died of natural causes. Her heart had simply given out. Though Porter had already convinced me to expect as much, I was still relieved to hear it.

When he asked me if I had any preferences regarding her remains, I admitted that I hadn't thought of it yet. So he gave me a phone number for the funeral home in Anacortes with whom the county had a contract, and suggested I call them about how to proceed. Then he offered his sympathies again, and wished me a good day.

I checked my copy of Paige's will, and saw that she'd asked to be cremated. So I called the funeral home and spoke with a very sympathetic man who took my credit card number, and asked when I might want to come for the urn. I explained that, living on Orcas, it might be several days or more before I could do so. He expressed even more sympathy when he heard I'd be coming by ferry, and assured me there was no rush. I hung up feeling very little, except empty. It had been a pretty draining day.

When Jen got home from penning up my ducks and chickens after her shift at Darvill's, I asked how her aching muscles were coming along, and was relieved to hear that her long hot bath had been very helpful. She told me she felt a-okay and ready to report for duty again. So, I gave her the news about Paige first, since I'm a big fan of leading with the upsides.

Then I told her about Lisa's return.

She heaved a sigh. "This is *exactly* what I didn't want to happen." Then she gave me a brave little smile. "So it's moving night after all! I'll get started on emptying the fridge and cleaning out the kitchen, if you'll—"

"What? No, I just told you, we can stay here. She's looking forward to our company."

"She's looking forward to *your* company. She hardly knows me."

"Oh, Jen," I said, managing not to roll my eyes. "I know this arrangement hasn't always been that comfortable for you, but I've loved having you here, and so has she—right from the start. She was so excited when I asked if you could move in. Why can't you just believe that?"

She shook her head, biting her lip.

"And she'll be delighted to get to know you better," I went on. "She's one of the friendliest, most welcoming people I've ever met. They liked her so much at the prison that they asked her to join the staff, right?"

"And that's supposed to make me feel *better?*" Jen asked.

I looked at her, confused. "Yes?"

"Look, hon, even if she thinks I'm a rock star for some reason, *I* don't know *her*. And this is exactly *not* how I'd hoped to do this. 'Hi, Ms. Cannon! Sorry we're still shacked up in your home—a whole year after you paid top dollar for us to remodel that guesthouse. But enough about me; how was your trip to…well, prison, I guess? Cam tells me you did amazing things there—while I was here slinging packages off a truck.'"

Wow! I thought. I'd never even guessed that she was this intimidated by Lisa.

"I mean, think about it," Jen pled. "If this doesn't turn out to be the love fest you're expecting, where am I even supposed to go if we're still living down the hall? Her guesthouse? Wouldn't that be a little less awkward if we were just already living there?" She seemed completely panicked.

"I'm...sorry," I said carefully. "I didn't realize you felt this way. Sure—we'll go to the guesthouse. Most of our stuff's still over there, and I cleaned up everything here except the kitchen this afternoon." I shrugged. "Let's just grab whatever's left, and go."

Jen gazed back at me, looking contrite and sad. "No, hon, *I'm* sorry. I shouldn't be dumping this on you after such a terrible week. But you know how I feel about flakes—which is what we look like now, whether she minds or not."

"This week's been hard for you too, mostly because of me, and your feelings matter to me too. So, really: let's just go. That *was* the plan."

She frowned. "She really wants us here? She said that?"

I nodded. "Very clearly."

"Well then, I guess it wouldn't look much better if we reacted to that by moving out."

I shrugged again. "I think anything we decide will be fine with her."

"Okay. Let's stay," Jen said, as if I'd just confirmed her statement. "I'll just pretend that she's a super important customer at the Barnacle. But if things get awkward, I'm counting on you to bail me out, okay?"

"Jen Darling has *never* needed bailing out. Just make her one of your fabulous drinks, and one of your delicious meals. She'll love you." I gave her a quick hug, which she returned enthusiastically as James appeared from somewhere to twine himself around our ankles, apparently having decided it was safe to join us now.

"Okay, then!" Jen said brightly. "Since it looks like the evening's free, shall we have a drink?" She turned around, grabbed our last half bottle of Pinot off the counter, then reached up for two wine glasses from Lisa's elegant hanging rack. "So, hon, how was *your* day?"

During our call that night, Kip shared my relief about the coroner's report, and was sympathetic when I told him about Lisa's call. But when I described Jen's weird meltdown over our aborted move to the guesthouse, he got very quiet.

Like, *very* quiet.

"You still there?" I asked.

"Yes. I'm…just having a little debate with myself."

"About what?"

"Well, I prefer to avoid unnecessary trouble by tending my own relationships, and letting other people tend theirs. Which is why I've been careful to stay out of your friendship with Jen." He paused again. "Should I just stick to that approach, do you think?"

"I don't know. Should you?" I was more than a little intrigued. "It seems kind of late for that now."

"Okay, yes. But here's the problem: the idea of being your boyfriend tattling on your best friend—who may already see me as a rival—makes everything inside me squirm. So, if you think I should stop, now's the time to help me out by saying so. Okay?"

"Oh, I think it's way too late to stop now," I said. "But I can keep a secret if you can. She'll never hear a word from me—unless you're going to tell me she's a vampire. Because then I'm moving a lot farther away than the guesthouse."

He rewarded this with a grim little laugh. "No. She's a wonderful person, and no threat to anyone but maybe herself. It's just that she's a lot less sure of all that than she pretends to be."

"Yeah. I've been getting that for a while now. Do you know why?"

He sighed. "I've known Jen since elementary school. Not super well; she was a few grades behind me. But, you know, a couple hundred kids on a small island. Everybody knows pretty much everybody else. And Jen's always been…a bit more visible than most."

"Yes," I said, smiling. "I'd agree with that."

"Has she ever talked with you about her parents?"

"Well…no, actually," which surprised me now that he'd called my attention to it. Kind of a lot, in fact. "They'd be here on Orcas, wouldn't they?"

"Not anymore," he said. "Her dad left when Jen was barely in grade school. And he didn't leave them with much to make it by on. Then her mom left the island maybe ten years ago. She needed help as she got older, but she and Jen had never been on good terms. So she went to live with a younger sister somewhere. Some other state, I think."

"Jen's never said a thing to me about any of this!" I couldn't believe it hadn't come up.

"She wouldn't have. Not anymore. But back when we were all teenagers, Jen made no real secret of how ignored and disapproved of she felt at home; I'm thinking her mom was a lot more focused on trying to survive and taking care of a child on her own than on taking any real joy in Jen. Kids usually blame themselves for everything going wrong around them, you know. It's about preserving an illusion of control, apparently. Adolescent Psych 101. But nothing Jen did—or could do—was ever good enough to win her mom's approval, much less fix anything at home. You see what I'm getting at?"

"Wow," I murmured. "I would never have guessed. Jen's so cheerful and confident and…lovable!"

"Oh yeah. She's been polishing that act since grade school. And it was never even us she was really hiding from, you know. Even now, it's still mostly herself she's trying to fool; the rest of us are all just collateral targets."

"I've always wondered why some guy hadn't snatched her up ages ago. Is she hiding from them too?"

"Got it in one—but only from the ones who might work out. Losers are no threat to her. She can have her fun with them, knowing it'll all fall apart long before they get close to the parts of her story even she doesn't want to see."

"Oh my god! She went straight for Kevin—like a bee to honey, the minute he showed up in that obnoxious RV!"

"Yup," he said. "And how long did that last?"

"But she really seems to envy what you and I have. I mean, deeply. So why hide from it that way?"

"Oh, she wants it all right. She always has. But to get it, she has to push past everything she learned growing up in her mom's house about what happens to people who fall in love. So there she hangs, caught between her longings and her deepest fears. That's called *approach-avoidance behavior*, according to last semester's psych class."

This was breaking my heart. Poor Jen! "Isn't there some way to help her get past that?"

"No. Believe me, countless others have tried. I know half a dozen real decent guys on this island who've had it bad for her at one time or another over the years. She sent every one of them packing, or just ignored them completely in favor of good-looking, horny jerks like your old friend Kevin."

Yikes! I thought. *My old "friend" Kevin?* "So…are you wondering what that poor choice means about me now, Mr. *Adolescent Psych 101?* I was with him for years."

"Hell no," he growled. "You traded him for me—which just proves what a fine head you've got on your shoulders, doesn't it?" When we'd shared a chuckle about that, he added, "Once is a learning experience, love. Over and over again is a strategy. Deep down, I don't think Jen believes she'd survive learning the kinds of things about herself that Kevin seems to have helped you learn."

I shook my head in amazement. "Is all this what they've been teaching you down there? Because if it is, maybe I should look into becoming a social worker too. It seems pretty useful all of a sudden."

"One social worker per household is the recommended dosage. Two can cause brain damage. That's what people say down here, anyway. But, yes, I'm definitely seeing a lot of things in new and much more useful ways now."

"Well, this is quite an eye-opener for me too," I said. "But I still don't see the connection to her panic tonight. Lisa's not some potential boyfriend."

"No, but it's the same problem from a different angle. I think Jen Darling is about three times better than anybody else at everything she does because she was raised to believe she'll never be good enough at all. So people who seem so much more than good enough, like you and Lisa, push her panic button."

"You think *I* push Jen's panic button?" I asked. Just when he'd been seeming so smart! "We're best friends—and great roommates. I can't imagine two people more comfortable together—except for you and me, of course," I rushed to add. "What makes you think Jen is scared of me?"

"I didn't say she was," he said patiently. "I think she's scared of *losing* you, and has been for years now—which is why she's afraid of Lisa coming back to share that house with you. She's been fine with me ever since I left for Portland. But you watch; she'll panic again when I graduate and come back up there to stay."

"No she won't! That's crazy!"

"Is it?" he said. "Have you really never noticed how little life she seems to have anymore, except as an appendage of yours?"

"That's not fair! The pandemic ended all her jobs. How's that her fault?"

"Nothing about this is her fault. But it is her *problem*, and she was already hanging off you like a second coat by the time your play was finished—which was well before the pandemic shut down anything."

"What are you even *talking* about?"

"I'm talking about your starring roles in a whole string of local murders, and then in one of the most talked-about plays Lisa's theater group ever put on, and even that red dress you wore to the closing party; not to mention the great job you got to *keep* through the whole pandemic, and the beautiful house you let poor Jen come live in with you when she was down to one part-time delivery gig. Now you're a locally landed heiress too. How do you imagine all that has made a woman who's afraid of never being good enough feel—about you or herself?"

"Oh! What are you— So it's my fault now?" I spluttered. "Her meltdown tonight was because of a party dress I wore, *once*, more than three years ago?" I felt indignant. "Do you have any idea how ridiculous you sound?"

"People talked about that dress for *months*, love. You made a much bigger splash that night than you may realize, and one of your new acolytes was definitely Jen Darling. She talked about that dress more than anybody."

My head almost literally spun as I tried to make any sense of this. "Did I make you jealous by wearing that dress? Is *that* what this is about?"

He actually laughed for some reason. Quietly, but still… "Is it time to pause this conversation, maybe?"

"Oh no you don't," I said. "We're not pausing anything until you explain… whatever you're trying to say here."

He sighed again. "Okay, I'll be as plain as I can if you'll try not to rip me a new one—before I'm finished. Okay?"

"I'll listen till you're done." I braced myself for who-knew-what next.

"Thanks," he said. "So, the morning you called in that first murder on Lisa's property, I met an attractive, charming, very frightened and utterly helpless waif who couldn't have been more perfect material for

Jen Darling. Taking you under her wing must have made her feel *good enough* in ways no one ever had.

"But then, you did something that surprised us both, I think. You grew and changed, and mastered all that helpless fear somehow. Jen's never managed a trick like that herself; and I still don't quite understand how you did it all so fast. But you're one of the most fearless, genuine people I've ever met now; and, in case you wish to know, it was watching you make that transformation that really made me fall in love with you. But do you know what that makes you to Jen now?"

"A better person?" I asked, mollified a little by all the praise, but still completely in the dark about where this was going, or how we'd even gotten here to start with.

"I suspect it makes you a uniquely important friend who she's not sure of being good enough for anymore. She longs for all sorts of things you have now; and—from her perspective, anyway—you no longer seem to need anything she can offer. You've one-upped her, love, however unwittingly. And I'd bet pretty heavily that deep inside where she's afraid to look, she's just fearing the day when someone who *is* good enough for you comes around and convinces you to leave her where her mother always did: in the not-good-enough bin."

"I would never do that," I said.

"I know. And neither I nor Lisa would ever want you to. But does Jen know that?"

"Yes she does," I insisted. "And especially after all she's done for me this week, I know she loves me just as much."

"I think you're right," he said gently. "But if *I'm* right, love is exactly the problem. She was taught by people with much deeper access to her heart than you or I have to fear love, not to trust it."

I wanted so badly to deny what he was saying. But it was starting to fit too well. Better and better, as I thought about it. "Well… That's really sad."

"I'm sorry, love. I really am. And I could be wrong."

I didn't think he was, though. "So…I kind of can't believe you've just been sitting on all this, and never said anything till now."

"Honey, I meant it when I said I'm the last person who should be telling you any of this. If Jen ever gets a whiff of this conversation, she'll declare war on me. I'm not kidding. She won't stop until she's made sure one of us has lost you. So I hope this makes navigating the waters over there a little easier, but I also hope that you'll forget this talk ever happened, okay?"

"I'll do my best. But thank you for risking it. And for putting up with my—"

"Don't even," he cut in. "Your willingness to fight for people you love and believe in is nothing to put up with. It's just another thing to love you for."

The rest of our conversation was too gooey to report. But when we hung up at last, I lay there on my bed for a long time, thinking through what he'd said, and how uncomfortable it must have been to say at all. My secrets weren't at all like his or Jen's. I knew that. Trying to share them wouldn't clear up anything. It would just leave everything more broken than I'd found it. But I still couldn't help feeling sad for all of us caught in a world so full of painful secrets.

CHAPTER 6

At four forty-five sharp the next afternoon, I stood at the tiny Orcas Island airport, my hair being buffeted by the wind as a small yellow-and-white Kenmore Air plane bumped gently down onto the runway, turned, and taxied to a stop not far beyond the chain-link fence I was leaning on. The pilot hopped out and walked around to open the passenger cabin door, as the terminal's lone desk attendant came out to start loading checked baggage from the plane onto a rolling cart.

Lisa was the third passenger to make her way down the narrow staircase. Her pale hair was longer now, and streaked with gray—which might have shocked me if not for the monthly Zoom calls we'd been having. Regular blue jeans and a sweatshirt now replaced her once elegantly tailored if understated outdoorsy gear. This was and wasn't the Lisa Cannon I'd known. But when her eyes landed on me, the warm smile I remembered bloomed across her face.

"Cam!" she called, waving as she stepped onto the tarmac and hurried forward to pull me into a hug. "Oh, it's so good to see you." She stood back and looked me over. "You look fabulous!"

I glanced down at the small carry-on bag she was holding. "That's not all you have, is it?"

"Of course not," she laughed. "Do I seem *that* changed?" She looked back to where the terminal attendant was still placing items on the cart. "I think we're supposed to get the checked ones inside."

As we walked into the terminal's tiny waiting room, I asked, "If you're not too tired, can I treat you to a glass of wine before we go home? There's a great new wine bar in town called Roots."

Her brows rose slightly. "That sounds lovely. Thank you."

"There's also something I'd like to talk with you about," I confessed. She looked concerned. "Everything's okay, I hope?"

"Everything is fine. But, well, strange and unexpected too. Which is why I thought it would be nice to sit down with a glass of wine."

"Well, it is five o'clock, I believe," she said with a smile. "Let's go catch up."

We drove the half-mile into town, and arrived just in time to snag the last available outdoor table.

"So," Lisa said quietly once we sat down. "I see Kathryn Taylor Chocolates did not survive the pandemic."

"No. This place was empty for a while. Then Roots was crowdfunded. I was a backer."

A server appeared at my elbow. "Hi ladies, what can I get you?"

"House red for me," I said. "And an order of truffled popcorn, please."

Lisa gave me a quizzical glance, then, to my surprise, ordered the same. "You know this place, and I trust your taste," she said when the server had left.

I was flattered. "There's not a mediocre wine on the menu."

"So," she said, after the wine was delivered and we'd toasted and sipped, "I'm dying to hear whatever you've waylaid me to discuss; but can I just say first how really wonderful it is to see you looking so happy, and…well, self-possessed."

"Thank you," I said. "You look great too."

She glanced down at her jeans and sweatshirt with an easy laugh. "That's very kind of you."

I studied her. "No, I mean it. You look—I don't know. Comfortable." Her gray-streaked hair wasn't as expensively cut and styled as it had been once. And if she was wearing makeup, I couldn't spot it, which was probably why the tiny lines around her eyes and mouth were more noticeable than they'd been three-plus years ago. Her casual clothes were rumpled from the flight, and her posture wasn't quite as… controlled, I guess, as it used to be.

But the whole effect was one of not just honesty or comfort, but substance. She'd always been so skillfully, expensively put together. And I'd always thought she looked great. But only now, with that performative mask gone, did I realize how artificial, even brittle, it had been. She didn't just seem more attractive now, but almost regal in some quiet way as she watched me study her with a look of quiet amusement in her eyes.

"In fact, you seem better than ever, which seems surprising." I flinched at my unintended candor. "I'm sorry; that didn't come out right, but...I guess that maybe I'd just wondered..."

"If a year at Camp Cupcake might have turned me into Sheila?" she asked, now openly grinning.

"No! Of course not." My cheeks were flaming. "I just meant..." I glanced around, but in this crowd, it was almost hard to hear ourselves, much less other conversations. "You aren't even just a little bitter about what Sheila and Derek have put you through?"

She leaned back, still smiling. "No. If anything, I'm grateful."

I felt my mouth drop open in surprise. "*Why?*"

"Cam, I have a confession to make. I was worried too, about how much these chaotic years might have changed *you*. And I can't tell you how relieved and happy I am to see they haven't, somehow. I don't know how you've done it, but I hope you'll keep it up." As I wondered if that was a compliment, or some kind of ironic sarcasm I was just too dim to recognize, she added, "That's just the kind of giant question you were always so good at asking. And I don't think we have the time to do it justice now. But the short answer is that, in a way, all this just finished what you started."

"What I started?" I *had* seen that first murder, and called it in; but the trouble hadn't started there.

"Do you remember the conversation we had at my home the day after Derek pulled that stunt at *Salon Confidential's* opening?"

I thought back, and did remember, sort of. "Just after you'd been..." I glanced around again and left it there.

She nodded. "Do you remember what I said, about how you'd been mentoring me?"

"Mentoring *you?*" Had she said that?

Lisa laughed quietly. "Of course you don't. Well, I said you'd helped me to remember the young woman I'd been once, long ago, whose un-jaded faith, vitality and vision had set all my later successes in motion. Is this ringing any bells yet?"

"Some of it." Though, honestly, not very much.

Her smile grew sadder. "I said I'd lost that younger me somewhere in the world she and I had made together, and that I hoped to find her again now that all the *success* I'd been struggling to keep hold of had finally collapsed." She leaned toward me, looking like a schoolgirl with the world's best secret. "And guess who I found waiting for me at Camp Cupcake?"

"That younger you?"

She nodded. "And that's a much longer tale. But if we don't stop now, I'm afraid we'll never get to what you brought me here to talk about. So let's just save the rest of this for some lengthier, less public occasion, and get to your news, shall we?"

Which was when I realized my miscalculation. It had been such a lovely evening that we'd grabbed this outside table—practically rubbing elbows with the crowd around us. Discussion of my unexpected inheritance right here on the sidewalk… Well, that probably wanted a *less public* occasion too.

"You know, I hadn't realized it would be this crowded," I told her. "Maybe when we've finished our wine, we should just head back to the house after all?"

"That sounds like a fine plan," she said, taking a handful of popcorn. "You do still know how to carry the suspense clear through act three, I see." I gave her a nervous smile, hoping she wasn't going to ask how my new play was— "Heard anything from Emerald City now that theaters are reopening?" she asked.

I groaned inwardly. "No. And, honestly, I hope they've got lots of other things to deal with first."

Lisa gave me a wry look. "Still having trouble finding it then."

It wasn't like my struggle with writer's block had never come up during three years of phone and Zoom calls. But I'd been avoiding the subject for a while now.

"I still haven't really even started it…again." She didn't look scandalized, at least, or even all that surprised. Had she expected this? "My third try crashed and burned back in February. I've, uh, had lots of distractions since then."

"Interesting," she said, then, more breezily, "So, should we get the check?"

"Sure. But, just to be clear, I'm paying."

She looked amused again as I flagged down a server.

As we waited for the check, I said, "Speaking of theater, the booster ladies are all dying to know what your plans for Orcas Rep are now.

And so am I."

She gave me an impish grin. "All right—if you promise not to tell them, or anybody else yet. I'll need to manage this transition rather carefully."

That unsettled me. "You're not stepping down or anything, I hope."

"Oh no. Though I'm not going to reconvene the professional troupe. From here on, Orcas Rep will be a true community theater with auditions open to any and all island residents who are interested."

"Wow! That's a really big change. I mean…it's going to affect the, uh, well, the quality of our productions some, isn't it?"

"I certainly hope so." She reached for another handful of popcorn without volunteering anything more.

"Do you have a show in mind yet?" I asked at last.

"Oh yes." She gave me a wicked look. "*One Flew Over the Cuckoo's Nest*, with an all-female cast."

I gaped at her again. "Are you serious? *Here?* And with an amateur cast?"

Don't get me wrong, there was lots of very edgy entertainment here on Orcas, and plenty of people who loved it. But Orcas Rep's audiences tended to be older and more traditional; this was not what they'd come to expect from us.

"That's kind of a giant branding shift, isn't it?" I added.

"Except for Nurse Ratched," she said, ignoring my questions. "He'll be a man, of course."

I began to laugh. I couldn't help myself.

Such a production might win critical acclaim in Seattle, with a professional cast. But here? From our new *amateur* community theater? We might have to rename the play *Swan Song*.

Fifteen minutes later, we were up the street, getting back into Tigress.

"Sorry about all the suspense," I said, pulling away from the curb. "That wasn't my plan."

"Anticipation makes everything better," said Lisa. "So what's going on?"

"Well, so, the day after Paige died, I got a call from a lawyer here in town."

I filled her in from there, trying to make it sound less crazy than I had with Kip. And, I'll admit, it was satisfying to see her do the gaping for once.

"Well, I didn't see this one coming," she said. "But I suppose I should have. Paige clearly had an extremely high opinion of you right from the start."

Really! I thought. Had Paige talked even to Lisa about me?

"So, she has no family at all?" Lisa went on. "They're sure?"

I shook my head. "Apparently."

"And, forgive me if this sounds crass," she said, "but is there much money?"

"More than I'll ever need, I think. She was a lot wealthier than she seemed."

Lisa nodded thoughtfully. "So, you own a house and farm now. And the funds to support them. That's *very* exciting news! I'm so happy for you."

"Thanks. But I just want to make it clear that I see no reason why this should affect my responsibilities to you in any way."

Lisa blinked at me, looking puzzled. "Well…thank you. But unless I've misunderstood, you no longer need the income, do you?"

"No. But that's beside the point. You've been unbelievably generous and supportive to me, and I *love* working for you. You've literally changed my life—in too many ways to list. There's no way I'm going to abandon you now, just as you've come home to put your own life back together."

I darted another look her way, and found her puzzled look replaced by one of amazement. "Cam, are you worried about letting *me* down?"

"Of course not." I looked back at the road. "I'm here for you one hundred percent, exactly like I was before any of this happened."

Lisa was silent for a moment, then said, "I'd forgotten what an impossible creature you really are. And I'm deeply touched. But I think we should discuss this a little further. When we reach the house, all right?"

"Sure." Something had clearly gone sideways here. I just had no idea what.

☙

As we drove the length of Crow Valley, Lisa gazed out the windows with obvious delight. "It's just all so beautiful," she murmured as West Sound's harbor came into view.

Ten minutes later, we pulled into her driveway above Massacre Bay, and drove down to her house. But as I parked, she said, "No one's staying at the A-frame right now, are they?"

"No." I wondered why she'd even ask. Did she think Kip might be visiting or something? I suppressed a blush. "I just use it as a studio."

"Good. Let's go down there then."

"Should I…bring your things?" I asked, hoping she hadn't decided to move in there just because Jen and I were still in the main house.

"Oh, no." She laughed. "Just to talk, I mean."

She smiled around at everything as we walked down the trail, and when the little A-frame appeared, her face lit up even more. "I had such plans for this little place once," she said as we stepped onto the porch and I opened the door.

I hadn't been back there since the day I'd gotten Margaret Rosen's call, and was a bit embarrassed now to find my used teacup still sitting by my forgotten laptop on the table. The bed up in the loft would still be unmade too, I realized.

Lisa gazed around before going to sit in the rocking chair. "I'm so happy you're still using this place."

I sat at the table. "So, did I say something wrong back in the car?"

She looked startled. "No, Cam, everything you said was impossibly kind. I'm just trying to respond without…breaking things I don't want broken."

"What are you afraid of breaking?"

She looked away for a moment. "As you know, I mentored quite a few young women back in Seattle, trying to help them recognize their power, and learn how to embrace it in a world so defined by the assumed importance of men." She looked back at me sadly. "As we both know, I failed catastrophically on one occasion. Though most of those talented young women went on to do great things." Her face grew even more sober. "But I see all that very differently now."

"Why?" I didn't see why she should look so sad about any of that.

"I thought I was training them to find and own themselves. But now I understand that I was only teaching them to perfect a role like the one I performed then, to out-perform the pompous men around me. I'm sure I trained at least a few of those young women to lose themselves as badly as I'd done myself." She gazed out through the A-frame's wall of windows. "It's no accident that when I came here to hide from Derek and his associates, I started up a theater. That's what I'd been best at all along. I just didn't know it then." She turned back to me. "Paige even tried to tell me that, in her oblique way. More than once. I see that too now."

"But your theater changed my life," I said, not sure if I should interrupt.

"That's exactly what I was afraid of," she said, "before getting back here today and seeing how undamaged you appear to be."

"Undamaged? I've never felt happier or more at peace with myself."

"Yes. It shows. Maybe we're both lucky that my arrest yanked me out of your life when it did. But I'm betting your condition has more to do with Paige Berry's influence than mine."

That was a little alarming. I couldn't believe Paige had shared any of our secrets with Lisa—and not told me, anyway. But then, Paige had chosen not to tell me lots of things I'd have thought she would. "What makes you think that?"

"In retrospect, Paige's advice tended to be a good deal wiser than mine. I had no idea then what frivolous kinds of 'success' I'd been peddling—here and elsewhere. I only saw that after finding myself surrounded by women who weren't fighting for prestige or wealth and power, or even for respect. But by the time I met them, they were just fighting for their lives in one way or another. Those women showed me back to my better self—if not always gently—while there was still time to become her again. And I will always be grateful to them for that."

"Wow," I breathed. "So, who are you...becoming now?"

"That, I would still prefer to save for later." Lisa got up and walked over to the windows, looking down at the bay below, the last light of the day fading on the water. "What's important to me now is *your* path."

"*Mine?* You just said I seem fine."

She turned back to smile at me, more sharply this time. "You do. But I think your path has reached another turning point—a really large one. And I'm concerned that you may not even realize it."

"What turning point?"

She nodded grimly. "See? You've had three years to write a play for Emerald City Rep. During a pandemic, with less than ever to distract you. And yet, oddly, you can't seem to get it started."

I looked down, wanting to vanish. As in actually vanish, like I'd used to.

"I'm not saying that to shame you," Lisa said urgently. "That play's unwillingness to come is not a failure, Cam; it's a signpost. Don't be ashamed of it. Read it."

"Well…" I made a helpless gesture. "I've been trying to read that signpost for three years now, but—"

"No." She shook her head. "If writing plays were what you *wanted* to be doing, Cam, you'd have written one by now. Likely more than one. You were never lazy. You aren't even fearful—not anymore. You *are* very talented. But I know a lot more about turning corners now than I ever did before. And I'm hopeful you'll embrace this one, instead of resisting it."

"How am I resisting it? What am I even resisting?"

She tilted her head, and gave me the sweetest smile yet. *"Change,* Cam. We all do. Derek and Sheila didn't put me in jail. Resisting change put me there. Don't make that same mistake."

☙

OUR CONVERSATION GOT EVEN STRANGER from there, and harder.

By the time we walked back over to her house together, lighting the path with our phones, my whole world had flipped onto its side *again*. I'd lost count of how many times that made now in, what—a week? I felt numb in the head, and, despite Lisa's best efforts to prevent it, kind of devastated. Nothing ever seemed to go the way I had expected anymore, and I was wondering if things ever would again.

As Lisa's front porch came into view, I saw Jen's little truck parked next to Tigress, and almost groaned aloud. It was dinnertime by now. She'd have come home from work, found my car there, but no sign of us, and probably conjured up all sorts of unhappy ideas about what *that* meant. Well… Wouldn't she be amazed when I told her.

The front door opened before we'd even reached the porch, and Jen stepped out, wearing a cute little black dress, green tights, and shiny Doc Martens. Her copper curls shone. "Well, hi guys!" she said, grinning from ear to ear as she came out to meet us. "Welcome home, Lisa!"

"Thank you, Jen." Their smiles seemed almost eerily matched.

"I hope this part of your trip was smoother?" Jen asked.

"It was," said Lisa. "And don't you look lovely!"

"Oh, this old thing?" Jen teased, doing a sort of half pirouette. I'd have rolled my eyes if I'd had the energy. "So, you guys must be ready for a drink."

"That sounds delightful," said Lisa.

"Come on in then." Jen led us through the door and waved us toward the living room. "I'll get you guys set up, and then put dinner on." Happily, her charm offensive now seemed dialed down to just six or seven. "I wasn't sure when you'd be back, but everything's ready to go."

As Jen headed back to the kitchen, Lisa gazed around at the house as if unable to believe what she was seeing. Then she turned to me. "What do *you* need right now?"

"I...don't know. But I'm not sure I'm up to doing this dance tonight." I flicked my gaze toward the kitchen.

Lisa nodded. "Why don't you go take a moment to decompress. I'll handle Jen, and then just follow your lead when you get back."

"Thanks." I went to tell Jen I was freshening up, then headed back to my room. I *was* hungry—it was well after seven—but eating almost anywhere else seemed like a much better idea now.

As soon as my bedroom door was closed, I pulled out my phone and called the Kingfish in West Sound. When the hostess told me very sympathetically that their back room required a party of at least five people, but that she could seat us at the bar, I explained my desire for privacy, and asked how much it would cost me to *rent* the back room till they closed. I was an heiress now. Maybe it was time to own that.

A moment later, I returned to the living room where Jen and Lisa were seated on the couch with colorful martinis of some kind, laughing away at whatever I'd missed. James was even there, sitting in Lisa's lap, which surprised me, and stung a little. *Don't get attached*, I thought at him, in case cats really were telepathic. I put on the best smile I could manufacture, and went down to join them. "So, Jen," I said, "Lisa's probably too nice to tell us so, but I bet she's a lot more worn out than she's letting on." I gave Lisa a pointed look. "She may just want to get some sleep?"

"Well..." said Lisa, "since Cam's seen fit to out me, I'm afraid she's right, Jen. Would you be very disappointed if I took a raincheck on dinner?"

Jen looked back and forth between us, clearly mystified.

"Why don't you and I just go out somewhere now?" I asked Jen.

"Give Lisa some time and space to get reacquainted with her house?"

I could see Jen tensing up. "Okay…"

"My treat," I said. "You ready?"

"I guess so." She sounded half afraid to breathe.

"Have a lovely night, you two," said Lisa. "See you in the morning!"

"Sleep well." I waved to Lisa, and my cat, as we headed for the door.

We hadn't even finished climbing into Tigress before Jen said, "Oh my god, what the hell just happened there? Are you guys all right? … Am *I* in trouble?"

"We're all fine," I said wearily. "Just get in."

She buckled in and shut her door without taking her eyes off me. "I knew this would happen. I just knew it. Where have you been?"

"I'll explain. Once we're at the restaurant, though. I don't have the brains left to drive and talk at the same time right now."

"Where are we going?" she asked.

"The Kingfish."

She turned to me with big eyes.

"I said, *my treat.*"

⁂

Ten minutes later, we walked into the Kingfish, and I gave the hostess my name.

"Right this way, Ms. Tate!" she said brightly.

Jen's eyes widened again as we were walked past several small tables and booths in their main dining room to the much larger table in their empty back room, with its lovely harbor views. After settling us with menus, the hostess took our drink orders and said our server would be right along.

"So, what was that pretty drink you guys were having?"

She looked…embarrassed? "Something new."

"Well, yeah. What's it called?"

She sighed. "Ray of Sunshine. Sorry you didn't get to try one."

Oh.

After a moment of awkward silence, Jen asked, "What's happening?"

"I need to talk, with someone. And I can't think of anyone who's ever listened to me better than you do."

This startled her back into silence—for a moment. "So, where were you?"

"At the A-frame. Talking." I watched her face. "I don't think Lisa needs me working for her anymore."

Jen gaped at me. "Because we didn't move?"

"No! Jen..." I groaned. "Just set that down, please? She's never cared when we move out—or even if we ever do, apparently."

"Then why'd she fire you?"

"She didn't fire me. I still have the job, and the salary, and the guest-house if we want it—as her *guests*—for as long as we need it."

Jen's mouth closed. Her brows climbed back down. "Okay, sorry, I'm...not clear on..."

"I know. I'm doing a terrible job at this. At everything lately."

"No you're not, hon," she said. "Just start over. I'll shut up."

So I went back through my whole conversation with Lisa—about the play I couldn't write, and signposts, and how she thought I was missing some huge corner by resisting change—even though there'd been nothing in my life I'd wanted changed at all before Paige died. Except the writer's block, of course, which Lisa didn't think I really wanted to change either. And how Lisa didn't want to be the reason that I missed the next big chapter of my life.

"She thinks she's *standing in your way?*" Jen asked when I finally fell silent. She seemed only slightly less surprised than when she'd thought I'd been fired.

"Not exactly," I said, as our wine arrived.

We sheepishly told the server that we hadn't looked over the menu yet. So she came back after we'd had time to pore over all their tasty choices, and answered a few questions before taking our orders.

"So...what is it that she *doesn't* think she's standing in the way of?" Jen asked as if we'd never been interrupted.

"What I really want to do." I frowned, taking a sip of my delicious Orcas Project Tempranillo.

"Oh! Well...what's that?" Jen asked.

"See, that's the weirdest part of all!" I exclaimed. "Lisa has no idea. She insists there's something else I want to do, but then says I'm the only one who knows what that is. But I don't! I just wanted to go right on doing what I've been doing all along."

"Which was...working for Lisa," Jen said uncertainly.

"Well, yes."

"Okay. But doing what, exactly?" she pressed.

"What do you mean, *what*? You've lived with me for years now! You know what I do for her."

Jen looked thoughtful. "Since I got there, that's mostly been a monthly phone call, shuffling some paper around every now and then, writing a play that's never gotten off the ground, and a big house remodel." She shrugged. "Am I missing anything? Because while that's a pretty cherry deal for what you're getting paid, she may have a point. It doesn't sound all that exciting."

"Okay, stop," I said. "Nothing happened *anywhere* during the pandemic. But with Lisa back, I should be helping her manage all kinds of things again. Except now she thinks that would keep me from moving on to something *better* that neither one of us can even name. That's just crazy. Isn't it?"

"I don't know. I mean, what isn't crazy these days? But I'm still not seeing the problem. If she hasn't fired you, why not just keep doing it then, if that's what you want?"

"The problem," I said in mounting frustration, "is that she said—straight out—that there's not really anything she needs my help with now that she's back home with no homicidal ex-husbands, murder sprees, or pharmaceutical companies to manage anymore. All she's got left to handle is Orcas Rep. And she says that should be no problem at all compared to everything she was doing before."

"So, you're still employed…to do what then?"

"Exactly! See? That's what I'm saying." I took a slightly larger sip of wine. "She was unbelievably nice about it—because, Lisa Cannon: what else would she be? She went on and on about how crucial my help has been, and how much better her whole life is now because of me, and how she'd be so delighted to have whatever help I'd like to give her with Orcas Rep's upcoming season—which sounds like quite a doozy, by the way, though I'm not supposed to say that." *I should probably nurse this wine,* I thought. "You and I are both welcome to keep living there for now, and she'll even go on paying me until I figure out what I want to do. But it seems very clear that I'm supposed to want to do something *else* as soon as possible." I sighed, and looked across at my best friend. "Is she just trying to fire me super nicely?"

Jen shook her head. "Nothing you've ever told me about her makes her seem like the type who'd do things that way, though you're right, this does sound kind of gaslighty."

"That's not it," I said. "I know she really cares about me. That's too clear to question. I think she's just…caught in a tough situation, and doesn't know any better than I do what to do about it."

"Did you ask her what she thinks you should be doing now? I mean, until you figure out what's next?"

"Of course I did."

"What did she say?"

"She asked what kind of condition Paige's place was in. And since she knew Paige too, I just said, 'about what you'd expect,' and she said maybe I should spend some time up there sorting all that out, and just let things 'percolate.'" I made scare quotes in the air with my fingers.

"Just what we've been doing!" Jen said.

"Yep. *That* is apparently my job now."

There was a light tap on the door frame, and the server entered with our food—which was mercifully and deliciously distracting. Jen ordered a second glass of wine, but I told the server I'd stop with one. We'd driven here in Tigress, and no one but me would be driving her home. Not even Jen.

Jen was clearly just as hungry as I'd been, and we spent the next twenty minutes totally absorbed in savoring our meals. The chef there so knew what he was doing. We both ordered dessert, of course, because that's the most important food group. And as we waited for it to arrive, Jen said, "So, I've been thinking while we ate, and I have something to propose."

"*You've* figured out what I really want to do?" I asked with faux excitement.

"No. And you're probably not going to like it, but just hear me out, okay?"

"Of course. You've been hearing me out all evening. Fire away."

"Okay, we both know how much more awkward being at Lisa's is for me now than it is—or was, at least—for you."

I nodded. "Yes. In fact, I meant to mention that you probably don't need to work at charming her quite as hard as you were doing back there."

"Oh, I know," she moaned, dropping her face briefly into her hands. "I thought at first that's why you were dragging me off to dinner like that. I'm so sorry." It was even harder to watch this after my talk with Kip the night before.

"Hey, don't beat yourself up about it. I just—"

"Yes, yes," Jen cut in, looking up again. "I know. And she really does seem very nice. I should get to know her better—and I'd like to—but after everything you've just told me, I really can't see how continuing to live there will be anything but really, really uncomfortable for either of us. In her house or the guesthouse," she added, clearly seeing what I was about to say.

"You have somewhere else in mind?" She still had almost no more work yet than she'd had when she'd first moved in. And it seemed hard to believe she'd be more comfortable letting me pay the bulk of our rent than she'd been with letting Lisa do that.

"Well, yes! Isn't it obvious? You own a *house* now, Cam. A giant one!"

It was my turn to gape. "You're saying we move up *there*? Into that shambles?"

"Why not? I think Lisa's nailed it. We can loiter around at her place now with our hands in our pockets, waiting for her to need something. Or we can go up to your new place and turn our full attention to getting it really back in shape. We'll make so much faster progress if we're waking up and going to sleep there. The animals would like it better too—and it'll be easier to take care of them."

And you won't have Lisa competing for my attention all day... Yep.

I had no idea what to say. It seemed like such an absurd idea, though I wasn't quite sure exactly why, since lots of what she'd just said was also true. I mean, the thought of sleeping in any of those dusty, half-cleaned-out little bedrooms at the Berry Farm gave me the creeps. That place had to be the capital of the spider kingdom. I'd definitely be buying new bedding before even thinking about lying down in there.

"You aren't saying no," Jen said, hopefully.

"I'm not saying anything. You'd seriously rather give up that brand-new guesthouse we spent all last year remodeling in exchange for Paige's giant dumpster mansion?"

"It's not a dumpster anymore. We dealt with the dumpster phase last week."

"By dragging half her furniture out to the barn. I'm not sure that's *dealing* with it."

"And there's another plus!" said Jen. "We won't need to go buy furniture."

I rolled my eyes.

"Look," she said, "can't we just go up there tomorrow morning and figure out what makes sense with all the pieces right in front of us?"

Our server picked that moment to sweep in with desserts, which wasn't really fair. It's amazing how a few bites of really good crème brûlée can affect a person's judgment.

☙

Lisa's bedroom door had been closed when we got home from the Kingfish, and it was still closed when Jen and I got up the next morning. Maybe she really had been tired. After grabbing a quick toaster breakfast, I went out and saw to Master Bun, giving him fresh food and water, checking his bedding, and apologizing for neglecting him so much recently.

He seemed to forgive me. Or at least, he munched enthusiastically on his new veggies in what seemed a very forgiving way.

After that, I grabbed James, without any consult this time, and carried him down to the A-frame. I didn't want him to be in Lisa's hair all day, or on her lap either. When I'd filled his bowls, I told him to behave while I was gone—because even cats enjoy a good joke sometimes. Then I headed back to the house. Lisa's door was still closed, so I left her a note in the kitchen about where we'd gone, and went out to find Jen already waiting in her little truck to drive us both up to the Berry Farm.

First, we dealt with the animals, and as we let the ducks and chickens out, Jen chatted with them just like she'd done with Jinx and Pep. Apparently, she and the birds had bonded too since she'd started coming up to pen them in at night. She was expert at finding eggs, and teased some of the hens who apparently liked to hide their output. Jen even cooed at all the angora rabbits as we cleaned out their hutches and refilled their food and water, though they were shy creatures, not hand-raised like my little fluffbutt had been.

But when we went to tend to the goats, she turned standoffish. "I'll take the eggs inside," she said, as I set Clara up for milking.

I was nearly done by the time she got back. She stood in the doorway of the milking parlor, arms crossed over her chest, frowning.

"Did you have some kind of childhood trauma involving goats?" I asked, grinning to be sure she knew it was a joke, which it *sort of* was. I hoped.

"No," she said defiantly. "Those demonic eyes just don't appeal to me any more than their perfume does." She shuddered. "Please tell me you don't plan to keep them."

I shrugged, feeling very differently about these ladies than Jen seemed to, though I'll admit that Chuck, the billy goat, had never appealed to me much either. He really was a stinky troublemaker, and noisy to boot. But Clara and her kids smelled good to me—actually, all the nannies did. Earthy, but in a good way, like hay and sunshine. And was there anything on earth cuter than a couple of baby goats? "I don't know. We could see if Marliese knows anyone who's looking for goats."

"I'm sure Lum Farm would be super happy to take them," she said.

It had clearly been a mistake to tease her about this. I picked up the pail and let Clara out of the milking stand. "Speaking of demons, let's go in and see what mischief Sam and Harry have been up to."

"Right," Jen said as we started toward the house. "Maybe you can sweeten the deal with Lum Farm by offering to toss them in too. Seems worth a try."

"I'm a little confused. I thought you were eager to come live on a farm?" I asked as we reached the porch.

She didn't dignify *this* jab with an answer.

As we walked inside, I looked up and around the high-ceilinged foyer as if Sam and Harry might be crouched up there somewhere, waiting to pounce. But this morning they weren't even waiting by their empty bowls in the kitchen.

"For house cats, they sure don't seem to spend much time in the house," I said, getting their bag of food out. "I wonder where they're always hiding."

"I don't know what you're talking about." Jen stooped to pick up their water bowl and headed for the sink. "I see them slinking around here all the time."

"Really! Where?"

"Well…" She paused to think. "Following you around, mostly."

I stared at her. "Following me? When?"

"When not? You haven't noticed?"

"No! Not once."

"Well, I don't mean like trailing at your feet. You know how shy they are. But nearly every time I've come to find you, there they were, huddled in a corner or crouched up on the wainscoting somewhere behind you, leering at you like they do. I almost mentioned it last Saturday when Kip was here. But, you know: there was so much going on that day."

"Well, that's not creepy or anything," I said, filling their bowls. Was that really why I never saw them anywhere—because they were always behind me? Stalking me like prey?

"It's pretty funny, actually," Jen said. "Like they think you're dangerous or something. Maybe it's because they smell James on you?"

"You're really selling this idea. Coming up to sleep here every night with demon goats and leering cats. How can Lisa's guesthouse compete with that?"

"Sorry." She laughed. "I'm not staying on message very well, am I? I'll stop dissing your animals."

"How about the rabbits?" I asked. "Have they been stalking me too?"

She shook her head. "They stay in their hutches, far as I can tell."

"Hatching all their little rabbit plots," I muttered, thinking of those long incisors. Wherever I put Master Bun's hutch, it would be nowhere near theirs. Probably on the covered porch. Right by the kitchen door.

"Why don't we go up and pick out bedrooms?" Jen started for the foyer doorway. "That should be more fun, right?"

"I have not agreed to do this," I said, following her out.

"Not yet," she said, breezily.

As we reached the staircase, I thought about the tantrum I'd thrown here just the other day. That whole episode still made no sense to me, but the place did seem awfully big now. "Do we really want to live in an old boardinghouse?"

"Did it feel that way to you when Paige lived here?" Jen asked, flipping on the landing's big central light.

I came to stand beside her. "Well…no, I guess. I never thought so, anyway."

"I don't think it'll feel that way once we're living here either. When we've really cleaned it out and refurnished it, it'll just feel like a house with lots of character again."

I again couldn't help smiling at all her talk of "we." Could this really be where she and I were going to live? Could I even imagine that? And even if I could, what would happen once Kip came back with his degree? Had he been right about that? *Slow down, Cam*, I told myself. This was only about where I should go to "percolate"—not where I was going to live forever.

I glanced over at the nearest door on our left. "I'm not spending a single night here until that bathroom's been scrubbed to a gleaming shine."

"I bet I've cleaned more bathrooms than you've cut heads of hair," said Jen. "That one won't even be a challenge. Next objection?"

"Someplace safe to sleep?"

She made a sweeping gesture at the doorways all around us. "There's a bed in every one of them—complete with mattresses." This fact had been confirmed on Saturday as she and Kip had carried everything piled on top of them into the barn.

"Yeah, but mattresses full of what?" I asked, imagining the terrifying array of creatures that might have moved in since those bedrooms had last been used for anything but storage. "Are any of them even comfortable to lie on?"

"Let's go see!" Jen said, walking to the nearest doorway on our right.

I followed her into a room with interesting wallpaper—if a little faded and water stained in places now. Its north-facing windows let in very little light, and looked out onto nothing but a tiny corner of the pond, nearly hidden behind a bushy wall of cedars. It reminded me of the guesthouse rooms before we'd remodeled. "Too large, and…beige?"

Jen laughed, squeezing around me to head back out the door. "More flair, less space! You just haven't gotten over that A-frame yet, have you."

As I followed her out, she stopped and gazed all the way down the landing—at the door to the one room none of us had touched yet.

But I shook my head. "Not that one. I can't even imagine it."

She nodded. "I had to ask." Then she headed straight across the landing.

I followed her into a slightly smaller but much brighter room. Sunlight poured through not one but two windows onto wallpaper of buttery cream in narrow satiny stripes. The queen-sized bed frame we'd unburied here had beautifully carved maple head and foot boards, and a thick, fairly clean-looking mattress of pale green. Jen grinned at me. "Better flair?"

"Much nicer flair. But…maybe still a little big?" Jen wasn't wrong: I'd never found anyplace I liked better than the A-frame. I just liked to feel a space fit around me like a warm, soft coat. A space I could fill enough to make it mine.

Jen gave me a dubious look. "I think I've read this story. You're looking for the room that's 'just right.' But didn't that girl end up eaten by three bears?"

"I don't think they ate her. Did they?"

She gestured to the mattress. "Want to try it on, just in case?"

"You first," I said, imagining mice or termites or scorpions boiling out of it when I lay down.

Jen rolled her eyes, then turned and fell back on the mattress with open arms like they do in the commercials. It swallowed her. Not completely, of course, but it looked softer than an underfilled waterbed. "Help me out of here." She stretched her arms up to me. "This one may not be for you." When I had pulled her up, she said, "Let's try next door. It's the smallest, I think."

The next room was just about the perfect size. And, like Paige's rooms, it had a nice view of the gardens and the curve of hillside beyond them, even a little bit of water view past that. Lots of light streamed through the casement windows here as well, and its wallpaper was the prettiest yet: tiny vine roses, not too busy—like a pattern from some Victorian maiden's sketchbook. "I actually love this room." I sat down carefully on the double mattress of its rosewood bed. Nothing came swarming or scuttling out of it, and I didn't get swallowed, or bounced off. It felt firm, but giving. There might even be enough room to fit Kip in here, if we were careful.

There were cobwebs in a couple corners of the ceiling and the window frames, and it was as dusty as the rest of the rooms. But there was a lovely old dark wooden bureau against the wall beyond the foot of the bed. Finding things to finish out the rest wouldn't be hard, from what I remembered seeing them carry to the barn.

"Is this it?" Jen asked, trying unsuccessfully to hide an excited smile.

I looked around the room again and sighed. "I loved visiting this house when Paige was here. I just never imagined living here myself."

"Maybe you don't want to imagine it," Jen said. "Because that would mean she's really gone."

Hmm... Was Jen not the only one here hiding things from herself? "I know," I said, thinking of what my mom had told me. "But she's still here." I patted my heart. "And she lived in this house, and loved it for so many years. In some way, she'll always still be here as well, I guess."

"Especially if you are too. She left you her home. She wanted you to have it."

I looked down and nodded, thinking of what Lisa had said yesterday. "So…maybe I should stop trying so hard to resist that."

☙

JEN DROVE ME BACK TO Lisa's on her way to town for a giant load of cleaning supplies. My job was to pack the essentials from our bedrooms here, the guesthouse, and the A-frame into Tigress and rejoin her back up at the Berry Farm with James. We'd decided to come back tomorrow for the rest of it, along with Master Bun and his hutch.

When I walked into the house, Lisa was down in the living room. She looked up and smiled. "Hi there! Did you two have fun last night?"

"Yes," I said, having hoped she might be out somewhere by now. "It was…a very nice meal. Did you sleep well?"

"I slept wonderfully, thanks. I really was exhausted, it turns out."

If there was some graceful way to do this, I couldn't see it. "Right. So, things have taken an unexpected turn for us." Lisa's brows rose slightly. "It looks like… We've decided to move up to Paige's farm. Tonight, actually."

"I see." Lisa's smile melted. "I hope I didn't give either of you the impression that I'm trying to get rid of you. If I did—"

"No! I know. And you didn't. I just needed time to sort things out last night. But I do understand. We both do. This move wasn't even my idea, it was Jen's."

"Was it." Lisa stood up, and came to me. "I'm so glad she's been here for you while all of this was happening. I hope you'll tell her that, okay?"

I nodded, wishing I had thought more about how to handle this.

"Would it be all right to give you a hug goodbye?" Lisa asked.

"Of course." I put my arms around her. "I'm so grateful for everything you've done."

"Me too." She gave me a squeeze. "Our friendship means so much to me. Please don't be a stranger."

"I won't," I said, as we let go of each other. "I promise."

"Is there anything I can do right now to help you?"

I shook my head. "You've already done it, by being so understanding." Then another difficulty occurred to me. A pretty major one. "Um, so, would it be all right if I keep using the Porsche for a week or two? Until I can get another car?"

"Seriously?" she asked. "You think I'd make you walk all your things up there?"

My cheeks warmed with embarrassment. Everything about this was so awkward. "No, of course not. I just meant—"

Lisa raised a hand to stop me. "There is a problem, though. That's not actually my car to lend you anymore."

"It's…not?" Who else's car had I been driving all this time?

"No. I've made plans to give it to a friend. The pink slip is already signed over, I'm afraid."

"Oh." My heart sank. So many goodbyes. "Well, we can just use Jen's truck for now."

Lisa shook her head. "Just wait here for a minute. I'll be right back." She turned and walked down the hallway toward her bedroom as I stood watching in confusion. I'd been driving Tigress for so long that I'd almost forgotten she wasn't mine.

Lisa returned a second later, carrying what I only realized was a pink slip as she handed it to me—and I saw my name written in beside her signature.

"*What?* No!" I held it out to her. "That's ridiculous. I mean, thank you! But, Lisa…I can afford a car now."

"As you explained so sweetly in that very car just yesterday, money's never been the point between us, has it?"

"Well, no, but—"

"I did my best to tell you how much you've meant to me, and in how many different ways, since Sheila unwittingly brought us together. And I hope you heard that as clearly as you seem to have heard that I'm in less need of an assistant than I used to be. I meant to free you, Cam, not push you away. And I want you to have this car that you've become fond of enough to name—because that will help *me* to feel a tiny bit better about this transition. Can I have that? Or must I just be the person who takes things you love away now?"

"I… I'm sorry." I threw my arms around her again almost without meaning to. "Thank you."

"Thank *you*, Cam." We hugged each other hard, and then she let me go.

CHAPTER 7

My mind went on sorting through what had just happened as I gathered our things from the bedrooms and the kitchen, then walked out to the guesthouse to box up whatever we'd need right away from there. As I combed through its drawers and closets and cabinets, I finally admitted to myself that I had never really wanted to live in this pleasant but bland little hutch for humans. It would never have been mine either.

When everything was loaded into Tigress, I went to get the cat carrier, and headed back down to the A-frame for the most daunting part of today's mission.

For most cats, including James, seeing the cat carrier show up means just one thing: a trip to the vet—where terrible things happen. So trickery is crucial. And, as any cat will tell you, tricking them is infinitely harder than tricking a chicken, a goat, or even a dog. Every cat owner I've met seems to have her own technique. Mine was to move his bowl into the bathroom, and then put something really tasty in it, because the next part needs to happen in a space as small and secure as possible. I bet you're wondering why James hadn't just learned to see through the whole moving food bowl trick itself by now. But food—especially extra tasty food—has pretty much the same effect on a cat's judgment that crème brûlée had had on mine last night.

So, once James was in there, blissing out over the tuna in his bowl, I closed him inside and went out to get the carrier. What came next is too unpleasant to describe—especially if you've never owned a cat. Fun fact: a cat really can make himself as wide, in all directions, as a turkey platter—but with claws—when you're trying to push him through the narrow door of that carrier. In the end, though, humans are *almost* always still the winner of these contests.

A few traumatic minutes later, I drove away from Lisa's house with most of our possessions and James in his carrier on the front passenger seat, whining all the way up to the Berry Farm. When we arrived, I locked him into the second parlor with his freshly filled food and water bowls, a litter box, and no evil vet in sight, which must have been even more confusing for him. But no cat's life can be catnip and sunbeams all the time.

With that taken care of, I went upstairs to find Jen in our bathroom with an armory of sponges, bristle brushes, squirt bottles, bleach wipes, Swifters, dingy towels, and rinse buckets, scrubbing everything back into shape. And, to my amazement, the room looked and smelled great.

There wasn't a single item left on any of its gleaming porcelain or marble surfaces except for a few vanilla-scented candles burning cheerfully that looked too new to have come from anywhere here. There were even brand new towels! Our own toiletries were still in a box down in my car, of course. But I could hardly wait to try out the now-lovely clawfoot tub that had still made me shudder just this morning.

"You have superpowers!" I exclaimed.

"No superpowers; this is just pure science, hon. I'll be done here any minute. If you want to take some of this stuff into your room, we can clean that up next."

"Why don't we do your room next?"

"Already done," Jen said. "You snooze, you lose."

I'd been gone an hour and a half at most, and Jen had bought all this stuff and cleaned two rooms already? "Not just superpowers. Miracles! You are so hired!"

She grinned. "So this doesn't seem as crazy to you as it did last night?"

"Well, yes, of course it does. But it doesn't seem as scary. Although…I hope the water in there doesn't come out all rusty or anything. Does it?"

"This house wasn't abandoned twenty years ago. There's been someone…" She shut her mouth and looked contrite.

"You're allowed to say it. There was someone living here. And now there is again. Those towels are lovely, by the way. I didn't even know there was a place to buy them here. Did they come from Ray's?"

"No…" she said, going back to her scrubbing. "I found them in a drawer in Paige's room." She looked back at me. "Is it all right that I went in there?"

"Well, yes. Of course. I mean, *I've* been in there—when I found her address ledger." I looked away and shrugged. "I know we'll have to clean that room out too. It's just…"

"I know. I could do it for you, if that would be easier."

"No. Really." I looked back at her and smiled. "I'll grow up any minute now."

"Well then, is it okay to tell you that I found a whole cabinet of nice clean bedding in her wardrobe too? Because either we use those, or we'll have to wash some. If the washer and dryer even work. I guess we'd better find out. If it doesn't…well, I guess we can't ask to use Lisa's now…"

"Oh this is stupid," I said. "Yes, sure, let's use Paige's linens. They're my linens now. All this is. And Lisa took it like a saint, actually. She's excited for us, and asked me to say how grateful she is to you."

"For what?" Jen asked skeptically.

"For all the ways you've helped me get through everything that's happened. And I don't think she just meant last night either. Or last week. The last few years would have been awful for me without you there."

An embarrassed yet pleased smile was blooming on Jen's face. "Well, it seemed like the least I could do. And I always try to do the least I can."

"Oh, that's obvious," I said, waving at all her cleaning supplies. "In fact, Lisa's so okay with this move that she gave me the pink slip to Tigress this morning."

"She *did?*"

I nodded.

"Wow. That's really generous of her."

"It is. So, she's *not* ticked off at either of us."

"Well, that's a big relief. So, you want to go down and start unloading *your* car while I finish this up?" she teased.

"Sure. Where do you want your stuff?"

"In the beige room you didn't like," she said cheerfully.

"Seriously?"

"I actually enjoy some space," she said. "And it's closest to this bathroom. Plus, since it faces north, I'll never have the morning sun in my face when I'm trying to sleep off a late shift at the Barnacle—if that ever happens again. Don't worry, hon, it'll look great when I'm done with it."

"Oh, I believe you." I glanced around again at the job she'd done.

She opened her mouth to say something more, but froze, looking past me out the door. Then she put a finger to her lips and made a *turn around* gesture with her other hand.

I turned in alarm, but found nothing there at first. Then I saw them, side by side behind the farthest stairwell railing, with their hooded eyes trained right on me. "Oh! You ninnies!" I said to Sam and Harry, striding out to shoo them away. "What is your problem?" Before I'd gone four steps, they slid like quicksilver through the railing and down the stairs. I turned back to Jen, now smirking in the doorway. "What is that even about?" I demanded, as if she'd been in on it too.

Jen shook her head. "Did you bring James?"

"Yeah."

"Where is he?"

"Locked in the second parlor with his things. Don't worry, I closed and latched both sets of doors. He'll be fine in there." Though I was more concerned than ever now about how Harry and Sam might treat him—or what they might teach him.

"I'll go down with you when it's time to check on him in case there's a brush-up to deal with."

"Thanks. I sure hope they get along. Because if they don't, it's not James I'll be booting out of here."

"True that!" Jen said.

As I went back downstairs and through the foyer on my way to the car, I looked everywhere for those dumb cats—especially behind me—but they'd vanished, of course. I didn't check on James, because sliding one of those huge pocket doors open, even just a little, might give the sneaky duo a chance to race into his quarantine chamber. And I didn't need to manage a cat fight before I'd even unpacked our things. He'd be fine in there, until dinner anyway.

After bringing things up from Tigress, Jen and I cleaned my room, and then enjoyed a little scavenger hunt for other furnishings to finish out our bedrooms. We began by dragging two wardrobes from rooms we hadn't chosen into those we had—which pretty much filled all the space left in my room. Finally, Jen declared that it was time to open up a bottle, wash out two of Paige's many mismatched but interesting wine glasses, and start working on our first dinner in not-Lisa's house—which would be essentially the dinner she'd intended to make for Lisa's homecoming last night, which I was looking forward to this time.

"But first," I said, "I think it's time to go see how James has been adjusting. Want to come referee?"

"Let's do it!" Jen said.

Downstairs, after looking around for any sign of Harry and Sam—which we didn't find even behind me, of course—I went to the parlor's closed pocket door and said, "Hey in there, tough guy. How's it going?" I put my ear to the wood, but heard no response of any kind from James. "You awake in there, little man?" I asked. Still nothing. I looked back at Jen. "Just help me make sure he doesn't come racing out before I can get in there, okay?"

She nodded, and positioned herself.

"Time to rejoin the world, okay?" I said a little louder, and slid one panel of the door a couple inches into its recess. When James didn't appear, I glanced at Jen and slid the opening a little wider. Still nothing. So I slid the door all the way, and finally saw James standing underneath a table beside his empty food bowl, looking up at me in silence. "Hey, buddy, why so quiet? Is this place feeling strange?" As he turned away to look at something well back in the room, my gaze followed his. Then I gasped as Jen hurried in beside me to gape as well at Sam and Harry, staring back at us from just in front of the dining room's still tightly closed pocket doors.

For a moment, all three cats just looked back and forth at us, and at each other, and at us again—as if James were saying, "Who are these guys? Do I have to share my food with them?" and Sam and Harry were asking me, "You have a cat? You sure don't act like a cat person."

"They don't seem to be fighting," Jen whispered.

She was right. They all looked more confused than hostile, which was a nicer surprise than their presence here. "I made so sure these doors were closed—they're still closed. And we've seen these two since I did it."

"Have I mentioned that they're kind of creepy?" Jen asked.

"If you didn't, I did."

At that moment, all three of them turned to look back at us.

"This is just the weirdest thing!" I'd always joked about how cats can walk through walls, but I'd never meant it quite this literally. This was really giving me the willies. I leaned down and looked at James, patting my leg gently. "Hey, little man, wanna come say hi?"

James gazed across the room again at Sam and Harry, then sauntered over to me, shooting them glances all along the way. I held my arms out, and he jumped right into them, which told me he was not as nonchalant as he pretended. Then I stood up and walked further in to have a word with his two visitors. But they just slid quickly and silently around Jen and me, and raced out through the open pocket door, heading for the foyer.

I exchanged a helpless look with Jen before gazing down at James. "So, what do you think of your new housemates, hmm? Were they kind of scary?"

He just stared up at me, then shrugged out of my arms and leapt back down to the floor to start pacing almost casually around, sniffing at the carpet and other things I couldn't see. I looked up at Jen again. "Should I try keeping him in my room for tonight?"

"You're the cat lady here. But we just saw how keeping cats where you want them works." She gave me a sympathetic shrug. "I'm going to go make those drinks."

༄

THE BRUSSELS SPROUTS WERE WASHED and trimmed, the pancetta was cubed, the lettuce was torn for salad, and the pork tenderloin was seasoned. Jen kept expressing her pleasure at the vast amount of counter space that had been hidden under all that garbage—though she loathed the terrible old electric stove. She cursed and swore as she tried to control burner temperature under a relish she was sautéing, while also trying to keep the risotto at the right temperature on an adjacent burner. "I could just cry, thinking about that beautiful Wolf gas range back at Lisa's," she said, as she opened the oven to slide in the pork loin.

And minutes later, as if to prove her point, that current-hogging stove sent our whole dinner right down the tubes. She'd just gotten the Brussels sprouts going in her precious air fryer when a fuse blew, plunging the whole kitchen into darkness. I had never before heard such a blue streak from Jen as she turned her phone's flashlight on and went racing out the back porch door to go reset the breaker in the root cellar. By the time the lights came back on and she hustled back in, the damage had been done. Everything on the stovetop was burnt, and everything in the oven and the air fryer was underdone and impossible to fix properly.

"At least we have prosecco!" Jen exclaimed, going to pull the bottle she'd bought in town out of Paige's big old fridge.

A short while later, we were seated by a crackling fire back in the second parlor, finishing off the bottle, and satisfying our hunger with a box of crackers. "How in the world did she cook on that thing?" Jen wondered.

"I only ever had tea here, maybe she didn't eat. That might explain why she kept leaving her vegetables on my porch." I sipped my glass of bubbly delight and grabbed another cracker. "But seriously—that stove probably worked fine for her. She didn't have anything crazy like an air fryer."

"Or a telephone, or a computer…" Jen pointed out. "I cannot live without that air fryer. Or a gas stove, honestly."

"Gas stoves are being phased out…" I started, then hesitated. I didn't like electric much either.

Jen nodded. "I know. But hon, though electric may be the future, we're living in a house of the past."

"Yeah. I'd rather have a gas stove too," I admitted, "or propane, at least. But I'll start looking for an electrician in the morning, and see if we can at least get that fuse box updated to work in this century."

"Good luck finding one before winter," Jen said, taking a sip of her prosecco. "I can price new stoves, and work on arranging for propane up here. Just give me a budget and I'll take care of all the legwork." Then she seemed to catch herself. "I mean, if that's okay with you. I don't mean to be spending your money," she said uncertainly.

"Hang on." I set my glass on the coffee table. "I don't want the money Paige left me making things all weird between us. So let's just talk about this, and get that out of the way."

"Well…fine. But didn't we kind of have that talk when I moved in with you three years ago?"

"Yeah. But that wasn't really my money, not like this is. So, first, after managing Lisa's bills all these years, I'm pretty aware of how much money it'll take to keep this big house up, and all its grounds. I'm just going to say—to you, and no one else, please—that I have way more money now than I'll ever need to live on. So if we decide there's something more we need up here, like a gas stove, for instance, it's not going to beggar me. If you were worried about that, you can let that go now."

"Okay. Good to know."

"Second," I said, "I have more money now than most people I know do. That's no fault of mine, and my head doesn't feel any bigger than it ever has. I know how you feel about even the appearance of freeloading. But from the day you moved in with me at Lisa's, you did as much or more work around her place than I did, and things are already going that way up here too. So, the way I see it, you're bringing as much value to our lives as I am—no matter how the money happens to be distributed, right?"

"If you say so."

She sounded almost like an obedient schoolgirl. And I could just hear Kip's voice in my head saying, *You can't fix this, Cam.* But that sure didn't mean I wasn't going to try. "I do say so," I told her. "You have never sponged, and you never will. I don't even think you're capable of it. So I'm counting on you to own the value of *your work* here, not just my money. Can you do that?"

She nodded.

"Good. That's important to me. And most important of all: though I may own this house, as long as we're both living here, it's going to be *our* home, not just mine. Whatever *we* decide to do, we'll do together. And while I don't want anyone spending my money without telling me, you should never be even a little bit uncomfortable about proposing things. Since I am the one who benefits from the value of this house, any repairs or improvements we decide to make will be paid for by me, never by you. If I agree to do something, it'll be because I want to. Does that all make sense?"

"Absolutely," said Jen.

"I don't ever want money to be this awkward unspoken thing between us," I said. "We're living together, and I want that to continue working just as well as it always has."

"Me too!"

"Good." I picked up my drink and took a sip, trying to think of anything more I'd missed. "I promise to be clear and honest with you about any issues that might come up, financial or otherwise. You'll never have to worry about how I really feel, okay?"

"Way better than okay." Then she grinned. "But you do *totally* want a ginormous six-burner gas range."

I laughed. "You're probably right. So, by all means, get on that ASAP."

☙

I WOKE UP THE NEXT morning in a strange if very comfortable bed, and peered around me at a lovely little room washed in morning sunlight. This was my new life—and I realized that, weirdly, once I'd finished tending to the menagerie outside, there would be no other urgent tasks ahead of me for…well, the foreseeable future! Everything but this was gone now, and the sudden transition from life I'd just lost and this one felt oddly magical. I really could do anything I wanted now.

So, why not drive Tigress down to the ferry landing, and go get her reregistered at the courthouse in Friday Harbor on San Juan Island? It might take all day—or even longer if I got really unlucky. But would that matter now? Where was the rush anymore? I could just think of it as a recreational excursion!

Inter-island ferry travel was a slightly different thing than ferry travel to the mainland. It was much less expensive, for one thing, and there were no vehicle reservations at all, which made things much easier. You just showed up as early as possible and waited in line for first-come, first-serve boarding—like things had been done back in the old days. But there were fewer daily inter-island sailings these days, and every time an Anacortes-bound ferry broke down or couldn't scrape up a full crew, they'd just yank the inter-island boat out of service—often without warning—and use it, or its crew, to fill the mainland service gap. If that left people unable to reach important appointments, or stranded on some other island overnight, too bad, so sad.

But that day just went on being magical, and I managed to get through the forty-minute sailings there and back in just a single day. I even had time for a relaxed lunch in Friday Harbor, and a turn through the town's two amazing bookstores. When I got home that evening, Tigress was truly mine. And so was my life, as it had never been before.

Of course, even magical lives rarely go as simply as one might hope. A few days later, my briefly idyllic bubble was burst by an almost unbearably cute young male goat. Paige's note to me had mentioned going to see Laurie at Lum Farm about "banding" baby Nick. I'd already met her once, and gotten all kinds of really useful insight on caring for our goats. But now, sadly, it was time to go see her again, and act on one of her most unpleasant instructions.

Do I have to explain what banding a young male goat is? I'd rather not. Suffice it to say that, with Lum Farm's generous assistance, Nick would never become a billy, which ought to mean that I could keep him at the Berry Farm without ever having to deal with such a situation again.

To my tremendous relief—after checking with her bosses—Laurie not only took little Nick's banding off my hands, but offered to give the nannies, Freddy, Ginger, and Klinka, a new home at Lum Farm too, along with the infamous Chuck. I'd decided I couldn't bear to let the adorable, playful kids go…and Jen had already produced two batches of delicious chevre, which had turned out to be amazingly fast and easy to make. So Clara would be staying with us on the Berry Farm too.

When I asked Laurie if she happened to want some angora rabbits as well, she'd looked thoughtful, and pulled her phone out again. By that afternoon, the Berry Farm had nine fewer animals for me to take care of.

Jen was at least as thrilled about all this as I was. And who could blame her? So many fewer animals to care for freed us up to make more runs to the dump, do days and days of deeper cleaning, and start the fun work of rearranging furniture and deciding how to decorate all those beautiful rooms.

I offered to hire people for all this work, of course, but Jen's answer was always the same. "Sweat equity, hon." Well, I sure wasn't going to sit around doing my nails while she worked that way on *my* house; so, basically, she made a lot of extra work for both of us. She was my bestie, though, and it was all great exercise, which made the flood of scones and chocolate muffins I kept rewarding us for our labor with a whole lot more guilt-free.

One afternoon, while cleaning the front parlor, Jen and I were moving a long, very heavy chest of drawers away from the wall to clean out the mass of spider webs and dead bugs that lurked behind pretty much every stationary object of any size here. As we dragged it out into the room, we discovered a hole, six or seven inches wide, crudely sawed through the wainscoting baseboard and the lath and plaster wall behind it.

"What on earth is that?" Jen exclaimed as we stood looking down at it.

"Do you think…there's something in there?" I asked nervously.

"Like what? The cask of Monte Crisco?"

"No, I mean something alive. Like a rat."

Jen rolled her eyes. "I haven't seen a rat dropping in this whole house yet. But I'll go look, if you're too scared to." She got down on hands and knees to crawl around behind the chest.

"I'm pretty sure that cask wasn't named Crisco," I said, a little stung by her remark. She knew very well I'd faced down murderers. Did I really have to deal with rats now too?

(And she was a fine one to talk anyway, I thought. Miss Afraid-of-Goats.)

"You're the writer. You would know," she said, pulling out her phone and turning on its flashlight before peering into the hole. "Oh wow! Look at that!"

"What is it?" I asked, stepping farther back.

Jen turned to grin up at me. "Not even termites!" She wriggled back out and stood up again. "No rodent droppings in there either. Wood looks dry and sound; not even any spider webs or mold to speak of, which seems surprising, but all definitely good news in a building this old."

"Okay. But what's it there for?"

"You knew Paige better than I did," Jen said. "You want to hazard a guess?"

She had a point. "Well, shouldn't we fix it, at least, before we put the chest back?"

"With what? Duct tape? This is a carpentry issue, and I'm no more a carpenter than I am a chimney sweep. We'll just have to put the chest back when we're done here and find someone to patch this later."

There were lots of spider webs to clean off the chest's back and around the short, carved legs that held it off the floor, as well as on the wall behind it. But, as Jen had said, none at all in the hole itself, though I'd have expected that to be the best lair of all for crawly things.

Finally, we rolled up our sleeves to go face the kitchen, or as Jen still liked to call it, "the heart of darkness." We did the easiest things first, like scouring old stains off the countertops, wiping down the insides of countless cabinets and shelves, and scrubbing out the double sink until it was completely white and even shiny—a thing I'd have thought impossible. But when it came to cleaning, Jen had years of expertise under her belt. I was getting quite an education.

"Well, I've got one good thing to say about this kitchen," Jen said after we'd been at it for a while. "I keep waiting for the rodent droppings to turn up here at least, but I still haven't seen a single one. I'm starting to think those two creepy cats must be amazing mousers. I can't think of any other reason this place isn't a rodent theme park."

Hmmm. Was that what Paige had seen in Sam and Harry? Did it mean I had to keep them too? Not that I'd actually decided to get rid of them…yet. Despite all their unpleasant habits, they seemed to be tolerating James far more politely than I'd feared.

And they were cats, after all. I liked cats.

Theoretically.

When all the "easy" stuff was finally done, we braced ourselves to level up, and pulled the fridge out of its alcove. What we found behind it was another hole hacked through the wall just like the last one, but slightly *above* the baseboard this time.

"Okay…what the heck is this about?" I asked.

Jen stared at it, rubbing her chin. "Could Paige have been looking for something?"

"Inside the walls? Like what?"

Jen shrugged and gave me a deadpan look. "Buried treasure? Maybe that's where all this money she left you came from. Out of all these little holes. *That's* where the deed to the diamond mine is."

"Very funny. But I'm serious. This is just too weird." I shook my head, thinking. "She did have a giant soft spot for animals. Like, any kind of animals. You think she was just trying to make it easier for the rats to get *in?*" I could just see them, pouring in here every winter to warm their little hands at Paige's oven or her fireplaces as she looked on fondly.

"Oh good heavens!" Jen exclaimed, gaping at me, wide-eyed. "I bet that's it!"

She didn't look like she was joking this time. "Letting rats in? Really?"

"No! Letting the *cats* in—to the walls!"

"What? Why would she—?"

"No rodent poop in this whole jumble of a house?" Jen said again. "The walls are where they live, and how they move around. And not even cats can get them there—unless…" She gestured at the hole.

"You're kidding me." But I knew she wasn't. This did seem like something Paige might have done. I could easily imagine her down on her hands and knees, hacking away with some little saw at her own woodwork as the cats stood by. *Now get in there, you two, and put an end to all this foolishness!* I brought a hand to my mouth and laughed. "Oh, Paige!"

"Come with me," Jen said, striding out into the foyer. I followed as she passed through the front parlor without pausing, and then into the second parlor, where she stopped and stood looking around the room.

"We moved everything in here when we cleaned," I said. "There wasn't any hole."

But she'd already turned to look behind us at the massive floor-to-ceiling bookshelf standing between the corner fireplace and the dining room pocket doors. "We didn't move that," she said, already walking toward it. It had been far too heavy to move without taking all the rows and rows of books down off it; and, like the front parlor chest, it too was held five inches off the floor on heavy, beveled wooden legs. Jen pulled her phone out and turned its flashlight on again as she lay down on the rug to look back into the shadows underneath. "There it is!" She got up and smiled at me triumphantly. "Cats really *can* walk through walls in this house. This is how the little buggers did it that night you left James in here."

"And how they keep disappearing everywhere else," I said, amazed. "Well, I'll find someone to get down here right away and have all these closed up."

"*What?*" Jen looked at me like I was crazy. "No, no, no. I mean, if you want to block off one or two—like in your bedroom, or—"

"There's one in my *bedroom?*" I cut in, horrified by the idea of being joined some dark night by those two furry little demons.

She gave me an annoyed look. "I have no idea. I just… Never mind. All I'm saying is, if these hidden holes are what's kept this house so rodent-free, we'd be idiots to get rid of them, or of those cats. We can start looking now, and if we find any of these where you don't want the cats to go, we can block them. But let's leave the rest." She looked back at the bookshelf and shook her head. "Who but Paige Berry would ever have thought up a thing like this?"

THE NEXT DAY, AT MY insistence, we looked under or behind whatever furniture was left upstairs for any more of Paige's little cat holes. Harry and Sam followed us the whole time, and meowed plaintively when we uncovered the first one behind an unused wardrobe in the small room across from mine. "Oh yes," I turned and said to them, "we're on to your little secret now." Sam turned away and paced out of the room, as if there must be something far more interesting out on the landing. But Harry went on glaring up at me defiantly, as if I'd just found a pack of cigarettes in his sock drawer. We found another one in the room next door to mine, behind the bed that swallowed people. Boy, was I ever glad I hadn't chosen that room.

Luckily, my room seemed cat-hole-free. Jen's room did have one, under the bed again, but she didn't seem to care. All she said was, "I'm a sound sleeper. And they don't seem to mind me as much as they do you." She assured me that if we ever needed to use the other rooms for guests or anything, we'd just block the holes up temporarily. So I agreed to leave them.

There were only two upstairs rooms left to clean now: Paige's—which I'd developed a weird phobia of thinking about, much less entering—and the room just to the right of hers on the landing's north side. As Jen and I were midway through deep cleaning that one, she asked, "What are we going to do with all these rooms? It's not like three or four of our friends are all going to come stay overnight."

"Slumber party at Jen and Cam's house!" I joked, clearing cobwebs from the ceiling with an extendable duster.

"Right. That sounds like us. But seriously, what should we do with them?"

I shrugged. "You're the one who talked me into this move. Haven't you got any ideas?"

"Not really, unless you want to open up an inn," she laughed.

"No thank you! Even what's left of Paige's little farm is keeping me plenty busy without taking on the care and feeding of a bunch of humans too. I hear they can be even more trouble than goats."

"Well, if you kept handling Clara and her kids, I'd be happy to take care of the humans," she said. "Those shouldn't need milking, at least."

She was wiping down a window sill with her back to me, so I couldn't see her face, but…was that just a joke? "Would you like to run an inn?"

She turned around, looking startled. "Heck no. That business is way too risky anyway, unless…" She shook her head and turned back to her cleaning.

"Unless what?"

"Nothing," she said, still scrubbing.

"No, seriously, what were you going to say?"

She turned back around, looking put upon. "Well, I was going to say, unless you have lots of money to work with. But then I realized how that would sound, and it's not what I meant."

"Hey." I gave her a reproachful smile. "Didn't we talk about this our first night here?"

"Yes, I know." She went back to window cleaning. "Sorry."

"All right then," I said, primly, as if we'd settled something.

Over a lunch of bacon, lettuce, tomato, and avocado sandwiches down in our newly beautified kitchen, Jen looked at me uncertainly. "You know, there's only one room left up there to clean."

I sighed, and set my sandwich down. "I know."

She watched me.

"All right," I said. "It's long past time."

After lunch, we walked upstairs with armloads of collapsed cardboard boxes. I was grateful for Jen's company. It felt like a layer of insulation between me and the presence I was sure would fill that room for me. But as we leaned our boxes against the wall outside the doorway, I still didn't feel ready to go in there and just cart everything off without a moment to say goodbye somehow to all these last, most intimate pieces of Paige's life. When we were finished here, this would just be one more empty room like all the others. Paige would be completely gone.

I turned to Jen. "Can I have a couple minutes first?"

"Of course." She gave me a quick hug, and started back toward her room. "Come get me whenever you're ready."

I drew a long breath, and walked back into Paige's room for the first time since I'd come here looking for her address book. It hadn't seemed nearly as hard that time. But I'd just been looking for a thing then, not coming to dispose of her this way.

I hadn't thought much last time about how neatly made her bed was. I wondered if the woman who'd left the rest of her house in such a mess had always made her bed so perfectly, or if this had been part of her private goodbye on that last morning.

There were a few books and an empty water glass on her maple burl nightstand, underneath a small frosted glass lamp shaped like a spiral of art nouveau lilies, and I went to see what she'd been reading. On top was a tiny green book called *Fail Better!*, which turned out to be a collection of short quotes about the value of failing. Did she think she'd failed at something? The second book was a thin photographic history of Orcas Island; and the last and thickest book was entitled *Shamanic Voices: A Survey of Visionary Narratives* by Joan Halifax, Ph.D. I flipped through that one for several minutes, but if any of the "maps" Paige had mentioned in her letter were in there, I didn't find them.

Above the bed's carved maple headboard hung a large Japanese silk fan washed in pale, watery colors with a little school of fish swimming across its pleated surface. Had she ever been to Japan, I wondered?

I turned around to gaze at the contents of her art deco vanity which, amid some little jars of her own herbal unguents, creams, and lotions, included two tiny, exquisite blown glass perfume bottles. Their insides held nothing now but the frost of long-evaporated scents. Beside them lay a gorgeously inlaid comb and hand mirror set, and a small pile of the organic-looking "goddess jewelry" Paige had always worn to festive events. High above these, tucked in between the vanity's large oval mirror and its beveled frame, were several tiny black and white photographs, all clearly very old. They were mostly portrait shots of lovely young women she must once have known. Tacked onto the mirror frame across from them was a beautiful engraved gold comb—the kind for holding hair up, not for untangling it—and tucked into its slender tines was a slightly larger black and white portrait of a young man who looked strangely familiar. I slid it carefully free, then lifted it closer before recognizing his face from the framed photo I'd found while Kip was here. The one that Paige's cats had knocked onto the floor and broken.

As if summoned by the thought, I heard a tiny sneeze behind me, and turned to find Sam and Harry standing in the doorway, gazing up at me intently.

"I'm sorry." The words were barely more than whispered, and had come out of nowhere. I wasn't even sure what I'd meant. That I too was sorry their mistress was gone? Or sorry that I'd come here now to erase even her private nest? Sorry...that I'd felt such dislike for these two cats without even wondering what her absence made *them* feel? Or all of those, and more.

I shooed the cats gently away as I went to the door and called for Jen. This was too much, and too hard. If I went on looking through Paige's things this way, I'd still be here at dinnertime. Or tomorrow.

"Let's just box all this up and move it to the room next door," I said as Jen approached. "I'll look through it all later."

"Okay, but…" She slowed to a halt amidst the ankle-swirl of cats, which now included James. He'd shown up from somewhere too. It relieved me to see them all getting along so comfortably, but it unnerved me too. From what I knew, that wasn't how cats were in general, and Harry and Sam had seemed especially unwelcoming—with me, at least. "If we're just going to move it all next door… Well, is this still too soon?" Jen asked.

I shook my head. "It'll help, I think, to do this in stages. Let's just get the room emptied and cleaned up today. I'll go through it all in batches, later."

"Right. Let's go then." She shooed the cats away more forcefully as she leaned down to pick up some boxes. "Let's start back in the office?"

It took me a few minutes to realize how smart she'd been—again. Almost everything back there was much less personal and difficult to deal with. Like the three-drawer filing cabinet stuffed with manila folders full of old paperwork. I'd have thrown it all out right then if I'd been sure there wasn't a stock certificate or some long-lost letter from President Truman tucked in there somewhere too. The little rolltop desk held only old stationery supplies, a plain, workman-like fountain pen, some pretty little ink bottles, sticks of green metallic sealing wax, a little box of "forever" stamps, and a small stack of the fine paper her note to me had been penned on. At the back of its wide, shallow front drawer, I found a couple of programs and a poster from *Salon Confidential*, which brought a brief lump to my throat.

In very little time we were finished there, and back to Paige's bedroom.

In the bottom drawer of her gorgeous antique dresser I found carefully folded clothes unlike any I had ever seen her wear. Beautiful silk or brocade blouses, scarves, and a few dresses clearly made for a much more slender woman, in styles from a century I hardly remembered. In the small top drawer of her vanity, I found a little hinged red leather box filled with jewelry that seemed unlike Paige too. Delicate garnet earrings, a fine gold chain from which a little opal pendant dangled. There was more, but I closed the box and shoved it quickly down into a tangle of decorative woolen scarves we'd pulled out of her wardrobe. The more I saw, the more I felt the loss of things I'd never been around to see.

"Let's get this bedding off of here," said Jen, reaching down to pull the comforter away from the bed. As I went to help her, there was a jarring thud against the window beside it, and we both looked up startled at a large, thrashing mass of coal-black feathers scrabbling against the lower panes before sliding down and out of sight.

"That was a raven!" Jen exclaimed in astonishment.

Before I could reply, one of the cats let out a yowl of fear or outrage from outside the door.

"*What the hell?*" I yelled, afraid that Sam and Harry had finally turned on James as we rushed out to the landing. But we found no sign of any cats at all there now.

And then, a soft, shuddering roar began coming from the walls around us.

I turned in fright, looking everywhere as my arms began to tingle, swiftly followed by my face and legs. *No, no, no!* I told myself, struggling to get past the fright and keep from vanishing right in front of Jen—who, judging from the width of her eyes, was as terrified as I was.

"Oh my god, it's just the central heating!" She turned to me, visibly limp with relief. "It's gone on for some reason."

I had no voice yet. I was still locked in a battle for control of myself.

Jen's expression shifted from relief to concern. "Are you...all right, Cam?"

"Yes!" I finally found the breath to say as the tingling in my face and limbs began receding. "Yes! I'm fine. All that was just so... What *was* that?"

"It's just air being forced through all the ducts and registers," she said.

"No, I mean *all* of that? What just happened in there?" I asked, swimming in the weakness of relief as well now—less because this scary noise had just turned out to be forced air heating than because I'd managed to suppress my long-dormant "gift" in the nick of time.

"Well, I guess a raven just tried to fly through that window for some reason…which scared off the cats?" She raised her hands and gave me a helpless shrug. "And then, by some coincidence, the heat came on, which it really shouldn't on a day this warm—or anytime at all until after August, I'd have thought. We'd better go down and make sure those cats haven't figured out how to bump the thermostat up or something."

"Yes. Let's do that," I said, almost entirely back into my body again. A dusty smell was filling the air, and I could feel a bit of the heat already. "But first, let's go make sure that raven didn't crack the glass."

The heat was running a lot less noisily now. But as we walked cautiously back into Paige's room, I heard a ruffling kind of crackle coming from underneath the bed—as if some huge spider there were drumming its legs against a candy wrapper. "What is that now?" I asked Jen.

"Well, let's find out." She went to grab the headboard, waving me toward the foot of the mattress. "Help me drag this out."

"Do we want to disturb whatever's under there?" I asked, looking for some way to grip the bed frame without actually putting my hands underneath it.

"Settle down. I'm pretty sure it's just something caught in a register. Grab the corners of the frame, not the mattress, and let's get this far enough from the wall to see what."

We dragged it a foot or two from the wall, which was enough to look back there and discover that Jen had been right. Something small and white was jammed beneath the register's louvered grill, rattling against the escaping air. Jen lay across the mattress and reached down to lift the grill and pull the obstacle out.

"Well, I'll be darned!" she said, handing me a badly mangled Polaroid of a young woman. It took me only seconds to recognize an even younger and prettier version of the Paige in that photo hung downstairs. "That's the photograph from the second parlor that disappeared before I could show it to you. Remember?"

"Oh. Yeah." I looked down at it again. "How'd it get up here?"

"I blame the cats, of course. At this point, I think it's safe to assume they're guilty almost any time things go sideways around here. And look—there's another one of their sneak-holes."

She was right. I shook my head and walked over to the window, relieved to see no cracked glass. I slid it open and peered down at the wraparound porch roof. There were no ravens on it, injured or otherwise, to my relief. I had a soft spot for birds, and hadn't wished it hurt just for scaring the crap out of me. I pulled my head back inside and closed the window just as the central heating went silent. "You know what? I'm done." I headed for the door.

"Understood," Jen said, joining me. "Let's go have a look at that thermostat, and then work on dinner, hmm?"

"Sounds great," I said, following her out onto the landing, unable to shake the feeling that, somehow, all that stuff had just happened because Paige was unhappy with me for trying to take her things out of that room.

Which was ridiculous, of course. But knowing that didn't help much.

Downstairs, we found the thermostat set just the way it should be, which seemed to clear the cats of any blame. This time, anyway. But that left Jen concerned about what else might be wrong with our heating system, or the big scary old furnace itself, down in the cold cellar underneath our kitchen. "If something like that happens again," she said, "we'll have to get the appliance repair guys on San Juan Island over here."

"I'll drink to that!" I said. "Right now, in fact. What's open?"

"A bottle of Pinot, I believe." She gestured at the kitchen door. "Shall we?"

CHAPTER 8

By the following morning, we'd put all that weirdness behind us. The rest of Paige's things got boxed up without any more strange incidents. When Jen pointed out that having it all piled in the smaller cat-hole room would make hanging new wallpaper there much harder, we moved it into the bed-that-swallows-people room instead. Then we brought a few of Paige's lovely old furnishings back in from the barn, and started moving everything around in the ground floor's three big rooms to make them feel more open, lively, and conversational. Because someday, we did plan to start having people over. A lot of really interesting and lovely art, glassware, books and tchotchkes had been buried in all that clutter she'd left behind. And it quickly became clear that a few more Oriental carpets would be needed too, which sent us to Kay's vintage shop in Eastsound. Talk about fun and fascinating places to get lost in!

The days began to pass more quickly; and with every one, I grew more excited about what a charming and cozy place this house could really be. I wasn't quite ready to admit it out loud yet, but Paige's big old ex-boardinghouse was starting to feel more and more like a real home after all.

Jen's excitement grew at least as fast as mine. Whenever she wasn't out delivering packages or working at Darvill's, she was home, moving or installing something, musing about where we might want extra lighting or what pretty views the windows had.

"We should have a bunch of people up here for Thanksgiving," she said one morning. "This dining room's just being wasted on the two of us. And there's not a better kitchen on the island for cooking a big holiday meal. Or there won't be once we get that stove worked out." Both the electrician on San Juan and the propane company had said it would be weeks or longer before they'd have time to get up here, so Jen had to use her air fryer in the dining room now to avoid blowing a fuse again when anything else in the kitchen was on.

A few days later, as we were rearranging the front parlor *again*, she kept waffling back and forth about whether things should be set up there for a big group conversation or smaller social clusters. I came *this close* to asking her who all these people we kept rearranging our furniture for were. But she was clearly having so much fun that I just kept my mouth shut, guessing all those years of working hospitality had just trained her to think that way.

Then, one evening, Jen got a text from Katrina at the Barnacle saying that they were finally expanding their open days and hours again, and asking if she'd consider coming back to tend bar and be their "cocktail consultant" again. She texted "YES" immediately, and then did a hilarious victory dance around the kitchen table, where we'd been having dinner.

"I'm so excited!" she practically screamed.

"Me too!" Then I pouted extravagantly and added, "But who'll cook me dinner now?"

"Oh, I'll make things up and leave them for you in the fridge, hon," she assured me. "I'm not letting my best friend starve."

It wasn't like I'd never learned to feed myself, of course. I'd just grown so used to having people around who were much better at it. "I don't know what they'd have done if you'd said no," I told her. "I still remember the first time I had one of your Ruby Sippers. It was amazing."

"Wow, I don't even remember that one. Was it sweet?"

"Kinda—cucumber vodka, both orange and raspberry liqueurs, and something citrus—lime, maybe. Just the right amount of sweet. Like you."

"Aw thanks. Yeah, I remember now: the one I stumped JoJo with."

"Yes," I said, my smile slipping a little. "You did, didn't you."

I tried to imagine what JoJo might say if he knew I was an heiress now. Something cuttingly clever, I was sure. But would he have been happy for me, as Lisa seemed to be, or just sad that I'd been sucked into the kind of privilege he'd grown so disgusted with? Not that my privilege was even near the same as his had been, of course. But I'd still have loved to show him what Jen and I were doing with this house, even if he just invented witty insults to reward me with…

And wow, so maudlin suddenly! "You know I don't really need you to make me dinner, right? I'll just come down whenever you're working and have you make me one of those fabulous charcuterie boards, with whatever ingenious cocktail you've invented that night."

"Oh, hon, that'd be so great!" She actually hugged herself in excitement as she beamed at me.

The next morning, Jen went off to give notice at her delivery job, and I decided it was time to face the growing pile of off-island tasks I'd been ignoring.

To begin with, I still hadn't gone to visit Paige's brokerage firm in Anacortes. Her checking account had provided me with more than enough money to cover things here for quite a while. But if any important investment decisions were needing to be made about those other accounts, Paige's broker would have no one to consult. And now that Jen and I were getting serious about restoring this house, I kind of wanted to know whether the balances on that schedule in the will had grown or shrunk during several years of pandemic turmoil.

We also needed new bedding and towels that weren't threadbare and ripped at the seams, curtains and drapes less faded and full of moth holes and spider droppings than the old ones were—where there were any at all—and new wallpaper for a few of the upstairs rooms, including Jen's bedroom. There was nowhere to buy any of these on Orcas Island itself; and I'd learned not to order such things online without having seen them in person first after a seemingly lovely set of gold brocade table napkins I bought had turned out to be blinding buttercup muslin with a "brocadey" pattern printed on them. So I needed to go do some window-shopping at mainland stores that carried any real selection of such things before coming back home sufficiently informed to order them safely online.

And, of course, there was still Paige's urn of ashes to be picked up at the mortuary.

So…there was an all-around fun-filled day in America to be faced and gotten over with. Since all my errands were in Anacortes, I didn't bother trying to get a vehicle reservation. I just walked on, which required no reservation at all, and called a fabulous taxi service at the other end called Mert's—named for the lovely man who'd founded it, and still drove one himself—who took me to the brokerage office on Commercial Street.

The investment adviser I met with was so much nicer than I'd imagined, and, without making me feel like a complete idiot, managed to walk me through a bewildering maze of legal forms, information about current market trends, a brief history of Paige's investment strategies, and various alternative options if I wished to handle any of that differently. The account balances on that schedule had grown considerably too. But a lot of things I'd found shocking a couple weeks ago didn't surprise me so much anymore—maybe because I was just permanently in shock now. So I just closed my mouth after a couple seconds, and told the man I'd be glad to go right on doing whatever they'd been doing. I was clearly going to be just fine for quite a while, it seemed—no matter what we did to the house.

I went window-shopping next, which was fun except for the mix of "giddy" and "guilty" I felt walking through those chi-chi stores, fingering silk napkins and damask drapes. Even after three years of driving a Porsche around, and being paid so well to live (for free) in that large, beautifully furnished waterfront home, I'd still seen myself as a card-carrying, lower-middle-class ex-salon worker. The Porsche, the house—even the job, as I'd just discovered—had all been owned by someone else, not by me. But was I still that person now? Could I keep this inheritance from changing me, or would I look into a mirror someday and see someone coiffed and dressed like Lisa used to be? Paige had been one of the most unaffected people I'd ever met, and I intended to follow her example. But...would I pull it off?

Finally, there was only one more errand left to do. I'd called the funeral home that morning to let them know I was coming. And the young man who met me there was so sweet and sadly sympathetic that I was tempted to comfort *him*. As he went to get the urn, I realized I still hadn't heard back from Paige's old friend, Elle Gascaux—or done anything more about planning her memorial service. I'd have to get on that as soon as I got home. The melancholy lad came back a moment later and invited me to inspect the urn. It was even prettier in person than it had looked in their online catalogue. When I told him so, he packed it back into its box, and handed it to me with the most sympathetic expression yet—and I knew why immediately! Who knew such a small urn could be so heavy? I was very glad I wouldn't have carry it any farther than out to the taxi, and up the long, bendy ramp onto my ferry home.

Remarkably, our boat pulled out right on time again—which made four in a row that month. Miraculous! I spent the voyage on a sunny bench out on the upper deck, watching rafts of gulls fly around against the sea and islands passing by. It felt kind of nice, in a strange way, to have Paige sitting next to me again. I picked up the box and held it in my arms for a while, imagining that I was holding her. Thanking her. Taking her home where she belonged.

I'd been planning to put Paige's urn up on the second parlor mantelpiece. But when I got back to the house and set it there, it just seemed...lonely and out of place. I sat down, gazing up at her for a while, and finally realized where she belonged.

The kitchen was a completely different room by now: spacious and bright and, well, a place to cook and eat food in. Every surface, visible or not, was spotless. And Paige's old pots and pans, mixing bowls and countertop appliances, ceramic spice jars, utensils, dishes and glassware all gleamed and sparkled in orderly arrangements on their shelves and counters, or in their glassed-in cabinets.

Back when she and I had still been dancing carefully around the subject of our secret gifts, I'd finally asked Paige what she really was; she'd said she was "a gardener." But, as I'd learned in time, her beds of giant kale and radishes, like my ability to vanish, were just the smallest part of what her gift was actually about. That huge crowd at her wake had been her real crop. And now it seemed so clear to me that this room—made for nourishing others—had been the heart of all that mess she'd left behind because it had been the real heart of her home.

I brought her urn to the kitchen and, with the help of a stepping stool, set it up between two beautiful glass punch bowls on the shelf above her fridge. I felt certain she'd want to be in the room where so much of her life had really happened, looking down as Jen cooked our meals every day and Sam and Harry wandered in and out to nibble; a room where I might even try to can some fruit from her little orchard someday, or make preserves as she had done. I know—me, cooking? But looking around at how we had transformed this kitchen, even that seemed possible.

With that taken care of, I went right up to my room to find Paige's address ledger, brought it down to the kitchen table, and started tracing all its little lines and arrows to their ultimate addresses. Half an hour later, I'd managed to transcribe most of our mailing list, confirming that everybody with the last name "Berry" had been crossed out and not replaced. I could do nothing more without knowing where and when the memorial would be.

Paige had not been religious in any conventional way, so I couldn't see having her memorial in a church. She'd been a pillar of the garden club, and someone's pretty garden would be just the thing—except that weather was a famous spoiler of outdoor events in these islands. Plus, lack of infrastructure might turn out to be a problem, especially without any idea of how many people would show up. I wasn't sure the senior center did memorial services…

And then it hit me: the perfect place, and with a lot of resonance for a theater booster club legend like Paige. Unfortunately, it was too late by then to call Madrona Farm. That would have to wait till morning. But they'd been big fans of Lisa's theater group—and of the booster ladies who'd supported it; and I was sure they'd want to host her memorial.

Once we had the date and place nailed down, all we'd need to do was write, address, seal, and send all those letters to all Paige's probably-still-living friends. If only she had acknowledged the existence of phones—or email, or the internet at all… That task could have been so much easier.

During our call before bed that night, I asked Kip if he'd like to come up for another visit this weekend—and, oh by the way, a mail-a-thon party in our increasingly beautiful new house. He almost hardly paused at all before saying yes.

೧೧

Just after eight-thirty on Friday evening, Kip drove up to the house, and I ran out to throw my arms around him as he got out of his truck. I'm here to tell you, this whole "absence makes the heart grow fonder" thing is a cliché for very good reasons. When we'd finished saying hello, I took his hand and led him up the front porch stairs. "Come see what've been up to."

He came in and glanced around the foyer, then looked through the pocket doors at the front parlor. "Wow! You guys have been busy!"

"Oh yes, we have." I pulled him toward the kitchen door. "Just look in here."

It was very satisfying to see his mouth fall open. "Unbelievable!" He gazed around for a minute, then said, "Let me see your hands." I held them up, and he made a show of studying my fingers. "Hmmm. There's no bone showing." He looked up and grinned at me. "Did Jen do all this work without you?"

I yanked my hands away and said with mock severity, "I'll have you know, I've worked beside her every step of the way."

He leaned in and kissed me. "Where is she, anyway?"

"At the Barnacle. They're finally ramping up again, and she's been hired to bartend. Katrina wanted to go over some things before she starts next week."

"She must be excited."

"Oh yeah. She should be back in an hour or so, though. She says hello."

Kip looked again around the kitchen. "Too bad. I skipped dinner to make the ferry." He looked back at me. "Want to go get something in town?"

"We could," I said, chagrined at his assumption that if Jen was gone, we needed to go out. "Or I could just make you something here."

He looked bemused. "You cook now too?"

Okay, I had clearly let myself get way too spoiled. "I fed myself for years before Jen moved in," I told him. "What would you like?" I prayed he wouldn't ask for any of the hundred things I had no idea how to cook.

He gave me a long, thoughtful smile. "What would you like to make me?"

Oh, wasn't he clever! So...what should it be? Chili and shredded cheese with chopped onions...or scrambled eggs and toast? Baby bok choy, perhaps? There was lots of food in the refrigerator; Jen had seen to that, of course. I just had no clear idea what to do with most of it. There'd be plenty of stuff for a salad to go with whatever I made, at least. And we had no end of desserts around here. But I really wanted to make him something...more special. And then I knew what—if we had the ingredients.

I looked in the pantry closet, and sure enough, there was a package of spaghetti, and, yes! Three cans of the special sauce I'd bought and put in here myself, I now recalled, obviously in preparation for a situation just like this. I grabbed one of them, and the spaghetti. "I'm going to cook you an old family delicacy."

"Is that so!"

"It's not anything gourmet," I warned him, "but it's got tons of sentimental value. It's called Daddy's spaghetti. My father taught me how to make it."

"Daddy's spaghetti." He grinned. "Can't wait to try it."

I would never in a million years have so much as mentioned Daddy's spaghetti to Kevin, but I was pretty sure Kip would like it fine. He'd been a cop, and cops ate anything, right? Donuts and cheeseburgers? This would be right down his alley.

After filling a pot with water and putting it on the terrible electric stove, I took him up to see our work on the second floor. He was just as impressed with the bathroom as I had been, and complimented all the other rooms. And when I showed him my charming new bedroomette, he looked around and said, "Cozy…"

"It'll be even cozier now that you're here," I said. The look he gave me reminded me of the pot I'd left on downstairs, which must be boiling by now.

And it was. I dumped in the noodles, gave them a stir, and set my timer as Sam and Harry ghosted through, heading for their food and water bowls, followed a few seconds later by James, who sauntered up to sniff at Kip's shoes and pant cuffs before going to his own food bowl well across the kitchen from those of his wicked new playmates.

As the noodles boiled, I started working on the sauce. Jen, of course, would have had a scratch sauce simmering for hours at the back of the stove, full of mushrooms and heirloom tomatoes grown by someone she knew, an obscene amount of garlic, and at least several herbs I'd never even heard of. It would never come out the same way twice, but it would be fantastically delicious every time.

I picked up my can of special sauce: Campbell's Tomato Soup.

She'll never know, I told myself. I'd have to destroy the evidence, of course. Hide the can in my room until she left for work at the bookstore tomorrow, then throw it away in town somewhere. But freedom has its costs. With a happy sigh, I set the soup can in the sink, unopened, and ran hot water over it for a minute. Then I drained the cooked noodles over it as well, and dumped them into a big serving bowl. Finally, I opened the can of soup, upended it over the noodles, and gave it all a good toss as Kip looked on in fascination.

At least, it looked like fascination.

"Can you grab a couple plates from that cupboard up there to your left?" I asked him. "And some silverware out of the drawer below it?"

"Sure," he said, glancing at the kitchen table. "Want some glasses out here too?"

"Wine glasses," I said, nodding at them. "But let's not eat not in here. Since this is a special occasion, we'll have it in the dining room."

"Oh, right," he said. "Got napkins somewhere?"

"Back there by those cookbooks." I waved in their direction. "But leave the dishes here, okay? It has to be served up right onto the plates. You can take that bottle of Cab on the counter out, though."

"Okay…" He set the plates on the counter next to me.

As he gathered the other things up and carried them out through the dining room door, I forked a big pile of the spaghetti onto each of our dinner plates, then went to get the butter dish and put about a tablespoon of butter over each of the piles, before salting them generously. The soup made a delicious sauce, of course, but it wasn't quite salty enough on its own.

When they were perfectly arranged, I carried our plates out to the long, darkly polished dining table, where Kip was now seated in… curious anticipation. I set a plate in front of him, and carried mine around to the spot across from his. I dashed back out for the serving dish, in case he wanted seconds. Then I closed the kitchen door behind me and took a seat.

"This is the first meal my adoptive dad ever made for me," I told Kip. "That I can remember, anyway." I smiled at the memory. Dad had cautioned me not to tell my mother, but with such a cheerful grin that I'd known this was a good secret, not a bad one like the secrets my life had been filled with before the Jonases had fostered, then adopted me. Mom had had some crazy notion about this not being suitable nutrition; but Dad and I knew better.

I leaned in to draw a deep breath of the spaghetti's sinfully delicious aroma, and my eyes nearly rolled back in my head with nostalgic delight. "To this day," I told Kip, "whenever Dad and I find ourselves dining alone, he whips up a batch of Daddy's spaghetti, and we scarf it down until our bellies burst."

"Sounds like you two had a lot of fun," Kip said, studying his plate with an amused expression before poking his fork into the mound of noodles and twisting up a mouthful. I watched him take that first bite, waiting for his smile of pure enjoyment. But his expression was more thoughtful than delighted as he chewed and swallowed. "Well, that tastes…real nutritious," he said at last, giving me a tentative smile. "There's a nice Spaghetti-O's thing going on there."

"I know, right?" I said cheerfully. "Isn't it great?"

He didn't answer. But to his credit, he put his fork right back into the pile for a second bite. And kept at it, workmanlike, till the plate was clean.

Hmm. Maybe you needed to be family to fully appreciate this feast. Or maybe he just needed more time. That was probably it.

I was serving myself a second plateful when the kitchen door opened and Jen stepped in—holding the empty soup can. "What in the *world* are you eating?" She stared incredulously at my plate, and then, in even greater horror, at Kip's.

Busted.

I just waved hello, and scooped up another forkful.

"It's… You…" She put a hand to her chest, as if she were feeling faint. "Do you really never want him to come back?"

"We were hungry," I said around a giant mouthful. "You weren't supposed to be home till later."

She looked at Kip and said, "I'm so sorry. I had no idea." But she was having a hard time keeping a straight face by now.

"Kip likes it," I said. Because, well, he hadn't actually said he didn't.

She snorted. "Kip likes *you*."

"In fact, I do," he said, giving her a sort of cautioning smile. Then he looked back at me. "I like you quite a lot. Thank you for dinner, love."

Jen shuddered dramatically. "I can't watch. I'm going to open another bottle of wine, and then I'll go make us a fire in the front parlor, if you guys are in the mood to socialize when you're…done here." She gave us a wink, and walked back into the kitchen.

"We'll be right there," I called after her. "I want to hear about your meeting. I hope you talked about the discount I should get now for letting you abandon me to dinner on my own."

"What sort of wine goes with glorified starch and soup?" she called back.

I snorted. "Oh, so you're at least giving me 'glorified' now?"

"Well, you did cook the noodles. So I'll give you credit for that."

"Gee, thanks."

Kip listened with a wry expression until we were done. "You two ought to get a sitcom."

"Oh, trust me, we've had one all along. There just aren't a lot of people tuning in yet."

"Am I right in guessing you guys haven't fixed the broken glass on that photo of Paige yet?"

"No. We've been so busy, I don't think it's even crossed my mind."

"That's what I thought." He rose from the table with his empty plate in hand. "If you don't mind cleaning up in there without me for a minute, I've got something in the truck for you."

"I love surprises."

A couple minutes later, as I was washing up our dishes at the sink—because, of course, we still hadn't got a dishwasher yet either—Kip came back in carrying a brand new picture frame still wrapped in cellophane from the store. "Let's just try moving the photo into this one. Lots easier than getting a new piece of glass cut to fit the frame it's in."

"That's brilliant!" I dried my hands and went to give him a kiss.

A short while later, Kip and I were sitting with Jen around the front parlor's cozy fireplace. Jen had found Kip a pair of pliers and a screwdriver which he was using to pry out tiny nails that held the backing onto the old frame. "They sure made all this a lot harder back then, didn't they?" he said, his tongue poking slightly out between his teeth in the cutest way as he tugged at the last stubborn nail.

"Just be careful of the photo against that broken glass," Jen said anxiously.

"I'll be cautious as a surgeon," Kip replied, as the nail came loose at last.

He handed the pliers to me, and set the frame down gently in his lap. "Who's got that screwdriver?" Jen handed it to him, and he wiggled it in carefully between the sheet of Masonite backing and the frame, then pried the backing slowly up and slid it out.

"Oh! What's that?" Jen asked, as we all leaned in to see a small, age-browned envelope that had been tucked between the frame's backing and the photo itself.

Kip reached down gingerly to remove it.

"That paper looks pretty brittle," I said.

Sure enough, as he closed two fingers on it, several little pieces of the envelope's flap cracked off like flakes of old house paint.

"Okay," Kip said, removing his hand. "You guys have a pair of tweezers?"

"Of course," said Jen, and dashed upstairs.

A minute later, she was back with a long-ish pair. Kip squeezed them closed and gently slid them in between the envelope and its flap. Then he let the tweezers open again, which lifted the flap away from the envelope just a little bit—and it broke right off along the crease. "Oh well," he said. "Let's hope whatever's in there is less fragile." After thinking for a moment, he pressed the tweezers closed again, and slid them into the envelope itself, then pried it slightly open the same way. The paper didn't crack this time. He lifted the tweezers, bringing the little envelope up with them, and swung it over his hand, then closed the tweezers so that the envelope slid off them into his upturned palm where it was easier to pick up. He squeezed its edges very gently between his fingers until it opened wide enough for him to peer inside. "Well…that's interesting," he said at last.

"What's in it?" Jen asked quietly.

"Is it a note?" I asked.

"No." He passed the envelope carefully to me. "Looks like a lock of hair."

"*Ohh!*" said Jen. "This guy must have been very important to Paige."

"Or her to him," I said, gazing down at it. "Depending on whose hair it is."

"I think we ought to get a Ziploc bag or something to put this in," said Kip, "before it comes apart completely." He looked at me. "If you want to keep it."

"Of course I do."

As Jen rose again, the sound of many cat feet hurrying across the hardwood floor made us all turn and look. Harry and Sam hurried in from the foyer, with James not far behind them, and all three trotted over to stare up at us in silence.

"Yes?" I asked them, wondering what to make of this sudden delegation.

"They're all looking at your hand," Jen said quietly.

Or at what's in it, I thought, realizing she was right, and feeling the skin prickle up my arms and down my neck—for reasons that had nothing to do with chameleoning this time. *What are you seeing?* I asked them in another stab at telepathic communication. But they just went on standing there, staring up at my hand until Jen came over and shooed them all away.

※

THAT NIGHT, AS KIP AND I lay side by side in my bed, staring at the ceiling, I asked, "Is it just me, or was that whole thing with the cats extremely weird?"

"It wasn't just you," said Kip. "That was...one of the creepier things I've ever seen, to tell the truth. And I've seen some creepy things before."

"Like what?"

He turned to look at me in the dim light of my tiny bedside lamp. "Do you really want me to answer that question? Tonight? Just before we turn the lights off?"

"Okay. Maybe later then."

We had put the envelope into a Ziploc bag, as Kip suggested, and then just tucked it back behind the photo in its new frame before Kip had bent its easy little metal tabs down and set it on a countertop in the kitchen. After that, the three of us had sat sipping wine as the fire burned down, and traded banter about everything except the envelope of hair, and those weird cats—which now included James, apparently.

I had no idea where, or if, I'd hang that photo now. Maybe in a closet somewhere.

"Cats are strange animals," Kip said. "They do all sorts of cat things for reasons no one's ever going to understand but them. No point in projecting our stuff on that. Whatever we imagine about them will just be wrong, I guarantee you." He grinned at me again. "That's even true of most people, I think."

I nodded. That all sounded very sensible. But my feelings weren't so sensible, and hadn't been much since Paige had died. "Those cats are stranger than most. And I've started wondering sometimes if they can see things I can't."

"Like what?"

I was tempted to ask if he really wanted me to answer that question right before we turned the lights off. But all I said was, "I don't know. They're just always showing up at the weirdest times, and behaving like…they're scared of something here. Or angry at it."

"And what do you think that could be?" he asked, sounding as if my words had been just as sensible as his.

"I don't know that either. But…a lot of times, it seems like me."

"You? What do you mean?"

"They always kind of cringe across the kitchen when I fill their food bowls, like I'm some kind of threat. They've done it since the first time I came here after Paige died. And now they follow me around the house. Jen noticed it before I did. Like they need to keep an eye on me." *Okay*, I thought. *This is where you say I'm crazy and run out of my room.*

But, of course, he wasn't Kevin. "Well, sure," he said. "After all those years, their owner's disappeared, and some stranger's come to take her place. Of course they're feeling threatened. But that's no reflection on you, love—any more than the things you imagine about those cats are any reflection on them."

I bit my lower lip. "Were you always this smart?"

He smiled without saying anything at all.

I reached out and pulled him closer. "I love you so much. Do you know that?"

"I do," he said. "I love you so much too—even after that spaghetti."

"Oh, you!" I swatted him away again. "Just don't ever let my father hear you say that."

He chuckled. "There's a lot of things I'll never let your father hear about."

☙

I WOKE UP WITH AN arm across Kip's lovely torso, and when his eyes finally opened too, we spent some time saying good morning a little more enthusiastically than we'd said goodnight. Then we dressed and went downstairs to find an amazing breakfast laid out in the kitchen.

"Didn't want you breaking out the Eggo waffles," Jen told me with a wicked grin.

Before I could think of any sufficient comeback, I saw a plate of… "Are those bear claws?" I exclaimed. "Did you *make* those?"

"With homemade almond paste and lemon glaze," she said smugly.

I glanced back to see Kip already lifting one into his mouth, and asked her, "Are you trying to steal my boyfriend again?"

"No, hon. I'm just trying to convince you not to keep cooking."

"Well…" I marched over and picked up one of the pastries. "It's working! Keep it up."

Scrambled eggs from our own chickens were lighter than air and sprinkled with chives, their little purple flowers, and shredded Cotswold cheese. Her smoked pork chops were smothered in homemade rhubarb-apple compote. There were poached bosc pears glazed in lavender honey, and grapefruit mimosas to wash down another of those devastating bear claws with. When we'd been stuffed into a state of bliss, Kip and I just sat, half dazed, at one end of the dining room table as Jen laid out our letter-writing campaign at the table's other end.

As I'd expected, the minute Erin Salazar had heard what I was calling about, she'd found and reserved a date for us at Madrona Farm in June. Jen and I had written up a nice invitation, and taken the file down to be printed up on lovely paper at the Office Cupboard in town. Jen was already addressing envelopes as we finally rolled down to join her.

"You really ought to open up a bed-and-breakfast," Kip told her. "The place would be famous in a single summer."

"You're too kind, sir," Jen said, blushing.

"No, I'm too serious. I grew up on this island, just like you, and I bet we both know everyplace there's ever been to eat around here. But I've never had a better breakfast than the one you just made us. And *thank you*, by the way. That was a real gift."

Jen looked at me. "I am really not trying to steal your boyfriend."

"I'm too full, and too happy, to be worried," I assured her.

But as the three of us sat there, writing out letters and getting them ready to mail, I could not stop thinking about what Kip had said to her. Because he was right. That was pretty much the best breakfast I'd ever had too—anywhere, not just on the island. But what really had my attention was the last thing he'd said to her: *That was a real gift.*

He'd meant a gift to us, of course. But that word meant other things to me. And I felt certain now that he'd been more right than he could have known. All this really was Jen's gift. Her special power. Not in quite the same way that mine or Paige's were, of course. But, now that I was paying attention, Jen's whole life seemed so clearly about making welcoming, comforting, joyful spaces for people to gather in and celebrate each other and themselves. It wasn't just amazing meals like this one, or her inventive cocktails. She'd been turning this house into someplace to share, not just with me, but with others, right from the beginning. She'd been telling me what she was—without ever hearing it herself. So I hadn't heard it either, until Kip had said it right out loud. *That was a real gift.*

Paige had told me more than once not to use my gift, but to let it use me—and said it again in the letter she'd left me before she died.

Let it use you.

Had she left this house not just for me, but for my gift to use?

I could barely think about the letters we were writing anymore. My mind was swirling now with new ideas. Huge ones.

☙

KIP LEFT SUNDAY AFTERNOON. EARLY Monday morning, I sat down with Jen and told her that I thought we really should, no joke, open a bed-and-breakfast.

After all the little hints she'd been dropping, I expected her to go crazy for the idea. But she resisted it so hard at first that it felt like I was trying to pull a fish out of the water with my bare hands.

"Since when are you interested in being an innkeeper?" she asked.

Well, I wasn't, exactly; I was interested in helping her be an innkeeper. But telling her that would shut the conversation down, so I tried another angle. "I really want to do something that matters with this huge gift Paige left me. But I still can't think of what. You said it yourself the other day: what are we going to use all these rooms for? I don't want my heirs just finding them piled full of my junk someday. But listening to you talk about what great views this place has, and how perfect that dining room would be to stage big meals in, and how we can arrange the furniture to encourage conversation has made me see that this place was literally made to be an inn."

"Hon, I wasn't trying to talk you into—"

"I know! And, if I was alone here, I might just sell it to someone who wanted to run an inn. But I've already got someone right here in the house who I think was made to be an innkeeper. It seems like the perfect marriage—staring me in the face this whole time. So, would you like to help me turn Paige's house back into what it was made to be?"

She looked at me like someone wondering whether to call 911. "It's not Paige's house," she said at last. "It's yours. And I'm still not seeing what would be in this plan for you."

Why had I thought she'd just leap up and shout *yes*? "I starting to love living here, and caring for the animals. Most of the time, anyway. And I'm getting interested in doing more gardening too, I think, now that I've got so much already well-developed garden to try it in. So I might enjoy being our groundskeeper too. I also love to furnish and decorate things—a lot. I learned so much when we were remodeling Lisa's guesthouse that I'd love to use again somewhere. In fact, I had more fun remodeling that house than I think I'd have had living there. And, honestly, I even love having the kind of company that shows up just long enough to be interesting, and then leaves again. I bet I'd enjoy all sorts of other things about having an inn too, if I had any idea what was involved, exactly—the way you so clearly do. Which is why I'm asking what you'd think about supplying that part of the formula."

"Our friendship matters to me. A lot," she said. "And I'm not sure working for friends is *ever* a very smart idea."

"Oh, no! Sorry. I meant a total partnership. Fully, legally, fifty-fifty; nobody working for anybody else. We'd be working together on *our* inn, more or less like we're doing now."

"Except I can't see how someone with no money to invest in *our* inn gets to be a fifty-fifty partner. This idea is super generous, Cam; and please don't take this the wrong way, but I doubt you have any idea how much money—or how much *risk*—would be involved just in turning this place into a functional inn, much less in maintaining it year after year. What if there's another pandemic? I'd say we could lose our shirts, except I don't have a shirt to lose, so that would all be you. You think I'd enjoy that?"

"I think you're already proving my point about how well you understand what's really involved in doing this," I said. "But it also sounds like you still don't understand how much your expertise and labor are really worth. I have tons of money right now that I have no more idea what to do with than I do this house, and I didn't earn any of it. It just fell on me out of the sky. Honestly, the value you'd be bringing to this project feels way more legit to me than my money-for-nothing does. You'd be *earning* your fifty percent. I'd just be supplying mine."

"No you wouldn't," she said. "Give me a break. You don't freeload any more than I do. What's going to happen is that you'll discover how much work an inn really is, and how much better at a lot of it you are than you thought you'd be. And a year or two from now, when all the fun decorating and remodeling is done, this place is going to end up running your life, not just mine; and you'll end up hating me for letting you agree to it."

I'd end up hating her…for letting me agree to…my own proposal…? It took me a minute to sort out that impressive maneuver, but as I did, I realized that she'd been responding to everything I'd suggested here as if it were something *she* would regret talking *me* into later. As if all of this had been her idea, not mine. Which was interesting.

"So let's make this simpler," I said. "Are you saying you don't want to try turning this place into an inn?"

"Do you have any idea how great the odds would be against our success?" she asked. Notably *not* an answer to my question. "I've seen a lot of inns come and go here. It's more a gamble than a business in a lot of ways."

It was as if she were trying to convince me we would fail. Which she probably was, I realized, if Kip's take on her was right. "I think it's a gamble I can afford to take," I said, "thanks to Paige."

"But why would you?"

I thought about that, hard. It wasn't like these weren't all good and valid questions she was raising. I was just less and less convinced they were the real ones. The thing was, only an answer I really believed as much as I wanted her to was going to work here.

"I think…it seems like a risk worth taking because I want to and I can. I've been trying to figure out how not to waste everything I've suddenly been given by someone I really cared about and wouldn't want to disappoint. And the only idea I've come up with yet that really makes me feel excited, and happy, is doing something creative and…" I groped for the right word, "constructive, I guess, with someone I enjoy and trust so much." I looked her in the eye. "But if any part of that doesn't feel good to you, just tell me no. And I'll keep thinking. No is a completely okay answer."

She went silent for a while, looking everywhere except at me before she finally said, "I guess it couldn't hurt to find out more about what would be involved." Then she looked straight at me. "But, Cam, I meant what I said about our friendship. I would hate to damage that. I mean really *hate* it. So, please, hon, let's just be real careful about this before jumping in, okay? And if you change your mind, I will be so fine with that!"

I looked at the expression on her face, and leaned over to give her a hug. "Nothing's ever going to hurt this friendship, Jen. And yes, if this ends up looking even a little bit unrealistic, we'll let it go. Okay?"

"Okay," she said, as if we'd just agreed to bungee jump into a live volcano.

☙

Shortly after our chat, Jen left for one of her last package delivery shifts, and I went to mail our memorial service invites at the post office.

When that was done, I drove to Lisa's house and rang her doorbell.

"Cam!" she said. "What a lovely surprise!"

"Good to see you," I said, a little shyly. "Are you busy?"

"Not at the moment. Would you like to come in?"

"Thanks." I followed her inside and down into the living room.

"So, how are you doing?" she asked as we settled on her couch. "Is everything going well up there?"

"I think so. That's part of why I'm here—I'd like to get your feedback on something."

"Sure. What's going on?"

"Jen and I are thinking of turning my place into a bed-and-breakfast."

Lisa's brows climbed half an inch. "Really! That's…quite an ambitious plan, after living there for just, what, a month now?" Her smile grew wry. "Have you even finished moving in?"

"We've been working very hard," I told her. "And the place is looking really good, I think. We need to have you up to see it."

"I'd like that. How's it going with Paige's menagerie?"

"Fine. It's gotten a lot smaller, actually. Lum Farm's adopted all the rabbits and most of the goats."

"Oh, well done. They're good people. So, was this B&B Jen's idea?"

"No," I said. "I had to talk her into it, actually. Pretty hard. And we're still not decided yet—we're going to look into it and see what we find out."

Lisa gave me a puzzled look. "Why would you have tried to talk her into it?"

"Why did you talk me out of staying here and working with you?"

She leaned back in apparent surprise before a broad smile bloomed on her face. "Well! Your blade's grown sharper since that conversation, hasn't it!" But she looked impressed, not offended, so I took it as a compliment. "If you don't mind, though, I'd like to hear more before doling out opinions. How did you come up with this idea?"

I couldn't tell her about all the things the word *gift* meant to me, of course, or about Paige's advice to let my gift use me. But I talked about how much I'd loved my life before Paige's death, and how uncomfortable I felt about all the things this inheritance seemed to be changing for me. I told her how unsure I'd been about whether I even *wanted* Paige's house, and how unlike a home it had felt—until recently, anyway—and my confusion about what to do with it now, or what Paige might have wanted done with it.

And then I told her about how much Jen had helped bring it back to life and make it beautiful again, and the way she kept talking about how it could be used, not just by us, but by all these other guests she kept imagining. I even started laying out Jen's long experience in local inn work, but Lisa stopped me there, saying she was well aware of Jen's impressive qualifications. So then, finally, I told Lisa about my conversation with Jen that morning.

"It just seems like what she's made to do," I finished. "Though she can't seem to admit that, even to herself."

Lisa sat looking at me thoughtfully for a minute. "It does sound like she resisted your proposal pretty strenuously."

I nodded. "I think she just wants this so much, it scares her."

"I see. Then…I have no wish to offend you, but I have to ask: are you sure you're not just trying to hand all your discomfort and confusion about this inheritance over to Jen, hoping that will resolve it for you?"

It was a surprising question, and a good one. I hadn't thought of that; but the answer I had given Jen still rang true for me. "Remember how she acted around you the night I brought you home?"

Lisa smiled sympathetically. "It was rather hard to miss."

"She has some of that around Kip too. Like she's afraid that she might lose me if someone…better comes along?" Lisa leaned forward attentively as I went on. "It seems like everything I've gotten involved with since…well, even before *Salon Confidential*, Jen's wanted to be involved in too."

"She does sound a little insecure," Lisa said gently. "Are you sure that's what you want in a business partner?"

I wasn't going to pass along what Kip had told me, even to Lisa. But I'd been thinking more since we'd had that conversation, and wasn't sure we'd got Jen right yet. "I'm not sure it's insecurity. Or not just that, anyway. I mean, she's actually one of the most confident people I've ever met. She's so good at so many things, and charismatic and pretty, and way wittier than me. But she's caring too. She's held me together like a pro since Paige died. None of that feels like insecurity to me."

"No," Lisa said. "So what do you think it is?"

"Honestly, I'm not sure why she's gotten so focused on being part of everything I'm doing. But she really is my best friend here. And this feels like a chance for *me* to be part of something *she's* doing. To use what I have in support of her for once. She'd be running this inn, mostly. I'd just be helping her. But here's the really important thing: this is the first idea I've had about what to do with everything Paige left me that makes me feel happy!" I smiled. "It feels so right—and I think something we can finally do *together*—as equals—will make me as happy as it'll make her. She'd be bringing the knowhow. I'd bring the resources."

Lisa was now giving me one of those fond looks that meant maybe I'd convinced her. Maybe?

"I am so honored that you've come to talk with me about this." She leaned back as if she'd held her breath the whole time I was talking. "And grateful as well."

"Grateful?"

"Yes. I've been worried I mishandled all of that before you left. I know my homecoming didn't go the way you'd hoped it would. But look at what you're already doing with that." She smiled in obvious relief. "Thank you for coming here and setting me at ease." She leaned forward with a much more businesslike smile. "Let me look into some things, and check with a few people, just to get my bearings. I've been gone a while and lots of things have changed, I'm sure. But then, maybe we should talk again, more practically, about what this new venture of yours might involve."

"That's just what I was hoping you'd say."

"I'd love to be of whatever help I can—as you have been to me, in so many ways."

CHAPTER 9

I returned from Lisa's even more excited about the B&B idea, and was walking toward the front porch completely lost in thought when the pulsing swoosh of large wings made me look up just in time to duck and yelp in alarm as an enormous raven dived straight at my face. It literally ruffled my hair as it swept by, inches above me. I threw my hands up over my head and whirled around to see it swoop up and land on one of the maple tree's lower branches, then rock around on its big black feet to look down at me. This had to be the same bird which had thrown itself at Paige's window a week or two before. Did birds get rabid, I wondered, backing toward the porch, afraid to even turn my back on this crazy bird.

I noticed a shiny object in its beak, glinting like metal in the dappled light. Whatever it was plunged to the grass as the raven opened its beak and started cawing at me angrily.

"Shoo!" I said quietly, wanting it to go but afraid of making it even angrier. "Get out of here."

The bird just tilted its head and stared at me with its black marble eyes. Then it started making stranger noises: loud clacking, followed by a *tok, tok, tok* sound. Then a raspy sort of noise with other bits of word-like sounds jammed into it. I had no idea what to make of this weird little symphony, but I was almost to the bottom porch step, and about to turn and dash inside when it shifted to something like a soft, cawing sneeze.

"Achoo... Achoo!" Did ravens sneeze when they had rabies?

The sounds continued changing. "Achoo" became *"An-cher, an-cher!"* It hardly even sounded birdish anymore. *"An...sher,"* it said very quietly, as if gargling for the sounds, deep in its throat. It leaned forward on its branch, as if trying to make me understand. *"An...sher war,"* it croaked.

"Are you talking?" I paused halfway up the steps, wondering if it was trying to tell me something.

"An...sher," it gargled again.

"Answer!" I exclaimed. "Are you saying answer?"

"An-ser! An-ser! Anser!" it gargled more loudly, flapping its wings again in agitation. *"Wwaarrr! Wwaaarr!"* it screamed, and swooped off the branch, not toward me this time, but straight down to spread its huge black wings and land just long enough to scoop the shiny object up with its beak. Then it leapt back into the air and flew straight for me again.

I spun around and raced up the rest of the stairs, grabbing at the front door handle in a panic as something hit the porch right beside me with a soft, metallic clang. I couldn't get the door to open. Was it locked? Why was it locked? We never locked our doors here! Had *I* done that for some reason? Why?

The bird began to caw again behind me, but it sounded farther away now. I shot a look over my shoulder, and saw that it had flown back into the maple tree to sit cawing its head off again. But even its cawing sounded different now, more like "gaw" than "caw."

"Gaw! Gaw! Gawn!"

I glanced down to see what it had thrown at me, and my mouth fell open. At my feet lay the engraved gold hair comb I'd found tacked to Paige's mirror the day we'd cleaned out her room. I looked back up at the bird in disbelief. "Where did you..." I'd packed this into one of those cardboard boxes still stacked up in the yellow room, as we were calling it now. I hadn't opened them again, or even gone into that room since then. "How did you get this?" I shouted at the bird.

It just leapt off its branch and flew up over the house, its large wings beating loudly as it cawed, *"Gawn! Gawn! Gawn!..."* and soared away.

I bent to pick up the comb, and turned to try the door one last time before going around to one of the back doors. But now the handle turned, and the door opened right away. Had I just been too panicked to operate a door handle? *Get a grip, Cam,* I thought wearily.

I walked inside and took the comb right upstairs to the yellow room, where I found the windows wide open, their curtains belling gently in the breeze. *What the…?* Flaps hung open on a number of the boxes stacked in front of them, and a few things had been pulled partway out.

"That you, Cam?" Jen called up from downstairs.

"Jen?" I called back, walking to the door. "What are you doing here?"

"Lunch break," she said, coming up the stairs. "They're already giving half my deliveries to other drivers now, so I had some extra time and came back here to make a sandwich." She joined me at the yellow room's doorway.

I waved an arm at the open windows. "Are the cats opening windows here now too?"

"No…" she said, giving me a strange look. "I did that."

"Why?"

"Well, it's been smelling a little musty in here since we piled up all these boxes, and I didn't want the things inside to mold. So I thought I'd air out the room a little… Is that a problem?"

"No, except that I just got attacked walking to the porch, by that raven who tried to smash through Paige's window. And it threw this at me." I held up the hair comb.

"Oh my god!" Jen stepped into the room and looked around with widened eyes. "Did it come in here?"

"I guess it must have." I waved the comb at her again. "And then it tried to peck my eyes out in the yard. Are you telling me you didn't even notice all that ruckus?"

"I was in the dining room. Eating my lunch. I heard a raven cawing, but I thought nothing of it. That's what ravens do. Why didn't you call for help?"

"I had no idea there was anybody here to help me. I didn't see your truck."

"Oh. Shoot. I parked it by the barn. I didn't want it in your way if you came home."

"Well, what a good thing it was just a crazy raven, and not a human serial killer. How ironic to be murdered on the porch while you ate a sandwich. Did you hear it trying to talk to me?"

Jen's brows shot up. "The raven?"

"Well, yes, it seemed… Am I just going literally crazy now?"

"About what?"

"About a bird talking?"

"Oh. No. Not a raven anyway. What did it say?"

"Wait a minute. *Ravens talk?*" I asked in disbelief.

She laughed. "Sometimes. They're mimics, like parrots, and incredibly intelligent. They can imitate human words. Haven't you ever seen the videos? They're everywhere online."

I stared at her. "Are you kidding?"

"No. I was kind of friends with a raven once, myself. I used to imitate the sounds he was making, and sometimes he seemed to try imitating me."

I felt my own eyebrows getting even higher. "You were on speaking terms…with a raven."

"For a while. When I was a kid." She looked amused by my astonishment. "Whenever I went out to chop firewood, he'd show up and sit above me in our tree making all kinds of noises at me. So one day, I started imitating everything he said to me; and he started imitating my imitations, and we'd keep that up until I finished the wood and went inside. It was hilarious. He wasn't any better at my language than I was at his, but we hung out quite a lot for months until one day he just didn't show up anymore." She shrugged. "Probably eaten by something. Very sad."

"Unbelievable. You seriously chopped firewood as a child? Like, regularly?"

She looked back as if I might be the one joking now. "Of course. Who didn't? So, what did the raven say to you?"

"Well…I'm still not sure it really said anything. But…first it seemed to be saying 'answer.' And then, I think it started saying 'gone.' Just before it threw this hair comb at me and flew away. I…really thought I might be going crazy."

"Maybe you should just come ask me next time you think that," said Jen.

"I think I just did. So…let's close these windows, huh? I don't want that bird going through my things again."

༻✦༺

THAT AFTERNOON, I FINALLY GOT around to hanging that reframed photo of Paige and her handsome young man on the foyer wall, near the kitchen door—well above the wainscoting this time. *Let's see if those dumb cats can knock it down here,* I thought, defiantly. After that, I went back upstairs to face all those boxes from Paige's room. Maybe the raven had thrown Paige's ornamental comb at me just to say it was time I stopped hiding from that task.

I started with the still-unopened boxes we'd found stashed under her bed. To my surprise, the first and heaviest one contained a large, truly hideous cuckoo clock. In addition to the usual door above its face, and elaborate Tyrolean woodwork, its top corners sported wooden turrets with mismatched windows through which little, crudely carved medieval figures made funny faces at me. I hung it on a closet door clothes hook, and tried pulling on its various weight chains and swinging its oak leaf pendulum, but couldn't get it to run. I could sure see why it had been stashed away under the bed, but wondered how and why she'd gotten it to begin with.

By dinner time I'd gone through all the boxes, and separated their contents into three piles. The first contained beautiful, interesting or useful things I wanted to keep, like the Japanese fan, some of her old jewelry, silk scarves, perfume bottles, interesting keepsakes, old photographs and books.

The second pile held beautiful, interesting or useful things I had no interest in keeping, like lovely old clothes that would never fit me, jewelry I would never wear, and curious but puzzling artifacts of her life like that ugly old clock. Those I meant to give away to anyone wanting them at her memorial service.

The third pile would just be taken straight to the Exchange or the dump. Ironically, the second and third piles went right back into boxes which I carried out to store in the barn until they could be disposed of. But having done even that much lifted a big weight inside me.

Jen came home that night from her shift at the Barnacle looking lighter too. She practically danced into the second parlor, where I was sitting reading a book, James on my lap, Master Bun snoozing by the unlit fireplace.

I set my book down and smiled at her. "Good shift?"

"Oh, does it show?" she asked, smiling back at me.

"You're not hiding it real well, if that was your plan. So what happened?"

"Nothing," she said, a little mysteriously, as she came to sit down next to me. "I just love being back in a job where I get to interact with people again. They're *so* much more enjoyable than boxes."

"I see. So, was there some particular not-a-box that put you in this mood, or was the whole crowd this much fun?"

"Well…" Jen said, looking away like that canary-feather-covered cat people talk about, "one of the dreamiest guys on the planet did sit at my bar all evening, behaving, if I may say so, most charmingly."

"Really! Tell me more!"

She bounced back up onto her feet. "I'm getting some wine." She glanced at my empty glass. "Want a refill?"

"Half a glass, or less; otherwise I won't sleep."

"Great!" She grabbed my glass and was off to the kitchen. Two minutes later, she was back. "I snuck a picture of him, hang on." She dug out her phone and opened her photos app. "Here you go. His name's Dylan." She handed the phone to me.

"Ooh! You're right!" He was slender and athletic looking, with neat, close-cropped hair, and clean-shaven. "He doesn't look like a local boy."

"Oh no," Jen said happily. "He's just moved here from Seattle to work for Rock Island—and took a serious pay cut to do it, apparently."

"Really! Why would anyone do that?"

"He said he's looking for a less toxic lifestyle?"

"Hmm…" Rock Island was Orcas's newest internet provider. About half a dozen people seemed to work there, and from what I'd seen the few times I'd gone in for help with my phone, it seemed a pretty low-key and lonely sort of job. "What was he doing in Seattle?"

"Some big entertainment software company. He told me the name like it was a big thing, but…" She shrugged. "What do I know about computer games? But apparently he's been making a fortune there for years now."

Yeah, this was so not adding up for me, and I wondered if this was one of the losers Kip had said Jen seemed to go for. "You're sure he wasn't just fired for some reason, and came here to hide and lick his wounds, or something?"

"Oh, I don't think so," she said. "He's renting a house over in Rosario while he looks for someplace to buy here. Does that sound like recently fired to you?"

"No, it doesn't," I had to admit.

"He seems really sincere," she said. "We talked off and on for hours, and half of it was about how much he struggled with the way people are living down there these days, about sleeping in beanbag chairs at work, and showering in the company gym on Sunday mornings. I'm pretty sure he's the real deal. He has a killer sense of humor too, by the way. And shady people aren't usually that funny—especially when they're trying to be."

"Interesting theory. What makes you think so?"

She shrugged again. "Shady people are too into themselves to understand what's really funny maybe? I don't know; I've just never seen people being laugh-out-loud funny while they're trying to get away with something. But Dylan is totally *hilarious* in this cute, self-deprecating way. He made me laugh about twenty times tonight." Her expression just then looked pretty smitten to me. Could this be something real—at last?

"I'm not crazy about people who like to say I told you so," I said, "but I'm pretty sure this is exactly what I told you would happen a few months ago. Remember?"

Jen looked confused. "That I'd meet a Seattle tech-bro named Dylan?"

"No, that new guys would be coming here as things opened up again, and that they'd flock to you when it happened."

Her smile vanished as her brows rose. "Oh, this is nothing like that. I didn't mean to..." She shook her head. "He's a new guy on the island kissing up to the local bartenders. Anyone who's ever tried to meet people in an unfamiliar town knows that old trick." She sighed. "It was a fun talk that made the evening fly by, but I didn't mean to make it sound that way. If I ever see him again, it'll be when he brings an actual date back to my bar. And trust me, he'll treat me just as charmingly then—to impress her. *Hey look! Me and the bartender are buddies!*"

I barely kept myself from gaping at this transition. And then I realized what I'd done. I'd called him a boyfriend—or as good as—too directly. It was almost scary how spot-on Kip's description had been. And now, just a few weeks later, here it was, happening right in front of me. My first instinct was to argue with her self-defeating conclusions. But fortunately, before I could think of what to say first, she moved right on to another topic completely.

"I've also been thinking a lot about our discussion this morning," she said, "and I'd like to apologize for freaking out about your idea like that. Taking advantage of your generosity is about the last thing I would ever want to do. But you're right; this place would make a really great inn. And if that's something you really want to look into… Well, it would be a complete blast to help you with something like that. I didn't mean to just shove your idea away."

"I know. And no apologies needed," I said, seeing so clearly how that moment and this one were just two chapters in the same story with her. I was really glad I hadn't tried to argue about her take on this guy at the bar. Here she was coming out of her panic this morning. Maybe if I just didn't keep poking at what had happened at the Barnacle tonight, she'd reconsider that too in time. "I did just kind of spring it on you out of the blue. But I'm glad you're open to it. I actually went down to bounce the idea off of Lisa this morning—just before the raven attack—and she seems to like it too."

"Oh," Jen said. "Did you guys…talk about the partnership idea?"

"Oh yes. And she agreed you'd be a very valuable partner."

"Well, that was nice of her," Jen said, less tensely.

"No, it wasn't *nice*. It was observant and smart. This is not a charity I'm proposing here. You're probably going to run more of this inn than I am. Your expertise is what we're counting on. So I'm serious; believe in your value to this partnership, okay?"

"Okay," she said, seeming to suppress a laugh. "I will be the most hardworking, brilliantly creative and intelligent innkeeper anyone in this county has ever seen; and when Marriott comes up here and offers me the penthouse suite in their flagship hotel in Seattle to leave you and come work for them instead, I will refuse because you *need* me, and I've totally got your back!"

"There!" I laughed. "Was that so hard?"

☙

As May marched toward June, the world itself seemed to be speeding up. Rumors of chaos in the wider world drifted our way: politics, economy, war, the global climate crisis. But on our islands, the seasons still changed, and the gentler rhythms of normal life continued to return. The delicate flowers and bright yellow-greens of spring gave way to whole fields of white daisy, orange poppies, and the darker foliage of summer.

Word was getting around about Lisa's new approach to Orcas Repertory. Most people I talked to seemed to find her plans exciting; and I'd heard a lot more from behind the scenes through Lisa herself, of course. Her booster ladies had adjusted to the idea of actual *community theater*, and auditions had been held for *Cuckoo's Nest*. Charles and Glory had both come back to the island to try out, and they'd both been cast, to my great relief on Lisa's behalf. Charles would be playing Nurse Ratched, and I knew he'd be spectacular. The show would be opening on July fourth weekend, and I could hardly wait to see it.

Tourist season was already in full swing by now, making a zoo out of Eastsound. But it was also great to see such things come back—especially for those whose livelihoods depended on the inns, restaurants, shops, and recreational businesses that were Orcas Island's only real industry these days. Jen and I began discussing the B&B idea with Lisa and other business-savvy friends around Orcas, including Jen's former innkeeping colleagues. They'd all seemed excited and very encouraging, and we'd decided to go for it.

We created a list of structural renovations needed to make the building work as a modern inn: upgrades to the kitchen, bedroom remodels upstairs to accommodate more in-room bathrooms, and a host of improvements to the house's plumbing and electrical systems. Then, with Lisa's help, we'd submitted permit applications and started trying to ferret out the necessary contractors to make all those changes later that summer—if, by some miracle, our permits were reviewed and approved in time to start work that soon.

In the meantime, Jen started working on the outlines of a business plan and marketing ideas. She was super excited about potential breakfast menus, and even wondered if we might want to offer dinners in the winter when nearly all the island's restaurants were closed down. "People visiting off-season would stay here just for that," she told me. "We could make a mint while everybody else is closed!" She'd be doing the actual cooking, of course, but I was completely ready to help chop or grate or mix things, along with serving as our waiting and dishwashing staff. Who knew? Maybe I'd even learn to cook a little better. Stranger things have happened in my life.

We were also going to need an internet connection now, which sent Jen down to Rock Island—where Dylan worked.

"Well, there's good news on the internet front," Jen told me when she came into the kitchen where I was having lunch. "Our location up here on this hilltop has great access to their transmission tower signals, so we won't have to spend your entire fortune getting fiber-optic cable laid all the way up here. We won't need much but a router, actually."

"Hurray!" I said. "Because we'll need my fortune to pay the contractors." And then...because I just couldn't help myself, "Was Dylan there?"

Jen gave me a kind of irritated look. "Yes. In fact, he was the only one there, naturally. The other guy on duty had taken the early lunch slot."

"Oh. And how did that go?"

She looked back at me with narrowed eyes. "Just fine. He was cheerful, knowledgeable, and very helpful—as I will state on his employee review at their website once we have an internet connection."

"So, when you walked in the door, he didn't say, 'Oh, it's just you again. I was hoping for someone more interesting?'"

"No," she said, patiently. "He was his usual charming self, and seemed delighted to see me—as any good salesman is supposed to. Just see how fond I seem of each and every customer who shows up here."

I shook my head. "You really are a hard nut to crack, aren't you?"

"Are you seriously suggesting that I should throw myself at our internet provider?" Jen asked with an edgy smile. "Do you have any idea how easy it would be for him to start sabotaging our connection or signal quality when things finally went wrong between us?"

"Only a shady guy would do that," I said. "And you told me he wasn't one."

She rolled her eyes. "It doesn't matter what kind of guy he is. This is a professional relationship. And I'm not the kind of fool who mixes business with pleasure."

No, I thought, *you're not* that *kind of fool.* "Well, that's very sensible."

"Oh, for heaven's sake, Cam. He's a very nice guy, and I look forward to working with him. Maybe we'll be friends. I'd love that. But I'm not throwing myself at the first non-obnoxious guy to cross my path just for showing up. Do I really seem that desperate to you?"

Oops. Now, there was a question I wasn't about to answer, as Kip's voice chimed up in my head again: *You really can't fix this, Cam...* "No, of course not. And I'm sorry," I said, speaking of fools. "I didn't mean—"

"I know," she cut in gently. "Of course you didn't. But...let's just give this one a rest, okay?"

I nodded, hoping I would not need to learn this lesson a third time.

PAIGE'S MEMORIAL SERVICE WAS ZOOMING toward us too. I was putting together a list of music for the service, menu choices for the caterer, and content for the programs. Responses to the invitations we'd mailed out to Paige's friends were starting to appear, along with several invites that were returned to sender, either because those addresses had changed, or because those people had died too. I threw a little party in my head when Elle Gascaux's reply finally arrived—weeks later than the first flurry, along with a *phone number*, thank goodness—and a very interesting note:

Dear Ms. Tate, thank you so very much for writing with this news. I am so sorry to learn that I will not see Paige in this world again. She was so dear to me, and mentioned you with great respect and affection on several occasions in our correspondence these past few years. I will be honored to attend, and to help conduct this celebration of her unspeakably remarkable life. I look forward very much to meeting you in person. Be well, Elle.

She'd mentioned me—to Elle—on several occasions? Was there anyone in the world that Paige had *not* talked me up with? I mean, seriously, how had I never known this was going on?

Just one week before the service, RSVPs continued pouring in from all over the country—all over the world, in fact—many of them from people we had not even sent invites to, which made me think that news of Paige's death must have gone viral somehow. I'd had no idea her reach was so vast. As energetic and dynamic as she'd been, Paige must have downsized herself considerably before I'd ever met her. Her memorial was going to be swamped, and I just hoped we'd have enough of everything, even *space*, to deal with that.

Roland Marcus was in a tizzy now, of course, about the two most crucially important items on anyone's agenda: the "purple azalea" color I'd suggested as a banner color, and "our" urgent need for his giant rental tent. He was the only person determined to make a crisis of the banner color. I thought the fabric he'd found was lovely. And I'd told him *NO* about the tent at least half a dozen times already. We had the farm's ample theater to move people into if the weather turned bad. But Roland kept insisting that holding *"Peggy's* memorial" in a *theater* would "make this great lady's death seem some kind of cheap amusement." I knew the only heartfelt word of his objection was "cheap."

He'd make less than half as much money without that tent. I'd stopped taking his calls. If he put it up anyhow and expected us to pay, I had an attorney now.

In addition to all of this, Jen and I were also getting ready for an after-gathering at the Berry Farm itself. I'd thought that might be nice for closer friends of Paige's who'd come a long way to be here, and wished to see her house one last time, and visit with each other for a while longer. And we had a barn full of mementos to give away as well. I'd planned to have the memorial service caterer do that gathering too, but Jen insisted this was an awesome chance to try out our new B&B menu items and advertise our inn's upcoming opening, so she was catering the after-gathering herself now.

I did have one more secret reason of my own for hosting that second event. Paige had once mentioned "others like ourselves" out there in the world somewhere. But she'd never brought it up again, and I'd never learned who or where they were before she'd suddenly gone beyond asking anymore. Her memorial service seemed like the best shot I had left of running into any of these mysterious others; but I had trouble imagining how or why they might reveal themselves to me. A smaller, more informal gathering at Paige's house seemed to lend itself better to that slight chance than a big mob scene at Madrona Farm did. There seemed nothing more that I could do than that.

☙

Just two days before the memorial, my mom called.

"Your dad's just tested positive for Covid," she said. "So we won't be coming to the memorial after all. I'm so sorry."

"Oh no!" I cried. "How's he feeling?"

"He's not too bad; and the doctor's already prescribed Paxlovid for him. But we don't want to be infecting all your guests. So, we'll have to come visit you another time, I'm afraid."

I could hear the stoic disappointment in her voice. "You have to," I said. "You're going to love this place."

"I know we will. Good luck this weekend, and we both send so much love."

I didn't have a lot of time to brood over it. Elle Gascaux was due in on the evening ferry; and before driving out to pick her up, I had to finalize the menu and the attendee count with the caterers, then drive by the Office Cupboard to pick up the programs. After getting all that done, I didn't even have time to drive home again before heading down Orcas Road to the ferry landing and pulling into the parking lot above the hotel there. Elle and I had agreed to text each other when the boat got near. But it was such a lovely evening that I just left the car and walked down to await her boat at dock.

As I reached the road, I could see the ferry at dock across the narrow channel on Shaw Island. As usual, there was a good crowd standing around the Orcas landing waiting room, holding wheelie suitcases and carrying backpacks, taking pictures of each other. It was so strange to see tourism so entirely back—though also very good news for Jen and me.

When the ferry pulled away from Shaw, heading for its big three-point turn out in the water before steaming to our landing here at Orcas, I texted Elle: *I'm waiting on the dock. Wearing blue jeans and a red T-shirt.*

But I needn't have worried. All the people waiting to get on the boat marched down the ramp and clustered just behind the gate. By the time the incoming walk-on passengers disembarked, I was nearly the only one still waiting up by the road.

Elle Gascaux was an old woman, of course, but dressed very colorfully, as any friend of Paige's would almost have to be. And she was barely more than five feet tall! But even across the distance between us, she projected an air of radiant calm as she walked up the ramp and smiled at me. I felt warm just seeing the easy joy on her face, as though I was being hugged before she'd even gotten near.

When she did reach me, she set her rolling suitcase on end and put out both hands for mine. I gave them to her and she squeezed them gently but firmly. "It's so wonderful to meet you finally, Camille." Her voice was low and melodious, with a faint French accent.

"You too. How were your travels? You must be exhausted." She'd flown to Seattle from New Orleans yesterday, spent the night in a hotel, then taken the airporter bus to Anacortes today.

She gave me a very Gallic shrug, tossing her white curls gently back from her heart-shaped face. "Eh, a glass of wine and I shall be entirely restored. Shall we go?"

I reached for her bag, but she shook her head. "No no, I am capable."

"It's a pretty steep walk up to the car," I warned her.

She grabbed the bag's handle and started walking. "The day I do not carry my own luggage is the day I finish travel for good," she said, sweetly but firmly.

So, I let it be. The day I began arguing with old ladies—particularly old friends of Paige's—was, well, not today, at least. "Just let me know if you change your mind. We're going up that hill there, behind the hotel."

"*Parfait.*"

She wasn't even breathing hard when we reached the car. I tried to cover my own huffing and puffing as I pressed the fob to unlock Tigress and open her back hatch.

Elle lifted her bag and laid it inside. "Lovely car," she said, appreciatively.

"Thank you." Funny how owning this car now made such compliments so much easier to take. I know…don't hate me.

I drove Elle up the road, then out through West Sound on Deer Harbor toward the Berry Farm. She sat in a comfortable silence mostly, admiring the scenery.

"It's been too long since I was here," she said, as we climbed the Berry Farm's long steep driveway. "I used to visit every few years, but it's been… Hmm. A decade or more now."

"Well, we're awfully far from New Orleans."

She grinned at my diplomacy. "And I am old now. Almost as old as Paige was. We of such great white-haired wisdom do not travel like we did when we were youth like you."

As we pulled up by the front porch, Jen stepped out of the house, drying her hands on a dishtowel. "You're here! Hello, Ms. Gascaux!"

"Oh, no, ma cherie!" Elle said, as she stepped down out of the car. "You must call me Elle."

She went to take Jen's hands as she'd taken mine.

Jen smiled and said, "Welcome, Elle. I'm Jen. Come on in. We're having nibbles in the front parlor, and I've got drinks all ready to mix up."

"Oh," I said to Elle, "I forgot to mention that Jen has been working on a new cocktail; but if you'd prefer a glass of wine—"

"A new cocktail is the *only* thing that would be better even than wine," Elle said, with a dimpled smile.

ELLE DID LET ME CARRY her luggage to her room, since we were practicing being a B&B and she was playing the role of a real guest. She did not, however, follow me up all those stairs to see her room, but just went with Jen into the front parlor. When I returned downstairs, they were in animated conversation, and a big platter of cheese and herbed crackers, rolled-up meats speared with adorable toothpicks, Castelvetrano olives, and Marcona almonds in rosemary oil sat on the table between three martini glasses, frosty and full, adorned with whimsical metal skewers. James sat sphinx-style before the unlit fireplace, looking for all the world as if he had no interest whatsoever in the platter, but just happened to be gazing in that direction.

Avidly.

"We almost didn't wait," Jen said with a grin, lifting her glass.

We toasted and sipped. It was complex, interesting of course; herbal, and only faintly sweet. "Fantastic. What's it called?" I knew better by now than to ask what was in it.

"I'm not sure yet. I'm toying with 'Berry Herbal,' but that isn't quite right."

"I'm not tasting berries," I said, after another sip.

Jen's grin widened. "Check out the garnish."

I pulled up my owl-adorned skewer and studied a basil leaf rolled around some dark, wrinkled little ball. "Is this a dried blueberry?"

"No," Elle said thoughtfully, before Jen could answer. "Juniper berry, if I am not mistaken."

"That's right!" Jen said, looking impressed.

"In gin, of course, but I find sage also," Elle said next, still thinking. She took another sip. "Sage liquor? And lavender, but also vinegar— could it be lavender shrub? But also St-Germain, I think. This is a very complex little treat! And bitters—but what kind? Not Angostura; something herbal."

Jen's mouth dropped open. "How are you…"

"Clever, using a cocktail shaker," the old lady went on, "so you get the sparkling water's minerals without so many bubbles."

Jen sank back against the sofa. "You just recited my whole recipe." She rolled her eyes to the ceiling. "At least the *quantities* are still a secret."

Elle smiled mischievously and reached over to pat Jen on the knee. "Don't fret, young lady. This is just a party trick of mine—I have a very sensitive palate, and I enjoy showing it off." She turned her pale gaze to me. "We all have our little talents, no?"

I nodded dumbly, covering my surprise and concern with another sip of Jen's most excellent (and as yet poorly named) cocktail. Was this what I'd been hoping for? Was Elle one of the others Paige had referred to? If so, she'd better not say too much with Jen sitting right beside us.

Be careful what you wish for, Cam, I told myself, afraid to look up from my glass. Was she some kind of super-taster? Or was the sensitive palate she'd mentioned just a small corner of some larger gift, like Paige had thought my ability to vanish was? Paige had talked with her about me, according to the letter she'd sent. Did she know my secret, or was she just guessing? And how was I going to let her know Jen wasn't in on it?

I looked up at last to see her still giving me a subtly quizzical look. "Oh yes!" I said. "Such quirks, so crazy—I mean so many quirks, ha-ha. Jen here is a gourmet all the way down. You should have seen how horrified she was the other night when I cooked my boyfriend a silly old spaghetti recipe for dinner! Miss Julia Child here almost threw me out." I smiled at Jen, maybe in apology. But she just looked at me like she was wondering if she'd made the cocktails *way* too strong. "And I'm a chatterer! Obviously." I took another sip just to stop myself from going on, and hoped I'd gotten my message across, at least.

Elle gave me a reassuring smile, though, and set her glass down to pick up a cracker and some cheese. "This is going to be a very charming bed-and-breakfast. I love how welcoming and homelike it feels."

"We're not quite done upstairs yet," I warned her, "and I'm afraid we're all going to have to share a bathroom."

"I am sure it will be splendid." She reached for a piece of rolled-up prosciutto. "Thank you again for this repast," she told Jen. "I had no chance for dinner before the ferry arrived, and could not bear the thought of supper from a vending machine. This is perfect."

"So, how did you and Paige meet?" Jen asked.

Elle picked up her drink and leaned back, cocking her head as if searching the air before her for memories. "We were just girls—in the old sense, I mean, when single women were all girls until they married. But I mean in our early twenties. Paige had just arrived in New Orleans on a grand adventure, traveling across the country—by herself—which was not a thing girls often did back then. And New Orleans was such a different place; rougher, wilder. Hardly suitable for an un-chaperoned young woman." She set her glass down and straightened her shoulders. "But Paige swept into town like a little hurricane, of course, marching into a jazz club on Bourbon Street and straight up to the bar to order whiskey and soda. Also not a thing expected of young women in those days. Not decent ones, at least."

"Wow," Jen said, looking awed.

"Oh yes. Mine was not the only attention gathered by her entrance," Elle continued. "I was at the bar as well, with my suitor at the time. He was clearly taken aback by her forthrightness from the start. But when the music began, Paige turned to me and said, 'That band is all white men! I thought they'd have *real* jazz on Bourbon Street!'" Elle's face broke into a radiant smile—almost a laugh. "Such reckless honesty, as if she'd no idea of the segregated South."

I put a hand to my mouth, almost afraid to hear what happened to her next.

"Since she was so clearly new in town, and a Yankee from New England—her accent said as much—I told her that colored men were not allowed to play on Bourbon Street; but that I could take her to a different club if *good* music was what she'd come for. My suitor…Roger, was it? Or Anthony?" She shook her curly head. "It doesn't matter. But he was horrified by the whole exchange. So I did him the favor of leaving with Paige instead." Elle smiled. "I did not see him again; he was entirely too comfortable with the world that was."

This was exactly the kind of story I'd been hoping to hear this weekend. I was fascinated.

"Paige and I did not separate that night until dawn closed the city down," Elle went on. "And I saw right away she had…a certain something that was very rare." Elle darted me another glance. "So, the following day, I persuaded her to leave her boardinghouse, and come stay with me a while. Though she had planned to visit our city for no more than a few nights, we had nearly three months of fun together before she moved on. I wanted her to settle there. But though we had become all but sisters, she told me one day that she knew her home was elsewhere." Elle looked around the room. "I was sad to see her go, but she promised to keep in touch, and tell me instantly when she discovered where this real home of hers might be.

"Her road to find it proved longer than either of us had guessed; but she kept that promise, and we shared many other adventures together, for decades and decades." Elle looked off at something only she could see. "And even after that, we wrote." Then she looked at me and chuckled. "One letter from her in particular would have amused you, I believe, Camille. I should have thought to bring it with me. It was quite a long report about your adventures with her purloined azaleas… And how hard you fought her—and everyone else—who dared suggest that a certain young deputy might be more than just a friend."

Jen snickered.

"Well, yes," I admitted. "I was a little slow to get that message." But there'd been so many messages for me to get back then, and they'd been way too tangled up to read very easily.

"He is…doing something else now, I believe?" said Elle. "This young man of yours?"

"Yes." Clearly she and Paige had continued corresponding until very recently. "He wanted to start helping people *out* of trouble instead of just punishing them for being in it. So he's mostly away at school these days, getting a degree in social work. He'll be here tomorrow night, though, for the service on Saturday; and he's excited to meet you."

"I look forward to meeting him as well," Elle said.

"Where did Paige go after she left New Orleans?" Jen asked, a bit too quickly, as if she was afraid Elle might ask about *her* love life next.

"She traveled west," Elle said, "through New Mexico and Arizona. She thought so highly of Sedona that I hoped briefly it might be her real home, since it was not all that far from me. But the desert did not keep her either, and she continued traveling for almost a year, never staying anywhere for long. I recall a postcard from San Francisco, where she was living on a houseboat." Elle smiled. "She was very cagey about that part of her journey, so I think there was a gentleman involved. But her next postcard was from Ashland, Oregon, I believe. So whatever happened in that houseboat did not last long."

The thought of Paige shacked up with some man on a houseboat seemed so weird to me—though I guessed it shouldn't have. She'd been just as much of a bohemian when I had known her. Except that bohemian had been a forceful woman in her eighties with goat-nibbled clothing and a penchant for kale.

"Eventually," Elle said, "I got a letter from this island, with a small photo of an empty boardinghouse half in ruins. On the back of it, she'd written just one word: 'Home.'" Elle smiled again, more sadly. "I remember staring at that little black and white picture for the longest time. I could see the color, could smell the trees, could hear the water." She looked around the room appreciatively. "I still see traces of that building here, even after all these years and changes." She stifled a yawn.

"We're keeping you up," Jen said.

"I'm having a wonderful time. But now, with some food in me, and your lovely drink, of course, I fear I'm not much longer for the land of the awake."

And it was two hours later in New Orleans, I realized. "Can I show you to your room?"

She nodded. "I do believe I might be ready to turn in. If you'll excuse me?"

"Of course," I said, getting up as she did. "I'll show you where everything is up there, and we'll get you settled in."

The stairs didn't seem any harder for her than the trek up to my car had been. But when we reached the upper landing and I pointed toward her door, she came to a sudden stop and turned to me in surprise. "Her room?"

Oh dear. It hadn't occurred to me, somehow, that this woman, who'd known Paige for so much longer than I had, might have as much trouble as I had seeing Paige's room without her inside it. "I'm sorry," I said, awkwardly. "That's just the biggest one, but there are several others here—as I guess you must know. It's no trouble to—"

"No, no, cherie," she said, softly, turning to look back at Paige's doorway. "I was just…taken by surprise. But it will be nice, perhaps, to sleep with her so near again, this one last time." She nodded to herself, and smiled gently. "Why don't we go in together, and see what you have done with it."

✢

I WORRIED I MIGHT SLEEP poorly with someone else in the house, but I didn't wake once until the sun was fully up and birdsong streamed through my cracked-open window. Which was around five in the morning this time of year. So, downstairs, I had the house to myself, as usual.

I put the coffee pot on, then went out to do the morning livestock duties. When I came back, I made myself a piece of sourdough toast and took it and my coffee out onto the covered porch behind the kitchen, as I'd been doing since the mornings had gotten warmer. I pulled Master Bun out of his hutch to let him sniff around while I sipped. When he began nuzzling my feet, I leaned down and picked him up. Of course, James arrived then too from whatever alternative dimension he'd slept in last night, and wanted space on my lap as well.

"You could snuggle with me all night if you wanted to, cat," I said, but let him jump up beside Master Bun. My lap was big enough for two.

Sam and Harry, as was their custom, watched me from the porch rail, well out of reach.

After a while, I heard someone moving around in the kitchen, and a few minutes later, Jen came out with her own mug. "Should be ready in about forty-five minutes," she told me.

"Sure looked delicious," I said, having seen her breakfast casserole in our fancy new fridge when I'd gotten the cream for my coffee.

She pulled up the chair beside mine and reached over to scritch behind Master Bun's silky ears. He leaned into her touch. "Any sign of our guest?"

"Not that I saw, though I've been out here for a while."

"Yeah. That's a long journey for someone her age."

"Hello?"

We both turned in surprise at the sound of Elle's call from somewhere in the kitchen. I quickly handed Master Bun to Jen, and just dumped James from my lap onto the porch as I stood up and went inside to find Elle peeking in the foyer door.

"Have I missed breakfast?" she asked.

"No!" said Jen, coming in behind me. "I just put it in the oven. You're up earlier than we expected."

"How'd you sleep?" I asked.

"Oh, quite wonderfully. I have just been looking at more old memories around your lovely house. However did you get it this clean?"

Jen laughed, as I wondered if Elle had been here more recently than I'd thought, or whether Paige had just always been so messy.

"It wasn't a quick job," Jen said.

"This lovely photo by the stairs out there is of her and George Harper, I assume?" Elle asked.

Jen and I looked at each other in surprise. "You know who that man is?" I asked.

"Oh…well, it is hard to be sure after so many years. He was gone before I ever had a chance to meet him. But this was one man Paige sent me many pictures of."

"Oh my god!" Jen said. "You have to tell us everything!" She bit her lip, and added, "I'm sorry—would you like some coffee first? Breakfast won't be out of the oven for about half an hour."

"Coffee would be lovely," Elle said. "But I may not have that much to tell you. And what little I know is mostly very sad."

"There are a lot of pictures of him around here," I said, "and we've been very curious."

"Cream or sugar?" Jen asked, already over at the pot, pouring Elle a cup.

Elle grinned. "Lots of both, please."

"Would you like to come and join us on the porch?" I asked her, gesturing at the door behind me. "It's a gorgeous morning."

"Sounds heavenly." She took her cup from Jen as we all headed back outside, where Jen went off to get a third chair.

"Look at all the darling little people," Elle cooed, smiling down at James as she wiggled her fingers at Master Bun—whom Jen had put back in his hutch, I was glad to see. James was lying in the sun a few feet away, ignoring me now, probably incensed by his rude ejection from my lap. "You are an animal person too then?" Elle asked me as she came back to sit down.

"Well, not like Paige, but yes."

"No one is like Paige," said Elle. "Or ever will be, I suppose."

We both fell silent as Jen reappeared with her chair and sat down beside us. "So then," she said to Elle, "who was George Harper?"

"Alas," Elle said. "He was the only man I think Paige ever truly cared for."

"I knew it!" Jen said to me. "The minute I saw that lock of hair." Elle looked up with raised brows, and Jen told her about what we'd found behind the photo. "I'm guessing it was his?"

"Most likely." Elle sighed. "A lock of his hair. After so many years. How strange that we can be so absent and so present in such ways, all at once."

"So…what happened?" I asked.

Elle looked down and shrugged. "Paige met him here, at a tavern, I think." She gave us a crooked smile. "She had an appetite for taverns in her younger days, if that is not already clear. But they were not drawn to each other at first, it seems." Elle looked up at me. "Much like you and your young man. Neither of them was what the other thought they were looking for. In time, however…" She smiled again and shook her head. "Life can surprise us. No?"

"Yes, it can," I said.

"But when they finally recognized each other, they fell very hard. I have dozens of letters from her somewhere, I am sure, which made that very clear."

"So…what went wrong?" I asked, wanting to know everything at once.

"He vanished," Elle said sadly. "They had an argument, and…he left the house that very day, never to be seen again."

"An argument about what?" I asked, astonished.

"I fear this is where my store of things to tell you ends," Elle said. "His departure devastated Paige. Everyone who's ever known her well, knows that much." Though *I* had not, obviously. "But Paige refused to speak about it, or about him, almost from the day he left—even to me. Or maybe she was just unable to." Elle looked at us apologetically. "There is one person I can think of who might know more. Her name is Florence Golding, and she was up here often in those days. She and Paige were very close back then."

Florence Golding… Where did I know that name from?

Then I knew, and sighed. "Her invitation to the memorial came back marked undeliverable."

"Really!" said Elle. "What address did you have?"

"I don't remember. It was from Paige's list; somewhere in L.A., maybe."

"Ah, well, that is why," said Elle. "She's lived in San Francisco for many years now. But have no worry. I contacted many of Paige's old friends to make sure they knew. Florence will be here, though I am not surprised she failed to let you know." Elle's grin faded. "She is…less attentive to such niceties than many of us are."

So then…Elle had been calling people. Would the whole *network* be here this weekend? And if they were, would I be able to tell? Would they let me know, somehow—or hide, as I was still doing now, even from Elle?

☙

AFTER A SCRUMPTIOUS BREAKFAST OF egg-tortilla-green chili-cheese casserole—one of my favorite treats from Jen's growing catalogue—I helped Jen wash up and then got out of her way. She'd asked Darvill's for the day off to start working on her giant list of offerings for tomorrow's gathering here, and Tracy had been more than happy to cover for her. She'd be in the kitchen all the way till dinner, I expected—and wouldn't want any help from the Daddy's spaghetti maven.

Kip wouldn't be arriving until evening, and I actually had very little left to do myself before tomorrow's service. So, Elle and I went out to stroll around the garden for a while. As we stepped down from the porch, I thanked her again for all she'd told us about Paige, and mentioned how sorry it had made me to know so little about the rest of her life.

"That's always how it is," said Elle. "When we knew my mother's end was near, I found a notebook, and sat with her to jot down what she had time to tell me. But her memory was already failing. We never have enough time with those we love. All we can do is make the most of what time we have." Elle turned to me with a strangely knowing smile. "So, your friend, Jen; she is extremely talented—if not in quite the way that you and I are." I almost forgot to keep walking as the moment I'd been hoping for, and avoiding, arrived. Elle must have noticed my uncomfortable reaction. "Paige was not a tattletale; but we were very close, and you were so important to her."

"So I've discovered," I said quietly, glancing at the evidence around us.

"She came to me only from concern about how best to be of help to you."

"So, what did Paige tell you about me? About…my gift, I mean." I braced myself to hear someone I'd barely met name my oddity out loud. But her answer took me by surprise.

"She told me that you have a powerful talent for drawing ragged ends together, and mending what's been broken. 'A shattered plate might almost be made whole again as she walks by.' Paige wrote that to me not long ago." Elle looked up to grin at me. "And look! Here you are creating a gathering place with your new inn, and reuniting all of Paige's old friends after so many years apart. I can see now what she meant!"

Not a word about vanishing or invisibility! Had Paige mentioned that part to her? And if not, should I? I wasn't sure what to say. It still seemed such a weird thing to bring up with someone I'd just met, even knowing she was gifted too. But that didn't keep me from trying to satisfy my own curiosity. "If it isn't too rude, can I ask what your gift is, Elle?"

"You saw last night," she said casually. "My senses are extremely keen. Not just taste, but all of them: hearing, sight, touch, smell, intuition, and a dozen more I would not know how to make you understand." She glanced my way again. "Very little gets by me." Oh...*that* wasn't unsettling, not a bit. Did I suddenly feel kind of exposed? "Though, if I'd learned to trust my gift a bit more than I did back then," she added with a wry expression, "I'd have known better than to waste any time at all on that man, Roger or whoever."

"Is that how you realized that Paige was gifted?" I asked.

"Oh, Paige was not someone I could have missed, even in a crowd. She clearly hadn't any slightest notion of her gift yet at that time. For me, though, it was like a sudden wash of daylight in the dark of night. I adored her instantly, for who could not have in the flower of her youth? And so charmingly oblivious of her effect on others! But the main reason I worked so hard to make her stay with me in New Orleans was that I wished to help her recognize this gift just waiting for a chance to *bloom* inside her—as it were."

This sounded like what Paige had done for me, back when I'd still been hiding from myself. "So you were Paige's mentor?" I asked, surprised by the idea, even though it made such perfect sense with all the rest of what Elle had told me.

"That is...an interesting word for it," she said uncertainly. "But there was nothing so formal about our exchange. This awakening I wished for her... It is not a thing one can just walk up and explain to someone who does not already know. As you understand, I think."

I nodded, remembering the long game of cat and mouse Paige had played so patiently with me before the night we'd finally spoken of it directly. "So, how did you make her see it then?"

"Oh, no, cherie. One does not make anyone see such a thing. I just *let* her see it. In New Orleans, there were—and are—many, many gifted people. I simply started introducing her to them, until she began to notice on her own that there was…something going on around her." Elle smiled and spread her arms. *"Et voilà!* Once she began to understand that *others* might really have such gifts, it was just one step farther to realize her own 'green thumb' might also be more than she'd assumed."

I tried to imagine living someplace with so many other people like us around… But, of course, Elle's approach had not been there for Paige and me to use.

"Once she started to embrace her gift…" Elle said wistfully. "Well, my garden never looked so good as it did those three months when she was staying with me." She gazed fondly around her at the house and grounds again. "Yours is very pretty too."

"Oh, it's nothing like what Paige's was, as I guess you'd know. I've just done my best to fill the space she left."

"Judging by the letter I received from her," said Elle, still looking at the garden, not at me, "I think she hoped that's what you'd do."

"She sent you a letter too?"

Elle gave me a probing look. "And to you as well then. But of course she would have." Elle nodded to herself. "Sadly, mine did not arrive until two days *after* your kind invitation did. In the confusion of her final days, I imagine, Paige had transposed two numbers of my zip code. It took the postal service some time to find me."

"What did it say? I mean, only if you want to tell me."

Elle looked thoughtful for a while. "It said goodbye," she said quietly. "In ways that would make no sense to anyone but me. And she thanked me, less for anything I'd done than for who we'd been together, she and I. And yours? If you wish to say?"

My gaze fell to the ground. Here at last was someone I could tell without any need to worry. "She…didn't say goodbye in mine. I don't know why. She just talked about some exciting journey to unknown territories, and how she'd been collecting maps for it. And that she looked forward to exchanging stories someday. I thought she meant when she came back, until… I didn't know she'd died yet, when I found the note." I looked up at Elle. "Do you know what any of it meant? Could she really be somewhere else now, traveling somehow?"

"Paige had been traveling long before the night I met her," Elle said.

"And I don't think she ever stopped, even once she'd settled here. Not inside, at least. But as to where she may be now…" Elle shook her head. "I never hazard guesses about things I cannot know."

Paige had said something like that to me once too. "Do you have any idea what kind of maps she was talking about?"

Elle smiled. "Oh, we are all collecting maps, ma cherie. And making them as well—every human being, however gifted. That never stops, from birth to death, if even then." She reached out to take my hand, and hugged me with her eyes, the way she could. "I am certain you already have a vast collection of them." I still had no idea what to make of all that, but I enjoyed the warmth of her smile until she let my hand drop, and we continued walking.

"So, your friend, Jen; she does not know," she said at last.

I shook my head.

"And how is that working?" she asked gently.

I shrugged. "Fine, I think. We've been close friends ever since I got here. She moved in with me three years ago, after the pandemic started, and we're closer than ever."

"Just…not close enough for that?" Elle asked lightly.

"Is anybody close enough for that? I mean, who's not like us?"

"Not many, no. But…she has noticed nothing in all that time?"

I shook my head. "There's not really anything for her to notice anymore. I mean, most of it's so invisible that even I don't see it happening—until afterward sometimes, I guess. And…" I could almost see Paige shaking her head at me. *Get over it, my girl.* "And the other part… My ability to vanish…literally…" I glanced nervously at Elle, who just gazed back at me without any sign of surprise. "Paige told you about that too?"

"Oh yes," said Elle. "Though she attached very little importance to that part of your gift."

"Well, yes; that's what she told me too. And I agree with her. Since she taught me to be less afraid of that part, I've learned how to control it pretty well, and I really just don't do it anymore. I have no reason to. So, honestly, what is there for Jen to notice?"

"Not much, perhaps, consciously. But people with or without gifts like ours have many other ways of knowing things—most of them unconscious, but no less powerful for that. So, are you certain that such a close friend might not notice something in those ways before you, or even she, is consciously aware of it? Can you be certain she has not already?"

I had no idea what to say. This had never occurred to me. "Okay, but even if she did, what am I supposed to do? Just walk up and say, *'Hey, Jen, I can disappear—like really!'* Then what? She'll just think I'm lying, and wonder why. Or that I'm crazy. That's what happened the one time I tried to tell someone I thought I was in love with. That relationship ended instantly, and painfully for me. Which doesn't matter anymore, because I'd been blind to what a jerk he really was. Later, I made sure he knew I wasn't lying or crazy by vanishing right in front of him. He went running off in terror, and I've never seen him again—which felt even better, honestly. Because I despise him now. But making something like that happen with Jen…" I shook my head. "I'd never get over that."

"Is Jen the kind of jerk this man was?" Elle asked gently.

"Of course not."

"Then perhaps she won't do what he did."

"Maybe not," I said. "But this is not like other secrets. You must know that. No one's going to believe it, and I still can't see any point in scaring her out of my life, or maybe even her mind," I added, remembering Sheila's reactions to my vanishing act, "by proving something about me that no one ever asked to know, and isn't even happening anymore."

"Ah," Elle said pleasantly. "Not even happening anymore. I see." She nodded to herself. "So, now that you no longer fear this gift you seem so frightened of sharing, it will just go away without ever altering anything around you again in ways your friend might notice?"

"Fine," I said, unable to hide my growing exasperation. "How would you tell her then, if you were me?"

Elle gave me a sympathetic smile. "If I were you, I would be very irritated with me too, right now. And I do not mean to suggest you do anything you do not wish to, much less presume to tell you how. People like us are a very private tribe for many extremely good reasons. None of your concerns are baseless. You know your own situation better than I can ever hope to, and may be entirely right. But I do wish to…challenge you to keep thinking through this issue. I am concerned about what may happen if Jen or others of such particular importance to you do notice someday—consciously, or, even worse, unconsciously."

The longer you've left them in darkness, the harder it may be for them to trust you if you must ever reveal the rest of your story for some reason."

Why had I imagined that meeting others like myself would be fun? "Well, I see your point. And I'll keep thinking about it." As if there'd be any way to *stop* thinking about it after this.

"Then, perhaps a change of subject is in order?" Elle asked with an apologetic smile. "If I may ask, was there more in Paige's letter?"

"In the letter?"

"Only if you wish to say."

"Well, not much," I said. "A lot of instructions about taking care of her estate while she was gone—which I didn't understand then either. And she told me again not to use my gift, but to let it use me."

Elle looked startled. "*That* was very good advice!" She gazed back at the house, as if considering it in some new way. "Which I may not be following nearly as well as you are…" she murmured more to herself than to me. "More and more, I see why Paige was so delighted with you. Take what I say with a grain of salt, of course, and follow your own counsel. That advice, I have no doubts about at all."

CHAPTER 10

Saturday dawned bright and sunny, and as soon as Elle, Kip, Jen, and I were done with breakfast, I darted back upstairs to change out of my goaty farm clothes into something more appropriate for the memorial service that afternoon. Leafing through my wardrobe, I came across the gorgeously absurd red sequined gown I'd worn to the closing night gala for *Salon Confidential*...and never since. The dress everyone had talked to Kip about for months, supposedly, and put stars of envy in Jen's eyes. Would I ever wear it again?

Not today, I thought with a silent laugh, and chose a pretty but more sober dress: long and light blue, with flowers. A garden dress. Paige would have liked that.

And with it...some of Paige's jewelry. I had kept her more delicate, older pieces in a box on my dresser. I opened it and pulled out an opal pendant with matching earrings. What more perfect time than now to wear these?

After a final glance in the mirror, I was out the door and gone.

One thing about memorial services is that, unlike weddings or theatrical performances, no one buys tickets or has to tell you they're coming; and I was worried that even the many RSVPs we'd gotten might represent only a fraction of the guests we'd actually have. Paige Berry had touched a lot of lives in her seven decades here. We'd put notices in the local papers and on community bulletin boards and Facebook pages, along with the island gossip network, but we really had no idea how many islanders might show up.

Jen had done her best to guesstimate our likeliest turnout. But it seemed clear to me by now that Elle hadn't been the only one out there making calls to people I had never heard of, much less invited. Jen had gone into a panic about whether there would be sufficient food at our after-gathering at the Berry Farm. Having been more a casual acquaintance than close friend of Paige's, she'd decided to skip the memorial service and spend the day making more food and gathering extra supplies to be sure her spread was ready for whatever crowd showed up.

Weirdly, she'd called Dylan late last night and asked if he'd be free to join her catering crew of one. Which he'd agreed to do, apparently. I had no idea what to make of that, but this time I'd possessed the discipline and wisdom to keep my mouth completely shut.

I left Kip at home to look after Elle until it was time for him to bring her down to Madrona Farm, while I went to inform Erin and José, as well as the caterer, that we might have some unknown number of extra guests. Then I went to beg two churches and the high school principal to loan us extra folding chairs—just in case. After that, I zoomed back to Madrona Farm.

José was already setting up mics and an array of outdoor speakers that would make Elle and others audible to our open-air audience; I trusted him to make all that work perfectly without me. But the list of recorded music and the slide show I had put together were being set up and operated by the booster ladies. And while they were mighty, and experienced…I needed to reassure myself that all of this was actually under control. It all reminded me uncomfortably of *Salon Confidential*'s opening night, although, thankfully, the star of *this* show would be Elle, not me—and, hopefully, we'd manage to avoid the law enforcement drama this time.

Happily, the day was clear and warming up nicely.

Roland Marcus was already there as well, installing two dozen twenty-five-foot-tall banners of shimmering lavender rayon—all belling gorgeously in the gentle breeze—on as many huge poles of PVC piping. For all the pain involved in working with him, he really was the best. To my further relief, there was no sign of his benighted rental tent, so I could check "call attorney" off my to-do list as well.

By twelve-thirty the seats were filling up, and there seemed nothing more I could do. So I found a chair on the aisle for myself, and saved another beside me for Kip. At twelve-forty, he walked in with Elle, who looked magnificent. Her outfit was not unlike the frilly, many-layered getups Paige had often worn—except that Elle's was well tailored in brightly colored silks, not hanging on her like a layered poncho of coarse fabrics woven out of goat hair and organic botanical fiber. The difference was stunning. Kip stopped to greet half a dozen people on his way, then came to slide in next to me. He took my hand as Elle strolled comfortably up onto the stage where her chair had been set up to one side of the podium.

At one o'clock precisely, the recorded background music faded out, and the audience grew quiet far more quickly and politely than any theater audience I could remember. As Elle stood and walked confidently to the podium, I glanced back across the crowd to see if we had many people standing, but was relieved to see none yet. I looked back at the stage just in time to see Elle reach up and adjust the mic a lot farther downward.

I'd forgotten to check that.

"Good afternoon," Elle said, "and thank you all for joining us here in this profoundly beautiful space on this perfect summer day to celebrate the life of our dear friend, Paige Berry." She gave the entire field of us that same smile she'd given me as she'd come off the ferry, and I was not the only one to smile back. Paige had chosen the perfect person for this task, because of course she had. "My name is Elle Gascaux, and I was deeply honored to learn Paige had asked that I officiate at today's memorial."

José had done his work perfectly. Her voice was clear, and the volume just right all around us.

"Paige and I go way back," she went on. "Farther back than many of you have been alive." Her smile widened as an answering chuckle murmured through the crowd. "I would like to say a few words about the extraordinary woman she was, and then I hope that we will hear from some of you who must also have stories of her to share with us. However," she cautioned, raising a schoolmarmish finger, "I'm going to put a strict time limit on these reminiscences, because we only have this venue reserved until midnight."

More chuckles.

Finally, Elle's smile gave way to a pleasant but frank expression. "I met Paige for the first time when she was not much more than twenty. She was passing through my home city of New Orleans on the long walkabout that would eventually bring her to this lovely island, where she spent the rest of her life. And I will begin by assuring you that

Paige already knew what she was looking for, even that long before she found it here. We met and fell into lifelong friendship at a jazz club on Bourbon Street, and had so many wonderful adventures together in the decades after that, that if I allowed myself even to get started here, I would be the one apologizing when none of you had gotten a word in edgewise yet at midnight."

There was another quiet ruffle of laughter.

"So then," she continued, "how to sum up such an indescribable woman and her equally indescribable life…" She paused, as if still trying to think that through. As a former actor myself, I was impressed at how good she was at this. "I'm going to go for the lowest-hanging piece of fruit, I think. Paige Berry was…a *gardener*." I saw people nodding, some with grins, others very soberly. I felt a little startled to hear Elle use the exact word Paige had used to explain herself to me. Had she used that phrase with everyone?

"So, let us stop and think about what that means," Elle said. "To begin with, I think we can acknowledge that *real* gardeners are rarely tidy people." This remark drew the biggest ripple of laughter yet. We'd all known Paige—and what a perfect place to start. "Their fingernails tend to be ragged, if not dark with soil. They come in at the end of a day with bits of twig and dried leaves tangled in their hair. Their arms and faces are sunburnt and dotted with dirt and insect bites. Their clothes are filthy, and their shoes are caked with mud. And it's not just that they don't seem to care. They don't even notice!" The laughter was no longer dying completely down before swelling up again. "But *look* at what they've done out there! The beauty and the life they have drawn up out of that messy soil, the flowers for our tables, the nutritious food and fruit! The meals and homes they have provided for all kinds of creatures you and I so rarely even think of!" It had grown suddenly… so quiet. "Who here…" Elle said as quietly as we were now, "who here has ever seen one of Paige's gardens, or eaten anything she grew? Raise your hands."

Almost everyone's shot up, including mine. And I saw tears now, mixed in with the laughter of some around me. Kip was staring up at Elle with his mouth hanging slightly open. I thought about the giant bags of vegetables she was always bringing me…and how I'd rolled my eyes about it every time. My eyes began welling too.

"So then…you understand," Elle went on. "And I am so blessed just to be in the company of this many people who have had even a single bite…" She trailed off, and I realized that although Elle was still smiling, there were tears on her cheeks too now. "A single bite," she said again, "of the *feast* I have been privileged to enjoy at Paige's table for close to seventy years. I will admit as well that I am envious of you. Of all the ready access you have had these many years to a woman unlike any I have ever met or heard of. Or expect to meet again."

Elle bowed her head, and paused. Then she said, more quietly, "I do not wish to cheapen my admiration and respect for this amazing friend by editing her story now, in any way. As I've already said, true gardeners are not tidy people. For all that they do God's work outside in the garden, they also leave a mess inside their own homes sometimes, or in the homes of others. Paige made mistakes. She had regrets. There may be people here today who know more about some of those than I do. But, even that was…just another sign of her sincere and genuine humanity: that she was never afraid to be as much like us as she was not like us in other ways. *She* did not ever even try to edit her story for the sake of pride. And I will miss all of her—including the untidy parts."

Elle looked up at us again, almost defiantly. "But one last thing I will say before turning this podium over to you, who knew her in so many ways that I did not. Though Paige is no longer with us as she was," she said, more forcefully, "neither is she truly gone. As long as there is one of us alive who knew her, and remembers her, she and her gardens go on in the world. Still growing, even now." We were all silent now. Lost in some much bigger understanding of what we'd had, and what we'd just lost, in Paige.

"Thank you," Elle said at last, "for the honor of your attention." She smiled again, for the first time in what had seemed a whole lot longer than the few minutes that had actually passed. "And now, I invite any of you who wish to enrich our memory of Paige with stories of your own to come up here and do so." Her smile became an edgy grin. "But remember, *mes amis*, there is a time limit. And I will not hesitate to come and drag you off this stage myself if you get too lost in what you are saying—not that I will blame you in the slightest as I do so."

This warning drew another little wave of laughter—to everyone's relief—as she left the podium, and walked down off the platform instead of sitting back down in her seat up there. As she reached the ground and glanced around, I realized that there was not a chair left down here for her to sit in. So I stood, and waved her over to take mine; but Kip stood up too and gently pushed me back down into my seat as Elle arrived to take his. Kip squeezed my shoulder, then went to stand somewhere farther back.

The first person to walk up was a woman I didn't know. She was in her sixties, maybe, and spoke very quietly and self-consciously of her first airplane trip as a young woman, to visit a new friend that Paige had introduced her to. She'd been so terrified of flying, though, that Paige had offered to go with her, and calmed her down so thoroughly during the flight that she'd gone on later to acquire her own pilot's license. I had a hard time even picturing Paige flying anywhere herself, though she must have if she'd visited Elle so many times.

Next up was a nervous little delegation of booster ladies who treated us to a slightly over-lengthy collage of "funny stories" about how Paige had made every project they'd worked on both delightful and efficient. The funniest part of it, I thought, was the way her death seemed to have altered things that…I remembered differently.

Porter got up and told a version of the azalea caper story that ended up being more about the reconciliation it had caused between himself and Paige than about the caper part—to my relief.

And then there was a man who introduced himself as just "an old friend from far away." He spoke about his youthful friendship with Paige so fondly, yet so vaguely, that I really wanted to pull him aside later and ask some pointed questions. He'd given us no name at all. But would a man who'd disappeared so mysteriously so long ago even want us to know who he was? Wouldn't it be amazing if George Harper had come back in disguise to say goodbye to his now-deceased true love? Or had I just read too many romance novels? There did seem some basis for a play script here, though! If he showed up at the after-gathering, I would definitely have to ply him with a few of Jen's cocktails and get the real story there.

There were many more tales, and people were generally very well-behaved when it came to time limits; afraid, perhaps, of getting that schoolmarm finger shaken in their direction. But when there was finally a brief pause in the flow of speakers, Elle jumped on the opportunity to go up and move things along, as Kip came back to take her place beside me.

"Thank you all, so much, for those heartwarming stories! But now, let us have a moment to reflect on Paige's life with a slideshow and an eclectic set of some of her favorite music prepared by Paige's dear friend, Ms. Camille Tate." She gestured graciously at me.

Kip clapped loudly, of course; I blushed, trying not to squirm, as people looked around at me. I'd just asked her to introduce the slide show, not me. Happily, the music came up right on cue, and everyone's attention was drawn back to the images of Paige appearing on a large shaded screen behind the stage platform.

I'd started with photos of Paige we'd found while cleaning out her house, taken back when she'd been young and lovely. And the first song was a short but absolutely perfect piece I'd found by Googling *gardener*. It was called "Gardens," by someone named Trevor Hall, and was heartbreakingly beautiful, with lyrics about a man who wanted all his gardens to speak for him when he was gone. The last line was about being born by dying, and was so powerful that I completely lost it for a minute. It was like he'd written it specifically for Paige!

From there, fortunately, the photos became more recent, and mostly more comical. I'd filled out the few pictures of her I and others had taken during the production of *Salon Confidential* with photos I'd collected from her many other friends around the island—especially Porter. As the big band swing piece I'd followed "Gardens" with segued into 1980s techno-pop hits, Kip leaned over and whispered in my ear: "This is great! But…The Cars? The *Human League?*"

"Clearly you never went through her cassette collection," I whispered back.

"She had cassettes? What did she play them on?"

"A cassette deck, obviously," I whispered. "Now hush. We're distracting people."

When the slide show ended, Elle retook the stage and invited everyone to stay for the refreshments that had been quietly set up in the field behind us all by the caterers. She also asked everyone to check the back of their programs for other information—meaning our after-gathering at the Berry Farm. We'd addressed that invitation to "close friends of Paige's, and visitors from off-island," hoping that every last one of the local people there wouldn't classify themselves as close friends.

As people started getting up and milling around, I raced over to tell Elle how amazing she had been before the crowd of others wanting to meet and congratulate her could beat me there. Then I went to find

Erin and José Salazar, who'd surprised me that morning with the news that they'd decided not to charge us—meaning me—anything at all for hosting this event! They felt Paige had contributed so much volunteer time to so many events there at the Farm that her fees had all been paid long ago. I'd been too stunned, and too frantic still, to say more than "Thank you!" But I wanted to thank them again, a little more cogently, for a job so well done before I left to see how Jen was doing back at home.

☙

I WALKED INTO THE KITCHEN braced for an outtake from *Titanic*, the movie, but found Jen and Dylan working at a line of baking sheets, quietly arranging fresh berries and chocolate shavings on little custard tarts in a state of almost disturbing calm.

Dylan looked up with a tentative smile, and waved. "You must be Cam. Nice to meet you."

It was the first time I'd actually seen him in person, and I have to say, his picture hadn't done him justice. He was taller than I'd realized, and looked rather dashing, I thought, in plain black slacks and a white shirt, open at the collar—as if he'd looked through his wardrobe for a catering costume. "And you must be Dylan," I said. "Thanks so much for helping us out on such short notice."

"My pleasure. All part of Rock Island's new incentive program: internet with a free Netflix subscription and spontaneous catering help."

Hmm. This must be the sense of humor Jen had mentioned. I was *very* curious to know how he'd really gone overnight from counter-guy at Rock Island to auxiliary catering staff here. But I knew better than to try touching this spring-loaded subject again—especially now.

"How'd it go?" Jen asked.

"It was amazing. I'm really sorry now that you weren't there. Elle's speech—wow. I'll see if I can make her do it again for you. So, how's it going here?"

"Way better than I expected," Jen said, glancing at Dylan, who smiled again in a...weirdly self-satisfied way? Or was I misreading that?

"Great," I said to Jen. "Kip should be bringing Elle back any time now." I glanced again at Dylan. "I'd love to tell you more about the service, if you can afford to take a couple minutes out on the porch, so we don't disturb your helper here?"

She gave me a look, but said, "Sure," and wiped her hands off on a towel.

When we were outside, far enough down the porch to be out of easy earshot, I asked her, "Are things really going okay?"

"Oh, yes! Dylan's been amazing help. He's so smart! Every time I turn around he's found some new, efficient way of doing things. I don't know how I'd have gotten all this done without him."

"Well, good! I'm glad to hear that; you just seemed…"

She sighed, and looked away. "Okay, I'm a little worried he must think that I'm an idiot by now. Does it show that much?"

"Oh, Jen! No, he doesn't, because you're not. I mean, if you were, who would know better than me, right? And if he's half as smart as you say, he knows that too." I gave her a little hug. "You're just tired, and who can blame you? The last few days have been a pretty wild ride. But it's nearly done, and everything is going great—thanks as much to you as anyone."

She smiled at me—almost as if she couldn't help it.

"Okay," I went on. "I won't distract you any longer. I'm going to go take a look in the barn, and make sure there's nothing left in there that should be going on the giveaway table inside."

"Have a look, but I don't think there is, unless you want to get rid of that spinning wheel or the loom. And I'm not sure we should be carrying them back into the dining room at this point anyway."

"No, I'm keeping those for now. They might be interesting as décor somewhere in the inn." I turned to go. "Now go easier on yourself, okay?"

"Okay," she said with a weak smile, heading back into the kitchen.

Not half an hour later, Kip and Elle returned, and warned me that the horde was coming right behind them. We'd cleared off a grassy field around behind the house for parking, and as Kip began directing new arrivals there, I tried to greet people as they approached the house, and get names attached to faces—most of which were unfamiliar. *How many of you are gifted?* I wondered. There was no way to tell, of course. Lisa was also among the first to show up, and immediately asked what she could do to help. But I told her that Jen seemed to have everything under control.

And that was true. Dylan had gotten a whole line of folding tables spread out on a stretch of lawn between the front porch and the chicken coop in minutes flat not long after I'd gotten home. They were spread now with an amazing array of fruit and cheese, tiny pastries, savory tarts, and little sandwiches, nuts and candies, along with paper and plastic dishes, cups and utensils—all elegantly displayed. He'd even brought out most of the chairs from inside the house for our elderly guests to sit on. A need that hadn't occurred to me until now.

I had just finished greeting Verna and Porter, who'd arrived with several additional cases of good wine, when I saw the mystery man who'd spoken about himself and Paige back at the memorial service walking with surprising ease up our steep drive. We'd been forced to start having people park down the hill now.

"Hello!" I said, as he approached. "You made it!" He looked a bit startled by my greeting. "I'm Cam," I said, extending my hand, which he shook warmly. "And I so enjoyed your touching story about Paige. But, I'm so sorry; I've misplaced your name."

"Emile Fisher," he said with a little nod. "Thank you for having us all here."

Emile Fisher? For a moment, I was disappointed. But then it occurred to me that a man who didn't want to be recognized wouldn't use his real name. Duh. "My pleasure. Can I get you a drink?"

"A glass of wine would be very welcome," he said, walking with me toward the house. "Something white and not too dry, if you have it?"

"We've got a lot of wine. Let's go see."

I walked him into the house and steered him toward the front parlor, where there was still a couch for us to sit on, before going to the kitchen. Dylan was restocking trays while Jen tended tables outside. "Hi Dylan," I said. "Would you know if we have a sweet white wine in here anywhere?"

"You bet," he said with a charming smile, and walked right over to a large assortment of bottles on one counter, snagging a bottle of Riesling almost as if he'd known I was coming. Yes indeed. This was one together young man.

As Dylan poured a glass for my guest, I poured myself a small splash of Syrah, and went back out to join Mr. "Fisher" in the parlor.

"Cheers," I said, as we both raised our glasses before sipping.

"Lovely! Thank you. So…have all of your guests been treated to a sit-down like this, or am I special for some reason?"

Realizing that I wasn't being too subtle, I decided just to lean into that. "Well, no. I'll confess that I've been hoping I might get to hear a little more of that charming story." I gave him an *oh what the hell* kind of smile. "Were you and Paige really…just friends?"

He looked chagrined. "Was I that obvious?"

Bingo! "Probably not to anyone but me. Paige and I were very close. But our friendship was always so focused on what was happening now that I never thought much about her past until she wasn't here to ask anymore. I've felt so sad about that, and was hoping I might learn more about that part of her life today, while you're all still here. I hope this doesn't sound too rude, but I'm betting that not many people here can tell me what it was like to be in love with her."

There. I'd done it. He would either tell, or he'd run.

"Well," he chuckled. "I hope it won't offend you if I say that right now you remind me of Paige yourself. That's just the sort of question she'd have asked—and just the way she would have asked it."

"Really!" I said, surprised. "I'm quite flattered."

He looked down and sighed. "Our affair was brief, to tell the truth."

My heart almost stopped. Had I been right? Was this really him?

"I'm so sorry," I said quietly, trying not to let my desperate interest show. "If this is too difficult…"

"Oh, no." He looked up again, waving my concern away. "It was too brief, really, to have hurt me very deeply—either of us, I'm fairly certain." And yet, here he was decades later, all the way from…I'd forgotten to ask where. He looked up and around the parlor. "I do still remember this room, though. It was very different then, of course."

When he said nothing more, I worried that I'd pushed too hard too fast. "Would you like to see more of the house?" Maybe stepping back for a few minutes would keep him from bolting altogether.

"That would be…well, very interesting, I guess," he said, a little sadly. As we stood up and headed back toward the foyer, he added, "I'm amazed that she spent the whole rest of her life here, in this house. She was one of the most adventurous people I'd ever met, and yet…" He shook his head. "I've lived in a dozen different places since then, and had at least that many different lives. While she stayed here. Who'd have guessed?"

A dozen different lives… And how many different names to go with them? Oh my. What would I even say to him, if… But just as we reached the stairs, he stopped and stared at something, looking almost frozen. I followed his stricken gaze to the photo I'd forgotten was still hanging there—of Paige and George Harper.

Oh no, I thought. *If this is him, he'll bolt for sure now. He'll think I knew all along. Unless...* "That's Paige," I said, thinking fast. "As I guess you know. But we have no idea who the man is. Do you know him?" If he thought I didn't know, would he stick around?

To my surprise, he nodded, now looking completely desolate. "Oh yes. That's the guy before me. Never met him, but...Paige still had that photo and half a dozen others like it up all around the house." He looked down, clearly quite embarrassed now. "And look," he said, putting on a smile—or trying to. "She still does."

Both my hands had somehow ended up over my mouth. I lowered them and said, "I'm so sorry! I had no idea." Which was true enough. I'd gotten this about as wrong as I could get it. "I didn't mean to—"

"I know," he cut me off, smiling bravely now. "Not your fault. How could you have known? But, if you wouldn't mind, I could use some air. Shall we go talk outside?"

"Of course," I said, already leading him toward the front door. "Really, please forgive me."

"There is nothing to forgive." But at the doorway, he stopped and turned to look up and around again—at everything *except* the photo. "I wonder if that torch is what kept her locked up here for all these years." He shook his head. "I hope not. He did not deserve that kind of love."

Like you did, I thought bleakly, following him out onto the porch, and feeling more awful than I'd felt since the night I'd wronged Colin several years ago. Clearly, things had not worked out for this man like they had for Colin and Priya.

༄

Mr. Fisher didn't leave the gathering in a huff, though I would not have blamed him if he had. We sat down on the porch steps, and I tried to help by explaining that she hadn't left that picture hanging there; I'd just found it in a closet. He laughed about how ironic it was that I should have hung it back up just in time for his visit after all those years, and then apologized for being "wretched." I didn't even try to extract any more information from the poor man. But he said enough on his own to make it clear he knew little more than I did about George, except that Paige's absent former lover had been standing there between himself and her until the day he too had finally left her, and the island, for good.

To my relief, a woman walked past as we were sitting there, and called his name with obvious delight. He reacted in kind, and went down the steps to talk with her, as I went back inside to have another look at that ill-fated photo.

Why? I asked the man who looked so happy up there, standing next to Paige. *What kind of idiot wins Paige Berry's heart, then leaves?* And then, I heard hushed voices from upstairs.

"Well, I have no idea," whispered one of them—a very elderly woman, judging by the quaver in her voice. "I could never have expected this! But that was her room, which is quite upsetting."

"Do you think the girl knows?" asked a second voice, also female, but maybe not so old.

"Oh, I doubt it," said the first voice. "But we must still try to do something, don't you think? Especially if it's her."

I had no idea what all this was about, but they sounded pretty distressed. I thought I'd better go up and find out why.

I started up the stairs very quietly, then walked more loudly so they'd know that I was coming. As I reached the upper landing, I did my actressy best to look startled. "Oh! I'm sorry. I just needed something from my room, and didn't know anyone was here." *Too much explaining?* I wondered. Probably. But it wasn't like I'd had time to rehearse.

"Oh, hello!" said the younger woman—younger as in maybe just seventy-five or so, not ninety or more like the woman standing next to her. She had short, straight salt-and-pepper hair, round glasses that reminded me of Margaret Rosen's, and was avoiding direct eye contact with me. "If your room's up here, then I guess you must be Cam? I mean, you can't be the other one." She chuckled nervously. "She's out serving that delicious food. So, we just came up to use the bathroom, and were admiring what you've done with Paige's house. I hope you don't mind."

Okay...she was explaining too much too. Interesting. What were we all dancing around?

"Oh, I don't mind at all," I said cheerfully. "Any friend of Paige's is welcome to look around here all they want. I bet you've known this place a lot longer than I have, right?"

"Oh! Yes, dear," said the older woman, seeming startled, as if she'd just noticed I was there. She was almost as short as Elle, but stick-thin, and hunched, with a dark, polished wood cane, and a great cloud of tangled curly hair, all snowy white. "We haven't visited here for…at least twenty years, I think. But it's amazing how much the same it is."

"And yet," her companion said, "how much it's changed as well." She looked blank for a minute, then said, "Oh! I'm sorry. I'm Diane Franklin, and this is my dear friend, Simone Wade. We're here from Los Angeles, and very sorry for your loss."

"Yes, we are indeed," Simone murmured, gazing woefully around again, as if already starting to forget that I was here still. "Very, very sorry."

"Thank you," I said, "I'm sorry for yours too. Is there…anything that I can help you with?"

"Oh no," Diane said crisply. "The bathroom was very nice and clean. We're so glad to have used it, aren't we, Simone?"

Simone looked back at us, seeming as startled as before. "Yes, yes. Very glad indeed."

The name Diane Franklin seemed naggingly familiar, and this time I knew why more quickly. "I'm so glad you made it here! Your invitation came back to us as undeliverable."

"Ah, yes. We were so glad that Elle called us in time. What address was that?"

"Lincoln, Nebraska?" I said.

"Oh my!" She laughed, more genuinely this time. "Who ever gave you that one? I haven't lived there since I was a child."

"It was the latest entry I could find in Paige's…address book."

"Well, let me update that then." She reached down to dig with meticulous care through her purse, and pulled out a business card to hand to me. It said *Diane Franklin, Data Analyst*, with her mailing address, phone number, and email address. Oh my goodness! They all had phone numbers—and *email!* I made a mental note to start collecting that information from anyone I could. If Elle had called these two, then they might be gifted as well, and I didn't want to have to keep writing all these people physical letters if I wanted to follow up with any of them. "We've heard you plan to start a bed-and-breakfast here," Diane continued. "Simone and I would be very interested in coming back for a visit when that happens. Have you got any kind of mailing list?"

"Oh! Well…I'm not sure yet." That kind of thing was Jen's department more than mine. "But I'm sure we'll have one soon."

"Would you put me on it when you do, please?" Diane asked.

"I'd be delighted to. Thank you."

"Yes…" Simone said quietly, gazing back at Paige's room now. "We should be on your mailing list. Let's do that, shall we?"

"Well… Okay then. We definitely shall." I smiled at both of them, though Diane still wouldn't look me in the eye. "Are you sure there's nothing I can do for you?"

Simone shook her head, facing us again. "Nothing you can do," she said sadly. "But I guess we'll see…"

"All right then," I said, "I'll just get that thing I came for, and let you two keep exploring. See you later!" I wriggled my fingers at them as I started toward my room for nothing. But Simone didn't seem to notice, and Diane just smiled and waved without looking at my face.

☙

I CAME BACK OUT OF my room a minute later—with a random book in hand, just in case. But there was no sign of the ladies now. I looked around to be sure, surprised that Simone could even have moved so fast. Finally, I shrugged and headed for the staircase, where I looked down and saw them walking out onto the porch. They'd clearly wasted no time getting out of here.

I left the house too, hoping that any of that amazing food Jen had been serving for almost an hour now was still left for me to try. My small sip of Syrah had been very tasty, but even wine as good as Porter's didn't pass for dinner.

I'd just filled my little paper plate, and was going kind of crazy over Jen's precious little wedges of Gruyère and onion quiche, when I looked up and saw Lisa maybe fifty feet away, talking to the most amazingly beautiful old woman I had ever seen. I mean, seriously: Grace Kelly and Audrey Hepburn spliced together by the world's best plastic surgeon, but at eighty-five going on thirty. That was someone I absolutely needed to meet…as soon as this quiche was finished. And the little ham and apple tart beside it, and that tangy-looking little chicken skewer I'd laid them down against.

And one of those custard pastries there'd been no room for in this first helping. But then, my very next stop would be that conversation over there.

I may even have snagged a second one of those little custard tarts, because I doubted there'd be any left by the time I made it back. And besides, Jen had been standing right there serving people for an hour by now, probably wondering why I wasn't interested in even trying any of what she'd been slaving over for two days. So I felt responsible to make it very clear how interested I really was. The smile Jen gave me as I took that second tart proved I was right.

With all that done, I walked casually toward Lisa and her dazzling companion. Not straight at them, but close enough to catch Lisa's eye—as if I'd just been off to feed the chickens when I'd noticed them. It worked perfectly: Lisa noticed me and waved me over to join them.

"Oh, hi!" I said—to Lisa first, of course, because I wanted us to go on being friends. And then I turned to her new acquaintance, trying not to stare.

Okay, yes, now that I was close enough to see them, she did have wrinkles; but they were all so tiny, and somehow delicate, that they just…didn't matter. Her makeup was salon-perfect, yet practically invisible as well somehow. Her full, silky hair, drawn back into a simple ponytail, was pure silver-white, but I should never even have thought the word "old" in her direction. She was *ageless*. We've all heard that term, of course. I'd been in the beauty business quite a while before I came here, and let me tell you, that word was a biggie in the industry. I'd just never really understood what it meant, or even believed that it existed, to be honest—until now. *This* was what it meant.

"Cam," said Lisa. "This is Florence Golding, an old friend of Paige's from San Francisco."

"Oh!" I exclaimed. "You're Florence! Elle told me about you."

"Did she really." Florence smiled as if we'd just shared some private little joke. "How kind of her. At least, I hope it was?" Even her voice was like music.

"Oh, yes, of course!" I couldn't actually remember what Elle had said. But what could anybody possibly have said about this woman but nice things?

"This is Cam Tate," said Lisa, completing the introduction.

"Yes, of course," said Florence. "I saw you at the memorial service— which was absolutely lovely, by the way." Her perfectly shaped red lips turned up charmingly as she smiled and raised a hand for me to shake—or kiss, or… I resisted an urge to curtsey, and settled for the handshake. "Lisa and I have been talking about you, and the inn you plan to open."

"You have?" I looked back and forth between them as if she'd just told me I might be up for a Tony Award.

"I think it's a wonderful idea!" And I was suddenly sure that Kip had been right; we were going to be rich and famous all over Orcas by the end of summer. "I'm certain Paige would be delighted too. Back in her youth, this house was filled with guests nearly year round." Those movie poster lips turned up again. "We liked to tease her about running the busiest and least profitable inn on Orcas Island." She sighed, perfectly. "We had such fun back then, Paige and I. It would make me so happy to see you and your friend Jen revive that tradition."

I was literally speechless. And then I noticed what was sitting on the grass to one side of her graceful ankle, and ruined everything. "The ugly clock!" I blurted. "You're taking *that?*" As my back-brain registered what I'd just said, my face caught fire in embarrassment. But Florence just threw her head back and laughed in delight, as if I'd told the most charming little joke she'd ever heard.

The wave of relief I felt was…well, pretty strange, actually. I mean, yes, I was relieved that she'd found my rude remark funny instead of insulting. But, suddenly, I realized how I'd been acting. I glanced at Lisa, and found her watching me with an expression almost as uncomfortable as the one that was probably on my face.

"I know the poor thing's rather gauche," said Florence, as if nothing was amiss. "But that's sort of why I bought it for Paige to begin with. I hoped she'd find it funny. Which she did, I guess… For a while."

"Wait," I said, *"you* gave this clock to Paige?"

She nodded sadly. "And you're entirely right, dear. It's a very ugly clock. But now it's coming home with me for sentimental reasons, clearly, not aesthetic ones."

She was still as pretty as she'd been two minutes earlier. But…that was all she was now: just a charming, gorgeous woman who'd aged unbelievably well. I wasn't sure what had changed; but my starstruck behavior seemed…well, more than a little embarrassing now.

"Back to your inn, though," said Florence, "one small bit of advice: Jen is a treasure. If I weren't so eager to see you succeed, I'd steal her from you and have her down to cook for me in San Francisco. So, fire everybody else before you fire her."

"Thank you. But right now at least, 'everybody else' is just me, so her job should be safe."

Florence rewarded me with a graceful little laugh.

"Florence has a wealth of good advice," Lisa said. "And she's surprisingly well-informed about a lot of things here in San Juan County. So perhaps you two should talk, while I go sample some of this brilliant food everyone's talking about." She looked back at Florence with a smile. "It's been such a pleasure meeting you. I hope we'll be talking again soon."

"I've no doubt we will," she said. "I look forward to it."

As Lisa left us, Florence looked back at me. "You have some very impressive friends, dear—besides Paige, I mean—which suggests impressive things about you too."

"Well…thank you," I said, wondering what *she'd* made of my fawning behavior during the last few minutes. "So, you've kept track of things here? All the way from San Francisco?"

She gave an elegant shrug. "San Francisco, Seattle, Los Angeles… It's all the same coastline. And, as I mentioned, this island has held a special place in my heart for a very long time. I still have many friends up here." She drew a deep breath and looked away. "One fewer now, though. The most important one."

"I know," I said. "I wish I'd known her half as well as all of you did."

Florence turned back to smile at me. "I think you may be overestimating our importance to her—or underestimating your own. She left all of this to you, after all, which suggests that you and she must have shared a bond at least as great as any of us did. Paige and I fell largely out of touch so many years ago. Perhaps you can tell *me* how or even who she's been more recently?"

"I'd be thrilled to exchange stories with you. I want so much to know more about all the things I should have asked her when I could have."

Florence nodded. "We should stay in touch."

"Yes, please. There's one story I'm particularly curious about right now," I said. "And I've been told you might be the one to ask."

Her brows rose prettily. "Which one is that?"

"What happened with her and George Harper?"

Florence leaned back slightly, almost as if I'd slapped her, her eyes wide and her mouth open. It was the first ungraceful thing I'd seen her do. She recovered almost instantly, though, and smiled again. But it was a harder smile now, one that didn't reach her eyes. "And who was it that directed you to me with that question?"

Clearly I'd made some kind of mistake again. "We found old photographs of him around the house," I said, trying not to make an even bigger mess of whatever I'd just stumbled into. "When Elle arrived, she saw one of them, and told us who he was. But when we asked her to tell us more, she said he'd gone before she'd had a chance to meet him, but that you had been around back then, and might know more." I shook my head. "That's all."

Florence seemed to study me for a moment, then visibly relaxed. "I'm sorry." She looked down and shook her head. "That's just…such a sad story. And so dreadfully complicated." She looked back up at me. "It's still painful for me, actually. And I will tell you someday, if you really want me to; but this is not the time or place. You have other guests to meet and care for, and it's actually time for me to go. I've another friend on San Juan Island who's expecting my arrival tonight. Perhaps we could have this conversation when I come back to see your inn sometime? Because I'd really like to. Would that be all right?"

"Sure," I said, feeling like a child out of her depth at some party for indulgent adults who all knew things she didn't. "I hope you will." But I doubted it would happen. I'd botched pretty much every encounter I'd had this afternoon.

Florence gave me another of those flawless Hollywood smiles, and thanked me for such a lovely memorial service, and for having everyone back up to the house. Then she picked up the ugly clock and made her departure as I looked around at all these people who knew everything I wanted to find out about Paige—and would be leaving any minute now for their far corners of the world again.

I needed Kip. I'd been embroiled with one thing or another since I'd seen him helping to get cars parked, and had no idea where he'd gone. But Jen was right where she'd been the whole time, so I went to ask her.

"Hi!" she said. The lines of people wanting food had all but vanished now, and she seemed more relaxed than she'd been all day. "Who was that movie star I saw you talking to?"

"An old friend of Paige's," I said, not unaware of the irony there.

Jen smirked at me. "Well, she sure stands out from all these other aunties hobbling around."

"*Jen!*" I cast a glance around to see who might have overheard that. But there was no one very close just then. "Aunties," I said, amused, actually. "That does fit, doesn't it."

Jen grinned. "It's like an auntie convention. I can hardly wait for the awards ceremony."

"Awards for what?"

"Oh, you know: whitest hair; most elegant bifocals, longest cane…"

"Oh, stop that!" I said, glancing around again. "Seriously. Someone's going to hear us, and then I'll never see a single one of them again."

"Where would you see them *again?*" she asked. "*Your* funeral?"

"They knew Paige. Like I never will now."

"Oh. I'm sorry, hon. That was…"

"Don't worry," I told her. "I've said so much worse today, over and over again. I can't seem to open my mouth without finding both feet already shoved inside it."

"Really!" Jen said. "What happened?"

"Ugh…we can talk about that later, when there aren't so many people still waiting for me to offend them or make a fool of myself. And by the way, that movie star was Florence Golding from San Francisco."

"Oh! The one Elle mentioned? Did you ask her about George?"

"Yes… And that's one of the faux pas we can talk about later. But she did ask me to tell you you're brilliant, and that I should fire everybody else at our inn before getting rid of you."

Jen laughed. "Well, that's so nice to hear!"

"Do you know where Kip has gone?"

"Hm… Not sure. I saw him a while ago, talking to Elle. They were walking off somewhere, out past the orchard, I think."

"Ah. I'll go see if I can find them." As I walked away, I glanced back. "And thank you, Jen! You're the big hit of the day, and a total genius—as I think I may have pointed out a while back."

She grinned and shrugged.

I'd hardly started searching for Kip again when Lisa caught up with me, and asked if I had a moment to talk before she too went home.

"Of course," I said.

She walked us away from others. "How was the rest of your talk with Florence?"

"Oh. It was…fine, I think?"

"Good. She was quite an unexpected find, with a surprising number of friends up here—some of them very influential. So, if she's really behind this inn of yours, you might want to lean into that, and stay in touch with her."

I nodded, feeling worse and worse about how that exchange had gone. "I'll give it my best," I said. "And...about my, uh..."

Lisa nodded. "Yes. I was going to ask you what that was all about." She leaned closer. "I'm sorry to say this, but you were reminding me a little of Jen, the night I came home."

I grimaced and looked down. "I have no idea where that came from. I've been...kind of stressed today, and I'd had nothing to eat since breakfast but a sip of wine until just before I joined you two. Then, I guess I crammed a little too much food in too fast, so...maybe it was just some kind of blood-sugar spasm or something?"

Lisa shrugged. "Well, we all have our off moments—as I'd know better than most. I just wanted to make sure there wasn't some bigger problem. That's a woman you don't want to lose track of, if you can help it. She could do a lot for your inn, before and after it opens." She patted me on the shoulder. "You've done a magnificent job with all of this. The memorial service was...kind of life-changing, for me at least. That woman, Elle, is someone I'd give a lot to know better. And this gathering is just perfect. Florence was right. I had no idea what a talent Jen is. You're batting a thousand, Cam; it's a thrill to watch."

"Thanks. We still need to have you up here for dinner. And not like this." I nodded at the gathering, and noticed Kip and Elle walking back into view, their heads still together.

Lisa saw me spot them. "I look forward to it—I'll call soon."

After she walked off, I looked back to see Kip shake Elle's hand. Then he headed off toward the food table, of course. But Elle turned to look right at me from clear across the field with a giant smile on her face, and beckoned me to come over.

When I reached her, she took both my hands in hers. "I have just had the most delightful time getting to know your beautiful young man. He is so much more than charming, Camille, and I am so happy for you both!"

"Thank you," I said, wondering why more people in this crowd could not have been as easy to talk with as Elle always was. "I feel so lucky that he and I...didn't miss each other."

Elle nodded, her smile softening. "I am happy for that too." Then she stretched up on her toes, and leaned up to whisper in my ear. "But if you tell no one else your secret, cherie, you must tell him someday. True love cannot abide a wall." She pulled away and settled back onto her feet. "And now, unless you need me for something more, I think I will turn in early. Tomorrow is another long day of travel."

"Oh, yes," I said. "But you may want lock your door. There's no telling who here might be wandering around the house before this ends."

"I shall follow your advice," she said cheerfully, and blew me a kiss as she turned and walked off toward the house.

☙

JEN, KIP, AND I SPENT a quiet evening at the house. Elle had indeed gone to sleep upstairs well before the last of our guests had said goodbye; and after helping us take care of the major cleanup tasks, Dylan had wished us good night and gone as well. Nobody was hungry after Jen's feast, of course. So Kip built a small fire in the front parlor for some cozy atmosphere, even though it wasn't a bit cold in June, and Jen brought out a bottle of wine. We all sat together, sipping at it slowly and reflecting on the highlights of an amazing day.

Jen talked mostly about her adventures in the kitchen, and Dylan's brilliant help, and how happy she was about everyone's responses to her fabulous buffet. Kip reminded us that he'd predicted her success, and, with an almost straight face, congratulated us again on going all in on *his* bed-and-breakfast idea.

I told them about my conversation with poor Emile Fisher, and about the two strange ladies I'd met upstairs. But I couldn't bring myself to revisit the embarrassing performance with Florence Golding—except to tell Jen that, no, I'd learned nothing more about the George Harper story from her either. I'd met a few more interesting people before the party ended; but if anyone there but Elle had been "gifted," I hadn't learned who they were.

Kip was more talkative than any of us that night. He'd spent most of his day with Elle, and she had clearly made a huge impression on him. He just couldn't get over her eulogy for Paige, and kept telling Jen how sorry he was that she hadn't gotten to hear it—as if, what? That was going to make her feel better about slaving all day in the kitchen? "It was the most amazing thing I've ever heard," he said *again*, then shook his head, and looked back at me. "Honestly, honey, I mostly just thought of Paige as a wackadoodle busybody, and never really understood your friendship with her—until Elle just...yanked my eyes open. It never even crossed my mind she might be doing such magic tricks right in front of us all that time." He looked down and sighed. "I get it now, though. Better late than never, I guess."

And, okay, that got my attention. I could remember nothing in Elle's speech that had pointed even vaguely to Paige's deeper secrets. So... "What magic tricks?" I asked him.

He gave me a surprised look. "The way she was always helping people while pretending to do something else. To *be* something else." He looked away, nodding to himself. "You know, I bet she actually *wanted* people to think she was just some batty old eccentric. If they'd seen her for what she really was—what she was really doing—people would have kept their guard up around her before she got anywhere with them." He looked back at me. "I hope I wasn't the only one who saw what Elle was really saying with all that stuff about gardens and food and everything, was I?"

Kip had been surprising me a lot since he'd gone off to school, but this was a whole new level. Could all this really just have come from Elle's speech? "Is this what you and Elle talked about during your walk?" I asked, certain there had to be more to it.

"Well, yes, partly. I mean, this whole idea of...I don't know, *stealth-helping*, I guess, has real implications for my own practice of social work someday. Getting past people's defenses against...well, just being *seen*, much less helped..." He trailed off, shaking his head again. "There's a kind of real genius in how she did what she did around here—without anybody even noticing! You and she were close; you must have seen this, right?" he asked me. "Am I making it up? Elle didn't think so," he added before I could even think about how to answer—which was just as well. Because I wasn't sure I *had* seen it half so clearly as he seemed to now.

"Wow," Jen said quietly. "I wish I *had* heard that speech."

"What else did you two talk about?" I asked, more than just intrigued now.

"Oh...all kinds of things." He shrugged, as if not knowing where to begin. "That woman is the real deal. We need to keep in touch with her."

I could not disagree with that, and was glad I had her phone number. I hadn't managed to get many others—besides Diane's, anyway. And I seriously doubted we'd want to keep in touch with her and Simone anywhere near as badly.

The subject came up yet again after we'd all turned in that night. Kip and I had just gotten into bed. He rolled onto his side to face me. "I didn't want to say this in front of Jen, because…well, you know. But Elle also told me how Paige kind of did her thing for us too when I wasn't looking."

"What do you mean?" I asked, really wishing now that I'd been less focused on meeting Paige's friends, and asked him about that walk with Elle a lot earlier.

"Well… She said Paige helped convince you to, uh…give me a chance, I guess?"

I felt my eyebrows shoot up before I could stop them. "She told you *that?*"

He grinned, and nodded. "Guess I've got more to thank Paige for than I realized, huh?"

Well, yes, I thought. Paige had definitely done lots more than I'd wanted her to at the time to nudge me in the right direction—and about as gently as her goats nudged me when they got impatient.

Kip chuckled and rolled back to gaze up at the ceiling. "I wondered for a long time what made you turn around so quickly like that, just when I was sure I'd lost you. I'd have bought that woman flowers, if I'd known."

"Well, I hope you don't think that was my only reason," I said, scooting nearer to wrap my arms around him. "I deserve some credit too, don't I?"

"Oh, that's not what I meant," he said, returning my embrace. "So… how thick are these walls, anyway?" he whispered as we snuggled closer in my double bed against the wall right next to Elle's suite.

"Are you serious?" I laughed, quietly. "How can you even have the energy after this day?"

"I'm feeling a second wind." He drew me closer. "I've missed you."

"I've missed you too. A *lot.*"

Then we quietly, oh so quietly and sweetly, got reacquainted.

Later, though, well after we'd finished that most private of conversations, I lay staring up into the dark as Kip snored softly beside me, and thought about what Elle had whispered into my ear. *You must tell him someday, cherie.*

I still had no idea how, and couldn't avoid thoughts of Kevin's shocked and angry reaction the night he'd called me crazy, and I'd run away to Orcas.

Kip wasn't Kevin. Not even close. And I understood now that I'd been even more afraid of my gift and of myself than Kevin had been that night, which wasn't true anymore either. But there was no longer any chance I'd just vanish right in front of Kip someday by accident. So why risk driving him away by calling his attention to something there was no way he'd believe anyway?

Then I had another awful thought.

Could that have been what happened between Paige and George? Had she tried to tell him about her gift one day—and just scared him right out of her life? Was that why no one who ought to have known what happened wanted to talk about it?

I appreciated Elle's concern. And saw her point, I guessed. But…if sharing everything with Kip but that one small, nearly irrelevant oddity of mine was not enough, then we'd probably never make it anyhow. Paige had never told her secret to anybody here but me. And Kip was right: look at all she'd done—without anybody knowing.

CHAPTER 11

A few days after the memorial service, Lisa dropped by the house to say she'd been discussing our plans for the inn with a "knowledgeable friend," and shown them materials from our permit application. When I asked who this person was, Lisa smiled apologetically and told me she was not at liberty to say. But she assured me that their expertise was beyond question, and that they thought our applications would fly right through without any problem. "So," she said, "I think it should be safe to commit ASAP to any preparations that can be legally initiated without the actual permit—like lining up contractors to start with."

All that seemed more than a little strange, since everyone we'd talked to about this, including Lisa herself, had advised us that the San Juan County planning department was in perpetual disarray, and no permit, even for a dog house, "flew right through" in much less than six months, if not a year—and usually with *lots* of problems. When I asked her what had changed, she just said something about golden keys to back doors, and suggested I not look a gift horse in the mouth. I was tempted to ask if she was sure these back doors were legit. But I could not believe she'd flirt with any more legal troubles, so I thanked her, and left it at that.

And, just weeks later, as July nudged June aside, we were notified that our permits had, in fact, all been approved—with inexplicable speed. When Lisa came by to gloat, I didn't even ask. She was clearly never going to tell me. But I knew we had her to thank somehow.

As the July Fourth weekend approached, tourists began pouring out of ferries onto our summer island in bigger droves than ever, and Jen and I went into overdrive, contacting all those carpenters, plumbers and electricians we'd put on notice in late May, and moving ourselves, James and Master Bun into the guesthouse down at Lisa's, finally completing the circuit that had shorted out that spring. As Sam and Harry realized we were trying to hunt them down, they made themselves scarcer than ever. So I finally just moved their food bowls out to a corner of the foyer where no one should actually be hammering or sawing, and wished them luck. We'd still be coming every day to tend the outdoor animals, after all. Maybe being stuck there through the coming uproar would convince them to cooperate with me a little more.

Kip came back up from Portland on the Fourth itself to join us for the weekend. He'd been unable to get a vehicle reservation this time, so I and Tigress were waiting at the landing to pluck him from the roaring mob of other walk-ons surging off the boat. We'd gotten Lisa's permission to enjoy a nostalgic retreat in her little A-frame. That arrangement had the added benefit of leaving our guesthouse quarters clear for Jen and Dylan to continue working on the inn's website together—or whatever else they might decide to do. Jen still kept assuring me that they were nothing but friends and business associates, though that was not the vibe I'd been getting from Dylan.

Kip and I enjoyed several hours of blissful peace and quiet before dressing up to go out with them for dinner at New Leaf, and then to the opening night performance of Lisa's play!

New Leaf was mobbed, of course, but my order of crispy confit duck leg with pickled cherries was indescribably delicious. Jen was clearly taking careful mental notes on everything we'd ordered as Dylan worked to charm her. But the more wit and intelligence he poured on, the more interested Jen seemed to become in her food. I saw Kip observing all of this in watchful silence.

The play was an interesting experience—especially for me. The July Fourth crowd filled the house for this first performance—as Lisa had intended, obviously. And the performances were far better than I'd feared they might be with a cast made up mostly of local beginners; some of them were jaw-droppingly powerful. Charles, of course, was spectacular as a male Nurse Ratched.

Even though Lisa had altered nothing but the script's pronouns and a very few lines, seeing a group of *women* confined to that abusive asylum—for mostly questionable reasons—and systematically destroyed there by a sadistic man in a caretaker's uniform told a *very* different story than the movie I'd seen years before. What a brilliant idea this had been.

Still, Orcas Rep had always been known for comedies—like the one I'd written, and the two I'd managed to produce for her before the pandemic. So it was kind of jarring for me to see such a dark and emotionally painful story unfold on a stage I'd had only uplifting memories of. The audience seemed very engaged, gasping or groaning in disgust in all the right places. But this was a holiday crowd, and I wondered nervously whether anyone could really be enjoying this. My answer came with the standing ovation and thundering applause the cast received at curtain call.

Out in the lobby afterward, I pulled Lisa aside just long enough to ask, quietly, how she'd gotten such amazing performances out of so many newer actors. She'd leaned close and said, "Almost everyone has painful stories of their own to bring to things like this. I just took an interest in those too, and encouraged them to tell those stories through this one." She gave me a wry smile. "And it didn't hurt that the director herself actually knew something about the material for once."

To see her smiling like that, after such a comment… I didn't know whether to laugh along, or cry. So I gave her a hug instead.

As we drove back to town for the island's first Fourth of July community fireworks display in three years, I was eager to talk about Lisa's changes to the play. But Dylan beat me to it, super eloquently, and, as far as I could tell, very sincerely. Listening to him, I just shook my head and thought, *Wow, Jen, you have finally found a keeper of your very own!* But Kip, I noticed, still looked more uncomfortable than impressed.

The Eastsound waterfront was packed to capacity. Main Street was completely closed to cars, and swarmed with partiers. There were deputies standing near their parked vehicles at nearly every corner. As we carried our blankets and bottled waters down to the small beachside park at the west end of town, I spotted Deputy Sherman, and waved. She smiled and waved back. She and I had come so far from where we'd started in the bad old days. I told the others I'd catch up, and jogged over to talk with her.

"You're lookin' sharp," she said as I approached. "Love those shoes!" She was in standard-issue uniform boots, of course, not her fabulous Fluevogs, so I just said thanks. "Been out to dinner?" she asked, keeping a wary eye on the swirling crowd around us.

"Yes," I said, "and to Lisa's new play! Tonight was their opening."

"Yeah, I was a little worried when I heard about that." She gave me one of her lopsided grins. "We don't have the staff these days to cover this circus *and* a hostage situation down in Crow Valley tonight."

I laughed, and told her all the loonies had been up on stage this time. This won me another smile. "So, how was it?" she asked.

"Sensational! Standing ovation—and not just to be polite."

"Hey!" she yelled, waving at someone beyond me. "Not here! Put those away, or I'll write you a ticket!"

I turned around to see a teenage boy drop his sparkler on the asphalt and start trying to stamp it out. "I'd better let you get back to this," I said. "Next time you see Sheriff Clarke, tell him I said hello."

"I'm sure he'll be relieved to hear that's all you had to say." She gave me only the hint of a grin this time, and a clipped wave goodbye.

I hurried back down Main Street and eventually spotted the others sitting on our blanket amidst a carpet of expectant partiers already filling the lawn. As I wove my way through the crowd, surrounded by a million of those glowy little necklaces and bracelets and wands that kids always get from somewhere before things like this, everything from John Philip Sousa to Pink Floyd blared from speakers at the park's edges. I reached Kip, Dylan and Jen as the guys traded horror stories about coping with Seattle traffic these days, while Jen looked on in almost convincing interest from behind them.

I sat down beside her and murmured, "How's it going?"

"I'm excited to see fireworks again."

"Me too! This feels like an old-school holiday. So exotic and exciting! And just think: more than half of these people are staying at expensive inns!"

"That *is* festive!" Jen agreed. "Or it should be next year, anyway."

The music suddenly stopped mid-song. Then, without fanfare or warning, a cluster of rockets soared up off the barge moored out past Indian Island, and burst into a giant bouquet of red chrysanthemums high above the water. Everyone cheered, and we were off to the races!

It was after sunset, but the sky was still far from dark as volley after volley of sparkly confections shimmered and crackled over the sound in front of a yellow crescent moon. But just ten minutes later the display suddenly tapered off and dribbled to a halt. This didn't worry us at first. We figured it was just the pause that always came before a grand finale of explosions and light that often went on longer than the prologue had.

But the pause got longer... And longer.

We were all starting to wonder if that could really be it, when two more rocket trails shot up from the barge. "Here we go!" Jen said, sounding relieved.

But they each burst into just a single little ball of red light, which drifted slowly back down toward the water.

"Those look like distress flares," Dylan said, apprehensively.

"Something's gone wrong out there," Kip agreed.

A minute later another rocket trail shot up from the barge, this time producing nothing but a tiny spray of green and golden sparks—the kind of cheap bottle rocket you could buy at any roadside fireworks stand in Skagit County, where such things were still legal in an age of yearly wildfires.

"Looks like they're stalling for time," said Dylan. He looked back at Jen and me. "Unless this is how it usually goes out here?"

"No," said Jen. "It was always a pretty good show before."

"If I was still a deputy, I'd be able to find out what's going on," said Kip just as a young man popped up out of some low evergreens right at the water's edge, and started making semaphore-like gestures at the distant barge. These had no effect that I could see, if they were even being seen out there.

Then the Pink Floyd tune from before started up briefly, but was cut abruptly off again as a second young man crawled up out of that same low clump of evergreens with an electric guitar in one hand and a portable amp in the other. He set the amp down on the grass in front of everyone, and started playing a decent, if extremely loud version of Jimi Hendrix's Star-Spangled Banner. But when he was done, he just unplugged his guitar from the amp, and walked away without a word, or even a bow.

"Was that...part of the show?" Jen asked. "Or just... Who was that even?"

"That cannot be it," I said. "Can it?"

Soon, though, everyone was up and milling around, folding up their blankets, grabbing their coolers, and meandering back toward the street, laughing or scratching their heads.

"These fireworks shows are community funded," Jen said, as we got up and followed suit. "After three years of pandemic, maybe they just couldn't drum up the same kind of support?"

"So, what?" I laughed. "The team they hired just gave us half a show and stopped?"

"The world still isn't working as well as it used to," Kip said.

As Kip and I reached the street, I looked back, and realized that Jen and Dylan had stopped a ways behind us. They were talking about something, and not too happily, it seemed.

Kip had turned around now too, and stood watching them beside me. "Three, two, one…" he said under his breath.

"What does that mean? Is something going on here I don't know about?"

He shook his head. "All that's going on is a nice young man trying harder and harder to impress Jen all evening, without seeing she's just felt more and more left behind."

As he said this, Jen gave Dylan a quick, clearly uncomfortable little hug, and turned away to walk toward us as Dylan watched her go in equally clear confusion. As she drew closer, Jen looked straight at me with an expression of naked panic. *What on earth?*

"What just happened?" I asked her.

"He asked me out. On a date."

"What did you say?"

Dylan finally started walking toward us too.

She sighed, seeming to pull herself together. "With everything we've got to do now that the inn is really starting up, I just don't have the extra bandwidth for a relationship. I can't give him what he deserves right now, so I just asked if we could wait a while."

"Oh," I said. Dylan was hardly ten feet away now; what else could I say?

Inside, though, I was groaning. Here she was, pushing away what she most wanted again. It seemed almost like a replay of me and Kip before we'd finally got it right. Were Jen and I that much alike? Was that why we got along so well?

I gave Dylan a sympathetic smile, and we all continued steering through the raucous crowd on our way to where I'd parked Tigress.

❦

WHILE JULY PASSED IN SUNLIT splendor, Lisa helped us refine our business plan and shore up dozens of other financial, legal and bureaucratic preparations as the house remodel started. I was continuously amazed at how much our building crew managed to get done in a day. They worked like demons—in part, I think, because they hadn't believed our permits would come through before the end of summer, and had committed to other projects now being squeezed into the same slot of time.

Our first priority was getting bathrooms for every guest room. Paige's little office space was converted into one for the Blue Heron Suite, as we renamed her bedroom. The original bathroom by the stairwell no longer opened onto the upstairs landing, but into the former "yellow room," now named the Dragonfly. We had its cat-hole covered over too, of course, and gave it a fine new mattress that *didn't* eat people. On the landing's other side, the room next to Jen's became two bathrooms. One adjoined the Orca Room, our smallest guest room, and the other, for Jen and me to share, opened into both Jen's room and the landing.

Almost right away, we started hearing from the work crew about materials or small tools suddenly missing or popping up where no one could have left them, and even about strange noises in the walls or ceiling. Then, during the double bathroom conversion, they found an attic space apparently sealed up during the building's earlier renovation, which was full of squirrel nests. Scattered in and around those, they found not only some of their own missing items, but old photographs, a paint color wheel of Jen's, and bits of Paige's older jewelry I just thought I'd lost somewhere. "Not the kind of stuff squirrels usually go for," the contractor told me, sounding puzzled. "But we've patched up the places they were getting in and out through, and put an entry hatch in the shared bath ceiling so you can keep an eye on things up there." Another mystery solved, I thought, wondering what squirrels had wanted in the first place with screwdrivers, color wheels, and old photographs of Paige.

As August approached, it was the kitchen's turn for a facelift. New permitting limitations forbade us to keep any of our personal food in the same refrigerator or storage spaces as food for our paying guests, or to share the meals we made for them, or even to sit down and eat our own food with them during any meal they were paying for—which bummed Jen out. She loved socializing with her customers, as I'd discovered the first time she'd waited on Colin and me at the Barnacle. So, along with all the other upgrades our commercial inn kitchen required, we built a small cookhouse out on the wraparound porch, with its own small stove, sink and fridge. All these improvements required giant upgrades to the house's electrical and plumbing systems too, of course. Happily, the huge old furnace in the cold cellar still passed inspection—though we didn't mention its tendency to come on for no good reason every now and then—which meant we could put off replacing that. For a while, anyway.

I watched the bills pile up with varying degrees of anxiety, even though I had ample funds to pay them. I was never going to get used to spending such amounts of money, and couldn't help wondering what might happen to my newfound financial independence if this whole venture *didn't* pan out.

I said nothing to Jen about such worries, though. She was just more excited every day. And that's exactly how I wanted things to stay.

The summer tourist season would be over well before all this remodeling, not to mention the painting and landscaping after it, was finally done. But we planned to try a "soft opening" in the fall, inviting personal acquaintances and members of our nascent mailing list to come be test-guests during the winter. We didn't expect many takers at that time of year, but even a few would help us find and work out our bugs before being hammered—hopefully—when we opened officially next spring.

Finally, one day in early September, all that work on the house and its grounds was done! It felt surreal to be moving out of Lisa's guesthouse and back up to our *real* home. "All these showers!" Jen exclaimed gleefully as we went from new bathroom to new bathroom upstairs.

We hardly saw Sam and Harry at first, but within a couple days, they started showing up again to stare at me sullenly as I filled their bowls or cleaned out their barely-used litter box. The remodel had clearly been hard for them; despite myself, I felt a little guilty.

I invited my parents out that very week for their long-postponed visit. They were, of course, one hundred percent charmed with the place, and everything we'd done with it. I even managed to finagle a dinner alone with Dad while Jen and my mom went out to get better acquainted over dinner in town. Dad and I didn't talk nearly as often by phone as Mom and I did, and it was really nice to catch up on a lot of things with him. Guess what I cooked?

Two days after they left, the Berry Farm website Jen and Dylan had been tinkering with all summer finally went privately live—meaning that the three of us could see and use it now, though no one else would be able find it yet. Happily, Dylan had gone right on helping with our website after Jen had turned him down. Their friendship seemed cordial and entirely professional, as if no other agenda had ever crossed their minds.

I have to say, the site he'd designed for us was pretty chic. But there were still a couple of entertaining glitches to work out. My favorite involved a lovely photo of the inn on our home page with a big button in the center that said, "See what awaits you at the Berry Farm!" Pressing it caused the whole website to crash and go dark—which made me hoot with laughter the first time it happened, as Dylan blushed, and Jen rolled her eyes. Within an hour, he'd found some glitch in the code and had the button working right, launching a gorgeous slide show of our rooms, public spaces, and Jen's beautiful food, just like it was supposed to.

Our website went really live the next day; now anyone could find proof that we were actually supposed to exist—if they knew where to look, which we were *not* doing anything to advertise yet. But we did send off an email to our mailing list about the inn's soft opening as of October first.

None of us really expected much if any response, but the very next day Jen and I were surprised by an email from Diane Franklin asking to book the Blue Heron Suite for herself and Simone starting October second—so we'd have "a day to breathe," she said. They wanted to stay for at least a week, but she asked if it would be possible for them to leave their departure date open. I couldn't quite wrap my head around the fact that after so much planning, dreaming and preparation, this was really going to happen—*now*.

"Aren't those the two weird aunties you found upstairs after Paige's memorial service?" Jen asked.

I nodded, marveling at her memory. I'd given her Diane's card the night of our party—over three months ago. But with so few people on our list yet, maybe they were *all* memorable for Jen.

"Well," she mused, "I guess we say yes to the open departure date? It's not like we have other guests banging down our door yet. And they do want our most expensive room for at least a week!" She pumped her fists in the air. "Woohoo! First booking! Look at us go!"

CHAPTER 12

My last encounter with Simone and Diane had been on a perfect summer day in June. Now my windshield wipers were batting wind-driven rain off the windshield as I went to pick them up at the Orcas ferry landing. (And no, innkeepers don't usually trot off to pick up their guests at the ferry, but since these aunties were our first-ever paying guests, we decided to make an exception.) (Well, two exceptions: we'd also decided to serve them dinners, and eat with them, sidestepping the regulations against doing so by not charging them for those meals. No laws against having friends over for dinner!) It had been a very pleasant if cool autumn until our first big rainstorm had blown in just yesterday; as I parked as close to the ramp as it was possible to get, I hoped the ladies weren't regretting their reservation now.

Their ferry was running right on time, at least, which was some small compensation. And, as it arrived—in the late afternoon on a nasty day like this one, well after tourist season—I saw almost no one aboard it. As the crew finished tying up the ship at dock, there were less than half a dozen walk-on passengers huddled at the front of the main car deck, waiting to disembark. It wasn't hard to tell which of them were Diane and Simone. Even under their heavy rain parkas, Simone's small, hunched figure and dark, sturdy cane were impossible to mistake. As their fellow walk-ons hurried up the ramp, crouched against the rain, the two old aunties trailed slowly behind them, Diane supporting Simone by an elbow as she caned her way up the rain-slicked cement walkway.

I went down to intercept them, and took Simone's small suitcase. But by the time we got all the way back up to the road, cars were already driving off the boat, and we had to wait another couple minutes in the rain before the ferry employee directing traffic stopped them, and waved us across the street toward my car. The ladies seemed cheerful, though, as I unlocked Tigress with my fob and helped get their luggage up into her back cargo space.

"Would you mind if we just kept our parkas on?" Diane asked.

"Not at all," I said. "Tigress can handle a little shower now and then."

"Tigress?"

"Oh." I smiled. "That's the car's name." I'd never needed to explain that to a stranger before, and it seemed a little silly now. That's when I noticed that, although Diane was smiling too, she wasn't really looking at me. I hoped I hadn't embarrassed her already.

As Diane helped Simone up into back seat, I got in and started the engine to get the heater running for them. Then I realized how dusty the dashboard had gotten driving up and down the Berry Farm's long gravel drive all summer, and grabbed a tissue from my purse to clean it off a little as Diane closed Simone's door, and came in to sit on the front passenger seat. As I signaled to pull out, Diane said, "Your new car is so lovely. Did you get it from someone here on the island?"

I turned to look at her in surprise, but someone tapped their horn behind me, waiting for my space. So I pulled out, turned around, and got underway. "Someone here gave it to me, actually. Last spring. How do you…"

"Oh, sorry." She looked flustered. "I'm always doing that, I'm afraid; jumping into conversations no one's actually been having yet but me."

"Um…sorry. I'm not sure what you mean."

She gave me a quick, apologetic smile, with everything but her averted eyes, and asked, "Are you familiar by any chance with the word 'neurodivergent'?"

"I think I've heard it?"

She bobbed her head. "Or perhaps the phrase 'on the spectrum'?"

"You mean, like autism?"

"Well, that's one kind of neurodivergence, yes. I'm a high-functioning neurodivergent person with a high sensitivity to observational data from which I tend to construct probable conclusions very quickly, and sometimes share them…prematurely." Her eyes very briefly darted almost but not quite in my direction. "It's probably best you know that, since we will be with you for a week, if not longer."

"I appreciate that. Is there anything we should know or do to make your stay more comfortable?"

"Not really, except try not to worry about it." Everything but her eyes turned toward me again. "People tend to assign all kinds of meaning to my difficulty with eye contact, but there isn't any, really. It's just uncomfortable for me. With anyone, not just you."

"I'm sorry," I said. "But thank you for letting me know."

"It seemed advisable. Thank you for understanding."

"This is really intriguing. Is it something you're comfortable talking about?"

"Oh yes," she said. "If you are."

"I'd love to, actually. So, can I ask how you knew I'd recently been given this car?"

"I didn't know it had been *given* to you. But you are rather precious about it: dusting off the dashboard, giving it a name. People rarely do things like that with such enthusiasm after the novelty of a new acquisition has worn off. As it happens, I'm a Porsche fan myself, and this model is over five years old. But I noticed your May registration stickers, and saw that your plates were much too new to be original to the car, so—"

"Wait," I cut in. "How can you know my plates are new?"

"Your plate number begins with a C," she said, as if that were obvious.

"What does that tell you?"

"From what I've seen on our way here from the airport, license plates in Washington are released in alphabetical and numerical order. I've seen a great many later model cars today with plates beginning in A or B. So, clearly, a C plate must not be original to a five-year-old car."

"That's amazing!" I said. "But I still can't see how you knew I got it from someone here."

"Again, I didn't know—which is why I asked. But your mileage is extremely low after five years, which suggests it hasn't been driven nearly as much as it should have been on the mainland. And I've certainly noticed how difficult travel is to and from these islands. So it seemed sensible to assume you probably hadn't bought the car somewhere else."

I shook my head in disbelief. "You got all of that in the time it took to get us in the car?" Then I remembered what was written on her business card. "That's right, you're a data analyst, aren't you."

"That is correct," she said ruefully. "Rather compulsively, I'm afraid."

"Well, you must be the best one in the world."

"Not officially; but in the top few dozen, I'm fairly sure."

"Isn't all this lovely…" Simone said dreamily behind us, gazing out her window at the gray, stormy landscape going by. "Such pretty autumn colors."

"I'm so sorry you weren't here to see it in the sunshine just two days ago," I said.

"Oh no," she said quietly. "I've always loved the rain. And isn't it remarkable how so many plants put on their brightest colors just as they are dying every year?"

"Uh…yes, now that you mention it." What an interesting pair of guests we'd started with. "And what did you do?" I asked Simone. "Or are you still working too?" Because, with these two, who could tell?

"Simone?" Diane asked, when she didn't answer.

"I'm sorry, what?" Simone asked. I looked into the rearview mirror, and saw the same startled expression I remembered from our previous meeting in June.

"Ms. Tate asked what you used to do for work," said Diane.

"Oh… Well, many different things, I guess." She paused again, still looking out the window. "I was working with the police when I met you, wasn't I, Diane?"

"That's right," said Diane. "And wasn't that a happy bit of luck?"

"Yes indeed," Simone said sleepily. "Very happy. All this time."

I was beginning to have an idea about this pair. Was Diane the caretaker of an older friend with dementia? It would explain a lot of things—about last June's encounter, as well as this one. I couldn't believe they'd come to stay here without even mentioning that to us, and I wasn't about to ask Diane right here in front of Simone; but I'd have to do it when we got to the inn and I could pull her aside.

"Simone," Diane said, pleasantly, "can you rejoin us, please?"

"I'm sorry, what?" asked Simone.

"Come back, dear. It would be nice to have your company while we're all in the car."

Okay… Just when I'd been sure things couldn't get much stranger…

"In the… Oh! I'm so sorry," Simone said to Diane. I saw her look at me in the mirror. "My apologies, Ms. Tate. Certain things tend to lull me into…well, something that's not quite sleep. Moving cars are one of them. It's a problem I've had all my life, and quite embarrassing sometimes. I hope I haven't alarmed you."

"No, of course not," I said, amazed at this transition. She sure sounded present and alert now. How weird was *this?* "And, please, just call me Cam."

"Thank you, Cam," said Simone. "Let's just be Simone and Diane then too. Much cozier that way, isn't it?"

"Great," I said. "I'm so glad you'll be here for the week. You both seem like such fascinating people. I'd love to get to know you better."

"That sounds very nice," Diane said.

"Yes. Lovely!" chirped Simone.

"My boyfriend is away at college to get a degree in social work right now," I told them, "but he used to be a sheriff's deputy here on Orcas. What kind of work were you two doing with law enforcement when you met?"

In the mirror, I saw Simone glance uncertainly at Diane, who, after a short pause, said, "We were assisting in an investigation, actually, shortly after I'd come to L.A. But there's not much that we're allowed to say about it—even after all this time." She half-turned to me, the way she did, and asked, "Do you know what a nondisclosure agreement is?"

"Oh, yes, I had to sign one with my previous employer. The one who gave me this car, actually." And I'd signed another one before helping with an investigation that I couldn't talk to them about either. Was life funny, or what?

"Well then, you understand," said Diane. "Simone and I have worked together on all sorts of things since then. But most of them involved NDAs as well. So, I'm afraid our work will be a pretty boring topic for conversation."

"Got it," I said. "But you're both data analysts then?"

Simone said nothing, and I was just about to apologize for asking more questions right after they'd told me not to when Diane said, "No, actually. Simone has a different kind of gift for uncovering information that even I am unable to discern."

"Yes," Simone, said, sounding oddly relieved. "I just gather data for Diane to analyze."

But I'd kind of stopped listening at the word *gift*, as it occurred to me that these strange aunties might be even stranger than I'd thought. How had it taken me so long to see something this obvious? "You know, I didn't think to ask last time, but how did you two meet Paige?"

"Simone?" Diane asked.

"Yes, well, I'm the one who introduced her to Diane. I met Paige when I was just a girl. She was passing through Los Angeles during that long trip Elle talked about at the memorial service, and Paige came to some party my mother threw. I can't even recall the occasion now. Paige and I just took an instant liking to each other."

"How old were you?" I asked.

"Oh...maybe fourteen, fifteen?"

So...if Paige had been twenty-ish, that made Simone five or six years *younger?* Yet Paige had never looked as old as Simone did. Well, people were different. And all those years of living in L.A. might not have been as healthy as life in these islands was for Paige.

"We've just been in touch, off and on, ever since then," Simone added.

Yes. That sure sounded like "network." And, suddenly, their visit meant even more to me.

⁂

JEN GREETED OUR INAUGURAL GUESTS with warmth, enthusiasm, and more apologies for the weather, before ushering us inside. I helped Diane and Simone carry their luggage upstairs to the Blue Heron Suite, thanked them for their compliments on how beautifully we'd transformed it, and let them know I'd be sleeping right next door if they required assistance during the night.

Meanwhile, Jen laid out *hors d'oeuvres* and four glasses of her latest custom cocktail in the second parlor, and when we came back downstairs to join her, Diane's quirks went on display again as she regaled us with a quick etymology of the phrase *hors d'oeuvres*—which apparently just meant "appetizers" in French. Then she asked, "Who here likes threes and fives so much?" and started pointing out all the places in our carefully decorated parlor where everything from paintings and photos, to candles, *objets d'art*, clusters of books, and even groups of furniture were arranged in clusters of three or five. I'd been responsible for nearly all of that, unwittingly, and could not un-see it now—not there in the parlor, or throughout the house.

In addition to her issue with direct eye contact, it turned out that Diane was also averse to quite a few flavors and food textures. I watched

Jen struggling not to roll her eyes as Diane sat in front of her delectable assembly of fine soft cheeses (including her homemade chevre), honeycomb, and fresh figs, eating only grapes and an occasional cracker—except for the cocktail, which she either enjoyed, or just convincingly pretended to. So there *were* things we'd need to watch out for after all. Happily, birdlike Simone made up for most of that by eating almost everything in sight. Watching her down one treat after another, I wanted to make sure she knew this wasn't dinner, but could see no polite way to do it.

Far and away the biggest shock that evening, however, was when Sam and Harry strolled into the room and walked up to Simone, purring and twining themselves around her ankles. Jen and I couldn't help gaping openly as Simone cooed down at them, then patted her lap, and chuckled in quiet delight as they *jumped up to sit in it and knead her skirt!* I felt sure I'd have noticed in the car if she had bathed in tuna. Catnip then? I couldn't understand it. Happily, James arrived just minutes later, and not wishing to be one-upped, leapt into my own, clearly more exclusive lap. *He* at least understood where the food in his bowl came from—even if the troublemakers over there didn't seem to care. Jen and I just kept looking over at each other until she finally shook her head, and excused herself to go start work on dinner.

Given the weather, I offered to drive the ladies wherever they wanted to go tomorrow, and asked what they might want to see or do around the island. But they insisted they were homebodies who just preferred to putter around the house, read books, sit by the fire and listen to the rain. *Really?* I thought. *You flew here from L.A. to sit in our house listening to the rain?* I mean, yes, I knew that California had been suffering historic drought for years now, but could mere rain really be that exciting to them? No, they were surely just being polite.

I finally excused myself as well to "help Jen" in the kitchen. Not that she wanted any help from me, of course. But I hadn't had a chance to debrief her about our conversation in the car on our way here. Jen couldn't believe they'd come up here to sit around the house for a week either. But once I'd filled her in on Diane's neurodivergence, and Simone's weird trance disorder, whatever that was, she grew more relaxed, if no less mystified.

Fortunately, Diane seemed to love everything about Jen's miso broth salmon bowls, and even the hot sake wine with it. Thin, frail Simone did herself proud too—*again*—as our once-antisocial cats circled her dining room chair, purring and rubbing their cheeks against its legs and hers from time to time. Where was all that food going? And, for that matter, where had our two untrusting house cats gone, and who had replaced them with these cuddly imposters? If all this wasn't proof of extra-natural powers, I couldn't think what was.

Diane also loved the fortune cookies Jen served after dinner, though she read her own fortune silently, then tucked it away in some hidden pocket. Mine read *You will soon go on an adventure*, which was so vague as to be completely useless. When was I not having some adventure?

"Ha!" Jen cried, when she cracked her own cookie open. *"You enjoy the company of many; you have never met a stranger.* It's true!"

"Simone?" I asked, wondering if she'd even respond.

But she opened her cookie as well, and smiled down at its message. *"A journey over water will bring important tidings.* Just so, I think." She gave Jen a mischievous grin. "Are these cookies manufactured here on the island?"

After dinner, we sat, somewhat tipsy, around the front parlor's blazing fireplace until Simone looked up suddenly, then rose and left the room without a word to any of us. I followed her into the foyer and watched her climb the stairs into the upper landing as if someone up there had summoned her. When I went back to the parlor, Diane had risen too, and was thanking Jen for such a lovely meal, but saying she really ought to go turn in as well. So, when Jen and I had finished cleaning up the kitchen, that's what we did too.

Between entertaining such interesting inn guests, Jen's filling dinner, and ample cups of hot sake, I had barely enough consciousness left to lie down and turn off my reading lamp. Minutes later, as I teetered at the edge of sleep, James leapt up to join me on the bed, rousing me just long enough to hear what seemed to be extremely quiet footsteps passing outside my door. I thought vaguely that with the aunties having turned in so long ago, it must be Jen walking toward their room now, and wondered why she would be doing such a thing. But I fell asleep before I could think any further about it.

I woke much later to muffled voices in the darkness, and peered at my bedside clock. Who was up, and why, at nearly one a.m., I wondered, then recalled the two old ladies lodging in the next room. Was there a problem? Should I go see?

I sat up, rubbing my eyes, then rose and pulled on a robe before stepping quietly to my doorway. I rested my hand on the doorknob as I listened. James had woken briefly as I'd left the bed, but seemed to be asleep again already. *Way to be a guard cat*, I thought.

Finally, I carefully opened the door, peeked out into the inky landing, and saw a line of pale light beneath the Blue Heron Suite's closed door. They were clearly awake in there, with a flashlight on, or something, which did not seem like good news at one in the morning. I stepped out into the landing hoping to glean some better idea of what the problem was, and tiptoed a few more steps in their direction just before their door rattled, then began to open.

This startled me enough to set my gift in motion, and in my half-awake condition, I must have half-decided just to let it happen. So there I was, chameleoned, unable to do anything but stand and watch. Moving in this state was no longer a problem for me. But my bedroom door was nearly closed behind me, and I had no idea whether I could convince their minds not to see that open if I tried to go back through it. I did back slowly toward the wall, at least. If they came this way, I didn't want them walking into me.

"Are you sure it's really gone?" Diane whispered, holding her phone—its flashlight on, but mostly covered by her hand.

"If it weren't, I would know," Simone whispered back.

Had they lost something?

"So, where now then, do you think?" Diane asked.

Simone gazed around for just a minute, and then, to my alarm, looked straight at me. As if she could see me. Now I really was frozen with fear. No one had ever done that to me before when I was invisible. After a second, though, she tilted her head, then turned back to Diane. "I'm not sure. I thought maybe there was something, but…if so, it's something else. This house is old and large enough to have more than one, I guess."

What on earth was this about? I had no idea what either of their gifts really were, exactly, though there seemed no doubt that they were gifted. But if Simone's ability had some power to get past mine…this could get very awkward in a hurry.

Just then, a long, plaintive meow came from the stairwell behind me. I turned to see Harry and Sam standing at the top of it, switching their tails back and forth as they gazed at Simone. She walked past me on her way to them, followed closely by Diane.

"Hello my little beauties," Simone whispered, bending stiffly down to run her hand along their backs and tails. "What brings *you* here now? Is there something I should know?"

Harry meowed quietly again; Simone straightened slowly as Diane looked back and forth between her and the cats. Sam twined himself around her ankles once more as Harry turned around and descended several steps before looking back up at Simone. When Sam turned to follow Harry down the stairs again, Simone whispered, "All right, dears. I'll come see then." She and Diane started after the cats. But just a few stairs down, she added, "This had better not just be a rat or something, loves. This old body won't soon forgive the two of you for dragging it down there just to have me force it to come up again."

I was just fine with talking to cats. I did it all the time with James. But those cats had surely *not* just really talked to her. I wasn't going there. Not yet, at least.

There was no way I'd just be going back into my room to sleep now either. I stepped silently away from the wall and headed for the stairs as well.

I followed their whispers down and through the foyer into the front parlor, then stopped well back from the open pocket doors. They'd all halted in the second parlor, standing in the glow of Diane's now less shuttered phone beside a set of low bookshelves underneath the room's north windows. Simone turned slowly around, seeming to search the shadows for something, then stopped abruptly and stared back down at the shelves.

"It's here," she said in the sing-song voice I remembered from our car ride. "It's…sitting. Right here. And…crying."

I could make no sense of this. What could be sitting on a bookshelf, crying?

"So much grief," Simone moaned. "Lost… Lost, and so…terribly alone. Where…"

"Is it her?" Diane asked anxiously. "Can you tell?"

Simone didn't respond at first. But then she made a helpless gesture, and said, "I'm just so…confused…and so alone now. The house is…full of chaos." It sounded as if Simone might be crying. "What is happening to my home? Why is it being torn apart? Where is—" She fell abruptly silent, then turned to look directly at me, just as she had upstairs.

A thrill of fear prickled down my arms as I realized the cats were staring at me too. Had my gift failed for some reason? Should I run, or speak to them?

"It's gone," Simone said to Diane, much less dreamily. "Something's scared it off, I think." She straightened, and took a few steps back in my direction, followed by the cats, then peered around the dark front parlor as if still looking for me. "There's something here again," she whispered, glancing briefly back as Diane came to her, holding her phone up to better light the room. "Something else… Something strange. This house is a very busy place."

Unable to stand it any longer, I turned and snuck from the room as quietly and quickly as possible, scurried up the stairs, and reached for visibility again as soon as I got to the darkened upper landing. After enduring the moment of fiery prickling across my body that still accompanied the transition, I turned around and started right back down the stairs, yawning loudly and rubbing at my eyes. Diane, Simone and the cats were all standing in the foyer now, watching me descend. I stopped, trying my best to look startled, and said, "My goodness! Everybody's up! What's going on?"

For a moment, they just went on staring. Even the cats.

"I'm so sorry if we've disturbed you," Diane said. "Have we woken Jen as well?"

"I don't think so." I started down again. "She's a much sounder sleeper than I am. Is everyone okay?"

"Yes," Diane said. "Simone sleepwalks sometimes, and I always come along to watch out for her, but I try to let her wake up on her own."

"It's less traumatic that way," Simone said, nodding in agreement. "I'm so sorry that we woke you, dear."

"Yes, but since we have," Diane added, "would it be terrible to ask if you could make Simone a cup of hot chocolate or steamed milk to help her back to sleep? She lies awake for such a long while sometimes after these unfortunate outings."

"Sure…" I said, trying to think of what we even had. "Would a powdered mix be okay?"

"Oh yes, of course," Simone said. "Whatever's easiest. It's very kind of you."

I smiled, and waved her concern away as I turned and started for the kitchen door.

"Might we keep you company in there?" Diane asked.

I looked back to see her smiling awkwardly, eyes averted, as usual. "Yes, of course."

A minute later, as I searched out powdered cocoa mix in our new, expanded pantry, the two aunties settled into chairs at the little kitchen table while Sam and Harry prowled over to inspect their food bowls.

"So, you and Paige were clearly very close," said Diane.

"Well, yes," I answered, thinking that it shouldn't take a data analyst to see that.

"Then, maybe you can help clear up some things that always puzzled me about her."

If it puzzled someone with her abilities, I didn't see what help I was likely to be. But I said, "Sure," as I emerged with a bag of little marshmallows and *three* packets of hot chocolate mix, because was I really going to make Simone's cup and let everybody else just watch her drink it? I didn't think so.

"Oh," Diane said, seeing what I was holding, "might I have tea instead? I'm sorry to be such a bother."

"Not at all!" I said, as cheerfully as I could manage. Of course it's fine to have a tea party at one in the morning! This is just what I wanted to be doing with my night! "What kind of tea?"

"Do you have chamomile? Or mint?"

I had both, so I grabbed the box of mint, not wanting to be still working this out when the sun rose. "You had a question about Paige?" I prompted Diane.

"Yes," Diane said. "To begin with, she grew the biggest vegetables I've ever seen."

"Oh yes," I said, going to the fridge for milk. Whatever the instructions on those little packets say, no real human being likes powdered cocoa made with water. I eyeballed two cups' worth and poured it into a small saucepan, then set it to simmer on our fabulous new ginormous propane stove. "As Elle mentioned at the memorial, her knack for gardening was legendary," I added, wondering what all of this could be about.

"Oh, it was indeed," Diane agreed. "And, as you know, I'm a person who likes to make sense of what I'm seeing. But every time I asked her how she made things grow that way, she just refused to tell me. Did she say anything to you, by chance?"

I looked over at her as I went to get the kettle, wondering why on earth Paige would have refused to answer such a question for Diane. Had she just not liked her? And how was I supposed to answer? "Well, you know," I said, filling the kettle at the sink, "I always just took those things for granted. Everybody here did. She just understood plants, I guess?"

"Hmmm…" Diane said, looking away. "Maybe so. But that wasn't the only thing about her that seemed strange to me."

I smiled. "What *wasn't* strange about Paige Berry?"

Diane nodded. "Well, yes. But did you ever notice how she always seemed to show up just as someone needed her for something—or to know a bit more than she should?" She shook her head. "I pride myself on being able to see what's really going on. But I never could make sense of her, which has always disturbed me." Everything but her gaze turned back in my direction. "Did she ever say anything to you that might shed light on any of this?"

I turned on a second burner for the kettle, wondering what the heck Diane was playing at. It seemed almost as if she were *trying* to make me talk about… And then I got it, and almost laughed again. How ridiculous had this gotten? Me trying to figure out if they were "in the club" while they were doing the same about me?

Well, they'd tipped their hand now, and I thought she knew it. Of course she did. She saw everything at a glance. Maybe that was her whole gift. Why not just tip mine too, and get this over with? It wasn't like I didn't have a million questions to ask *them!* I gave the milk a quick stir, then turned around to face her. "Are you asking about Paige's weird ability to nurture and communicate with, well, almost everything alive?" Diane's face showed no surprise at all. It didn't even change. "Did she really never say a word to either of you about her gift?"

"So, you *are* gifted too then," Diane said.

I nodded. Why not? Our cards were on the table now.

"That's what everyone's assumed," Diane said, then gestured at the room around us. "None of this makes any sense otherwise. But she'd never said so, not to anyone I know of, at least, so…I just needed to be sure."

"I know the feeling," I said, keeping an eye on the milk while also watching the kettle. I'd need to grab it off the burner before it started whistling and woke Jen up too. This would be a very bad moment for that. "Paige told me there were others out there, but she never told me who or where they were either."

"It's a very private thing," Simone said softly. "There's a lot of pain connected to these gifts for most of us, before we come to understand and accept them, anyway. And even then... It's just not the sort of thing that can be trotted out most of the time, is it."

"We try to respect each other's privacy," said Diane.

"I understand," I said. "All of that. Mine was painful too, even traumatic—until Paige came along. But I spent the whole day of her memorial service trying to figure out who else there might be one of us, and came up empty-handed. You can't know how badly I've wanted this moment to come."

"Oh, we know, dear," said Simone. "We've all been there." She gave me the sweetest smile. "Welcome to the table."

And just then the kettle started screaming. I yanked it off the burner, looking up as if I might be able to see Jen wake up right through the ceiling.

"She doesn't know then," said Diane, who of course hadn't missed my glance.

I looked down again and shook my head.

"Well then, we have lots to talk about. But there's no point in starting now just to have her wake and come down to see what's happening, like you did..." Diane gave me a much stranger smile than usual. "If that's what really happened?"

Oh crap. She'd just figured the rest out too, hadn't she? These gifts caused so much trouble.

"We can talk about that in the morning too, unless you'd rather not," Diane said. "Right now, though, we should probably *all* drink our cozy beverages and try to get some sleep."

❧

I WOKE UP THE NEXT morning feeling cotton-headed. The hot chocolate had been very ineffective—for me, at least. I hadn't slept again until just an hour or two before dawn. James still snoozed away beside me, making his adorable little cat-snores as I got up and went downstairs to tend the farm animals, and then help Jen set up for breakfast.

Jen, of course, was chipper as a little bird this morning—which I hoped meant I didn't need to worry about whether she'd heard anything she shouldn't have in the night. Once breakfast for our guests was in the oven, she and I sat down in the kitchen, like good and proper innkeepers, to have our separate meal made from our separate food supply out on the kitchen porch. As I pulled the lid off of a strawberry yogurt and grabbed a spoon from the drawer, Jen said, "There'll be extra French toast casserole if you want."

"What if they want seconds?" I asked.

"They're not going to want seconds. They're old ladies."

"Were you not sitting right there while Simone plowed through your *hors d'oeuvres* yesterday—and then wolfed down dinner too?"

"They won't eat that way now, though," Jen insisted. "Old ladies can't stand eating in the morning—especially old ladies who ate like Simone did last night."

I shrugged. "Have it your way. I didn't have the best night's sleep, though, so I'm just going to stick with yogurt, thanks."

As we served our guests *their* breakfast, I watched Diane cut her French toast casserole into a perfect grid of little squares, then eat them one by one in order, as Simone just swept her maple-syrup-covered portion up in practically one piece, groaning with delight.

"Looks like you enjoyed that," I said to her cheerfully, when I came out to refill their orange juice glasses and coffee cups.

"Oh, yes, dear!" Simone said. "That Jen's a genius, isn't she?"

"It's very good," Diane agreed—which was high praise, from her.

"I do believe that we could each eat another helping," Simone said. "If that's permissible?"

"We have plenty," I assured them, promising to come right back with more.

"Told you so," Jen said, when I returned to the kitchen with the empty serving platter.

"You did not," I said. "You tried to give *me* that casserole. I think you need to get that memory of yours looked at."

"You, me, whatever—it's so hard to keep it all straight," she said, laughing as she dished up two more hearty servings.

After breakfast, Jen and I cleaned up before she headed down to Darvill's for the day. We had talked about whether she should leave her other jobs when the inn opened, but she hadn't thought leaving all her best employers in the lurch before we even knew if this was going to work was such a good idea. I couldn't quarrel with her logic.

She'd been gone about three minutes when Diane and Simone came down to the front parlor where I was sitting with a book before the fire, and asked if this might be a good time to resume our conversation from the night before.

"I thought you'd never ask."

They hadn't even gotten settled on the little couch before Sam and Harry padded in and looked up at Simone for permission to come aboard. She patted the seat between herself and Diane this time, and they jumped up to arrange themselves there like the most well-mannered little felines on the island.

"Before we get started," I said, "can I ask something?"

The aunties both nodded.

"Since day one, those two have been the most unfriendly, skittish, destructive house cats I've ever met," I said. "But then you walk in, Simone, and…" I gestured at them, snuggled there at her side. "What's up with that?"

"Oh, I'm so sorry," she said. "I promise I'm not trying to steal your friends away."

"They're not my friends. They never have been—they're monsters. But they sure love you!"

"Well…" She smiled down at them and ran her fingers lightly through Harry's black fur. "I seem to live half in the otherworld these days, and so do they." She looked up at me again. "Most animals do, actually. These young fellows just see me there as well as here—the same way I see them. It makes everything so much easier for all of us."

Right… "So, when you say, half in the otherworld," I asked, uncertainly, "where is that, exactly?"

"Oh, the otherworld's right here! We're the ones who are somewhere else."

"How… Um, I don't understand."

"I know," she said sympathetically. "I don't really either, even after all this time. The fact that, for some reason, I experience more of the world than others do doesn't mean I understand any of it. I was quite lost before Diane came along. She's the one who knows how to make any sense of all the bewildering little pieces I run into there. But I'll do what I can to explain."

"Thank you," I said.

Simone nodded. "Human beings seem to think—understandably, I suppose—that this life we experience is where all the big important things are happening, and whatever else may exist before or after this is either nothing at all, or just some endless, empty, boring void where almost nothing ever happens. But, from what I know, it's the other way around. Most of everything is really happening in the otherworld. What we call our 'real lives' is just...like little terrariums. This life we know *is* the otherworld, but with nearly all of what's really happening in the rest of it cut out. Pared *down* to the tiny things that we experience." She looked over at Diane, as if for help.

"I'm as deaf and blind to everything she's trying to describe right now as you or anybody else is," Diane said. "I depend on Simone for any access to what she's describing. But I can tell you how I've come to think about it. Are you aware of all these new virtual reality games so popular with younger people now?"

"You mean, with the goggles and everything?" I asked.

"Yes, precisely. I've tried one or two of them out, actually. Professional curiosity. You sit down in a *real* room somewhere, and don all that equipment to exchange this giant, infinitely diverse world we live in for some small, relatively flatter, cruder, emptier diorama that you can enjoy a cruder, emptier, flatter illusion of moving through and interacting with."

"Yes!" Simone quavered. "Can you imagine? It's like we've found a way to make our lives here even smaller!"

"From what I've learned by working with Simone," Diane went on, "our so-called real world is to the otherworld Simone knows as those little VR goggle worlds are to what you and I experience as real life. For Simone, at least, the world you and I live in is like a small aquarium set up in one corner of a living room inside a house, on a planet, in a solar system, et cetera."

"But that aquarium is and isn't somewhere different than the living room!" Simone interjected. "Do you see? Both our world and the otherworld are and aren't separate places."

Next to this, my little disappearing trick suddenly seemed like child's play. "So, when Paige said she'd be traveling to unfamiliar territory," I said, "you mean that she's, what, escaped this aquarium to go hiking out in...all of that?"

Both women looked at me in silence, then at each other, very uncomfortably, it seemed.

"Yes," Diane said finally. "Except that every now and then, people run into trouble, and get stuck halfway out of the aquarium. So to speak. That is really why Simone and I have come here."

"What do you mean?" I asked, already pretty sure that I didn't want to hear the answer. Though, of course, I also did.

"When did Paige tell you this?" Diane asked. "About traveling, I mean."

I told them about the letter she'd left me, while they glanced at each other, nodding. When I was finished, we all just stared at one another for a moment. Then I said, "You're not saying you think Paige is stuck that way. Are you?"

"We're still not sure yet," Simone said, sadly. "But when we were here in June I went up to see her room…and was very surprised to discover *someone* there who clearly is."

"And it's Paige?" I asked again, more dismayed by the second.

"That's what we've come to learn, and hopefully to do something about," Diane said. "Simone can…communicate with what's on either side of this divide."

"Well then, can't you just ask them who they are?" I demanded.

"No, I'm sorry," Simone said. "It doesn't work that way. There are no words there—except for mine. I think maybe words are something we made up here, just for here. Sometimes there aren't even faces, voices, anything. Touching the otherworld is more like…sharing a dream. Fleeting images and feelings, wordless understandings. You know how disjointed and confusing dreams can be. Your cats are better at communicating that way than I will ever be. They and most other animals still use the language of that place. All I can do is give Diane as much as I can fit to words, and hope that she'll find meaning in it."

"No. No, *I'm* sorry," I said, holding tears back for the first time since last spring. "It can't be her. She wouldn't…have that kind of trouble. She was too wise. She had maps. She told me so!"

"Please, try to be calm," Diane said. "We need your help, and just being able to ask you for it puts us so much farther ahead. We can't ask most people for any help at all. Not with a ghost."

Oh my god… I thought. *We have a ghost? A real ghost… Paige's ghost?* "What can I do?" I managed.

"First," said Diane, "I need to know a number of things."

"Okay," I said, no longer looking at anyone as I struggled to control my feelings.

"To start with, did Paige ever speak of being troubled here by strange experiences, or any disturbing presence in the house?"

I shook my head, sure I'd have remembered her mentioning anything like that. I looked up to catch Diane and Simone exchange another concerned look.

"Then, have *you* experienced anything strange here since her death?" Diane asked.

"Don't even think about those ghost stories in books and on TV," Simone added. "That's all rubbish. We mean little things: strange thoughts or feelings, unusually vivid dreams, odd animal behavior, even the slightest—"

"Yes," I cut her off, wondering how I could have missed so much... But then, I hadn't met these women yet, or heard any of what they'd just told me. So, of course, I'd just dismissed it all.

I told them everything I could remember: my weird emotional tantrums and nightmares after Paige died; the skittish behavior of so many animals, from Sam and Harry, to the goats, to the homicidal/suicidal raven—even the squirrel nests full of stolen items. I told them about the footsteps and other noises, what had happened when we'd gone to clear her room out, the furnace, and all the accidents we'd blamed these poor cats for—including the photograph of Paige and George Harper that kept getting smashed when no one seemed to be around. And then, I thought of something much more recent.

"Last night, Simone, you were looking at that set of bookshelves in the second parlor, and talked about someone who was crying, and upset. About the house." A tiny, knowing smile turned Diane's lips up at their corners, but Simone's mouth dropped wide open, so I guess Diane had kept that secret to herself. I nodded, not quite meeting Simone's eyes. "That other presence you kept feeling; that was me, I'm pretty sure. We can talk about that in a minute. But I'm wondering what you saw there."

"I *saw* nothing," she said. "But I felt someone—or, no, I *was* someone sitting there with others in some terrible distress. I can't tell you more than that. It was just feelings without words or images at all. Anything you heard me say was just me, trying to tell Diane."

I nodded, miserably. "That spot, where those shelves are, is where

Paige's couch used to be. She always used to sit there with Jinx and Pep, her little dogs, on either side of her. And it's also where I had one of the first, and worst, experiences of…grief…for something lost. Or some*one* lost, I guess."

Diane looked across at Simone, and I finally realized that she was actually *looking* at Simone. In the eyes, as she seemed to do with no one else. "It's not looking good, my dear," Diane murmured. "It all seems to have started after Paige's death, just as we feared. Most of what Cam's just told us seems focused on places that were particular to her. And last night, you asked what was being done to your home. You complained of chaos. This house has been substantially remodeled in the past few months, and cleared of most of what was in it before that." She turned to me, her eyes averted slightly once again. "The dream you had of being lost in Paige's house…"

"Yes," I whispered, feeling only devastated now.

"That could have been Paige too, if she's lost herself somehow."

"A thing that happens, sometimes," Simone said dolefully. "She may not remember where she left herself, or even who that self was."

"We have to help her," I said.

Simone sighed and looked away. "Well…now that we seem more sure of who I'm reaching out for, I will try again. But not today. Last night took so much out of me, and I am not a girl anymore. I need at least a night of uninterrupted sleep first." She looked at me, apologetically. "There is another room up there, I believe, large enough for Diane and me. The Dragonfly, if I recall correctly."

"Yes," I said. "Do you two want to move there?"

She nodded. "Paige is very much still in the lovely room that you have given us, I think. And I suspect that I will sleep more soundly almost anywhere else."

☙

As I helped Simone and Diane move out of the Blue Heron Suite into the Dragonfly Room, they told me about how difficult being gifted had made their lives as children. Simone's bewildering access to the otherworld and Diane's compulsion to see patterns and guess their meaning had led them both, again and again, to discover things they weren't meant to know.

"It was an endless nightmare," Simone said as she folded her clothes into the top drawer of their new bureau. "With my attention always fading in and out between the otherworld and this one, people thought that I was brain damaged. And I never knew what it was even safe to know, much less to say. When I wasn't being punished for being too spot-on about someone's awful secret, I was being called crazy for talking about things that made no sense to anybody."

I sure understood what being called crazy felt like.

"It was much the same for me," said Diane, "except that all my divergent tics made me seem not just like a snoop, but a freak as well. And then..." She paused as if debating whether to go on, then sighed. "I was showing off for my mother one day, telling her all about patterns I'd detected in my father's behavior...which ended their marriage." I looked up at her from the shallow plastic tub of fresh towels I'd just pulled from underneath their bed, and barely managed to mask my startled sympathy in time. "Until I met Simone," she went on, "I had no idea there were any others like me."

"It was a lucky day for both of us," Simone said. "I've still met no one else who understands me and my life the way Diane does."

Their stories and the physical work of helping them change rooms was already pulling me out of the state I'd fallen into downstairs. "I guess I was luckier," I said. "My secret was easier to keep. Since no one ever remembers I was there, it just erased itself."

We'd already talked about my ability to chameleon by then. Simone had seemed as amazed by the idea that a person could actually just disappear as I'd been about what she did, until I'd mentioned Paige's suggestion that it only really happened in the minds of those around me, not in the real world—whatever "the real world" meant anymore.

"Well, of course," Diane said, straightening and aligning the towels I'd just put out in their bathroom. "It's not only our abilities that work that way. 'Reality,' as we know it, is constructed as much or more *inside* our heads than *outside* them."

"Would the cats talk to me too if I had your ability to hear them?" I asked Simone.

"No, dear," she said, patiently. "Animals and I communicate in the otherworld, not in this one. But since your lucky brain doesn't perceive it, you aren't even there for them to talk to, so I can't see why they'd think of trying."

Well...it was comforting to know they weren't just wondering why

I'd never talk to them.

When we were finished in the Dragonfly Room, I went to change the bedding and towels in their previous suite. But both aunties and all three cats—James had finally left his beauty rest to join us—trailed along. Apparently whatever Simone experienced in this room didn't bother her as long as she wasn't trying to sleep.

As I started stripping the bed, Diane—who did certainly like explaining things—began telling me about ghosts. From what she'd learned with Simone, she said, her best theory was that ghosts were kind of like our own gifts.

"They only happen, or perhaps only exist, in the minds of living creatures who perceive them," she said as I shook out a fresh set of sheets. "They've been reduced to something like pure thought, without any *tangible* presence beyond that of…atomic particles, for instance. That 'cloud of thought' can interact with almost nothing but living minds that it encounters."

"Well, wait a minute," I said, tugging the bed out from the wall to start tucking in the bottom sheet. "Then what about all the *physical* things this one's done?" I couldn't bring myself to call it Paige. Not yet, at least.

"Like what?" Diane asked, as if I hadn't just told them both downstairs.

"Like the footsteps, and thumps inside the walls. The broken picture! All the little things it seems to have moved around here in the house. And the heating coming on like that, the day we tried to clear this room!"

"Well, recording devices would probably not have picked up those footsteps any more than they captured that incident at the prison you told us about. The furnace is a more interesting question… Thoughts are, in part, the product of countless tiny electrical discharges in the brain—at least, while we're still living in this state. But I've seen things to suggest a cloud of 'ghostly thought' may still generate some kind of charge—especially when the presence is excited or distressed. It might not require more than a stray electron or two to short out a computer chip, or other extremely fine electrical connections."

I snorted at that idea. "That old furnace doesn't have anything like computer chips in it."

"But its wiring and its thermostat include fine electrical connections," Diane said. "As for thumps, moved items, and that broken picture," she went on, "you did hear cats yowling just before or after many of those events. And the little floorboard entrances you showed us are apparently there precisely to address the presence of other creatures in these walls. Weren't many of your misplaced items found upstairs in squirrel nests?"

So, we'd been right to blame the cats. Why didn't that surprise me? "Yes," I said, frowning.

Seeing my expression, she said, "I'm not suggesting that these events had nothing to do with Paige. Animals have minds as vulnerable as our own. The raven that kept assailing you was likely channeling the same kind of intrusive thoughts and feelings that fueled your nightmares and fits of emotion. And it was carrying an item Paige may remember and want back; so did it fly through those open windows just because it was attracted by something shiny? Or because Paige wanted it to find something she already knew was in those boxes? Did the sullen distrust of these cats reflect their own feelings toward you, or the ghost's?"

Oh…these questions were not making me feel better. Had Paige really used the cats to spy on me? Is that why they'd followed me around like that? But why would she have distrusted me? I straightened out the coverlet on her bed. "Could Paige have forgotten who *I* am?" I asked Simone. "Does she not want me here now?"

"I don't know," she said. "Answers like that are Diane's department."

"It's very hard to parse a ghost's intentions," said Diane. "As Simone told you earlier, they seem to occupy a disjointed and irrational kind of dream state, and can use little to express themselves but what's already in our minds, or in their immediate environments. So it's almost impossible to be sure where our own thoughts or feelings end and theirs begin. But useful clues are rarely found in any single detail. The patterns I must find if we're to help free Paige will come only from the largest and broadest possible assembly of data. So you must tell me if any other details occur to you, no matter how slight or irrelevant they may seem."

"And, if you can find those patterns, we can fix this?" I asked as I plumped the pillows.

"I hope so," said Diane. "We have had luck at such things before. But first, we must determine what has kept her here."

"Unfinished business, usually," said Simone. "And I don't just mean laundry left out on the line. It takes something big, and usually painful, to interrupt what's normally an almost instant trip from one here to the other."

Diane nodded. "I'm interested in knowing more about this photograph that kept getting broken. I assume it's the one downstairs in the foyer?"

"Yes," I said.

"I don't suppose you can tell me who that man beside Paige is, can you?"

I turned to look at her in surprise. "You don't know?"

"No…"

"That's George Harper."

Simone's mouth fell open again, and even Diane's brows rose slightly. "Well, of course!" gasped Simone. "I'd forgotten all about that… situation."

"There's a lock of hair behind it, in an envelope," I said.

"Oh, my," said Diane. "Why didn't you tell us this to start with?"

"I just assumed you'd know," I said. "Everybody else seems to."

"Well, yes," said Simone. "I've heard she was in love once with a boy who left, and that it was the reason she had never married. But I've never heard more than that. She certainly never spoke of him to us."

"No," said Diane. "And we did visit here from time to time over the years."

"I found it stacked along with lots of other photographs and paintings when we were clearing these rooms out. I'm not sure when it had actually been hung up on a wall."

"You don't know more about whatever happened there, do you?" Diane asked me, keenly.

"No. And Elle didn't either. But she said a friend of Paige's might. But when I met her after the memorial and asked her about him, she said it was too painful and complicated to talk about then."

"Who?" asked Diane.

"Florence Golding."

"Oh dear. Florence," Simone said, looking at Diane again. "Do you think we should?"

"I think we have to," said Diane, with clear distaste. "That young man seems as good a candidate for Paige's unfinished business as any I can think of. And if Florence really cared for her as much as she likes to pretend, I'd think she'd have to help us."

"I don't know how to contact her," I told them. "I could try calling Elle to get her number."

"No need." Diane looked like she'd taken a big bite of lemon. "I have it. But it may be better if I let you make the call. She's not always pleased to hear from me. May I just text you her contact?"

"Okay…" I said, dying to know what that was all about; but, by the looks she and Simone were exchanging, I thought I'd better not.

A moment later, I had the phone to my ear, hoping Florence would answer a number that would not be anywhere on *her* contacts list.

"Hello?" she said.

"Oh! Um, hi, Florence! Thank you for—it's Cam. Camille Tate, I mean. We met at—"

"Cam! Hello! And give me just a moment, please, while I add you to my phone." I waited, trying to pull myself together before she said, "There. Now I'll know next time. And what a pleasant surprise! I heard your inn is open—at least partially. And your website is quite charming. How's everything going?"

And, again, I couldn't think of what to say. How could she have known about our soft opening? She hadn't had me put her on the mailing list, obviously. And it wasn't mentioned on the website—how had she even found it already?

"Cam? Are you still there?" she asked.

"Yes! I am, and thanks for asking. The inn is going very well so far. In fact, we have our first two guests already, and…I'm sorry to bother you about this again. But they're very interested in a picture of George Harper downstairs, but, of course, I don't have much to tell them, so, I hope you don't mind, but I told them maybe you would know? Is this…still a bad time to ask…about it?"

After another pause, she asked, in a very neutral tone, "Did Lisa give you my number?"

"Uh, no." *Crap.* I clearly wasn't supposed to tell her who had. That's why I was making the call. But if she asked—

"May I ask who these guests of yours are?" she asked.

I shot a panicked look at Diane. Refusing to tell her would have to be far more offensive than anything else I could say. So I said, "Simone Wade, and—"

"Diane and Simone?" she cut in, sounding startled. "Have you got a ghost?"

I yanked the phone from my ear. "She knows! About the ghost!"

"No I don't," I heard Florence say, rather loudly, and put the phone back to my ear. "But I think I want to. Have you got space for another guest, dear?"

"Uh...yes. Certainly."

"Please book me into the nicest room available. I'll be right there." And she hung up.

I looked back at Diane and Simone in complete confusion. "She says—"

"Oh, we know," said Diane. "She talks quite loudly when she gets excited. We heard everything."

"How did she know about the ghost?"

"I don't think she did. But she knows what we do, and I didn't realize you'd begin by announcing our presence here, or I'd have…" She sighed. "But I suppose I should have seen that coming. Oh well, she's on her way. That's what matters now."

CHAPTER 13

Florence called me back less than an hour later, much more graciously this time, and apologized for having been so abrupt before. She promised to explain everything when she got here, just as I received a text containing her travel itinerary, which I read as we continued talking. She was flying—*tomorrow*—from San Francisco to Seattle, and from there to Eastsound by private plane! I asked her if she'd need a ride from there to the inn, and she said, "Yes please, dear; around five p.m.? That would be just lovely."

"I'll see you there, then."

"Thank you, Cam. Don't do anything exciting without me! Bye for now." And she hung up.

I shoved the phone back in my pocket, dazed by the speed of it all, and went to tell Diane and Simone the news. They seemed grudgingly pleased that we'd be able to move ahead so quickly, but less than thrilled by the prospect of Florence's imminent arrival. And I just… really had to ask. "So, what I should know about your history with Florence?"

Diane made some odd waffling gestures with her hands. "Many years ago, while performing some analysis for a client I had no reason to suspect of any connection to Florence, I uncovered some tracks she…hadn't meant to leave behind."

"She wasn't very nice about it," said Simone. "And neither were we, to be honest. But that's all water long under the bridge now. And all we should probably say about it."

Oh yes, I thought. *You're so clearly over it*. "Okay. Thank you."

Keeping my mouth shut around Jen that evening about, well, everything I'd learned that day, was really, really difficult—especially after I told her that the aunties had moved from the Blue Heron Suite to the Dragonfly Room.

"Weren't they comfortable in there?" she asked, obviously dismayed that our nicest, most expensive room had been rejected after just one night. "Is there some problem we need to fix?"

Well, actually… "Not really. I think they just…wanted to be closer to the stairs, maybe."

"Closer to the stairs?" Jen looked even more nonplussed. "Why?"

"Well…I suppose that…after walking up all those stairs, walking the whole length of the landing too, just to reach their room, was too much for Simone…maybe?" Wanting to move on before this got any worse, I distracted her brilliantly by saying, "But it's not actually a problem, because I've rebooked the Blue Heron Suite already. Remember Florence Golding?"

Jen looked at me even more strangely for a moment before shaking her head.

"The movie-star auntie from our memorial after-party gathering?" I prompted.

"Oh! Sure," she said, and smiled. "She's coming too?"

"Yes," I said. "Tomorrow!"

"*Tomorrow?*" Jen said in alarm.

"I've already remade the Blue Heron," I assured her.

"Well, thanks, hon; but I'm going to have to rethink my meal plans now. I haven't shopped for three this week, and I've just made a batch of zucchini-pecan muffins that won't be enough now either. And of course we have to give her dinners too. How long is she staying?"

"I'm…not actually sure yet? It all happened…really fast."

Jen rolled her eyes. "What the heck is going on around here?"

And there was a question I *really* couldn't answer. "We're getting a lot of business! If this keeps up, maybe you can drop one of your other jobs."

"If this keeps up, I may end up in a loony bin and have to drop all of them." But she was grinning now. So we were out of the woods, for a minute, at least.

Diane and Simone came down to join us for dinner that night, just having realized that these evening meals had been omitted from their bill somehow. We explained the regulations, and our clever work-around. So, of course, Simone suggested they just pay us under the table. But we told her we were fans of simple hospitality, and we'd hear no more about it. Even Diane seemed rather charmed by this, and ate at least a bit of nearly everything Jen served. Afterward, while Jen was in the kitchen, the aunties and I agreed to give ourselves a rest tomorrow until we'd heard whatever Florence had to tell us.

I arrived at Eastsound's airport the next day around four forty-five. The rain had cleared that afternoon, because not even Mother Nature wanted to displease Florence Golding. At five p.m. exactly, a small, unmarked but elegant white twin engine plane touched down and taxied off the runway. The pilot came around to open its passenger hatch, pulled down a folding set of stairs, and Florence swirled out and down onto the tarmac in a cloud of glamorous charisma, wearing a pair of those big black sunglasses you see on tabloid covers. I say swirled, because that's just what she did, somehow. She wasn't wearing petticoats or anything. But her dress had clearly been designed somehow to swish around her legs as if she were.

I climbed out of Tigress, super glad I hadn't needed to pick her up in a Kia, or a pickup truck like Jen's, and waved to her. She tilted her sunglasses down a smidge—like they do in Hollywood—and waved back as she sauntered toward me. The pilot followed with her luggage. I had no idea what Florence did, or had done, for a living. But it must have been something important, because she was clearly very used to moving through the world this way.

Determined not to disgrace myself by playing fan girl this time, I took a deep breath as she arrived, and stuck out my hand. "Welcome back," I said, in a cheerful, casual, not at all overawed way as she shook the hand I'd offered.

"Thanks so much for coming down. It's just so ridiculous that one *still* can't get a taxi anywhere in these islands."

"Oh, I think we have taxis now. But I'm happy to do this." I fobbed my back hatch open for the pilot, who lifted her luggage into the car for us, and waited.

Florence shook her head. "Those are vans, dear. Not taxis. And I don't do vans—or Uber. The people who drive them think you'll tip better if they chat with you the whole way there, and about nothing. A real taxi driver understands the value of silence."

"Oh…" I said, feeling my careful balance slipping. Didn't we have car taxis? "Well, yes, I guess. I hadn't thought about it that way."

"Shall we?" she asked pleasantly. "I don't want to keep you standing out here in this chill."

"Oh, ah, yes," I said, opening the passenger door for her before trotting around to climb in on my side. She handed the pilot a tip and climbed inside as well. "I'm so used to it, I hardly notice anymore," I went on, apologetically. Because, of course, it wasn't *Florence* who'd left *me* standing out in *that chill*. And yet, all I wanted was for her to think highly of me. And of our inn, of course. Which she'd been in such favor of last time we'd met. I didn't want her changing her mind about that.

And there I was, doing it again, I realized! Fawning. I'd never been a fawner. Not with Lisa, or the director of Emerald City Repertory, or any of my old salon's wealthiest and most important customers. *What is your problem with this woman?* I asked myself as I drove out of the airport onto Mt. Baker Road.

As I turned up Enchanted Forest, Florence turned to me and smiled. "You do have some kind of knack, then?"

"A knack?" I said. "For what?"

Florence rewarded this question with a little trill of laughter. "Oh, aren't you darling. Some special talent or ability, like Paige had?"

"Oh. She didn't tell you?"

Florence shook her head, a little sadly. "Paige and I lost touch quite a while ago. I've always regretted that." She smiled at me again. "But she left you everything, and now you're chasing down a ghost with Simone and Diane, and don't seem very startled by the idea. So, it seemed safe to assume you're one of us. I didn't mean to pry, though. I understand as well as anyone how private such things are. So, how's this?" she asked, as if in confidence between two girlfriends. "I won't tell you mine if you don't tell me yours?" Her smile widened at what was clearly meant to be a friendly little witticism, and…I smiled back, accepting it as that too, in spite of a feeling, farther down, that I should have asked her more.

When we reached the Berry Farm, Florence surprised me by going to take her own, not tiny, suitcase from the back. From the moment she walked in and looked around, she gushed about how wonderfully we'd restored the place, preserving its "historical charm" while making it so fresh and lively too. Of course, Jen was enchanted right out of her socks as she checked Florence in, because, really how could anybody not be?

And when Florence asked to leave her checkout date open too, Jen just said, "You bet! We'd love to have you all the way till Christmas!"

I did a double take, wondering if that was what I sounded like around this woman. But the question slid away somehow before I could really think about it more as Florence asked Jen whether there'd be dinner here, or if she should find someplace in town to eat. Jen explained our arrangement, and said that Florence would be more than welcome to join us in the dining room at seven. Florence said she still hadn't forgotten a single bite of all the fantastic things Jen had served the last time she was here, and would be thrilled to eat with us tonight. Jen just glowed, of course, as Florence picked up her suitcase and asked if I'd mind showing her the room.

"Of course." That was my job, after all. "May I carry that for you?"

She shook her head. "I can manage, thank you." She looked up toward the landing as we climbed the stairs. "It feels so much like coming home."

When she realized we'd put her in Paige's renovated room, she seemed genuinely moved, and gushed again about how beautifully we'd updated everything. I thanked her and, after urging her to let us know if we could get her anything else, left her to get settled.

I'd seen no sign of Diane or Simone the entire time.

Our dinner table was less congenial that night than it had been before. I watched Diane almost literally curdle as Florence swept in to join us, and from that moment, everyone's attention—not just mine—seemed to gravitate in Florence's direction. Jen's pear, prosciutto, brie and basil crêpes with fig preserves were as fabulous as everything else she served. Florence filled the air with cheerful, witty conversation, full of more praise for Jen's cooking—which Jen clearly couldn't get enough of. But Simone and Diane were quite subdued. And even I felt some strange tension in the air that went beyond whatever bad blood existed between our three guests. Was this Paige's ghost again? I wondered. And if not, then what?

Dinner ended with a plate of Jen's mouthwatering coconut macaroons, which prompted Florence to muse about the possibility of actually staying till Christmas, and ask if we offered any kind of discount to people who stayed for more than a month. Jen all but giggled with delight. I smiled to see her having so much fun. Diane and Simone excused themselves and went upstairs, followed only minutes later by

Florence.

When Jen and I were finished cleaning dinner up, she said she'd need to spend some more time prepping and cooking before she turned in, to adjust things for our extra guest. She didn't seem upset about that anymore, though. So I told her I'd go up and check to make sure Florence didn't need anything else before I turned in as well.

When I got upstairs, though, the Dragonfly Room's door was slightly open with no light on inside. And I heard voices coming from behind the closed door of the Blue Heron Suite.

As I approached the door, I heard Diane's voice, as close to raised as I had ever heard it. "Everybody in this house but Jen is gifted, Florence. So who are you performing for?"

I stopped and listened.

"Well, I've just met these girls," Florence said. "I'm only trying to make a good impression. Is there something wrong with that?"

"No," I heard Simone say. "But could you dial it down a bit, at least? You're laying it on so heavily that I'm surprised Cam hasn't noticed. She's quite bright, you know."

"I'm well aware of that," said Florence.

Listening to them talking about me now was uncomfortable, so I took the last few steps and knocked softly on the door.

Florence answered, and beamed when she saw me. "There you are! Now our quorum is complete. Do come in, please!"

I came in to see Diane and Simone sitting on the bed. Florence went to sit back on the chair before her vanity. Which left me—the youngster here—to slide down and sit cross-legged on the floor with my back against the room's little bureau. I took a moment to sort of test the air for strange sensations. But if Paige's ghost was here, I couldn't tell. "So," I said, "have we come up with a plan yet?"

"No," said Diane. "We've just been exchanging pleasantries until you got here."

"You were expecting me?" No one had told me about any meeting.

"You called me, dear," said Florence. "And given what we're about here, it was hard to imagine that you *wouldn't* come looking for us when you could."

Okay, she had a point—which I'd just proven by showing up. "So, do we get to hear about George Harper now?"

Everyone looked at Florence, who suddenly looked a lot more sober.

"I suppose that is what I was summoned for." Though no one had actually *summoned* her, I thought. She could just have answered a few questions on the phone. But if she wished to frame it that way... I thought again about what I'd just heard outside the door, and began to think about her differently. "So then," she said quietly, "as at least some of you know, I believe, I spent a lot of time with Paige here when we were young. And, one night, she and I were at the Upper Tavern..."

"Sorry?" I asked. "Not the Lower Tavern?"

Florence shook her head. "The Lower was given that name to distinguish it from the Upper, which was just west of town, and up a little rise. It's long gone now, but back then it was the real place to go, if you were young and fun. That night, Paige and I met a young, good-looking, if somewhat *less* fun young man we'd never seen around before. His name was George Harper, and he'd just washed ashore here, running, he said, from his strict, religious family in the Midwest. But as attractive as he was, it soon became clear that, running from religion or not, he was still a great deal too well-behaved for us." She gave us a naughty smile that said maybe a little too much about just *how* fun she and Paige must have been in those days.

※

FLORENCE TURNED OUT TO BE a pretty decent storyteller. She described so vividly the shy, quiet young man who'd arrived on Orcas Island back in the late fifties with a love of wild and remote places, and his books of poetry. He'd come to work as a warden with the newly created Fish and Wildlife Service, and that he'd been brought along to the tavern by friends that night, in spite of being a federal employee with the power to write citations, because word had gone around that he was a decent guy who wasn't into coming down on people who'd lived here long before he'd ever come ashore.

When he'd found local people hunting deer where they had always hunted but weren't supposed to anymore, or fishing in the places they had always fished, even without newfangled licenses, he'd been more prone to issue warnings than fines, Florence said. He'd saved his citation book for haughty tourists, or greedy locals who disregarded conservation law out of a sense of privilege rather than just trying to make ends meet as regular people always had.

"But, as nice as I'm making George sound," she told us, "he and

Paige bounced quite firmly *off* of each other to begin with."

She talked of how Paige had learned to hunt and trap, fish and dig for clams, and smoke, freeze, or can her food to last the winter—as well as how to grow and preserve the uncommonly voluptuous vegetables and fruits we all remembered. In the process, Florence said, Paige too had sometimes run afoul of the newly proliferating rules and regulations George was there to enforce. And when she hadn't been milling lumber or wielding tools up on her hilltop to turn an old abandoned boardinghouse into her "estate," she and Florence had apparently been quite the party-hearty girls.

It was so easy for me to imagine Paige that way as Florence talked, and to wish I could have known her then.

By contrast, George had been far too timid for Paige's tastes, and generally nervous about the very notion of romance. Florence doubted he'd had much experience with such matters during his upbringing in a fire-and-brimstone Christian home. He'd explained his reticence to others, and himself, with ethical pretenses around not dating people potentially under his authority as an officer of the law. But Florence smiled at us and said that he'd really just been embarrassed by a lack of savvy that made bold, brash, and flirtatious girls like Paige seem far out of his league, if not morally suspect, even.

But in time, Paige had begun to see George less as timid than sincere, less straightlaced than honorable and modest, and he had a terrific sense of humor. George and Paige had started talking about his love of nature and the out-of-doors—a love they'd shared in common—and as George had started growing more loquacious, Paige had found herself lighting up whenever he appeared.

"He started dropping by her property on his way to rounds in Deer Harbor," Florence said, "and Paige always welcomed his advice or help with her ongoing building projects. During one of my visits, George finally told me that he thought Paige was 'a mighty fine woman' who made him feel like no one else ever had. I began coming up to visit even more often then, just to watch their beautiful affair unfold until, one day, Paige told me that she thought George might really be the one." Florence wasn't really looking at us anymore, but at things in the past that only she could see. "The next time I visited," she said, "Paige sat me down and told me all about the day he'd come to help her harvest blackberries higher up the hill. They'd come back to the house to wash them and, on a whim, she invited him to stay for dinner. Over dessert, without warning or invitation, she gave him a peck on the cheek. He blushed, and stammered a bit—then kissed her back. And it wasn't just a peck."

Florence's eyes had reddened at the edges now. This was not the woman I'd picked up at the airport before dinner—or the one I'd met in June. This was some other woman I wanted to know better, even more than I had wished to please the woman who kept leaving me in dumbfounded awe. And that was when I realized that, since coming through this door tonight to join them, I had not once felt that childish adoration of her at all. So…what had changed?

A moment later, Florence seemed to remember we were there. "George was still there in the morning, and a few weeks later, he moved his last few things out of his boardinghouse in town, into this house, to live with her. From then on, they were inseparable. When I came up to visit, it was three of us, not two now. I was so envious."

"So, then…what went wrong?" I asked, hoping that she wasn't about to tell us how she'd come between them somehow. I wanted so much to like the woman Florence had turned into as she'd told this story.

"Well, it started with his job," she said. "There was a local man who'd parlayed his business as a realtor into a fortune and now ran a kind of hunting lodge for well-heeled outdoorsmen half a mile uphill from Paige's property. He encouraged his lodge guests to do just the kinds of things that George had no problem writing tickets for. As you might imagine, George and he were not good friends. The man threatened George periodically for a while; and, when that didn't work, he wrote angry letters to George's boss about how George persecuted his customers while refusing to penalize his own friends at all. And when that man found out that George's girlfriend lived just downhill from him, he began harassing Paige too, just to get at George.

"One day, the lodge owner showed up here, and told her he was quite sure her little compound must be out of compliance with laws and ordinances of some kind, implying that he might look into getting her thrown off her land.

"Well, everybody here knows what this place meant to her. She told George that night about their belligerent neighbor's visit, and asked him if he couldn't just try to be a little more even-handed with his ticket book. The lodge owner's complaints had already gotten George put on notice with his superiors, and Paige was worried he'd get transferred to some other post, who knew how far away, or even fired. She also pointed out that his reluctance to ticket friends was playing right into the hands of obnoxious people like that man.

"George promised he'd start holding everyone to the same standard. But handing out fines was his least favorite part of that job, and in time, Paige began to see that George's problem wasn't favoritism but a deeper dread of even mild confrontation. Far more than she'd ever realized. He just hated making people he was fond of unhappy."

Florence looked down at her folded hands, almost as if they were causing her pain now. "As we all know, Paige was not a timid person. Or averse to conflict she thought necessary or constructive. I don't think she knew how to live in fear of anything; and she began to wonder whether she could really share a life with someone who couldn't live as fearlessly and honestly as she did."

Florence fell silent again, looking almost fearful herself of whatever she had left to tell.

"As that bastard up her hill kept turning up the pressure," she said at last, "Paige's arguments with George became more frequent. But that's all they ended up being: *Paige's* arguments. George was gentle as a kitten, and didn't want to fight at all. He'd just apologize to her, berate himself, and commit to doing better—until he found himself in conflict with friends he'd caught in some infraction, and failed to hold them accountable again.

"I wasn't there as much by then. Visiting them was much less pleasant than it had been. But Paige wrote me many letters, and talked about it whenever we saw each other. She found herself increasingly upset, not by George's reticence to ticket people he sympathized with, but by his seeming allergy to offending anyone at all—including her. She'd come to realize what a master he was at dodging conflict with a noncommittal smile and a joke or a placating generality. He was a sweet, kind, well-intentioned, and generally sincere man—whom she'd fallen quite in love with. But in the middle of his internal garden, she now saw a noxious weed: fear of seeing, much less working through, anything uncomfortable.

"As Elle said at Paige's memorial, forthrightness had always been one of her most distinctive traits. Paige knew that any lifelong course their relationship might take would require both of them to face and work though all kinds of difficult passages. But now she wondered whether George was equipped for it. She was coming to see his fear of conflict as a kind of cowardly dishonesty—not just with her and others, but with himself. And that didn't just worry her. It made her angry. Did she want to live the rest of her life stuck in this fix with him? No, she did not. If they were to work out, she needed him to come out of hiding for her.

"Apparently, one morning not long after that, George started carping over breakfast about some new provocation from the lodge lord up the hill, and Paige decided it was time to force the issue. She told me later that she wasn't nice about it this time. She gave him both barrels about how they would never make it as a couple if he couldn't face an honest fight, and even shoved him in the chest to reinforce her point. She said she'd told him what she thought of cowardice and dishonesty disguised as kindness or patience, trying to make him fight back for once instead of just being meek and apologetic, leaving her to be the fishwife.

"But she said he'd just looked astonished and stung, then told her he was going to take the Fish and Wildlife boat over to Waldron for the day, and hoped they might try talking all this through more rationally when he came back that night."

Florence looked around at us, and spread her hands.

"She never saw him again. The boat he'd told her he was taking to Waldron was found days later on Lopez instead. And someone there said George had asked him for a ride out to the ferry landing.

"Paige could not believe he'd just run out on her after their first and only real fight. She feared the man who owned that lodge had finally made good on his threats somehow, but no evidence to support that theory was ever found." Florence looked down, and shook her head. "The authorities investigated his disappearance, but all they found was a man who was unhappy with his job, whose employers were unhappy with him, and who had just had a big fight with his girlfriend the day he'd left the islands. Just as lots of people did, when they found the reality of living here too out of sync with what they'd imagined.

"I'm not sure Paige ever forgave herself for driving him away. She hadn't meant to; and for years, I think, she didn't believe he really had left her for good. She kept expecting him to come back and say he'd just been thinking things through somewhere, and was sorry to have hurt her. But in time, that hope failed her too. She wouldn't even talk about it after that—to anyone. Not even me. But as we know, she never found another George. She hadn't left him. They hadn't broken up. They'd never even said goodbye. And no other man who ever came along…was him."

I thought again of Emile Fisher, and wondered how many others like him there had been.

"So," said Florence. "There's everything I knew, until recently."

"Until recently?" Diane asked, leaning forward with avid interest. "You've learned something more?"

Florence nodded, and looked at me as she stood and went to her wardrobe. "This," she said, opening one of its two doors and reaching inside, "is why I was so taken aback by your call yesterday, Cam." She turned around, holding out the ugly clock she'd taken from the giveaway table at our after-party.

"The *clock?*" I said. "What's that got to do with—"

"As I mentioned to you back in June," Florence cut in, "this was a gift from me to Paige, not long before things fell apart between herself and George." She came to sit back down, and placed the clock face up in her lap. "I got it for her as a joke, and to my delight, she thought it was hilarious, and loved it too. So when I saw it at your party, I took it home as a memento of the last time things were truly good between myself and Paige. May I ask where you found it, Cam?"

"It was…in a box beneath her bed," I said.

Florence looked back down at the clock in her lap with a rueful smile. "When I got it home, I tried to wind it up and make it work again, but, of course, it wouldn't."

"As we'd written on a note beside it on that table," I reminded her. "'Does not work.'"

"I saw the note. But I'm not one to take no for an answer—not without a fight. So, recently, I got out a screwdriver and opened up the back of it to see if I could figure out what needed fixing. The answer wasn't hard to find." She turned the clock over, removed its already loosened back panel, and poured what was behind it out onto the floor between her feet: a cascade of newsprint scraps and what looked like ancient mail mixed with little sheets of waste paper. As we all stared down at the pile, Florence looked back up at me. "I assume you weren't the one who put these there?"

"No! Of course not! I never even thought to look."

"Yes," Florence said, bleakly. "That's what I thought."

"What is it all?" asked Diane.

"Newspaper clippings about George's disappearance and the brief investigation afterward," said Florence, "along with correspondence between Paige, a couple of local journalists, and an investigating officer. The whole affair, piled together, stuffed into the funny clock I'd given her, and shoved into a box that I suspect has not been opened ever since." She sounded as if she'd just read her own obituary, though I had no idea why.

"That's marvelous!" said Diane. "This could be extremely helpful!"

"I'm glad that I could be of help," said Florence. "So now for the question I've been afraid to ask." It was Diane she turned to this time. "You have a ghost here, clearly. Please tell me that it isn't Paige."

Diane just looked back at her, as if unsure of what to say.

"Or tell me that it isn't about what happened with George, at least?" Florence asked with a strangely desperate intensity.

"Oh, I think it might be," said Simone. "After everything you've told us, I think it very likely is."

☙

THE STORM HAS GROWN TRULY *frightening—clouds so low and dark that it seems more like night than morning now. I hear the monstrous waves roaring toward me long before they come crashing down, tossing my small launch from side to side, up into the air, down into a yawning trough. The boat feels like an angry, bucking horse beneath me as I keep cranking the engine's throttle in a pointless effort to outrun the sea—and my own terrible distress.*

What fills me isn't fear, but grief. Unbearable loss. And shame. I've lost her in the storm. Just...left her... My cowardice has betrayed us both, and nothing matters now but finding her again. But where, in all this chaos. What if she's drowned? What if she's gone forever, because I was too frightened to reach out and pull her back aboard when I could have? How will I ever...

My misery is interrupted by the roaring of another engine as a larger boat appears. Or...not a boat—a car. A giant, rusting truck. Driven up and down across the cresting waves by...a dark-furred lion who pulls up beside my little rolling boat. The lion leans down to me with a friendly grin full of sharp teeth. "Need a ride, friend?"

"Can you help me find her?" I cry out against the storm's roar. "I left her in the water, and I can't find her now!"

"Hop in then!" says the lion, reaching down to pull me up into the truck's back seat. "She's on the fishing boat, you fool! Come, I'll get you there."

As I climb up to sit beside the lion, he turns and drives us toward the fishing boat I work on, where she's been all along. I remember with a surge of joy! She's been waiting on the fishing boat. For me.

We drive and drive across the frothing sea, right out of the storm and back into a lovely morning. Ahead of us is a low green island, and the harbor where my boat is docked.

We drive across the water, straight up onto the narrow gravel beach, and up the cliff face without pausing, then onto a two-lane road across the field above it. But...where is the fishing boat? We aren't driving toward the harbor.

"Oh, we'll get there," says the lion, his smile of reassurance full of pointy teeth. "Don't you worry."

I nod, feeling apprehensive as he drives and drives, and finally turns off on a narrow little road into the woods—barely more than a deer trail—and still we drive into the forest. My apprehension grows, but I am in the lion's debt.

We halt at last before a small lake surrounded by tall grass and shrubs... which rustle strangely, as if there are creatures crawling furtively around each time I look away. At the center of the pond there is an island, on which a cabin barely larger than an outhouse sits. Smoke curls from between the shingles of its mossy, half-rotten roof and through the cracks in its badly weathered, lichen-encrusted siding—as if the whole interior is smoldering, waiting to burst into flame if someone should be fool enough to open up its door. "Can you take me to the fishing boat?" I ask.

The lion turns and offers me another toothy smile. "This will only take a moment." He leaps from the truck to land on all four legs, and strides with sinuous strength toward the pond and then across the water as his car had driven on the sea. Whatever's in the grass resumes its rustling. At the island's shore, the lion stands up like a man, walks up to the cabin, and pulls open its lopsided door. There is no burst of fire, to my relief, or even glow of embers from inside—only darkness. The lion steps inside and shuts the door, leaving me to sit, and listen to the restless grass.

And then the little cabin's door creaks open. But I see no one inside.

"Take me to the fishing boat!" I cry. "Please," I add, for fear that I've antagonized him. We're too far from the harbor now. I can't reach the fishing boat without the lion's help. "I need to see her."

"She's here!" the lion's voice calls, pleasantly, from beyond the cabin's darkened door.

"No…" I say, bewildered. "She's on the fishing boat. You said so."

"She's here now, and she wants to speak with you. Come see for yourself."

I can't imagine why she'd be in there, but…I'd forgotten she was on the fishing boat until the lion reminded me. The lion knows things I don't know. Maybe he knows this as well.

I climb down from the lion's truck and walk to the pond, which is no longer full of water, but of grain—and sugar crystals that must just have made the rippled grain sparkle in my eyes. I walk across it just as the lion had, though my footing seems less sure than his had been; my feet sink into the shifting mass of grain and sugar which I fear might be turning into water after all. But I am closer to the island than the shore now, and too afraid to stop. If I don't reach the cabin, will she leave again?

When I look up, the lion is standing there, giving me a toothy smile and pulling the door wider as he gestures me inside ahead of him.

For a moment, there is only dark around me. Then the glow of embers after all, growing brighter, and the whole inside is burning—just as I had feared! She is nowhere to be seen, and I know the lion had deceived me, but too late. The lion roars and leaps to knock me back into a giant well of nothing where the ground should be. Mouth open, wordlessly, I plummet, turning in the air and blind, knowing that the fall will end at any second—but the pain will never stop.

I woke, gasping, and twisted in my covers, scrambling to catch hold of—anything. Beside me, James grumbled and shifted on…the bed… My bed. In my room.

I lay there as my breathing slowed, still feeling more grief than fear. I would never see Paige again; never get to tell her that I hadn't meant to leave her in the storm like that—just run away and— But…no. I hadn't, had I?

Just a dream. Let it go, I told myself. *You don't have to work that out. No lions. No burning cabins.* It was just… Morning! Oh my goodness, what time is it?

I turned to look at my bedside clock, and sat up in alarm. It was after breakfast time! I never slept this late! Why hadn't Jen come and got me up?

I struggled out of bed, earning an irritated look from James, who curled back into some more comfortable position and closed his eyes again. Then I stumbled over to where I'd left my clothes piled on a chair, feeling like crap, and not just because I'd left Jen to manage serving breakfast all alone.

After telling us her stories about Paige and everything else, Florence had handed her clock and its cargo over to Diane, who'd suggested we call it a night and start combing through Paige's stash of clippings and letters after breakfast today. Diane and Simone felt sure now that Paige's unfinished business had something to do with what had happened between her and George. But we still had no idea exactly what part of that had kept her here, or what, if anything, we could do to help her resolve it—though we hoped there might be something in the clock's contents that would shed light on that question.

And I sure hoped there was, because not five minutes after I'd laid down and turned off my light last night, the thumps and footsteps had begun. Even James had gotten agitated, sticking his head up and looking around, or leaping off the bed to go sniff at corners, peer under furniture, or pace back and forth along the windowsill, staring through the glass as if something might be out there trying to get in. I hadn't gotten to sleep until almost one o'clock, and then there'd been the dreams, only one of which I still remembered much of now.

We're trying, Paige, I thought as I pulled the last of my clothes on. *Cut us some slack, okay?*

As I left my room to head downstairs, I saw that all the other bedroom doors were closed. The house seemed almost unusually quiet now, but less in a peaceful way than like the quiet of a crouching beast waiting to pounce. Or maybe that was just echoes of last night still coloring my thoughts. Like Diane had said, it was hard to tell now where my feelings ended and Paige's ghostly distress began.

To my chagrin, there was no one in the kitchen, though *someone's* breakfast had already been cleaned up. Jen had filled Sam and Harry's bowls, but the cats themselves were nowhere to be seen either, and their food looked untouched. I found Jen's note on the kitchen table. *Florence and I had breakfast—together—and no food service monitors popped up to arrest me. She says the rest of you were up late, so I've left a continental spread out in the dining room for everyone—including you. Enjoy. (Really. They won't come for us on a first offense.) I've gone shopping to fill things out for our extra guest, and have some other errands after that. Should be back by 1:00. – Jen*

I took a peek into the dining room, but saw no sign of Florence there. Were all three aunties out on the grounds somewhere, already working on the clock stuff? Or were Diane and Simone still asleep? Considering the night *I'd* had, I thought Simone must be a wreck this morning. And I guessed Diane would not have slept much better, sharing that double bed with her.

I poured myself a cup of coffee, doctored it heavily with cream, and drank it down before going out to do the milking. Nick and Nora were well weaned by now, of course, and nearly fully grown. But if I didn't keep milking Clara, she'd dry up. We were all too addicted to Jen's fresh chèvre to let that happen.

I saw no aunties out on the grounds anywhere.

Back in the house, I found a perfect little buffet set up in the dining room, on the side table under the windows: a basket of Jen's delicious zucchini-pecan muffins and various breads with lots of tasty things to spread on them, plus a big plate of mixed fruit, a bowl of hard-boiled eggs, and another bowl of plain Greek yogurt with several appetizing add-ons to sprinkle over it, along with a selection of juices. Everything was iced and covered, of course, in case the food police should show up. I glanced around before I touched anything, but still seemed to be alone.

So I put a plate together for myself, poured a little glass of grapefruit juice, and sat down to eat, thinking about what a lucky thing it was that Jen had gone out this morning. She had a shift at the Barnacle tonight, but I'd been planning to take the aunties out "sightseeing" after breakfast so that we could look through the contents of that clock and continue strategizing or whatever else ghost-whisperers did, without Jen around to catch us at it. Now we'd have some time right here at the house for a while. This would be better, I assumed, since having our quarry nearby might be helpful—at least, when no one was trying to sleep.

I'd just taken my first bite of Jen's scrumptious muffin when Florence swept in through the second parlor pocket doors looking, as always, like a fashion plate.

She gave me a charming smile. "Good morning, sleepyhead."

"You look like you slept well," I told her, trying not to sound resentful.

"I did! That mattress is fabulous." She took another look at me. "You didn't?"

"No," I said, dabbing my napkin at the corners of my mouth to make sure I hadn't left any crumbs there. "Our friend was unusually restless last night. You really didn't notice?"

She shook her head, making her satiny ponytail bob prettily. "I'm not sensitive to that kind of thing. You are?"

"Apparently. Not like Simone, I mean. But… Or maybe, since it's Paige, I'm just getting special attention or something."

"Well, I'm so sorry to hear that," she said, seeming to mean it as she sat down across from me. I must have been getting used to her air of perfection now, because her presence didn't make me nearly as self-conscious and desperate to please as it had once. "Maybe we can start figuring out how to do something about all this today."

"I hope so. Jen's gone out to do some errands, and left a note saying she'll be back at one o'clock. So it looks like we can just get started here after all."

"I know," said Florence. "I asked her if she'd get me a few things while she was in town, to buy us some additional time."

Well, hadn't that been clever.

"I'm not going to torture you by describing what she made for me," Florence went on, glancing at my little dish of fruit and yogurt, "but I have to say again what a wonder that girl is in the kitchen. If you do well here—and I'm quite sure you will—she'll be one important reason why."

"Oh, she'll be the whole reason why. As far as I'm concerned, it's her inn, really. She's the one with all the experience here. I'm just supplying her with the resources to do it."

Florence studied me with a look of…was that approval? The giddy girl I'd been when we'd first met would have passed out from sheer glee. "Supplying the resources is not a trivial or ignoble contribution," she said. "Paige would be quite proud of what you're doing here. And especially of why you're doing it."

What a nice thing to say, I thought, feeling a little surprised. This woman was such a mystery. So entitled and sure of herself one minute, seemingly impervious to any of the struggles most mortals have to cope with; then so…well, kind, appreciative, even vulnerable the next—like the woman who had come close to crying last night as she'd told us Paige and George's story. Fabulous Florence had seemed almost as excited about our inn as Jen and I were, right from the start.

And then, a bunch of pieces all clicked into focus for me. Her interest in the inn, her unexpected knowledge of our soft opening and the website when I'd called her—out of the blue. *Did Lisa give you my number?* And now she was "quite sure" of our success? "You asked whether Lisa had given me your number when I called you," I said. "Have you two been in touch much since last summer?"

She gave me a small, secret smile. "Once or twice, perhaps."

"Are you Lisa's knowledgeable friend?"

Her smile got a little wider, but she shook her head. "I'm not sure what you're talking about. But I may have introduced Lisa to one or two old friends of mine around the neighborhood up here. Perhaps the person you're asking about was one of them?"

Wow. Was Florence behind why our permits had flown through with such speed? And…had I just gotten Lisa into trouble? "If they are," I rushed to add, "I have no idea who they'd be. Lisa's been entirely discreet. But a few things have gone…inexplicably well for us. And, well, if your friends had anything to do with that, I'd just like to say that we appreciate it very much."

"I'll let them know," she said. "And you'll forget we ever had this chat, won't you?"

"What chat?"

She smiled more openly this time. "You really are so much like Paige sometimes. The way she used to be, at least."

And, since we were suddenly all up close and personal… "Last night, when you brought the clock out, you seemed…upset? That Paige had put those things inside it?" Her smile hardly changed, yet it seemed more strained now. "Is there some connection there I'm missing?"

Before she could answer—or refuse to—we heard the sound of footsteps and the tap of Simone's cane coming through the parlors, and a moment later, the two women appeared, looking the way I felt, or worse.

"So…rough night?" Florence asked them, sounding just gun-shy enough about the question to make it seem at least a little less obnoxious than it might have otherwise.

Diane turned to look at Florence in all her usual perfection, and actually scowled. "Rougher than yours, by the look of it. Deaf and blind as a doornail must be very nice just now."

"How did you expect us to have slept in a house raging with grief and distress?" Simone asked, not even looking at Florence as she made her slow and steady way toward the buffet. "Did you really feel none of it—sleeping right there in her room?"

To my surprise, Florence just looked abashed. "I'm very sorry. I didn't mean to…"

But Diane just waved her apology aside as she followed Simone, and asked me, "How did you sleep, Cam?"

"Maybe not as poorly as you two did. But along with all the rest of it, I had some pretty awful nightmares."

All three aunties turned to look at me at once, as if I'd just coughed up a goldfish.

"Well, may we hear about those, if you wouldn't mind?" Diane asked, seeming to forget about the breakfast lineup behind her as she took the nearest chair at her end of the table. Simone threw half a dozen things hastily onto her plate, and sat as well.

"There's really only one I still remember."

"One is more than none," Diane said.

So I told them in as much detail as I could about the dream I'd woken from this morning. And as I did, Diane's face went slack, seeming to grow even more ashen than it had been when they walked in. By the time I finished, Simone's mouth was hanging open again too.

"But…that makes no sense…" Simone murmured. "I see nothing there that sounds much like Paige."

"No…it doesn't," Diane said, sounding almost as lost in thought as Simone usually did when she got distracted by the otherworld.

"In fact, all that about the fishing boat sounds more like—"

"Oh, Simone!" Diane groaned, dropping her head into her hands. "We've had this completely wrong! The entire time!" She looked up at me, and then around the table. "Last night, while all of that disturbance made it impossible for us to sleep anyway, Simone and I went through the things from inside Florence's clock, and Cam, your dream…it's full of…" She looked down and shook her head again in either disbelief or dismay. "This isn't Paige. I think it's *George's* ghost we're dealing with, and has been all along."

There was just time for my mouth and Florence's to fall open too before we heard the wailing screech of cats from the front of the house, followed by a loud thump and the sound of shattering glass. We all got up and rushed out through the parlors to see what had happened now—Florence and me in the lead, then Diane, and even further back, Simone. What we found were a very agitated Sam and Harry, switching tails and still yowling at us from the stairwell's midway landing, and, on the foyer floor to one side of the stairwell, the photo of Paige and George, with its new frame and glass completely shattered.

"Well," Diane said as Simone finally joined us, "I'd call this confirmation."

As she said it, the walls suddenly roared softly as the house's forced-air heating came on. Yes, it was October, and the weather was much cooler now.

But still.

❦

As we swept up the mess Sam and Harry had made, Diane described the useful bits of information she and Simone had found last night in the contents of Florence's clock.

The newspaper clippings contained the exact date and even approximate time of George's disappearance, along with some quotes from witnesses who'd been questioned by investigators. Apparently, "discussing an active investigation" hadn't been as big a concern back then. Several people who'd been at a harbor restaurant the morning George had tied up his boat there had overheard him asking after a local fisherman he was hoping to get work with. But the fisherman—a friend of George's—had never seen or heard from him that day. Some fellow named Leon Ackerman had given a hitchhiker calling himself George a ride to the Lopez ferry landing later. Those two items, combined with my description of the dream, were what had suddenly rearranged Diane's whole understanding of the situation.

First, she said, my dream had me trying to reach a fishing boat because the woman I'd abandoned would be aboard it. Diane had already seen a pattern in the mentions of George's inquiries about his fisherman friend. "If he felt his job performance was what had come between himself and Paige," she said, "he might have gone to see his friend on Lopez hoping to get a new, less confrontational job. Then he could have gone home to Paige that very night and told her he was done being a game warden at all: problem solved."

Diane's second moment of revelation had come from hearing about the lion who'd given me a ride out of the storm and into my doom. Lion and Leon had just seemed too close for coincidence to her, especially when both of them had offered rides.

"If you'd already seen those articles," she told me, "I'd have assumed your dream was just making use of what you'd read. But you hadn't. So where could that material have come from but George? It may have been smarter than any of us realized to have our meeting in a room where so much of him resides now. That has to have been what caused all that ruckus last night and inspired his messages to you, Cam."

"Okay," I said, "but why not send that dream to Simone, who's half there in…wherever he lives now, anyway?"

"Familiarity, most likely," said Simone. "These poor dears are more like clouds of blowing leaves than solid minds and bodies. Their existence is just a long, disjointed dream that comes and goes. We're as much ghosts in their flickering lives as they are to us. But you've been coming here enough for years now, dear, that he may have had time to become aware of and remember you as he can't have done with me yet. He might even have come to associate you with Paige, and trust you more because of that."

"Which is why he had her cats spying on me?" I asked. "Out of trust?"

"Or to try understanding what you were, and how to reach out to you," she said. "In fact, that's also likely to be why Paige's cats are so much more responsive to him than your James seems to be. Sam and Harry have been fixtures in George's long, confused dream for several years by now. But George's ghost may hardly even have noticed the presence of some new cat yet—or my presence either."

I'd been stalked by his ghost because he thought we knew each other better? (And why was my life always so *strange*?)

When we'd finished in the foyer, the four of us went back to the dining room.

"So, how long will Jen be gone again?" Diane asked me.

"Her note says one o'clock. But I wouldn't bet on that. Jen's a very efficient task manager. Noon might be a safer guess?"

"And it's almost eleven now," said Florence. "I'm sure I could come up with some way to lure her out of the house again, if you need me to."

"I'm sure you could," Diane said, grumpily. Then she looked contrite. "I'm sorry, Florence. I'm being a dreadful pill. I don't do well without sleep. But we owe you a considerable debt of gratitude. If you hadn't brought us what was in that clock, I shudder to think of how much more time and energy we might have wasted rowing in the wrong direction."

"Yes," said Simone. "The ghost seemed so much more present in Paige's most personal spaces, and so distressed that night about what was happening to its home—this house—that I didn't see who it could be but her. But, of course, George is simply focused on those places because that's where he'd grown used to finding her." She shook her head, sadly. "He must have been here all that time. This would be the only home he'd think of now."

"But Paige never said a word about a ghost here," I pointed out. "I can't believe she just wouldn't mention a thing like that to me, or to any of us, all that time. So if he's been here, why did no one notice until now?"

"I've been asking myself that same question," said Diane. "But perhaps it's not the right one. During our conversation last night, I mentioned how these presences are most likely to intrude on living people when there's something they need them to do, or stop doing. George may not have had any reason to bother Paige or anyone else here until her death suddenly threw his environment into chaos."

"That's what was conveyed to me in the parlor that night," Simone said. "Sound and chaos. What's happening to my home?" She looked apologetically at me. "Maybe when you and your friend came here and started carting Paige's things away and changing everything, George was finally given reason to complain."

"I'm just so relieved it isn't Paige," said Florence. "I don't know how to tell you."

That went triple for me, of course. It had taken a few minutes for the significance of our discovery to sink in, but then I'd suddenly felt almost light enough to fly—despite last night's awful sleep. Paige wasn't stuck here! She hadn't been spying on me through her cats, or wanting me out of her house. She was off traveling in the otherworld, just the way she'd wanted to.

But there was still someone trapped here, or some*thing* at least:

sweet, gentle, decent George Harper. The only man Paige had ever loved. So it didn't feel right to celebrate my relief about Paige yet. Not until we'd found a way to help him.

"Well, as important as this discovery is," said Diane, echoing my thoughts, "it still leaves us with the same question we had before: how can we free him from his half-existence in this house? We must try to find out what he thinks the problem is—or wants done about it." She looked over at Simone. "I know that you're exhausted, dear. But do you think you have the energy to try finding out?"

Simone heaved a sigh. "I can try. What would you like me to ask him?"

"Hmmm…" Diane looked thoughtful. "So many things it would be useful to know. Do we start with what's happening for him now, do you think? Or with what entrapped him here to start with?"

"He vanished, what, sixty or more years ago?" Simone asked her. "That's an eternity for the kind of creature he is now. After so much time, his bundle of leaves may be very scattered indeed. He may not even remember what got him stuck here. Probably best to start, anyway, with questions about recent concerns."

Diane nodded. "All right, then let's try to tell him that we understand who he is now, that we're friends of Paige's who care about him, and…" she shrugged, "just ask him what we can do to help."

"Can you do that?" I asked, surprised. "I mean, didn't you tell me you can't just ask questions and get answers that way? That they don't even have words there?"

Simone smiled wearily. "I believe I said there were no words there *but mine*, which in themselves aren't likely to mean anything to him. But the *thoughts* attached to every word that any of us ever speaks—the feelings, images, connections and intentions—those *are* the language of the otherworld. If Diane is right, and he eavesdropped on us last night, it was our intent he perceived: not our words. Which is why it's so much harder to tell falsehoods there, by the way. So, yes dear, I'm quite able to *ask* as many questions as I like, and even be understood by those in the otherworld. The challenge will lie in understanding George's responses, if any come, and finding words of my own that translate any of it sufficiently for Diane to make use of."

"So, shall we try then?" Diane asked.

Simone nodded. "Here and now is always best."

"Would you like us to leave?" Florence asked.

"Why?" Simone asked, seeming surprised by the question.

"For your concentration? Or his?" Florence said. "Will all our thoughts or feelings clutter up your...conversation?"

Simone smiled again. "Not unless you're having them in the otherworld with me. Which, given how well slept you appear, seems rather unlikely."

Florence blushed! It would never have occurred to me she was able to.

"But, if you wish," Simone went on, "I can talk aloud to let you follow along."

"No need, thank you," Florence said.

I said nothing, just waited for instructions. Like, you know: holding hands, lighting candles, drawing pentagrams with salt... But everyone just went on sitting there. I was just about to ask what we were waiting for when I realized that Simone had closed her eyes. So...had it started?

Several minutes later, we were all still sitting there, waiting for... something to happen. Séances were sure a lot more entertaining in the movies.

"No, dear..." Simone murmured, finally. I leaned in, waiting for the rest, but...

More silence.

Florence had started looking sleepy, while Diane kept watching Simone like I'd seen James watch nearby birds. At least I'd known what James was concentrating on so hard.

Lots more silence. *So much silence.*

"No! I'm sorry, dear!" Simone's eyes flew open. "George; I didn't— She's just... *Damn it."* She looked crossly over at Diane. "Well... That went poorly, I'm afraid."

At least there'd been no yowling cats or breaking glass this time.

"What happened?" Diane asked.

Yes! Thank you! I thought. I'd been dying to ask, as had Florence, from the look on her face. But since Simone had sliced her down to size like that, I think we'd both been afraid to open our mouths again.

Simone rolled her eyes and leaned back in her chair, wincing slightly as if stiff from sitting so still for that long. "It took a while to find him, actually," she said at last. "I think that after that tantrum in the foyer brought us all running, he may have gone off and hidden somewhere."

"More confrontation than he'd bargained for?" asked Florence.

To my relief, and maybe even Florence's, Simone just responded with a crooked grin. "He does seem a rather timid sort. I kept calling his name, and apologizing for having been so slow to recognize him, and eventually, he crept out of hiding, and asked me who *I* was." She glanced at me and Florence, and added, "In his way." Then she looked back at Diane. "I told him just what we agreed to: that we were friends of Paige's who wanted to help him, and asked if there were something we could do.

"But all this got me was confusion—waves of it. And then the statement, 'Paige is gone,' as if maybe I didn't know that, or he thought I was trying to trick him into something by claiming to be her friend. So I tried asking if changes to the house upset him; if we'd taken something away from here that mattered to him; if he didn't like it when we went in Paige's room. But no matter what I asked, he just kept sending me the same response: *Paige is gone.* So then, I made the rather stupid mistake, it seems, of asking if he knew that Paige had died." She made a helpless gesture with her hands. "It seems he hadn't known. Or perhaps my question meant something to him I hadn't intended it to. Whatever the case…there was such alarm. He fled in full-fledged panic, and I'm not sure I'll be allowed to tease him out again now."

"Paige died outside," I said. "They found her lying peacefully underneath the maple tree out off the front porch. Was George so trapped inside the house, or something, that he couldn't see what happened in the yard, and just thought Paige had gone out and would come back eventually?"

Simone shook her head. "Again, dear, the otherworld doesn't work like ours does. There's little there that you would recognize as space or time. It's like a dream: you know you're on a train until the instant you're in someone's house. You aren't really aware of anything except what's happening in the moment. If something dreadful happened to George all the way over on Lopez Island that day, that didn't keep him from being here. He may still be in both places now—and other places too. He may think he's been here forever, or that he's just arrived this moment—again every day, or every moment. If he wants to be out in the yard, he can be. If he was that day, he may not remember now. In the otherworld, everywhere is here, and here is everywhere. Every time is now, and now is every time—or not. It's…up to us, perhaps? I don't really know more than the tiny bits I've experienced from time to time. I'm still mostly here, in this little aquarium with Diane and all of you."

Diane sighed, looking down as if lost in thought. "Well, if we've chased him off, then maybe we can find out something more about what really happened back on Lopez the day he vanished."

"I might be able to learn quite a lot," Simone said, "if I could be where the doom implied at the end of Cam's dream actually happened. But how can we even find out where that might have been after so much time?"

"Property records," said Florence.

All of us turned to look at her.

"For all we know, Leon Ackerman may be dead by now. He probably is. But we know he lived on Lopez Island, and property records should tell us where. Possibly even where he moved to in the time since then, or even who his heirs were and where they live now, if they happen to be local still."

"Not a bad suggestion," Diane said.

"Well, where would we go looking for those?" I asked.

"At the county courthouse," said Florence. "I'll go to Friday Harbor and take care of that tomorrow."

"Good luck getting there and back on the inter-island ferry," I said. It was the first one they took out of service when there was a disruption—every other day, it seemed.

Florence smiled at me the way she did sometimes, like I was just the cutest thing. "I won't be needing ferries. I still have friends up here, remember?"

Well yes, of course she did. Hadn't we just discussed that fact this morning?

Jen got home just before one with three bags of groceries, which I helped her put away, and an armload of packages that she carried up to Florence. When she came down, I showed her what the cats had done *again* to that poor photo in the foyer, though nothing, obviously, about why they'd done it. I no longer blamed them, of course. But she sure did.

"Those awful creatures are going to end up at the shelter pretty soon," she growled, scowling at the somewhat mangled photo, and peering into the envelope to make sure the lock of hair had survived. "If things keep up this way, these ladies may never want to stay here again."

"Oh yes they will," I said, "as long as you're still cooking. Florence made that very clear to me again this morning. And it's not like they've been here every time this poor thing's gotten broken. For them, it's just a one-off."

She shook her head. "I suppose you're right. But it's clear that Simone and Diane aren't sleeping any better in the Dragonfly Room than they did in the Blue Heron Suite. Though Florence seems to be doing fine there. So it's probably not a problem with the beds."

"No," I said. "It's a problem with being old—as they've known for years by now."

"That may be their excuse," she said, "but what's up with your sleep all of a sudden?"

"Too much rich, delicious food too close to bedtime," I said, fending off a pang of guilt as I recalled my talk with Elle. But seriously, was telling Jen we were all dealing with a ghost going to set things right somehow? I could not imagine how.

"Okay, you get celery sandwiches and graham crackers tonight, then."

"Oh, come on. I haven't been complaining about it, have I? Though I am sorry about this morning. I'll start setting an alarm until my sleep patterns straighten themselves out again."

Just as soon as our ghost problem is taken care of, I added silently.

CHAPTER 14

Florence was gone before breakfast the next morning. She'd left a note for Jen and me saying that she'd be visiting an old friend on San Juan Island, and probably not back before dinner.

Was she flying again, I wondered, or just going on someone's yacht? What was it like to live that way? Were there costs as well as benefits? There must have been, at some point. But was she still paying them, or were they just buried in her past somewhere and forgotten now? I could not help wondering.

During a moment upstairs with Diane and Simone that afternoon, I asked them what Florence's particular ability actually was. Was it just the charisma, or something more? But they just glanced at each other, then said that wasn't for them to tell me—as if, charitably, I might not have understood that yet.

That evening, while Jen worked in the kitchen on tonight's salmon fillets in orange and honey sauce, I was sitting by the front parlor fire sharing a glass of wine with James (well, okay, the wine was only for me) when I saw a black car pull up outside. Before I had a chance to clear my lap so I could get up and investigate, the car was already driving away, and Florence swept into the house with an air of palpable excitement. She crooked her finger at me to follow as she passed through the foyer without slowing and headed up the stairs. I reached the upper landing in time to see her tap politely at the closed Dragonfly Room door, and joined her. The door was opened by Diane, who looked curiously at Florence, and invited us in.

As usual, Florence wasted no time getting to the point. "Leon Ackerman purchased a house four years before George disappeared, and subsequently left it to his daughter. Her name is Anna Levine, now divorced from her husband, Joseph Levine who, happily, did not manage to take the house from her during their settlement. Their brief liaison produced no children, so she lives there alone now. Here's the address." She handed Diane a slip of stiff paper with nothing on it but two lines of elegant handwriting. "Perhaps we should go pay her a visit in the morning?"

I expected Diane to be as flabbergasted at Florence's efficiency as I was, but she just nodded and said, "Well done. Thank you." As if she'd expected nothing less!

"How did you find all that out?" I asked Florence.

She gave me a pretty shrug. "People can be quite accommodating if approached correctly." She glanced almost imperceptibly in Diane's direction, as if to make sure she'd heard that, then added, "At dinner tonight, I'll make a small fuss about what fun I had in Friday Harbor today, and convince you two to go explore Lopez with me on the early boat tomorrow. So be prepared to play along, all right?" She turned to me without waiting for an answer. "And we will all be thrilled and grateful when you, my dear, offer to come along and be our local guide. I believe that should cover all our bases with Jen, and alert her to the holiday she'll enjoy tomorrow. Does that seem workable to everyone?"

"As long as you don't expect us to be as perky about it as you just were," Diane said.

"Well, obviously not," said Florence. "I'll want us all to be completely natural, of course. So you should probably surrender to the idea with your usual weary resignation."

Weirdly, that won a smile from Diane for the first time since she'd let us in.

"Do you have some local friend lined up to get us there?" I asked, pulling out my phone and finding the ferry website. "We don't need a vehicle reservation for the inter-island ferry, but our only options for Lopez on a weekday are six-forty-five in the morning, or twelve-forty in the afternoon. That won't leave us a lot of time before we have to catch the seven-thirty ferry home again—if it's still running when the time comes."

"Ah..." said Florence. "Unfortunately, we are going to need a car there, but none of my usual transportation options is equipped to bring that with us. And, before you even say the 'T' word, dear, allow me to observe that, given our real reasons for this adventure, we might want to travel unobserved at some point. As I may have mentioned, the so-called taxi drivers in these islands are a notoriously loquacious tribe. So, I fear that this time it must be the dreaded ferry."

"The twelve-forty sailing should be fine," said Simone. "We're going over for a brief chat with one young lady, aren't we? How long could that take?"

"It would depend on where that chat leads us next," Diane replied, as Florence nodded. "And, sadly, Florence is right about the taxi. If something terrible did happen to George that day, we may end up searching for a crime scene. But while last night was slightly better than the night before, I vote for the twelve-forty sailing too. If we need more time, we can just come back and tell Jen we had so much fun, we're going for another round the following day."

"That's settled then," said Florence. "Poor Jen will have to cook us breakfast after all."

Our little play at dinner went off without a hitch, and the next day, after a quick lunch of delicious sandwiches from the market at Orcas landing, the ferry arrived, fifteen minutes late but still in service…so far. After driving on, we left the car and went up to sit outside on an upper deck, where the temperature was brisk but tolerable, and the views were splendid as ever. As the ferry made a brief stop at Shaw Island, I went inside to buy us all bottled drinks from the vending machine. But as I was juggling them through a heavy breezeway door, I overheard an odd conversation between Diane and Florence, and paused just inside to listen.

"I was out of line, Diane. I know that, and I'm sorry. Can't we get over it?"

"Yes, you were," Diane said. "And I appreciate the apology. But I can't do what I'm here to do unless the results we get today are accurate, not just the ones you wanted somehow."

"Of course," Florence said dismissively. "I understand that, but I wish you'd said something earlier. A phone call would probably have been sufficient if I'd known."

"*I* still need to be there in person," Diane said, "as does Simone. And we may have need of what you do as well before the day is over, but just not there, okay?"

"Fine," Florence said, sounding impatient. "I promise to be good."

"I don't need you good. I need you off completely—at least where she's concerned."

"I get it, Diane. My goodness, you can be so tiresome."

Ha! "And there's the kettle calling the pot black."

Suddenly, there were people behind me wanting out as well. So I shouldered the door open and gave everyone their drinks, wondering what they'd been debating—and why they'd done it while I was gone. I knew they had their differences, and maybe they just didn't like airing them when I was there. But I was getting tired of always wondering what else was going on behind my back.

On Lopez, we drove off the ferry and up the steep hill from the island's little landing. A guy in a pickup truck heading the opposite direction waved at me. Did I know him? Caught off guard, I didn't think to wave back until after he'd passed.

Four other drivers waved at us as we headed to the address Florence had uncovered yesterday, following directions googled on my phone. "Did I leave my purse on the roof of the car or something?" I asked. "What's with all the waving?"

"Friendly island, maybe," Florence observed. "Rural places are like that."

"We don't do that on Orcas."

Not far down Center Road on the north end of the island, we turned left on Cross Road, right on Port Stanley, and, a few hundred feet later, left again onto a gravel driveway. That went for almost a quarter mile before ending at a low, weathered, ranch-style house painted a faded red brick color with dark green trim. A struggling garden of leggy calendula and spindly vegetables grew off to one side, nearly done for the season. There was no visible address, but my app said we'd arrived.

For a moment, we just sat looking at the battered old house.

"I'm not getting *friendly* or even *reasonable* feelings here," said Florence. "Are any of you?"

"No." Diane sighed. "But we should try, at least. People often reveal more than they intend to, even when they're turning you away."

"Let's just smile, and stick to the plan," Simone said. "We're working on a book for the historical museum, and her father was quoted in the papers about it. It makes perfect sense we'd want to talk with her."

We'd come up with this story while waiting for the ferry and, after dusting off my inner actor-and-playwright self, I'd spent some time mentally rehearsing my role on the way here. It had all seemed quite clever then.

"You two are needed up there, obviously," Florence said to Simone and Diane. "And Cam is our lead. But I don't think the person living in this house is going to like me much. Maybe I should just wait in the car."

"You may have a point," Diane said.

"Could you roll a window down before you go, dear?" Florence asked me.

When I'd done so, the three of us got out and headed for the porch. There was no doorbell, so Diane knocked softly. When nothing happened, she knocked again, slightly harder. We were about to admit defeat and leave when I heard approaching steps and the door was opened by a woman, maybe not quite sixty, with dark wiry hair gone half gray. She had a strong jaw, deeply seamed skin that had seen too many years of too much sun, a little too much makeup around her eyes, and the hardened look of chronic disappointment. She gazed at the three of us, unsmiling. "If you're here to sell me some religion, it's a waste of time. Please go."

"Oh. No," I said. "We're here looking for Anna Levine. Would that be you?"

"I guess it would be," she said, suspiciously. "What's this about?"

"Well, my name is Shelly Pierce," I said. "I'm a writer from Orcas Island, and I'm working with the historical museum there on a collection of personal histories from around San Juan County. The history I'm working on right now is of Paige Berry, a woman of some prominence on Orcas who passed away recently. Have you heard of her, by any chance?"

The woman tilted her head and looked at me, as if deciding whether I was sneaking up on something else, or just plain crazy. "Can't say I have. So, who are these two? Your fan club?"

I responded with a little laugh, as if that had been funny. "No. These are just friends of Paige's who might know better than I can how to follow up on anything you care to tell us."

"About what?" the woman said, clearly growing more impatient. "I just told you, I've never even heard of her."

"Oh. Yes, I'm sorry. An important passage in Ms. Berry's life involves the sudden disappearance of a man she was very close to named George

Harper, around sixty years ago. And, as it turns out, your father, Leon Ackerman, was quoted in several newspaper articles at the time about having talked with Mr. Harper that day as he gave him a ride to the ferry landing. We're just hoping you might be able to tell us something more about those conversations? Did your father ever mention them to you?"

She just stared at us, then shook her head. "I have no idea what you're talking about. My father never mentioned anything like that to me, and frankly, I have no idea who you are—except strangers invading my privacy. So, as I said before, please leave, and don't bother me again." With that, she shut the door, softly but firmly, in our faces.

We looked at each other. Then Diane shrugged, and we went back to the car.

"Well, that was rather brief," said Florence as we climbed back into our seats.

"But not a *total* waste of time, I think," Diane said, buckling herself in.

"It wasn't?" It had seemed like one to me.

"She certainly did know what we were talking about," said Diane. "Her body language betrayed that much in half a dozen ways."

"Yes," Simone agreed. "Her presence in the otherworld is almost nonexistent. But what there was got noticeably darker and more turbulent the minute you said George Harper's name. She's heard it before today, and not in any happy context."

"So, now we know there's something left for us to learn here, if we can figure out how," said Diane. "I'm afraid it won't be from her, though. The last thing we need is to be arrested for trespass."

"But you were very convincing, Cam!" said Simone. "I was impressed. What a lot of clever details you came up with."

"Not clever enough, obviously." I started Tigress up, put her in gear, and turned around.

"So what's our next move?" asked Florence.

"I'm not sure," Diane said. "I need some time to think. Maybe we should just go do some tourist things somewhere, if there are any here to do, so that we'll have something to tell Jen about tonight—speaking of convincing performances."

But a thousand feet back down the gravel drive, I pulled off to the side and parked.

"What's happening?" asked Florence.

"I'd like to give this one more try before we give up," I said, unbuckling my seatbelt and opening the door.

"What are you going to do?" asked Diane.

"Think about it," I said with a pointed smile.

"Oh!"

"Oh! Yes, of course!" said Simone.

"Oh, what?" asked Florence. "Is anybody going to fill me in here?"

I was delighted to have caught Florence Golding off guard. And the other two seemed fine with letting her wonder too. I gave Diane a wink as I shut my door again, and started walking back down the curving driveway toward Anna's house.

As soon as both the car and the house were out of sight, I chameleoned. The transition was still not all that comfortable, but it sure was nice to go right on moving in this state now that I wasn't paralyzed by my own fear anymore. I had no clear idea what I meant to find when I got back to Anna's house. But if Diane and Simone had been that sure Anna was lying, I thought it was worth a try to see if I could find some clue to what she'd been lying about.

The first thing I did when I reached her house was tiptoe around and look in the windows to see if I could find out where she was. I might be invisible, but I'd still have to open a door or window to get inside, and I didn't want to try it right where she was standing. Nor did I want to stumble into her by surprise.

There was no one in the living room, or in a dingy bedroom just behind that. I crept around the back corner of the house, and looked through a small window into what turned out to be her kitchen; and there she was—pacing around talking to someone on her phone! To whom, I wondered, and about what? I put my invisible ear against the glass and, thanks partly to Anna's clear agitation, had little trouble hearing every word.

"…know who they were, or why the hell now after all these years, but they sure seemed to know something, Rheena. … Yes, I know his head is all but empty, but you still better call Fair Haven and tell them Zeph isn't allowed any visitors you haven't approved. All either of us needs is for him to blurt out something stupid when… I don't know, say it's 'cause you're scared he might get Covid. What does it matter? If you tell them he's not to be visited, they have to do what you say. You're paying the bills there."

Oh my god! Bonanza! *I* was going to be the hero of our little group, for once!

Zeph. At Fair Haven, I thought, pulling away from the window and turning to hurry back to the car. *Zeph. At Fair Haven.*

Back at the car, I pulled the door open and jumped back inside. "Zeph at Fair Haven!" I said. "He knows something."

Florence just stared at me, and…was her mouth hanging open? Just a little, maybe? This was so much fun.

"Who is Zeph?" Diane asked. "And where is Fair Haven?"

"I have no idea," I said. "But I'm betting Fair Haven is a rest home. The problem is that, by the time we find it, someone named Rheena will probably already have called and told them Zeph can't have any visitors that she hasn't personally approved."

Florence was already working madly on her phone. "Yes. It's a nursing home right here on Lopez—and not a very nice one, by the look of it." She looked back up at me. "How did you do that?"

Diane was as straight-faced as ever, but I could see Simone struggling not to smile.

"People can be so accommodating if approached correctly," I said.

"Yes, very funny," Florence said with a patient smile. "But seriously, what did you just do?"

"Oh," I said breezily. "You know how private these things are." It made me a little nervous to play with her this way, but I was enjoying it too much to stop.

Florence finally laughed. "Are you actually related to Paige? Is that it? Or are you just channeling her right now?" Well, that was high praise! "All right, you win. I'll tell you mine if you tell me yours."

I was lucky to have gotten away with baiting her this long. It was time to be a gracious winner, before she started telling all her powerful friends to make things *harder* for Jen and me, instead of easier. "I vanish." Florence's eyes widened, along with her smile. "What do you do?" I asked her. A deal was a deal.

Her smile became sad, then left altogether. "I charm the hell out of people." Her gaze moved from me to the road in front of us. "So I think they'll let *me* see Zeph, no matter what Rheena may have told them. Let's find this Fair Haven." She twisted around to look back at Diane. "If that's all right with you?"

Diane gave her a slight smile, and spread her hands. "It seems your moment has come, Florence. As I believe I said it might."

☙

As I drove us back toward Port Stanley Road, my mind was abuzz with the implications of what I'd just learned. She charmed people? As in… Had Jen and I been under some kind of spell all this time? I thought back on all those episodes of embarrassingly giddy behavior, and felt…ill, honestly. And she could obviously turn it up or down—even off altogether. Had she done it to me? Reached in with her gift, and made me adore her? Made me make a fool of myself? This wasn't *funny*. She'd been gaslighting me—hardcore.

And I'd known! I could remember knowing now, several times, at least. But even that knowledge had just…slipped away. Every time.

Oh my god.

No wonder Diane and Simone didn't like her. Hadn't even wanted to call her. What was I supposed to do with this now? I didn't even want her sitting next to me in the car.

But here we were. Stuck together, at least for today.

I made myself breathe…and think.

Diane and Simone seemed like good people. I could not believe they'd have let Florence anywhere near this—or near me either—if they thought she was evil. I thought back again, reevaluating all of my exchanges with her. They hadn't all been giddy. In fact, almost none of them had been since…well, that first night, in Florence's room.

Who are you performing for? … I'm just trying to make a good impression…

Did Florence really just not understand the difference between making a good impression and literally *making* people like her? Could she be that out of touch? I couldn't believe that. She was so smart, so fast and effective at everything she did. None of that said "clueless" to me. But, now that I knew to look for it, it did seem she'd turned off whatever she'd been doing to me before that night I'd overheard Diane scold her for it. Had she turned it off with Jen as well? If she hadn't, I'd have to make sure she did now. But how was I to go about that?

Florence had used her ability, it seemed, to make things go well for Jen and me, and for our inn. And she did seem to really like us. Her excitement about what we were doing with the house still seemed genuine to me as I looked back on it. I didn't want to tick her off now and make her sorry she'd been helping, and start hurting us instead. Jen so clearly loved the inn—cooking fabulous meals, inventing brilliant cocktails, entertaining people, making it all work. I couldn't risk taking that away from her, especially when she'd never even know why it had turned sour. Would Florence really be that cruel? I'd never thought so. But had I even been allowed to?

I thought about the way she'd teared up over Paige and George's painful story. The nice, generous things she'd said to me the other morning about the inn, and my support of Jen there. She could be caring too, and kind. She'd been that way to both of us, on numerous occasions...

There was too much to untangle here. And it all just seemed too dangerous to think about—right now at least. We needed her to get George free and out of Paige's house. She'd clearly been using this talent of hers to help us, and there was still so much to do. I had to set this down, right? Set it down until I understood what I should do.

Just play nice, I told myself. First things first.

It took less than twenty minutes to follow the directions on Florence's phone to Fair Haven Nursing Home. It was a small cluster of dingy stucco buildings just off Fisherman Bay Road, several miles south of Lopez Village. Florence had me drop her off at the main entrance, and told me to go park somewhere out of sight until she called for us to come pick her up again.

That call came less than half an hour later. As she got back into the car, she gave us the name of a road, and said she thought we might find what we'd been looking for at the end of it. "I've already got directions on my phone," she told me, unsmiling now, as we pulled away from the nursing home and back on to Fisherman Bay Road.

"What happened in there?" Diane asked.

"Zeph is pretty far gone with dementia," Florence said grimly. "But there's still enough of him there to make it clear he wasn't very nice even in his prime. I just started reminiscing about that little shed by the pond where we'd spent so much time back in the good old days. He's used to not remembering things now. But he was clearly flattered by my descriptions of the fun we'd had out there together, and pretended that he did remember everything—and so much more. It wasn't long before he started coughing up all kinds of information about the still he'd used to run back in 'them woods'—and what a ladies' man he'd been back then." She shook her head, looking disgusted. "Not a man we need to feel sorry for."

She does have a conscience, I thought. *How many different women are tangled up in there?*

When we found the road, it was a two-track grass and gravel lane with a large "Private—Keep Out" sign posted to one side. I pulled off the main road and parked beside it. "This looks like a driveway," I said. "And assuming Rheena is Zeph's daughter, I'm betting she won't be pleased if we show up at her house too after that phone call from Anna. She may even know we've barged in on Zeph already. So, what now?"

"I'd rather no one knew we'd even been here," Diane agreed. "Maybe we'd be better off sneaking in after dark."

"Aren't you glad we're not dependent on a taxi now?" Florence asked me flatly. "It would be kind of hard to sneak in here that way."

She hadn't smiled, I realized, since we'd told our secrets to each other back on Anna's driveway. *She knows we're not going to be girlfriends now,* I thought, betting she'd always known we wouldn't be, once I found out. *That's why she'd tried so hard not to tell me.* For a second, I almost felt sorry for her. But whose idea would that sympathy turn out to be? Was she using her gift to play me, even now? "We'll have a pretty narrow window to do that and still make the seven-thirty ferry," I told Diane. "How dark does it need to be?"

"Oh, where's your spirit of adventure?" Florence asked, still without looking at me. "Is getting back to Orcas really the most important thing right now? Spending a night on Lopez could be fun, if that's what it takes."

Oh yeah, I thought. *Just look at all the fun on everybody's faces now.*

⁂

"Lopez Farm Cottages has two cabins available," Florence said, looking up from her phone. "I'm booking them now."

Oh great, I thought. "I'd better call Jen then, before she gets too far into making dinner. Any thoughts on how I should explain this to her?"

"Just tell her we're having too much fun to come home," said Florence. "And how we'll regret missing even one of her delicious dinners, of course; because I'm quite sure we'll find nothing half as good here tonight. All the best places will be closed this time of year."

"Speaking of which," said Simone, "who besides me is feeling peckish?"

"There's an ice creamery here that's pretty famous—locally at least," I said. "Shall we go find it?"

"That sounds like a great place to start," Simone said cheerfully. "But do call Jen first, of course."

While I was making our excuses to Jen, and apologizing for the change of plans, Florence found the Lopez Island Creamery for us too. It was in Lopez Village, of course, and, to our relief, open even in October.

After our cones, we wandered around the village's various shops, spending lots of time in the fantastic bookstore there, and across the street in a pharmacy-general store almost as fabulous as Ray's. There was an open coffee shop with scrumptious pastry, which Simone sampled as eagerly as she had the ice cream. But it took only an hour or so to exhaust the small town's still-open attractions—as well as Simone, I was pretty sure. And it was still many hours till dark. "Any ideas what we should do next?" I asked as we admired the weird old farm implements on display outside the historical museum. "The restaurant at the harbor looks like our only option for dinner on a weeknight now. But they're not serving dinner for a while yet."

"The bookstore clerk was telling me about some amazing views at the bottom of the island," Simone said. "Can any of them be driven to? I'd love to see more of this coastline, but I'm a bit walked out for hiking at this point."

"Let me look," I said, bringing up a map of the island on my phone, and scrolling around. "There seem to be a couple options. Shall we go have a look?"

"That sounds lovely," said Simone. "But, I'd love to pop back into that little café before we go and get one more of those excellent cookies for the road—just to tide me over."

☙

AFTER NIGHTFALL, WE DROVE SLOWLY down the private road for quite a while before we saw a house set well back to our right, screened by trees. We would probably have missed it completely if not for the lights in several of its windows. Diane immediately suggested I avoid the attention of anyone inside by turning off my headlights and slowing to a crawl. Fortunately, there was enough moonlight to let me pick my way forward until the house was far enough behind us to make headlights seem safe again.

A minute later, we found our way blocked by a barricade of sawn-up logs and small boulders, clearly dragged there to prevent anyone from driving farther. I parked Tigress as far to one side of the road as possible, and we all got out, lit up our phones, and went to see what was beyond the roadblock.

Remnants of the gravel track continued for a hundred feet or so before dwindling to an overgrown footpath barely wide enough for us to walk single file. I led while Florence took up the rear, with Simone and Diane in between. As we crept forward, careful of our footing, between dimly lit tree trunks rising out of tangled, leafless bushes and deadfall, I tried not to think about *The Blair Witch Project*, a cult horror film I'd seen with friends when I was back in school, in which three teenagers careen around some forest in the darkness until they're all dead—of what, they never really tell you. "Be careful," I called back quietly. "It's getting marshy up here."

Simone soon gave up even trying to use her cane. "I can make do without it for a short while," she assured us. "I'll just take it slow, and be extra careful. No need to worry."

Not much later, the scrubby forest we'd been walking through fell away, and I raised my flashlight to see knee-high grass and reeds stretching ten or twenty feet in nearly all directions. Beyond that, there was only darkness. I told the others to wait while I made my increasingly squishy way forward until the high grass gave way to shallow open water. "It's a pond," I told the aunties. I raised my phone again, pointing it in all directions, but the light wasn't strong enough to travel far. I saw vague suggestions of some structure farther off to my right, and started carefully in that direction along the pond's mucky shoreline. Minutes later, the object I'd been heading for grew clearer in the glow of my phone's light, and I stopped to stare in disbelief. "This is it!" I called back to the others.

As they came swishing slowly toward me, I went to take a closer look. Yes: without a doubt, this was the little shack from my dream. It wasn't on an island in the middle of the pond. But the steeply peaked, mossy shingle roof with its bent pipe chimney was exactly right, as were its weathered planks of siding, and the funny copper handle on its door, now green and black with verdigris. "That is so completely the shed from my dream," I said, as the others arrived. "And I guess this must be the pond."

"Simone," said Diane. "Would you—"

"I'm already on my way, dear."

"Should we look inside the shed?" asked Florence, moving toward it.

I followed, nervously, unable to keep from imaging George's skeleton tumbling out as she opened the door. But when we got there and pulled it open, there was nothing inside but a few bits of pipe and metal on a packed earth floor. No still now. No sign of the gaping open well I had been pushed into in the dream. No skeleton, of course. Just an all-but-empty shed.

"He's here," Simone said in that dreamy, sing-song voice that meant she was focused on the rest of here that none of us could see. "But he's not…the same."

"Not the same, how?" Diane asked quietly, going to steady her with an arm around her back and a hand on one of her elbows.

"He's been…waiting…for so long," Simone said. "He…doesn't know…"

She fell silent.

"Doesn't know what?" Diane asked, almost tenderly.

"That he's…at the house," she quavered, swaying lightly. "Wants to know… But… Mustn't…scare him off. This time…" She might almost have been talking in her sleep now. This was way more creepy than that other séance in the dining room.

"Can you ask him what he has been here waiting for?" Diane asked softly.

"I did…" said Simone.

We waited, but that seemed all she had to say.

"Oh!" Simone lurched, and turned to look behind her, seeming suddenly wide awake. "Who just poked me?" she demanded.

We all looked at one another. "None of us," said Diane.

"Ouch!" Simone rocked on her feet as if someone had shoved her from behind. "The water! Help me get down to the water."

"Is that safe?" I asked. "It's mud above my ankles down there."

"Oof!" Simone lurched to keep her balance. "Will you stop!" she exclaimed irritably. "You've waited sixty years! Just give me a moment."

She looked at me. "You're young and strong, dear. Will you help me get down to the water?"

I stared at her and said nothing. I so did not want to be the one who let Simone drown in this pond.

"Stand behind me and put your arms around my waist," Simone said to me, handing her useless cane to Diane. "And, if I lose my balance, make sure to pull me over backwards, not face forward."

Nodding dumbly, I handed my phone to Diane, wrapped my arms around the bottom of Simone's rib cage, and then, as Diane and Florence kept the phone lights trained on us, we began to lurch in tiny steps together closer to the pond's edge.

"Be careful with her," Diane said, pointlessly.

"Is he pushing you?" I asked Simone as we made our slow way forward.

"Yes. This George is quite impatient."

"*This* George?" I asked. "There's more than one?"

"This George is the other one, just in a different place. Dying here and finding Paige all the way back there seems to have left him spread quite thin, and I guess the connection's grown quite tenuous after all those years."

Okay...never mind. "So, George did die here then?"

"Oh yes. He's made that quite clear. And he's desperate to make sure she knows it."

"Who?"

"Paige, of course," Simone said, a bit impatiently. "That's what he's been waiting for, I think, someone to tell Paige."

"Oh dear," Diane said behind us. "That's...not going to happen now."

Simone lurched again, but I managed not to let us fall. "If he doesn't have any physical power, how does he keep pushing you?" I asked, feeling irritable myself now.

"Oh, my dear; have we not been over this? My brain controls my body. So George—"

"—doesn't need to push you from outside," I finished for her, feeling dense. "I get it now. But can't you stop him?"

"Yes, of course. I could just pull my attention fully back out of the otherworld. But then how would we learn what he wants found down there in the water?"

"Okay, well, here we are," I said, ignoring the chilly rush of new water back into my shoes. Simone was not complaining, so I wasn't going to either. "Now what?"

"Hold on tightly, dear. I need to ask him that."

I felt her slump a little in my arms. "Are you okay?" I asked. But she didn't answer. "Simone?"

"Is she okay?" Diane asked anxiously behind us.

Before I could turn and snap something regrettable, Simone asked, "Can you…see that?"

"See what?" I asked. "All I see is water." And that, just barely.

"There…" She raised a languid arm, and pointed down at the water just in front of us.

"I don't…" I twisted around as best I could without losing hold of her. "Can one of you get closer? We need more light."

Florence shoved through the weeds with surprising speed, given her age—whatever that actually was—and shined her phone down on the water where Simone was pointing.

"I think I see it," I told Florence. "Something metal in the water there. But I can't get it and hold Simone up at the same time."

Florence made a small exasperated sound, and splashed softly past us with her phone. Happily, even she had worn sensible shoes for this outing. Wading out very delicately, she stopped ahead of us, playing the phone's light across the silty bottom until she saw it too. One more careful step took her close enough to bend down and pull it up. "It's…a ring. Oh, good heavens, it's *his* ring!" she said, barely above a whisper. "I remember this."

"No…" Simone said from somewhere far away again. "Not that… There…" Oddly, she pointed to the very spot from which Florence had just pulled the ring. "Can't…you see it?" Simone murmured. "Shining… Like…a firefly."

Florence hadn't stopped staring at the ring. But I looked down again, and still saw nothing.

Simone groaned in her almost-sleep. "Just…sit me…down."

"What?" I asked.

"Sit me…in the water. … There…" She raised her arm again, slowly, and pointed right back at the same empty spot. "Please… There…"

I heard Diane rustling closer now as, with very little help from Simone, I waddled us another step or two out into the pond. But I saw no way of sitting her down there without risk of just dropping her in. So I sat us both down, keeping my arms around her as I did. The water felt even colder on my butt than it had on my ankles, and it smelled half-composted, at least. I'd brought no extra clothes, of course. So this was going to be a very uncomfortable evening, not to mention hard on Tigress's upholstery.

Without any complaint, Simone reached into the water between our legs, and pulled up a tiny, utterly unremarkable, oblong pebble. She held it up for me to see, and murmured, "You…can't see it…shine?"

I rolled my eyes, and looked up at Florence, who had tucked the ring away. "Can you help me get her standing again, please?"

In the end, it took all three of us to get Simone back up and onto shore as she squawked sleepily about not losing that stupid pebble—which, at her insistence, we'd handed to Diane for safekeeping.

"Simone, what do you think that stone is?" I asked.

She looked over at me like a child who'd just been woken from sound sleep. "It's…" She drew a deep breath, her eyes seeming to focus again. "…his finger."

"*What?*" all three of us asked in unison.

"Oh my goodness! It was with the ring?" Diane asked Florence as she pulled it from the pocket she had shoved it into, and held it under the light from her phone.

"Yes," Florence said. "Why?"

"She could be right!" Diane said. "I think it's a bone. A finger bone, I would imagine."

"Everyone stay where you are, please!" came a deep male voice from the darkness behind us. All of us but Simone twisted around in alarm as a painfully brilliant beam of light burst from a large flashlight in the hand of a very large sheriff's deputy. "Now, turn around very slowly, and then, don't any of you move."

☙

IT WAS REALLY PRETTY FRIGHTENING, at first. I'd witnessed a couple murders, been kidnapped, shot, and haunted by a ghost; but I'd never been arrested before.

The officer took a few steps toward us, swishing through the high grass, and played his flashlight across our faces, clearly surprised, and a little confused, to find three elderly ladies and me. "Whose vehicle is parked on the road back there?"

"Mine," I said, already scrambling to think how we were going to explain, well, any of this.

"Want to tell me what you ladies are doing here?" he asked me.

I looked at Diane, who looked at Florence, who looked back at Diane and shrugged.

"Ma'am?" the deputy asked, still looking at me. "I asked you a question."

Apparently, being the driver made me the spokesperson for our gang as well. "We...took a wrong turn...and got lost?" I tried, knowing instantly that I hadn't made the greatest choice.

The deputy's face hardened visibly. "So, you turned onto a clearly marked private road after dark, and just kept driving until the road ended, then got out of your car, and hiked further into the woods until you reached a pond, in the dark, and then..." He glanced pointedly at my soaking clothes, and then at poor, sopping, bedraggled Simone. "You kept hiking right into the pond, apparently, because you were lost?"

Yup. I'd sure picked the wrong lie to try first.

"Before you try fixing that story," the deputy continued, "you should know that the complaint we received also said you slowed down and turned out your headlights as you drove past the house back there. Is that correct?"

I saw Diane wince slightly.

"Yes," I said.

"Seems to me you ladies have worked incredibly hard to *stay* lost," he said, humorlessly. "So, let's start again, shall we? What are you all doing here?"

"Seeking justice for a murdered man!" Simone said, as if that should have been obvious.

All of us turned to gape at her, including the deputy, though his mouth wasn't hanging open nearly as far as all of ours were.

"Come again, ma'am?"

"Look at us!" Simone said, indignantly. "Do we look like criminals to you? Three old ladies and a girl?"

Had she really just called me a *girl?*

"Let's back up here," said the deputy. "Who's been murdered?"

"A poor, good man who just came to Lopez Island looking for a job!"

she said.

"Simone, dear," Diane said quietly. "It's time to come back now. We need you here."

"I am quite back!" Simone said. "Do I not look back to you, Diane?"

"Is she...all right?" the deputy asked.

"She gets confused sometimes," Florence said smoothly.

"Oh, stop it, all of you," Simone growled. "Nothing we can possibly say here is going to make any more sense than the truth does. Lying about it is just making us all look like liars."

Well...she wasn't wrong. But how much of the truth did she plan to tell him, I wondered, and where did she think *that* was going to get us?

The deputy was nodding, though. "She doesn't sound confused to me." He looked from one of us to the next. "In fact, that's the most sensible thing I've heard anybody say here so far. So let's just go with the truth then, okay? Starting with this murdered man. Does he have a name?"

"Yes. George Harper," said Simone. "We think he came here looking for work as a fisherman."

"Okay," said the deputy. "And when was that?"

Simone turned to Diane. "Do you remember the date in those articles?"

"No," said Diane, looking either resigned or disgusted now, I couldn't tell which.

"Well then," Simone said to the officer, "it was sometime in the early nineteen-sixties, anyway."

The deputy blinked at her. "The early...he came here *sixty years* ago?"

Simone nodded.

"Sorry, ma'am, but I was asking when you think the man was murdered."

"Well, the same day, of course," she said.

The officer looked confused again. "You're saying he was *murdered* sixty years ago?"

"Yes. Precisely," Simone said, sounding relieved that he was finally catching on.

He looked around at the rest of us now, clearly unsure of who exactly was confused here. "So...who do you think he was killed by?" he asked Simone.

"A man named Leon Ackerman, I believe," Simone said, crisply.

"That's an assumption, dear," Diane murmured. "The still seems to have belonged to the man in the nursing home, so—"

"What still?" the deputy asked.

"That shed, there." Simone gestured at it.

The officer waved his light toward it briefly. "There's a still in there?"

"Well, not anymore," said Simone.

He looked back at her. "But there was," he said. "Sixty years ago?"

"Yes! There, now we're getting somewhere."

Diane just rolled her eyes and turned to the man. "We're not sure yet who actually killed him. That's…part of what we're trying to find out here."

"So, you're here trying to figure out who killed this man sixty years ago?" The deputy was starting to sound exasperated. "And this Leon Ackerman, where is he now?"

"Oh, he's dead too," Simone said. "For many years now."

The deputy shook his head, clearly out of patience. "So you ladies are out here in the middle of the night trying to solve some cold case from sixty years ago? What are you, some kind of amateur detective club or something?"

"Yes!" I said, leaping at the chance to keep Simone from digging us even deeper in here. "That's exactly what we are. We're a…historical interest group from Orcas Island, and the man Simone is talking about was very important to a close friend of ours who died recently. We found a bunch of newspaper articles in her things about George Harper's disappearance on Lopez sixty years ago, and have been doing a lot of research about it. And, well, that's what led us here." I shot a warning glance at Simone, hoping she'd get the message. Then I turned back to the deputy, and hung my head in only partly fake embarrassment. "I know this is private property, sir. And that we shouldn't have just snuck in here like this. We're very sorry."

"Oh pish!" said Simone. "No, we're not sorry! We're here to help a man who's waited sixty years for vindication! And if you think we're just some silly amateur detective club, young man, we've got his finger bone right here to prove it's true."

"What are you doing, Simone!" Diane exclaimed.

I sighed and shook my head in defeat.

Simone swiveled angrily toward Diane. "I've just been *immersed* in his *despair*, Diane! He's been here all this time waiting for someone to know he didn't just run out on her. I'm not here to get us out of trouble. I'm here to get him out of hell! Aren't you? What else have we been doing all this time? Show that man the bone. He's an officer of the law—which is just what we need to get this record set straight, finally, isn't it? Can't we do that much for George, at least?"

"You have a *bone?*" the deputy asked, looking at Diane now. "From this murder victim?"

"Well..." Diane glanced back and forth between him and Simone, then raised her hands in helpless frustration and looked back at Florence, who'd been strangely silent all this time. "Can't you do anything?"

"I...don't think so," Florence said.

Diane glared at her, then shook her head and reached into her pocket for Simone's pebble, which I doubted would prove anything at all to the deputy, except further evidence of our lunacy. "Here it is," Diane said, holding the pebble out in grim resignation.

The deputy looked at all of us again, very uncertainly. "Would you bring it to me, please?"

Diane waded through the grass and gave it to him.

"Thank you, ma'am. Now would you step back to where you were, please?"

Diane rejoined us as the deputy raised his flashlight to examine the object in his hand more closely. He juggled the flashlight around so that he could scratch lightly at the pebble with the nail of his right index finger, then glanced up at us before looking at the "bone" again.

"You can test it if you want," said Simone. "You'll see. It's his. And the rest of him is in that pond somewhere as well, I'm sure." She waved at the dark stretch of water behind us.

He looked up at her sharply. "What makes you think..." His eyes narrowed slightly, and he held up the bone. "Where did this come from?"

"Right back there." Simone pointed behind her at the pond again.

"You...just found a finger bone—if that's what this is—in that pond, tonight, in the dark?"

"That's right," Simone said.

The deputy looked back at me. "Is she, or any of the rest of you, currently under the influence of...any kind of medication?"

Have we been doing shrooms, you mean? "Not that I'm aware of."

He gazed at me for another moment, then drew a deep breath and looked away, clearly thinking hard. Finally, he looked back at us. "Ladies, I'm not sure what's going on here; but the longer we talk, the more…concerned I become, and I'm afraid I need to bring you down to the substation for some further questioning."

Florence gave a small *hmph* of laughter. I just looked down, wondering how I was going to explain this to Jen.

Or Kip.

"Now, to be honest," the deputy said, "there isn't really room to transport all of you in my vehicle, and I'd rather not call in backup for three old ladies and a girl." I was *not* a *girl!* But then, he *was* just quoting Simone. "You folks don't seem too dangerous, and all we've really got for sure yet is a misdemeanor trespass violation. So, if you'd all be so kind, what I'd like to do here is go back to the road together, and just escort your vehicle to the substation. Can I trust you all to do that without making any *more* trouble for yourselves—or me?"

He looked at me, the *girl*, for an answer. So I assured him we would be very well behaved, and we all started back through the marsh grass to the footpath and from there to Tigress, who was now hemmed in by his patrol car.

After texting me the substation's address, he told me once again to drive myself and the aunties there while he followed along.

He stayed very close behind us. And if any friendly Lopez drivers waved at us, I couldn't see them in the dark.

Once we all got there, he documented our IDs and contact information, wrote us up citations for trespass, and told us that he would have to keep our "finger bone" for now—though it seemed clear he thought it would just prove to be a deer or rodent bone, if even that. Then he questioned us for a while longer, separately and together, trying to get a more complete picture of what the hell we were actually about. Happily, his insistence on keeping the bone had seemed to mollify Simone, so we managed to get through those conversations without her telling him she was a medium, or that I could disappear. Finally, he informed us that we would need to stay on Lopez until his superiors returned in the morning, and *apologized* for not having anyplace there at the substation to lock up more than one person at a time. When we told him we already had reservations at Lopez Farm Cottages, he "offered" to escort us there as well.

And who doesn't dream of being introduced to the lovely and charming proprietress of a surprisingly elegant lodging facility late at night with a police escort, right? Wet and muddy to boot? When we arrived, the deputy verified that we did, in fact, have two cottages reserved, then told us to expect the arrival of another deputy, probably quite early in the morning, to "further process" tonight's events with us. "Sleep tight, ladies," he said pleasantly as he made his departure. "And no more trouble before morning, okay?"

What a charming *boy*, I thought as we watched him drive away.

CHAPTER 15

As the four of us started down the long, winding, and fortunately well-lit gravel path to our cottages, Diane turned to Simone and said, "All right, so what just happened there?"

"Which there do you mean?"

"Any of them!" Diane said. "At the pond; blathering to that deputy—what is going on?"

"All right..." Simone said wearily. "Where to start..." We all walked along in silence, waiting for Simone to continue. "So, perhaps we'd better start with what I learned at the pond," she said at last. "George was there, of course, at the place he died, as is so often the case. But, apart from that, it was all very strange."

Apart from that? I thought. Was she serious?

"To begin with," she went on, "he seems to have no idea that he's at Paige's house. And even stranger, George at the pond didn't even seem to have the same...I don't know, *agenda*, I guess, as George at the house does—which leaves me suspecting that if I sought George out again back at the house now, he might have no memory there of anything that passed between us tonight. If I'm right about that—"

"Okay, wait, stop a moment," Florence said, breaking her strange, evening-long silence for the first time in quite a while. "I'm confused. You're talking about George at the pond and George at the house as if they're two different people."

"Not exactly, but yes, in a way," said Simone.

Oh, well that makes it all much clearer, I thought. And if even Florence was confused, what hope did I have of understanding any of this?

"It confused me too, at first," Simone said. "But I'm starting to have a theory, so hear me out, please." When no one objected, she continued. "George at the pond remembers the day of his death very clearly, and the people who did this to him. And I do think you were right, Diane. It seems there were two of them, not just Leon. This George was chock-full of very vivid impressions about that day. And George at the pond also seemed very concerned about finding some way to let Paige know he hadn't just run off. But that seemed to be *all* that George at the pond knows. He showed no sign of knowing he's been back at the house for so long, or that any time has passed at all since the day of his own demise, much less that Paige has died now—which I'd think he ought to, since my clumsy decision to tell him of her death at the house the other day is what sent him fleeing from us."

"Well," I said, at risk of displaying my ignorance again, "you told me how confusing a ghost's existence is—that whole blowing leaves thing. Couldn't he just have forgotten what happened in the dining room a few days ago?"

"I doubt he'd forget something as traumatic as that clearly was for him," Simone said. "Not this quickly, at least; though it's certainly not impossible. But after engaging George at home several times now, trying to find out anything at all about what happened to him, or what unfinished business he might need help resolving, I've never once encountered a hint anywhere in him of all the things that George at the pond tonight was so obsessed with. I don't think George at home knows any more about what happened sixty years ago, or what Paige might have made of it, than George at the pond seems to know about what's happening at home right now."

"Well, that is very strange," said Diane. "Have you ever seen—"

"No I haven't," Simone jumped in. "A presence can normally be summoned anywhere, if it can be summoned at all, and still be whatever it's been anywhere else."

By this time, we'd arrived at a semi-circle of adorable little cottages all facing an open field and the woods beyond. I was so tired, and so damp still, that I could hardly wait to go inside, shed these clothes, and get cleaned up. But I also wanted very badly to understand where all this with Simone was going. I mean, both our quest to free George and the Berry Farm's future seemed at stake here

"So, what's your theory then, about this anomaly?" Diane asked, as we all stood in a cluster outside our quarters for the night.

"I fear this will sound just as strange as the rest," Simone warned her. "But I wonder if, in the moment of his death here on Lopez, George's need to reach out to Paige might have occurred so suddenly and severely that in his urgency to be with her too, he...tore himself somehow."

"So...he *is* two different people now?" asked Florence.

"No!" said Simone. "It's the same George Harper, here and there, but divided within himself somehow into George Harper then, and George Harper now. I'm not talking about a physical kind of tear, but a tear in...intentional space, maybe? And if I'm right, this could well be what's kept him trapped here all this time."

"How do you mean?" asked Diane.

"My impression so far is that George at home knows Paige is gone now, and just wants her back," said Simone, "while George at the pond has no idea she's gone, but needs to let her know—sixty years ago— that he didn't abandon her. George—meaning *all* of him, of course— would need to resolve *both* of those problems to move on, since half of George can't just move on without the rest. Yet neither moment of him even knows the other, or its need, exists; and worst of all, neither of those needs is even addressable anymore. Paige isn't just gone; she's gone for good. George at home can't get her back now, any more than George at the pond can let her know what really happened in the past anymore."

"*Oh god...*" Florence whispered. It was too dark to tell, but...was she crying?

"So then, if it's hopeless," I said, "why did you bother putting on that show for the deputy?"

"That was not a *show*," she said, as severely as she'd ever spoken to me. "The moment of George residing at that pond has waited practically forever for any hope that Paige might know the truth about his disappearance. If I'm right about any of what I just said, he may remain trapped there for even longer into the future. But I tried to give him hope tonight that his message had finally been delivered to someone who might get it all the way to Paige. He doesn't know she's died. It's still that day sixty years ago for him, and may always be. But if even one part of George Harper can have at least a bit more peace now, that seemed worth whatever little trouble it caused us. Or it did to me, anyway."

Didn't I feel like a heel now.

"I'm sorry I was so short with you," Diane said to Simone, apparently feeling the same.

"There was a lot going on. I understand that," Simone assured her. "And, Cam, dear, please don't misunderstand me. I don't mean to say our cause is hopeless now. My theory is still only that, and even if it turns out to be right, the fact that I can't envision a solution doesn't mean there isn't one. As you must understand by now, the otherworld is so vast and different from this one that I will never have even an inkling of what's really possible or not there."

"Well, whatever lies ahead of us now," said Diane, "bed must come first for me. I am completely spent. Simone and I will see you two when the authorities arrive tomorrow. Good night."

"Good night," I said.

Florence said nothing to anyone, just turned and started for our cottage door. I followed, bracing myself to spend the night sharing a bed with her.

***

THE INTERIOR OF OUR COTTAGE was lovely. Clean, uncluttered modern elegance. Minimal but perfectly arranged décor. The bathroom was even nicer than ours at the inn, and the kitchenette had everything we'd need to make ourselves a small, tasty meal in the morning, including two savory scones, yogurt cups and homemade granola, canned beverages, and coffee.

The only problem with the space was that Florence and I were both in it, and there was nowhere to hide from each other but the bathroom—which would become problematic sooner or later.

Florence had gone to sit on what was now clearly her side of the bed, facing the little table and chairs by the front window, and started pulling off her damp shoes and socks.

"So," I asked, "could you have charmed that deputy into letting us go?" I wasn't eager to touch the issue, but dancing around it all night seemed even worse somehow.

Florence paused, then straightened without looking at me. "Is that what you'd have liked me to do?" she asked quietly. "Sweep our little inconvenience aside by bending him to my will?" Which, I noticed, was not an answer to my question.

"Arrest is just a little inconvenience to you?" I asked, ignoring her question too. Fair is fair."

She responded with a little grunt of laughter. "That wasn't an arrest, dear. Were you fingerprinted or photographed when I wasn't looking? Were any of our belongings confiscated? After ticketing us for a minor trespassing violation, that officer *escorted* us to this chic little cluster of cottages to spend the night under our own reconnaissance. That, sweet summer child, is not the usual course of events in an arrest, in case you didn't know. This, however," she gestured at the pretty room around us, "is definitely about as minor as inconvenience gets; in my experience anyway."

Okay…five points to Florence, none to me. Served me right, I supposed. Although I *had* certainly seen the inside of a prison once or twice. Well…once, actually. For about an hour. On the visitors' side.

"There wasn't anything to worry about anyway," she went on, sounding as tired as I felt. "Even if we had been arrested for some reason, anything short of murder charges would all have been dropped within a day or two without any help from me."

"Oh really," I said. "Why is that?"

She turned around, finally. "Half of the most important phones in American law enforcement, at both state and federal levels, have Diane and Simone's numbers on speed dial." My surprise clearly showed, because her smile widened noticeably. "Did you think they were just amateurs, ghost hunting door to door like paranormal Avon ladies?"

"The Feds hire ghost hunters?"

"Well, yes, of course; though that's not all Simone and Diane do. Their combined skill set is as useful for all sorts of other applications as it is hard to find. The minute their arrest had crossed any of countless desks right here in this county, they'd have been escorted out of jail with apologies."

"And what about you? Would you just have charmed your way out?"

The smile she gave me now was an overt smirk. "I'd have been in even better shape than them. My connections on this coast aren't confined to law enforcement."

Well, of course. Didn't I know that by now? I wasn't even going to ask her what I'd have done if we'd been arrested. Why hand her another easy win? "What's an Avon lady?"

Now she laughed out loud. "Weren't you in the salon business?"

Had Lisa told her that? "Yes," I said peevishly. "And I know what

Avon is. We wouldn't have been caught dead selling it. I've just never heard of Avon *ladies*."

"Before your time," she said wistfully, returning, finally, to the removal of her remaining shoe. "And they were a noble breed back then. So watch your tone, Miss Judgy."

I was being slaughtered here, and had a lot more damp clothes to get out of than she did. So I went to grab one of the classy gray velour bathrobes tied up attractively in a basket on the mantelpiece, and escaped into the bathroom for a while.

The shower was as splendid as the rest of the cabin.

When I came out, Florence was wearing the other robe, and sitting at that little round table, with the blinds drawn up, gazing out the window at the moonlit field outside. "I understand why you're upset," she said very quietly without turning to look at me. "And I don't blame you. But I didn't… I just…"

That was when I realized why she wasn't looking at me. Maybe even why she hadn't been looking at me before. She *was* crying. She'd been doing it off and on ever since we'd left the pond, I was certain now. I hadn't really seen this coming, and had no idea what to do. The suppressed resentment I'd been nursing all day was suddenly wavering. But after giving her the cold shoulder all day, I could hardly just go take her hand now and say, *Aww. What's wrong, girlfriend?*

"None of us asked to be what we are," she said, swiping briefly at her eyes, clearly struggling to pull herself back together. "But…I got the worst draw of them all." She lost her battle for composure all at once, laying her head down on her folded arms across the tabletop, and sobbing.

I did not go to sit down across from her, much less touch her, as I would have if it had been Jen in this condition. I still couldn't be sure this wasn't just another move in whatever game it was she played with people. But I did go sit down on her side of the bed, and waited to see if this was something real. I'd seen a human being mixed in there too, hadn't I?

Within a couple minutes, she'd pulled herself together. She lifted her head again, still not looking at me, but not crying anymore. She was… not nearly as pretty now as she'd always seemed before. In fact, thinking back, she'd looked tired, washed out, and kind of disheveled even before we'd left the substation. Even since we'd left the pond, maybe. I wasn't sure. It had been dark, and I'd been paying attention to a lot of other things.

"I really do like you. A lot," she said, looking not at me yet, but at my reflection in the darkened window glass. "I have from the moment we met, partly because you do remind me so much of Paige. And Paige was the best, most important friend I ever had. But in the last few days, I've come to like you more and more for your own sake. I really hoped..." Her voice grew rough again. "I should never have used my gift on you. I didn't...really mean to. Not so much, at least. And I'd already stopped doing that to you, before today. Or I was trying to, at least."

She finally turned around to look at me directly, and this time, I don't think I managed to hide my surprise. She looked...her age. Truly pretty once, but not anymore. Not in the same way, at least. That was partly her reddened, swollen eyes, of course, and the damage tears had done to her makeup. But...that wasn't all of it. She was letting me see her, as she never had before. And I had a hard time believing she'd have done that just to lure me back, or win an argument. But, still...

"I know that look," she said. "You'll never know if you can trust me now." She sighed deeply, and looked away again. "But, for what it's worth, I won't be able to do that to you anymore. It only works well when people have no idea there's anything to watch for. They mistake my desire for their own then, and why wouldn't they?" She looked back at me. "But once you know, you'll know. You'll still feel the compulsion, but only as an irritation, like Diane and Simone do, and nearly everyone else like us that I know. Even Paige did. You're safe now." She looked down with such...shame. "Ask Diane, if you wish to. She'll back me up."

"But, why did you do it at all? I've been desperate to meet others like me, ever since I met Paige and realized there were any. I'd have wanted to get to know you just for that. And I've found myself liking you for lots of other reasons too. I've seen how kind you can be, how caring and generous—and not just to me." I dared to give her a slight smile. "You cover those parts up a lot, but they leak through sometimes."

She bit her lip, as if she was afraid to smile back. "So does my gift. It's a lot harder for me to control than you might think. Because it's just so hard for me to tell sometimes where the line is between my own normal feelings and desires and the use of my... My *gift*," she said sourly.

I was startled by the similarity of her words to what Diane had told me about knowing where our own thoughts and feelings ended and a ghost's began.

"It's not a gift, though. It's a curse. I don't think I've ever met another gifted person who should not be on their knees every night thanking whatever powers there may be for not afflicting them with this."

Was this self-pity? From the woman who had "old friends" waiting under every rock to grant her merest whim, instantly? Whose "connections on this coast weren't limited to law enforcement"? "How is getting whatever you decide to want the worst curse ever?" I asked. "I'm pretty sure I've seen some worse ones."

Her face swung shut like a door. "Oh, yes. I do get what I want. And I won't apologize for that, to anyone. Getting everything I want is what the universe pays me in exchange for having taken away everything that might have made me happy. I have a thousand very useful friends, who just adore my gift, but haven't ever met me, and never can—with more always waiting in reserve. I have astonishing amounts of money that can buy me everything but freedom to be what I am, but never asked to be, out in the light. I am a gorgon who's had countless lovers, but never love. I'd say I've earned my perks, many times over—just like I did today."

"What did it cost you today? If you mean when I got ticked off because I found out you'd—"

She raised a hand to stop me, shook her head, and looked away again. "Losing your trust hurt, Cam. I won't pretend it didn't. But... no." She swallowed, hard. "I don't mean this as a barb of any kind, but you were nothing like the worst wound inflicted by my *gift* today." Before I could ask what else had happened, she stood and walked past me toward the bathroom. "These country deputies really do rise with the dawn. We should get some sleep while we can."

Ten minutes later, I lay under the blankets on my side of the bed and stared up at the darkened ceiling. *...everything but freedom to be what I am, but never asked to be. ...countless lovers, but never love.* So, this was what people meant when they talked about a "beautiful mess."

I was still awake well after she'd begun to snore quietly, thinking about what my life had been like before I'd fallen into this endless maze of rabbit holes. And of what Elle had said last spring about the risks of hiding my own truths from people I loved. I'd told her that I never did this anymore. Yet this afternoon, I'd done it for the second time in this month. *You think this gift will just go away...?*

In the chaos that had followed, I'd also missed my nightly call with Kip. And tomorrow I'd have to tell him some *harmless little fib* to explain why—as I'd done that afternoon with Jen. Nothing like the first I'd told them, or the last. As Elle had warned me, that didn't feel good here, in the dark without distractions. But until someone could convince me that such fibs were more dangerous than making Kip or Jen think I was crazy, or making myself some kind of impossible monster in their eyes by vanishing in front of them to prove it, I saw no alternative. Florence and I had that, at least, in common. We both wore masks in a world that had no room or tolerance for what we were. I had once feared what lay behind my own mask. That was the cost of gifts like ours, and pretending otherwise would just make life worse for Kip and Jen, as well as me. How could Elle not see that?

&

I WOKE UP JUST AFTER dawn, wondering what Jen would do with a morning when she didn't have to cook breakfast for anyone but herself—and what I was going to tell her about where we'd been and what we'd done here. She would want to know.

She wouldn't be milking Clara, I knew that much. So I hoped we'd get home by some reasonable hour this morning.

Finally, I slid out of bed as carefully and quietly as possible and tiptoed into the bathroom to don my mostly-dry clothes, which looked... not quite as bad as I'd feared. Then I tiptoed out again, pried the cottage door open silently, and went outside.

There were two plastic Adirondack chairs in front of each cottage. Ours happened to be right in front of a big hanging bird feeder at the field's edge, across the path. It was already swarming with chickadees, junkos and the nuthatches who also clung upside down to twigs in a tree above me, making their squawky little clown laughs. It was my most peaceful moment in ages.

A short time later, I heard quiet sounds of movement in our cabin, and went back inside to find the bed empty and the bathroom door closed. She was awake, which meant I could make us coffee, and some breakfast for myself.

I'd done all of that, and was partway through my scone before Florence emerged again—looking like a vision...though none of us had brought so much as a makeup bag on this "day trip."

"I thought you said your gift wouldn't work on me anymore," I said, not in an unfriendly way. I was just curious.

She gave me a wry look. "I said it wouldn't make you adore me anymore. Or that's what I meant to say, at least. If you really want to see me without any soft edges at all, dear, I imagine you can convince your mind to do that too, now that you know it's there to be done." Her smile widened slightly as she started for the kitchenette to get her own little treats from the small refrigerator. "But do you really want to do that—especially while you're eating?"

I almost laughed just as we were interrupted by a firm if quiet knock at our door.

I reached back and pushed the blinds aside far enough to see the porch, and who was standing there but Sheriff Clarke. I just managed not to groan. Had I wondered how this could get any more embarrassing? Now I knew. I got up and opened the door.

"Good morning, Sheriff." I did my best to smile pleasantly. "I'm so sorry to have pried you out of bed so early." And wasn't that the truth!

"Ms. Tate," he said, giving me a small, tight smile in return. "How do I keep managing to find *you* in the middle of things like this?"

"Dumb luck?" I tried.

"May I come in?"

"Of course." I stood aside to let him.

"Sheriff Clarke!" Florence said cheerfully, as if she'd invited him here for tea. She was...really looking good again, I had to admit. That curse of hers sure had its upsides. "Who knew we'd meet again so soon?"

I looked back and forth between them. "You've met?"

"At the courthouse, just the other day," said Clarke, clearly trying not to look as charmed as I felt sure he must be.

"Yes!" she said to me. "We happened to run into each other in a hallway on my way to the county clerk's office." She gave the sheriff an apologetic look. "I guess I was supposed to tell Cam hello for you, wasn't I. So sorry I forgot."

"You were there doing research, right?" Clarke asked. "Something to do with property records?"

"Yes," she said, bringing her scone and cup of coffee over to the little table by our front window. "Can we get you any coffee, Sheriff?"

I wondered who'd be making that coffee if he said yes, betting it would not be her.

"No, thank you. May I ask whose property records you were looking for, and why?"

She sat down to her breakfast. "A man, now deceased, named Leon Ackerman."

"Huh," said Clarke, as if this surprised him. "And did you find them?"

"I did," she said, looking down into her coffee mug as she lifted it to take a sip. "He owned a house right here on Lopez Island, it turns out."

"And here you are, just days later," Clarke said congenially. "What a coincidence. May I ask why Leon Ackerman's property records were of interest to you?"

She smiled back at him. "Did your deputy's report about last night not make that obvious? Several of us explained it to him pretty clearly, as I recall."

"Because you are all under the impression that he murdered someone named George Harper here on Lopez sixty years ago," Clarke said, looking dubious.

"Exactly," she said, and nibbled off a corner of her scone.

Clark nodded to himself. "Okay. We'll come back to that. But first, I'm curious about how Leon Ackerman's property records led you all to trespass on land owned by Rheena and Jack Henderson."

So that *had* been her house we'd driven past last night.

I must have made some little noise of surprise, because both Clarke and Florence looked at me. "Do those names mean something to you, Ms. Tate?" he asked.

"Yes, they do," Florence said, drawing his gaze back to her before I had a chance to answer. "And may I just save you some time by cutting to the chase here? This must be a busy morning for you. And we have nothing to hide."

"Very well," he said nodding at her appreciatively. "What's this chase then?"

"I believe you knew Paige Berry?" Florence asked.

"She and I were acquainted, yes. What does she have to do with this?"

"George Harper was the love of her life," Florence said, "before you were more than a child, I believe. And back when she and I were extremely close friends in our twenties, George disappeared one day without explanation—never to be seen again. That loss wounded her forever. As I believe Cam explained to your deputy last night, we found documents among Paige's things about the rather half-hearted investigation that followed his disappearance; and, out of care for the memory of someone we all loved, we decided to revisit the issue a bit more carefully. Following me so far?"

"Yes," he said, clearly interested now.

"Have you spoken with Diane and Simone next door yet?"

"No, Ms. Golding. I came here first." He glanced at me, kind of reproachfully, I thought. "Because your names both meant something to me."

"Then, I take it that Diane's name doesn't?" Florence asked.

He frowned at her. "Should it?"

She shook her head. "Probably not. But somewhere higher up the line, Sheriff, her name would have drawn attention long before mine did. She's a rather famous data analyst—at least, in certain circles."

"Of course she is." Clarke sighed, casting a weary look at me again. "And, if I may pop in here and have a whack," he said, looking back at Florence, "she found some string of previously overlooked clues in those old documents?"

"Right again, Sheriff." Florence smiled at him like he was just the brightest boy she'd ever met. "So Leon Ackerman was quoted in the papers back then about having offered George a ride to the Lopez ferry landing that morning sixty years ago, where, presumably, George sailed away from Paige and his whole life here for no reason."

"But your friend Diane didn't buy that story," Clarke said.

"She did not," said Florence. "So I used Leon's property records to find his daughter, Anna, who's still living in his house here. And yesterday, as you will doubtless discover upon looking further into this, we went to bother her at home about what, if anything, her father may have said to her at any point about that ride he gave to George. Still making sense?"

He nodded. "And…this all leads to Jack and Rheena Henderson's land how?"

"Leon's daughter had no idea what we were talking about, and wasn't all that happy to see us, as I'm sure you're not surprised to hear. But she sent us to an old friend of her father's named Zeph, currently residing at a nursing home here called Fair Haven, where I went to visit him yesterday afternoon."

Well, that part wasn't true…exactly. Though it wasn't quite a lie either. Anna had sent us there, however unintentionally. What a clever way with words Florence had.

"It seems that Zeph is Rheena's father," she went on, "or perhaps her father-in-law. Anna didn't make that part completely clear." No, she sure hadn't! This performance was a thing of beauty. "And, if he weren't so far gone to dementia, he would probably not have told me anywhere near as much about the still that he and Leon used to operate out by that pond on the Hendersons' property—or about any of the other things that used to go on out there. But, being a bit addled, he did; which is one reason we didn't just go to Rheena herself for permission to go have a look—being rather unsure whether or not she might turn out to be as…unreliable and dangerous a person as it seems her father may have been. So yes, we trespassed. Guilty as charged. And I'm sure that each of us will happily pay the fine. But Diane and Simone will confirm everything I've told you. And I think it very likely that if you look *carefully* this time, you'll find George Harper's remains somewhere in that pond."

Oh my god. The look on Clarke's face was worth all we'd been through!

He turned to look at me then.

"See?" I said, spreading my hands cheerfully. "Just like I said. Dumb luck!"

He looked up at the ceiling, shook his head, and laughed quietly before looking at me again. "I'm told Paige left everything to you."

I nodded, surprised, and a little disconcerted to hear that this news had made it all the way to Sheriff Clarke.

"Well, that makes as much sense as any of this," he said. "You two are like peas in the same pod." He shook his head again. "She was always getting tangled up in things that shouldn't have been any of her business either. Are you sure you two are not related?"

"What a crazy question," I said. "How would we have been related?"

He folded his arms, and wandered thoughtfully toward our kitchenette and back. Then he took another long breath, released a moment later in another long sigh. "So, if that thing you gave my deputy last night actually turns out to be a human finger bone…"

"Oh, I suspect it will," said Florence.

He turned to look at her. "I suppose you have some kind of training in forensic anatomy as well, Ms. Golding?"

She shook her head and smiled prettily. "The facts just seem to pile up in that direction."

"Well, I do have a little training of that sort," Clarke said grimly. "Not a lot; but a sheriff is expected to have some idea whether or not he's looking at human remains. That badly degraded little bone isn't much to go on, but it isn't obviously something else. So I'll be taking it over to the coroner in Anacortes this morning myself."

"I await his verdict with bated breath," said Florence as she took another little bite of scone.

"But even if it is a finger bone," he said, "we'll have no way of telling whose it is. Unless George had a DNA sample stashed away somewhere sixty years ago."

Oh! "We have a lock of his hair at home!" I said.

He stared at me, open-mouthed this time, then grunted another little chuckle. "Of course you do. May I ask one more thing then? How on earth did you even find that tiny bone, underwater in the dark like that?"

Florence glanced at me, then smiled up at him again. "More dumb luck."

He stared at her, then turned to look at me suspiciously. "You like doing this to me, don't you."

I gave him a helpless shrug. "Actually, I'd be very happy just to go home and run an inn for a while. That turns out to be a lot of work, you know."

"You're running an inn now?"

This was what he *hadn't* heard? Then again, our soft opening had only started, what? A week ago? "You bet!" I said, proudly. "The Berry Farm. That's what we're doing with Paige's house."

"Huh. I never thought of you as the innkeeper type. Weren't you an actress—and a playwright?"

"Oh, Sheriff Clarke." I laughed. "That's all such pre-pandemic reconnaissance. Sounds like you could use some better informants."

His brows rose slowly. "You realize, I trust, how complicated a whole lot of people's lives are going to get around here now if you've found a human gravesite in that pond." Was he blaming me for that, somehow?

"If this pans out," he said to both of us, "I'll have those trespassing citations waived. But, if I can ask you all for one last little favor, it would be extremely helpful if the bunch of you would stick around for a couple days, at least? It seems likely we'll have further questions, though at this point, I can't even guess what they might be."

"I've always loved these islands," Florence said. "And I have nowhere else pressing to go."

"I live here," I said cheerfully. "We…can go back to Orcas, at least, yes?"

He nodded. "Yes. Thank you. Guess I'd better go and see your friends now, though it looks like there's not much left to discuss." He turned to Florence. "Thank you, Ms. Golding. You've been much more helpful than I'd expected." Then he looked at me. "You, I will be seeing around somewhere, I'm sure." He tipped his hat, and let himself out.

When he was gone, I turned to Florence in amazement. "Wow! I mean, just…WOW! That was…mind-blowing."

Her smile managed to seem smug and sad all at once. "I'm not *just* a pretty face, you know."

༼༽

As we all leaned against the rail on our way back to Orcas, listening to the seagulls cry and watching water foam and swirl in our wake, I couldn't stop thinking about the way Florence had assembled all those pieces into such a seamless and convincing explanation without pointing even slightly at the parts of our actual path that no one would have believed. And yet…

"What happens when Anna tells them she never sent us to Zeph, and even told Rheena to have Fair Haven keep us from visiting him?" I asked her.

Florence's lips quirked into a little smile as she watched Shaw Island's shore go by. "She won't, of course. It would be her word against ours; and all the known facts work in favor of our credibility more than hers or Rheena's."

"Okay, but…*why?*" My mind was nowhere near as fast as hers.

"Well, to begin with," Florence said, "if Anna didn't send us to find Zeph, who did? They'd have a very hard time finding any other answer. If anything, they'd be more likely to assume that Anna just wanted to keep her friend Rheena from knowing she'd sent us to her father. But the main reason that no one's going to tell them about trying to stop us is that doing so would merely demonstrate their intent to cover something up."

Well, how obvious. Would I ever learn to think that way?

"But what about Jen?" I asked. "I mean, a sixty-year-old body found on Lopez is going to eclipse anything else on the local rumor mill, and probably even make the papers. How will I explain my involvement in something like that to her?"

"Tell her exactly what Florence told the sheriff this morning," said Diane. "What more brilliant story could you give her?"

I saw Florence trying *not* to smile, for once.

"Oh. Right," I said. "But she'll just ask why I was involved in all of that to start with."

Diane rolled her eyes. "You got involved in this because we dragged you into it—in case you've actually forgotten. You could even tell her that, until last night, you had no idea this was why we'd really come to stay at your inn."

"Because you actually didn't until that first night of our stay, did you?" Simone added.

"Well... No, I guess you're right."

Simone nodded. "Once you've made it clear that we got you into this, any other questions she has will be aimed at us, not at you."

These old aunties really were a very devious bunch.

"So," said Florence, "it looks like we'll be staying for a while longer now."

"Don't worry," I said. "We offer a special discount for this kind of thing."

When we got home, Jen was a little snippy with me about what was *really* going on, until I told her that I'd actually gotten tangled up in yet *another* murder mystery. Then she was all *ooh*s and *ahh*s as I went through everything these strange old aunties had really come up here to set right, leading to our conversation with Sheriff Clarke that morning.

"Well now I get the whole *'let's leave the end date open'* thing!" she said. "Oh, hon! You lead the most exciting life I've ever heard about! And I keep getting front row seats!" She was practically bouncing on her toes like a five-year-old who needs to pee. By the time I went upstairs to change out of those nasty clothes at last, Jen seemed put completely off the scent. *Phew!*

Finally, I called Kip to tell him the official version of our escapades on Lopez too, before one of his old law enforcement buddies spilled the beans. I was afraid he might get all alarmed and leave his studies to come racing home again. But when I made it clear that this murder had happened sixty years ago, and that all the perpetrators were either long dead, or in nursing homes with dementia, he seemed reassured that I was okay. After that, we had a lovely talk about his life, and how much we looked forward to seeing each other soon.

Of course, we still had the original problem to resolve: helping George out of our inn. Unfortunately, Jen had nowhere to be the next day until her evening shift at the Barnacle. So, the aunties puttered upstairs among themselves—still looking for some way to move things forward—while I was careful to do other things both inside and outside the house while Jen was paying attention.

There was no shortage of other things to keep me busy. Jen had not enjoyed having to cover for me with the goats during my unscheduled absence, and had indeed left the milking for me. And even though we were reaching the time of year when the whole garden's only real job was just dying, managing even that is a lot more work than non-gardeners assume. A good deal of how well plants are likely to do when they come up again next spring is determined by how well they were put to bed last fall. After a whole week with three aunties in the house, there was no small amount of laundry to do either.

I was carrying an armload of clean sheets and towels across the upstairs landing when I heard raised voices coming from behind the Dragonfly Room door, and…well, veered aside to listen in. Once a spy—well, *confidential informant*—always a spy, I'm afraid. And besides, I kept hearing such important little things whenever I eavesdropped lately.

"But Florence is right!" I heard Diane say. "And that's a rather giant hole in your entire theory. I can't believe we didn't see it sooner."

"Well, so much keeps happening, so quickly," Florence said. "I didn't think of it last night either. None of us did."

"Yes, of course," Diane growled. "I wasn't trying to assign blame. I'm just saying that if Simone's basic premise is in question, the whole rest of her plan becomes far too dangerous to continue discussing. I think we need to set this whole idea down, and try again from some completely different entry point."

"Before we've even tried to think Florence's question through?" Simone said, indignantly. "You only want to start over because you've disliked this plan since I suggested it."

"Okay, yes," Diane said. "I can't pretend to like a plan that might turn you into a ghost as well. If we lose you, Simone, who's left here to help George, or anybody else ever again? I'm worthless in this arena without you."

The laundry in my arms was getting very heavy. But this was clearly not a conversation I wanted to walk away from. I set down the laundry and tapped at the door. A second later, it was opened suddenly by Diane, who looked relieved—probably to find me and not Jen there.

"Is there a problem?" I asked her.

"Come in," she said, beckoning me through the door in agitation.

I walked in to find Simone propped up on pillows on the bed, and Florence sitting on the bureau with her feet dangling seven inches off the floor. Diane closed the door behind me, and went to stand leaning against the wall beside the window.

"I could hear you almost from the stairwell," I said. "What's going on?"

Diane huffed. "You remember Simone's theory last night about how George has developed two schizophrenic personalities here and at the pond, both trapped by their divergent desires and ignorance of each other, right?"

I nodded. "Yes, though I don't pretend to understand it all as well as you guys seem to."

"I'm in your camp on this one, dear," said Florence. "But I just seem to have shot an accidental hole in the idea."

"It was your dream about the lion and the storm that sent us off to find that pond last night," Diane said a little crossly. Was I being blamed for something now? "But, if Simone's new theory is correct, the only part of George that knows about that aspect of his story is George at the pond—who, as far as Simone can tell, has no idea that he's here at the house as well, or ever has been. While George here at the house seemingly has no idea that the pond or himself there exists at all, and remembers nothing about the events depicted in your dream."

"Okay…" I said. "And?"

"Who sent you that dream?" Diane asked. "George who would have known anything in it, but doesn't even know he's ever been here? Or

George who's here to put that dream into your mind, but seems to have no inkling of its contents?" She gazed at me, as if expecting I would have an answer—which, of course, I didn't. "So, now you see," Diane said at last with oddly angry satisfaction. "The theory we are trying to plan around is clearly flawed. But my dear Simone here just wants to try flying it to the moon anyway."

I was still thinking, though…that I really should have gone on with my laundry instead of listening at doors. But also… "I know I'm always asking stupid questions, and I'm sure this is another one, but… You guys say that in the otherworld, space and time don't matter, right?"

"No, dear," Simone said gently. "They matter just as much. They just don't work the same."

"Okay, right. That's what I meant. But everywhere is now, and every time is here?"

"You've…got that sideways, I think," Florence said with an encouraging smile. "But, yes, we understand. Go on."

"Okay." I sighed. "All I'm trying to ask is, if my dream had to come from George at the pond, does it really matter where he is? I mean, if everywhere is…here…there, then couldn't he have sent that dream from where he is to…anywhere it went?"

"Good try, Cam," said Diane. "But no. Not because of where *he* is, but because of where *you* were when you had the dream. George at the pond could not have sent a dream to you here without even knowing *here* existed—before or after he did it. So—"

"No!" Simone nearly shouted, bolting up from her throne of pillows. "She wasn't!"

She had our attention now. We just had no idea what she meant.

"She wasn't what?" Diane asked, more patiently than she'd seemed since I came in.

"She wasn't *here!*" said Simone. "At least, not completely. If Cam was dreaming, then, by definition, she was at least half in the otherworld—just as George's splintered self is. Half in, half out. While that dream lasted, they were all in the same place! Which answers everything! Cam, you are a genius!"

"I am?" It took some serious self-control not to giggle in delight.

CHAPTER 16

As soon as Jen had gone to work at the Barnacle, we gathered downstairs in the second parlor. That room was in the back of the house well hidden from the driveway, and separated by either the kitchen or the front parlor from any other entrance, which lowered our chances of being taken by surprise if Jen or anybody else showed up unexpectedly before we were done. We'd all been over the plan, to the extent there was one, and although Diane still disliked it deeply, for really good reasons, even she had come up with no better alternative.

Simone had needed some solution that would resolve *both* of George's unfinished pieces of business at the same instant, since neither splinter of him could "translate" into the otherworld by itself. But, again and again, she'd found just a single answer. Only simultaneous access to Paige herself could resolve all of George's different needs at once. So, Simone planned to try something she'd never even thought of, much less done before: create some kind of dream, like the one I'd had, that would allow "George now," "George then," and an already-translated Paige to be all together in one place, even for an instant.

And it got worse from there. Even if she found a way to do that—a giant *if*—it would have to be done not straddling the otherworld's edges, as she'd always done before, but completely immersed there. Otherwise, she said, it would be like sitting on the edge of a swimming pool with only her feet in the water, and trying to coordinate a pool-bottom surgery. She and the others involved would hardly be able to see or hear each other from opposite sides of the rippled surface—assuming she could even find and gather them to begin with from half-outside the pool. Only fully submerged could Simone even hope to see, hear, and speak directly enough to both Paige and all of George to help them navigate whatever might go on between them. But neither Simone nor Diane had ever heard of anyone who'd even tried such full immersion in the otherworld—and come back to tell about it, anyway.

None of us would have asked her to do this. Diane didn't want her to try. But Simone said she couldn't imagine living comfortably with the decision to walk away from George or Paige like that on her conscience. So…here we were, gathered beside her to give *her* as much access to *us* as possible, not the other way around. That much had been made very clear. If our presence turned out to be of any use at all, only she would know it when the moment came.

In other words, she was going off alone into the complete unknown, and none of us had any clue what might happen next, or how to help. That was the *real* plan, basically.

"So then…" Simone quavered when we were as settled around her as we could be, "a few last things to review before I leave all of you on your own. The first thing I'll try, just because it might be possible to do it from the *edge* of the pool in ways I know a little about already, is to find both aspects of George there, and try to bring him together by leashing both of him to me somehow. In case it's not obvious to the beginners here, I'll point out that, as with any work of this kind, what I'm trying to do will be more art than science, and I have no idea whether even this first part will work at all. If it does, though, be prepared! It seems very unlikely to me that George past and George now are separated that way for no reason. So being reunited, even through me, may be traumatic for either or both of him. I have no idea how George here at home may express that trauma—but he may do it *here* as much as there, and possibly through one or more of you. So if anything disturbing happens, try to remember that it's mostly in your minds, not in the tangible world. I know that's foolish advice, since it's hard even at the best of times to tell much difference between your mind and the tangible world, but maybe some of you can be ready to help others hold onto that awareness if they are having trouble doing it for themselves.

"If I manage to gather up all of George, the next thing I'll try is calling Paige to join us, which is not a thing I'd normally expect to succeed at. The only reason I can find and communicate with presences like George is that they're stuck halfway here where I am. Paige is all the way out of our little aquarium, and completely translated into the otherworld.

"But if you've ever been swimming, maybe you've noticed the difference between how sound travels into water from above the surface, and the way it travels when it's made underwater to start with: much louder and clearer, right? I'm hoping it'll work the same way once I'm *fully* submerged in a plane where all times are now and all places here. If I turn out to be right, I should just be able to call out her name from wherever we are, and she'll come. In reality…" Simone spread her hands. "We'll see."

She looked at me and James, who was sitting cooperatively in my lap for once. "If Sam or Harry do appear, you'll close the pocket doors and try your best to keep them near me?"

"Of course," I said. We'd been looking for them everywhere but, naturally, they'd picked this moment to disappear again to wherever they went—likely inside the walls somewhere. Other than Simone, our three cats were the only living creatures in the house who occupied both our "aquarium" and the larger otherworld at once. And Simone felt that, if they could be kept near her body until this was done, they might act as tethers she could follow between our aquarium and the plane she'd be immersed in, if she had to. But if something happened to Simone tonight while Sam and Harry played hooky, I was seriously going to take them right down to the animal shelter in the morning, and wish them good luck forever.

My James, though, was doing both of us proud—right now, at least.

Finally, Simone turned to Diane. "You know what you have meant to me, all these years, dear." Diane nodded, looking closed up as a fortress. "I understand," Simone said, "that I am risking you as much or more than myself by insisting on this, and if it all works out, I will embrace as much of your entirely justified anger as you wish to share. But…if this proves to be as…bad a plan as you have tried to convince me it is, I need to know—do you think you can forgive me?"

Diane gazed at her, hardly seeming to move or breathe, anger and sadness so evenly locked away behind her face that it was hard to guess which one was winning.

"I'm not looking for one answer or the other, dear," said Simone. "I just… Before I go; if…if I am unable to return, I just don't wish to be left wondering what I've done."

Diane's eyes were reddening now, and growing brighter. She shook her head. "I won't wait to forgive you then, dear. I forgive you now." Her eyes finally overflowed, but her impassive scowl remained unchanged.

Simone sighed very deeply, tears in her eyes too, and nodded gravely at Diane. "So, let's get started then," she said, leaning back against the cushions of her love seat and closing her eyes.

I got up and carried James over to her. "You want to take a nap with Simone, little man?" I asked him, scritching the silky fur on his head. "Will you do that, if I put you down?" He didn't answer, of course. I wasn't there in the otherworld to be answered. But he did like to sleep—a lot—and I'd been bothering him enough to keep him from it for a while. I lowered him gently into her lap, and stroked his back and tail for a while until, for a wonder, he began working himself around into a more comfortable position, and started kneading the fabric of her dress. A moment later, he laid his head down, purring very softly, and closed his eyes. I shook my head, wondering if she *had* been there in the otherworld to explain his job to him. Well, so far so good. I went back to my chair.

As I was learning to expect, nothing happened for a while except the silence. It was nearly sunset, and the view outside the parlor's windows was bathed in amber light and streaked with long, purplish shadows. *What a beautiful place our little aquarium is,* I thought. A raven pecked at something in the grass, then spread its wings and flew up toward the roof above us, out of my sight, as two wild rabbits loped tentatively out from underneath some rhododendron bushes.

Florence sat in an upholstered wingback chair to my left, gazing out at the view as well.

"I'm sorry. I need… I'll be right back," Diane said, getting up and walking out through the front parlor. I heard her go up the stairs, then across the upper landing above us. A few minutes later, I heard a toilet flush, and the scraping sound of a window being opened. A minute later, she was back and settling into her seat again as our wait continued.

And continued…

The light had gotten noticeably lower and rosier when Diane got up again and went to touch Simone's hand, gently. "Simone?" she whispered. "Are you all right?"

There was no response. Simone had told us that she'd probably have no attention to spare during all of this, which was why she'd gone over and over what she'd be trying to do, and how, and what we might or might not experience, before she'd gone away.

Diane sighed, and went back to her chair.

It was full twilight, and I was struggling to stay awake, when Diane said, "What was that?"

I startled up and looked at her.

"What was what?" asked Florence.

Diane was looking up at the ceiling now. "Don't you hear that?"

I looked up as well, and listened. But…there was just more silence. James slept on in Simone's lap, undisturbed as well.

"Someone's shouting!" Diane said, standing up, still staring at the ceiling.

"No. They're not," said Florence, glancing uncertainly at me. "I…think this may be one of those things Simone warned us about?"

Diane finally looked down at us. "Neither of you are hearing that?"

"What does it sound like?" I asked, hoping that telling us about whatever was happening in her head would help her…or me, maybe, deal with it.

"It's a child, I think!" She looked very distressed. "He's wailing now—for help. This is George, isn't it. It's happening." She shook her head. "All these years… This is the first time I've ever…"

"Can you shut it out?" Florence asked calmly. "Just tell your mind that it's not real, and to…stop believing it?"

"I don't know," said Diane. "I'm trying, but…"

Florence's expression was all but blank. But I could sense the fear in her, because I was asking myself the same question. Would *we* be able to ignore it? Right now, we were trying to reassure and support Diane; but what would happen if all three of us ended up fighting hallucinations thrown off by George as he struggled against whatever Simone was doing?

A loud thud came from the window to my right, and I turned to see a raven—the one I'd seen before?—scrabbling at the window sill with its black claws and flapping at the glass, as it had that day in Paige's room. "Florence?" I asked, "is there—"

"Yes!" she said. "The bird? I think it's real. What does it want?"

Diane was looking at it too. "We're all seeing that, right?"

Florence and I both nodded.

"The voice upstairs is gone now," Diane said.

I realized that James had woken up and was staring at the bird as well, just as it turned and veered up into the air, flying out of our sight. But the pattering sound of little feet on the hardwood floor made us turn again as Sam and Harry trotted into the room. They walked up to sniff Simone's feet and gaze at each other like two doctors in a consult, then looked up and meowed at James, who merely bobbed his head at them. Harry, then Sam leaped lightly up to join James on Simone's lap. And James didn't seem to mind. Now this was getting *really* strange.

"Oh god, *I* hear it now," Florence murmured, staring up at the ceiling as Diane had. "Someone's moaning, like they're in pain." She glanced sharply at me.

"I still can't hear it," I said.

"I can't either, this time," Diane said. "But it keeps coming from up there. Do you think... Should someone go up and see if there's... something more going on?"

"I don't think it's coming from anywhere but in here." I tapped at my head. "But...what the hell, I'll go up and make sure there's nothing to see. You two stay here, okay?"

"Seriously? You're going up alone?" asked Florence.

"Yes. Because we all know it's in our heads, so what does it matter where I go? I'm only going up to prove that we can let it go, right?"

"You're braver than I am," said Florence.

"I'll come if you wish," said Diane.

"No, I'm *fine*," I said again. "You two are the ones it's targeting for some reason. Just stay here to support each other, and make sure those cats don't leave Simone. I'll be right back."

Before anyone managed to talk me out of it, I walked into the front parlor, pulling the pocket doors closed behind me to keep the cats—especially James—from following me. Then I turned every light in the room on, walked out into the foyer and did the same, and finally climbed the stairs and turned on the central landing light too. Still no crying or moaning. No ravens flapping at the windows either. Just as I suspected. Nothing to see up here. It was all in our heads, as everyone had been telling me over and over. The question I was carefully not asking was, why *wasn't* George in my head too? Because everybody knows what happens if you're dumb enough to ask that kind of question, right?

I decided to turn on all the other lights up there before I went back down, and went from room to room flipping switches until I came to the Orca Room between the Blue Heron Suite and Jen's room. I reached for its door handle, and stopped. There was music coming from inside. Happy, jazzy big band swing music! Someone was partying in our only unoccupied room—which meant now I'd have to go in and kick them out. And I hated confrontations like this.

Because, as we all know, no one ever notices that they've walked into a dream. We never even think to ask, *Does this make sense?* No, you just slide in and go with it.

So, braced for an uncomfortable confrontation, I turned the door handle and walked in to deal with whoever had decided to throw a party in the Orca Room. Only, this wasn't three high school kids passing a joint around. There were at least…a hundred people there, all dressed to the nines in elegant party clothes right out of *I Love Lucy* or *The Lawrence Welk Show*. They were laughing over drinks, dancing like pros to the Andrews Sisters, and wolfing down plates of cake and chocolate-dipped strawberries. I caught a glimpse of a buffet table in the next room, and my mouth fell open. What a spread! They even had a champagne fountain. The joint was jumping!

It was hard just to get in the door, and as I started trying to squeeze further through the crowd, I bumped into a short, dark-haired teenage girl in a black velvet dress with a white lace collar who was talking to some other kids with her back to me. She turned around and stopped, staring at me in surprise. "Cam?"

"Do I know you?"

"What are you doing here?" the girl asked. "I had no idea you would come!" She turned with a hand up at the side of her mouth and called, "Hey, Mom! Cam's here!"

I had no idea why she knew me, but she seemed happy I'd come. "What's the occasion?"

"It's a party!" she said—as if that weren't obvious. "My mom's throwing it."

"Why's your mom throwing a party?"

The girl shrugged. "I don't know."

"Oh," I said, feeling strangely confused. "I'm sorry. This is very embarrassing, but, who are you again?"

The girl gaped at me, still smiling, but like she could not believe I was serious. "I'm Simone, silly! Didn't I just tell you it was my mom's party?" Without even looking away from me, she reached back to grab the hand of a teenage boy still talking to the other kids behind her, and pulled him around to face me. He blinked at me with pale blue eyes from under a mop of almost curly light brown hair. But...there was something off about his face. It blurred a little, every time he moved. Like a film of someone being played at the wrong speed, or double exposed. "George," said Simone, turning to face the boy, "this is my amazing friend, Cam! And *she* knows Paige too!" Simone looked back at me. "Did you bring a gift?"

"Was I supposed to bring a gift?" I asked her nervously. "I'm...not sure I knew this was a birthday party."

"I'm sure you brought one," said Simone. "It was on the invitation. Can we see it?"

"Yes," George said excitedly—his voice doing something kind of like his face did. *"Please,* can't we see what you brought?"

Had I brought a gift? What invitation? "Well...I'm so sorry, but I didn't—"

"Oh, you silly!" Simone laughed. "It's right there in your hand!"

"And it's so beautiful!" said George.

I looked down, and was astonished to see the most gorgeously wrapped present in my hands. The paper was all gold with flecks of rainbow in it. The ribbon seemed made of crushed rubies, and the bow was like the crown of spray on one of those huge ornamental fountains, all full of light!

"Who's it for?" I asked, still gazing down at it in wonder.

"It's for Paige," said George. "Who do you think?"

"Oh! Let's open it!" Simone cried, bouncing on her toes.

"Yes, I want to see!" said George, the frisson in his voice making the last word sound more like *sshssshheheee.*

"Are we supposed to open Paige's presents?" I asked, uncomfortably.

"Yes!" Simone said with almost alarming urgency.

"If you're sure then," I said, looking down again. I saw no seams in the paper, or tape to pull off. The ribbon didn't even seem to be cut or tied anywhere.

"Oh, hurry!" Simone said impatiently. "I can't wait to see what's in such a beautiful box!"

Then I remembered that, of course, there wasn't any tape or paper. You just opened it! And at the thought, the bow of fountain spray shot out in all directions, and the package unfurled to pop open just like one of those sunlit jellybean poppies in Paige's garden.

And everything went silent.

I looked up to find that the entire party had turned to look at me. George stood frozen, staring down at the open petals of wrapping in my hands with an expression of wonder. Simone gaped up at me with speechless joy. What had I done?

Looking back out at the sea of nearly motionless partygoers, I discovered one of them was Florence! And not far behind her was Diane! Had they gotten invitations too? Then I saw *Elle*—smiling at me in amazement; and way back behind her… Was that *JoJo?!* He looked just about to laugh, of course. There was a sudden rush of quiet sound, as if everyone were breathing in at once—which they were, I realized, just before the room erupted in a deafening cheer, as if this were midnight on New Year's Eve!

"I think that you must come see Mother," Simone said very solemnly as everybody else began to laugh and dance again. "She'll want to thank you for a gift like that, in person." She glanced back at George, then beckoned me to follow as the two of them turned and started weaving through the crowd toward the room with the buffet table. I hurried after them, still finding faces that I knew now, all around the room: people I'd known back in Seattle, even friends from high school. There was Porter! And Charles from Lisa's acting troupe! What were they all doing here? I had no time to stop and ask them, though. Simone and George were already in the next room, heading for a big set of glass French doors just beyond the buffet table. I hurried to catch up with them, and was surprised to discover there was no one else in there with all that delicious-looking food except the children, waiting patiently for me to join them now.

"She's in there." Simone pointed at the big French doors.

"Aren't you coming in with me?" I asked.

She shook her head. "George and I must go back to the party in case Paige comes."

"Paige isn't here?" I asked. "At her own party?"

"Not yet," said Simone. "But she's on her way, I'm sure."

"She's the guest of honor!" George told me. "Of course she'll be here; that's why we've all come." He looked back at Simone. "Can we go back now? I don't want to miss her."

"Come on. Let's go." She took his hand again, and they trotted back toward the other room without so much as goodbye.

I turned back to the French doors. The room beyond them looked elegant and well-lit by lots of floor-to-ceiling paned windows, but I saw no one in there. Was Simone's mother here anymore? I pushed one of the French doors open, and walked inside.

"Oh…wow!" I exclaimed quietly. The largest window on the far wall looked out on Cinderella's castle—the one at Disneyland, with the fireworks show going on above it.

"Hello, dear. I'm surprised to see you, but so glad you've come!"

I turned, and saw…*Simone!* Not the raven-haired teenager who'd just brought me to this room, but the snowy-haired old lady that I remembered suddenly—as I now remembered everything else, but so scrambled. "Where are we?" I asked, struggling to reorient myself. My gaze darted around the impossible room. "Is this…the otherworld?"

"No, dear. This is only my dream, as is the Simone who brought you to me. It's me you've really been talking to since you got here. And you, it seems, are the vital missing part of this whole plan." She gave me a rueful smile. "I should have seen it. Long ago."

"So, wait, everybody else here is only a figment of your dream?" I asked, wondering why, or how she could be dreaming about *JoJo*, or people I knew back in school?

"No, not all of them," she said, "largely thanks to you. But we have very little time, so no more questions; I need your help. You must use that gift you brought to help me call Paige here."

"I…don't. You mean that box I opened, or…my *gift?*"

"They are the same thing," she said.

"Well then… All I do is…vanish. How can that—"

"It's not just that," she said impatiently. "You told us so that first night in the kitchen when we talked about what Paige had told you—though none of us has bothered paying attention, sadly. You fit in, and help others to fit in, to come together—like the pieces of a broken plate, as Elle said. Is that not what *you* told us?"

"Okay, yes… But what—"

"Stop asking questions! Just open the gift, and use it! Please! I need you to teach my guests here a party game. It's called, 'Paige, where are you?'"

"Okay…" I said. "But…how is it played? Are there rules?"

"You already know the game! You've been playing it for years now. You've been playing it with *us* all week! Simply teach them to play it too—and quickly please. I am running out—of everything."

I was only more and more confused. "I need—"

"Just make one up then," she pled softly. "If you don't know it, your gift does. It will show you how it's played, but you must go out and do it now."

I was desperate not to fail her—or George, or anyone. "Okay. I'll teach them a game. 'Paige where are you.' Got it. See you later."

"I hope so, my dear," she said. "Sorry to be snippy. Now go on, and good luck!"

I turned and left her room, not even sure I knew any party games.

It couldn't be charades or anything like that, because we had no time, apparently. No pressure, right? So…it had to be easy and quick to learn and something lots and lots of people could play all at once. But *nothing* fitting that description came to mind as I walked past the buffet table except for the stupid Bunny Hop!

And suddenly, I imagined a whole room of people doing the Bunny Hop and shouting, *Where is Paige?* Good grief; could it be that simple? Well, it didn't matter because I was already walking back into the party room, and I had nothing else. Not even time to keep thinking.

I put my fingers between my lips, and produced the loudest, shrillest whistle I had ever heard, which made everybody stop and look at me again. Even the music stopped. For a second, I just looked back at them in astonishment, because I had no idea how to whistle like that in the waking world. But here, apparently, no problem.

"Okay, people. I think it's time to play a game! Don't you?" I shouted happily, trying to sound like a cheerleader, not a maniac, and braced myself for groans and catcalls. But no; everybody cheered again, and clapped their hands as Simone and George came running up, looking as excited as the rest.

"What's it called?" Simone asked me, grinning ear to ear.

"It's called, *'Hey, Paige! Where Are You!'*" I said loudly, so that everyone would hear.

"HEY, PAIGE, WHERE ARE YOU!" everyone shouted, laughing and clapping again.

Wow. Good crowd, at least.

"How's it played?" George asked.

Okay, gift, I thought. *How's it played?* I imagined that Bunny Hop again, and said, "When I say *go*, everybody turn to someone next to you, and ask, 'Are you Paige?' If they say no, they have to put both hands on your shoulders, and follow you to ask someone else if they're Paige." I looked up at the whole room now. "If that next person says no, they have to put their hands on the shoulders of the last person who said no, and all three of you find someone else to ask. Then…keep going. Does everybody get it?"

George nodded, grinning, as lots of others shouted yes, reminding me of that part too. "But while your line goes looking for new people," I said, "everybody in it has to shout, '*Hey, Paige, where are you?*' Because…that makes it harder for the other lines' questions and answers to be heard. So, you'll slow them down by shouting, see?"

"Does slowing them down help you win?" asked young Simone.

"Yes; how do you win?" George echoed her.

Winning, I thought. Why did everything have to be about winning? *How do you win…?*

"Eventually," I said, thinking hard, "since no one here is Paige—"

"Yet!" George corrected me.

"Yet," I said, nodding at him, "there should eventually be just one long line, shouting, '*Hey, Paige, where are you?*' Whoever is still at the head of that last huge line is the winner! So you always need to ask that question faster than the person you're meeting, because if you're the one who has to answer, not the one who asks—and assuming you're not Paige, of course—you're at the end of the line."

"And what's the prize for winning?" George asked eagerly.

"That…is a surprise," I said, partially because I had no idea. But also because I hoped and prayed that long before that final line was formed, Paige would have answered our call, and this dream would finally be over.

"*Are you Paige?!*" George turned to yell at Simone, who immediately looked crestfallen.

"Nope! Wait!" I said. "Not till I say *go*, remember?"

"Oh." George looked embarrassed. "Sorry Simone."

I smiled at them, and waited…and waited, until I saw George start to fidget. Then, very quietly, because, well, I sort of *wanted* George to win, I said, "Go."

The chaos was instantaneous. A hundred people all shouting, "*Are you Paige?"* as couples, then trios, dashed about to shout the question again. Simone's hands were back on George's shoulders as I watched him win the shouting match again with someone next to her. It seemed barely seconds before small lines started shouting, *"Hey Paige, where are you?"* In no time at all, those lines were long enough to start getting tangled in often hilarious train wrecks, with a lot of laughter. But, as those lines got longer, the question they were shouting got louder and louder too. I watched them all with tears welling in my eyes now; not from fear this time, but from hope that this might actually work.

Hey, Paige, I thought. *Are you listening? Please be listening.*

☙

THE PARTY ROOM NEVER QUITE seemed to run out of space for whatever all the people in it were doing, which was especially good as we got down to just three very long, very rowdy repurposed Bunny Hop lines, all shouting *"HEY, PAIGE, WHERE ARE YOU?"* loud enough to… No, I'm not even going to say it. But it had become extremely hard for the three remaining "fronters"—one of whom was George—to chase each other down and ask the dreaded question while trailing a line of thirty or forty other shouting, staggering people behind them.

It wouldn't be much longer before there was only one line left. And I'd still seen no sign anywhere of Paige.

If this didn't work, what would happen to Simone? Or to me? And Florence and Diane—if they'd really ended up here too. Would we all just wake up back at the Berry Farm no closer to a solution than before, or vanish into the otherworld forever? I tried not to imagine Jen coming home from her shift at the Barnacle to find all of us lying there in comas.

Paige, please! I thought more anxiously than ever as Simone's guests careened around me, shouting louder and laughing harder.

Then, it happened. The two remaining lines managed somehow to meet head on at last; and George beat his harried opponent to the question by a single word, forcing the other boy, when his panting had died down enough, to bow his head and say, "No. I am not." George thrust both his strangely blurring hands up in the air and whooped in victory as everybody cheered him—even those he had defeated. Which nearly broke my heart. Had he been happy like this even once in over sixty years? And now the game was finished, without Paige. How many more minutes of such happiness would this dream allow poor George before it collapsed—leaving him where? Haunting his pond and Paige's house again?

"All right th-then!" George said happily to the team he'd beaten. "Evvvererrybody to the back now—all of you. That's th-the rule."

Weirdly, even the defeated players cheered and scrambled to comply, so that a moment later, the entire party was back to dancing around the room, kicking up their feet in one enormous line and shouting, *"HEY PAIGE, WHERE ARE YOU?"* They were having too much fun to stop, which seemed a good way for us to end, I thought: too happily to see it coming.

And then, a nudge at my elbow made me turn to find young Simone looking at me solemnly. "Mother needs to speak with you."

My heart sank. Here it came. Would she offer me evacuation instructions, or just goodbyes?

Simone turned, and I followed her back the way we'd gone before.

We hadn't even made it to the buffet room when everything around us stopped, as fully and instantly as when I'd first opened up my gift. I felt it in my bones, like the vibration below hearing just before an earthquake or a coming train, or the way the world seems to bend before a giant gust of wind. I turned with everybody else to see the crowd of partygoers part before her. Old, but straight and hearty, just as I remembered, draped in layers of fringy, woven fiber clothing. She gazed around her in bemusement as she came farther into the stunned and silent room. Maybe it was just because I'd happened to stop in the buffet room doorway, but I caught her eye somehow. Her brows rose, and a corner of her lovely, crooked smile lifted slightly, as if to say, *Well, well, my girl; who'd have thought that I might see* you *here?*

And then, with a heart-rending wail of bottled pain, George rushed from the silent crowd, growing older and less blurred with every step, so that it was no longer a boy but a tall and lanky young man who threw his arms around her, as a man caught in a raging flood might throw his arms around a passing tree, and sobbed against her chest. She put her arms around him too, lowering her cheek to his, calmly, but bemused no longer. That was all any of us got to see before the room around us began to glow as if the sun were rising behind a wall of onion skin—and her voice came from everywhere inside me. *"Oh, my dear... Well done."*

I started weeping, and could not stop. Those five words are the only part of what passed between us in that instant that I know how to translate here. But our real conversation was…so much larger. It held everything I wished I'd told her after she'd died, and everything I wished I could have asked her too. She showed me all the people who had come together at the wake we'd thrown, at her memorial service and its after-gathering, at the inn that Jen and I had started at her house, and even at the party in this dream—not as things I'd made happen with my gift, but as things my gift had made through me.

The gift I'd spent nearly my whole lifetime so far trying to outrun.

All in the time it took Simone's amazing dream to flare up like a candle flame and die.

Which left me…somewhere dark. Staring up at…was that…a ceiling?

I tried to raise my head, but groaned and laid it down again. My neck felt like a fencepost made of pain, and a gong had just been struck inside my head. With a whispered moan, I tried again, more slowly, and found myself slumped in the chair I had been sitting in before I'd gone upstairs to… Except the house was dark now. There were no lights on anywhere, just shards of moonlight scattered near the windows.

I heard small movements around me, and memories of where I'd been during and before Simone's dream began trickling back. "Simone?" I asked softly. A very quiet sigh, but nothing more. "Florence?" I asked. "Diane? Who's here? Is everyone okay?"

A small whimper, like someone crying in their sleep off to my left. Then what sounded like…the fluttering of wings? I sat up, still wincing at the stiffness but a great deal more alert, and saw the darkened shapes of all three aunties slumped down in their places. But we were not alone. Other things were moving furtively in the darkened room. I froze in fear. *"Florence?"* I whispered more loudly, wanting her to be there most of all for some reason.

"Cam?" she said. "Why is it dark? Where has everybody…"

She was interrupted by the flap of wings again—big wings, like a duck, or—

I launched out of my chair and lunged for the nearest light switch, then spun around and stood gaping as at least a dozen birds, only two of them ravens, fluttered or flapped into the air to fly, scrabbling and thudding against the walls and ceiling in a panic. Three wild rabbits scampered for cover as well, and a squirrel leapt from Simone's love seat to dash through the front parlor and out the foyer pocket doorway, just beyond which, I heard the bleating of a *goat!*

"*Good god!*" gasped Florence, sitting up now too and staring wide-eyed at everything I was seeing. Which was comforting in that maybe I was not still trapped in some ghostly hallucination after all; but not so comforting in that my beautiful new inn was full of wild animals for some reason—and was there really a goat out in the foyer?

"Shoo! Shoo!!" Florence had gotten up now and was trying to wave creatures toward the pocket doorway.

"Ohhh…" Diane, groaned, turning over in her chair. "Where…"

I ran out to turn on more lights in the front parlor as I headed for the foyer, where I found the front door wide open and, yes, Clara standing near the still-closed—thank goodness—kitchen door, chewing something I didn't even want to know what it might be. "Why is the front door open?" I called back to Florence as I went to try bullying Clara back outside.

"Because you went running out of it," she said, trying to herd two of the rabbits through the front parlor's pocket doorway too now, "just before I found myself…doing some kind of Bunny Hop at a huge party, somewhere?"

"Oh good heavens!" I heard Diane exclaim from back inside the second parlor, likely awake enough now to notice all these animals. But I had Clara in a head lock now, and couldn't go and help Diane out too.

"Did I ever even go upstairs?" I asked Florence, dragging Clara closer to the door.

"No," said Florence. "You just— Where did it take *you?* Was Paige there too?"

"Yes!" I said, finally wrenching Clara out onto the porch. "So were you and Diane. And if it was me who talked you all into that Bunny Hop, then I think we were all in Simone's dream."

"Is that what it was?" asked Florence, as her rabbits finally bolted past me for the great outdoors. "But what are all these creatures doing in here? This can't just be what happens when you leave a door open around here, can it?"

"Florence! Cam! Come here!" cried Diane, still clear back in the second parlor. "I need you! Simone won't wake up!"

Florence and I shot each other a look. "Don't you run away now," I told Clara, and hurried with Florence back to the second parlor.

We arrived to find Diane bent over Simone, who was still unconscious on the love seat, and not looking well at all. Her skin was grayish, and her cheeks looked sunken. "Oh, my dear," Diane moaned, "please come back. It worked! You did so well. But we need you to come back now, dear. *I* need you!"

Florence put a hand over her mouth, looking horrified.

I knelt beside Diane, wondering where the cats had gone. Not even James was here. "Simone?" I said. "It's Cam. We did it. George is back with Paige. And Diane is right: we need you back." Where were the damn cats? They were supposed to be her tethers to this…place. They'd really seemed to understand that, before we'd all left. "Simone? Please. Can you just follow our voices back?"

"Oh, Simone!" Diane wept. "I'm not ready to lose you! You were right. I was wrong. Please…" she whispered. "Let me say that to you, face to face."

I heard the rustle of Florence's dress behind me, and turned to look up at her. She looked so fierce that I stood up and backed away. Diane looked up too, her face a tear-streaked mask of desperation now.

"*Simone,*" Florence said—and I felt the force of her will hit me like a sudden sickness of desire. "I can't have you on my conscience too." She sounded more desperate now than fierce. "I need you to come back, dear. It would mean the world to me." Tears splashed down her cheeks. "I'm sorry," she wept. "But I need you back as well, Simone. It is…*all I want.*"

I saw Diane's face go slack, as I suspect mine did too. I'd have rushed right back into the void myself at that moment to find Simone and bring her back, if I'd known how to. Not for Simone's sake, or for Diane's; but just because it was what Florence needed.

Neither Diane nor I was even looking at Simone now. We gazed up at Florence in a stupor. Her face was a mask of abject misery.

"Florence?" murmured Simone. And the whole sense of compulsion that had held me hardly breathing fell instantly away. I almost gasped for air as I turned to see Simone's eyes fluttering, but open. "That's… quite enough of that, dear. Thank you," Simone murmured.

"Oh, Simone! You were miraculous!" Diane cried, lunging in to wrap her in a hug as fierce as Florence's face had been just seconds earlier. "I know now! Paige spoke to me."

"Yes," Simone said, still sounding weak, but fully present now. "She spoke to everyone, I think." Her gaze moved up past Diane to Florence again. "Even…to the cats, it seems…"

I looked at Florence, who was crying even harder now. "I'm sorry!" she wept, looking wretchedly from one of us to another. *"I'm sorry!"* And she rushed from the room, through the front parlor into the foyer, and ran up the stairs.

CHAPTER 17

The aunties, I was discovering, had solutions for everything, and the basis for most of them seemed to be, *Things don't have to be as complicated as you're making them.* With Clara already outside, and Simone returned to us, it took me surprisingly little time to get the rest of our animal friends out of the house—mostly because that's where all of them except Clara really wanted to be anyway. And with them out of the mix, the mess wasn't so bad. A few feathers here and there, some rabbit pellets and a little bird poop, a ding in the woodwork here, a scuff in the hardwood flooring there; the general sense that, while we were gone, someone might have had a pillow fight downstairs—using a couple barnyards instead of pillows. But nothing Jen was likely to notice right away, at least.

Cleaning up the little patch or two of "offerings" that Clara had left in thanks for my hospitality was the biggest task; but it was a hardwood floor, and, being an inn, we had cleaning products and knew how to use them. The whole reclamation effort took me less than half an hour, which left almost two more hours before Jen was likely to get home from the Barnacle.

When I went back into the second parlor to see how Simone—and Diane, honestly—were recovering, Simone was looking much more like herself again. "If you have any trouble with Jen, just blame all this on us again. Tell her we wore you out all week so badly that you went up to take a nap, and when you came downstairs again, you couldn't get a straight answer out of us about whatever happened. That way, dear, she'll just have to come to us; and trust me, we can handle her."

There was always at least a touch of truth in the aunties' fabrications, which was part of what made them so effective. I was definitely learning things.

Diane's business for the rest of that evening was Simone, and who could blame her? None of us saw Florence again that night. And I decided to turn in early. If we were all asleep when Jen got home, then there'd be nothing more for me to deal with till morning. I walked into my room, already yawning, and there, asleep at the foot of my bed, was James. Using the same trick on me, I suspected. *Can't talk about it now. I'm sleeping.* But in the morning, there would be a reckoning.

In the morning, though, things moved along too quickly to leave any room for wondering about yesterday. Jen greeted me as usual when I joined her for our separate little breakfast in the kitchen, and said she'd found a note from Diane taped to the kitchen door that said they'd be needing to check out after breakfast, and would appreciate a ride back to the ferry landing before noon, if that wasn't too much trouble. I was just as surprised as she was.

"Did something happen yesterday?" Jen asked.

"Like…what?"

"Well, I don't know, or I wouldn't be asking you, would I? Their checkout just seems so abrupt. I hope nothing we did ticked them off."

"Oh! No, nothing I'm aware of, anyway." Though Sheriff Clarke had asked us all to stay around a while. Was Simone not feeling better after all? I would have to check on that as soon as either of them appeared for breakfast. "I'll drive them down, of course."

"Well, yes," she said, looking amused. "Unless you want them squeezed into the cab of my pickup. Are you okay this morning? You seem…kind of poorly slept again."

"Do I? No, I'm fine. Yesterday… I adore these ladies, but having them all here this long, and everything that tumbled out on Lopez Island…" I smiled at her. "It's not completely terrible that they've decided to go home, you know?"

"I'll miss them," Jen said. "But yes, I know." She sipped her coffee, thoughtfully. "Was there a bird in the house yesterday?"

I shot her a look. "I don't think so. Why?"

"I found a couple black feathers and some spots of bird poop on the staircase when I was coming down this morning." She gave me an inquisitive look.

"Well…I did take kind of a long nap. You could ask the aunties."

I went back to my breakfast, and so did Jen. But a minute later, she looked back at me. "Are you ever going to tell me what's really been going on here?"

"What are you talking about?" I asked, hoping my unreliable poker face was in working mode this morning.

"You've been spending a lot more time with these aunties of yours than any innkeeper should need to," she said. "Why's that?"

"Ah. Well… I think it's because they all knew Paige. For decades before I did, I mean. And you know how much I've wished I'd known more about her life. Remember when they told us about George? Even you were interested. I've just been milking them for more stories, that's all. And they've been very nice about letting me pester them."

"They don't seem very pestered to me. They asked you to go to Lopez with them—on a secret mission, apparently." She gave me another inquisitive look. "That doesn't seem a little weird to you?"

"Oh, well, that part, yes! *I* asked them why they'd dragged me into that. Several times."

"What did they say?"

"You know, they never really answered me. They're a very tricky bunch of ladies, actually." I turned and looked right at her, hoping to seem frank. "And now that you mention it, I think you may be right! I think they're up to more here than they've told either of us. I mean, look at how Florence just decided to show up right at the same time Diane and Simone were already here! That's just coincidence? I don't think so!"

"You're right," said Jen, thoughtfully. "Well… Don't get me wrong; I'm glad they're here. I've really enjoyed having them around. Especially Florence. But that's one weird bunch of aunties you have there."

"Don't I know it," I agreed.

And happily, that seemed to be that.

Florence came down for breakfast, looking as posh and perfect as ever. But she was much quieter than usual, responding graciously to anything we said to her, but never leaping in the way she liked to. I noticed she was wearing George's ring on a fine silver chain around her neck now, and wondered if that should have gone to Sheriff Clarke with the finger bone.

To my relief, Diane and Simone seemed just fine. Or as fine as usual, anyway. They thanked us profusely for "such a lovely stay"—*Diane*, and "All the marvelous food!"—*Simone*. And, when they settled up their bill with Jen right after "another lovely breakfast," Diane left an eye-popping tip, which seemed to relieve Jen of any concerns about their satisfaction.

"I think they just paid for all those dinners after all," Jen said as we washed up in the kitchen.

"But technically, they didn't," I said. "So there's no need to call the food police."

An hour later, after a last round of goodbyes and thank yous, Diane, Simone and I drove off in Tigress toward the ferry landing.

"So, your departure seems a little sudden," I said as we started down Deer Harbor Road. "Is there anything I ought to know?"

"Oh, no, dear," said Simone. "We just felt that, since our job is done, you might like to have your life back now, and get some peace and quiet."

"Well…thank you. Though, just for the record, we weren't in any hurry to get rid of you. I've really enjoyed having you both here, and, of course, I'm forever grateful for all you've done. I don't even know how to begin thanking you for everything."

"You already have," said Diane. "In more ways than you'll ever know."

Really? I thought, not quite clear on what I'd done, except around the edges. "But, should we let Sheriff Clarke know you're going? He did kind of ask us all to stick around."

"Already done," said Diane. "I had a brief exchange of emails this morning with one of his superiors in Seattle, and asked him to assure the sheriff of my full availability if he should have any further need of my assistance." Clarke had superiors in Seattle? And Diane was asking them for favors? Florence hadn't been exaggerating, had she. "But it seems unlikely that he will," Diane went on. "From what I was told this morning, both Rheena Henderson and Anna Levine have already been very cooperative, and informed investigators about the confession Anna's father made to her—in a drunken stupor, apparently, shortly before his death. Neither she nor Rheena is responsible for things their fathers did, and it seems they were both sensible enough to realize that lying about it now was just going to make more trouble, not less, for them."

"So…did your, um, associate in Seattle say anything about what they'd told Clarke, exactly?" I asked, hopefully.

"Oh yes. I think at this point, they see me more as a member of the investigative team than as a suspect or a witness. Anna and Rheena are all the witnesses they'll need. And the suspects are all beyond anybody's reach now."

"Right. So, I suppose you're not allowed to tell me what Anna or Rheena said."

"Oh! I'm sorry. Of course I can. I just…" Diane shook her head. "I'm so preoccupied right now. But, yes, according to the girls, George had tried to hitchhike to the home of his friend, the fisherman, as we'd surmised. And it seems that Leon only meant to offer him a ride, but he was on his way to deliver some replacement part for the illegal still that his friend, Zeph, was operating, and made the rather stupid decision to stop and take care of that on his way to deliver George. He was unaware, it seems, of what job George was leaving to become a fisherman. But, according to Anna, the fact of George's current employment had come to light there at the still somehow, and Zeph had clubbed George across the back of his head before Leon could do anything to stop him. Whether Zeph *meant* to kill him, no one's probably ever going to know, now. But after that, they just weighted George's wrapped-up body and threw it in the pond."

She gazed out the window for a moment.

"But, alcohol wasn't illegal in the nineteen-sixties," I said. "What was Zeph afraid George would do?"

"*Alcohol* was not illegal," Diane said, "but cooking up vast quantities of it to sell without a license or paying the state its share certainly was," Diane said.

"Ah."

"I can't help wondering how or why George would have been foolish enough to reveal the nature of a job that he was leaving anyway at such an inappropriate moment. Unless…" Diane shook her head. "From what Florence told us the other night, it seems that the main issue between him and Paige was his fear of confrontation. Wouldn't it be sadly ironic if, on his last day as a warden, he decided to step up and prove that he was not afraid to confront wrongdoing when he found it?"

"Do you think that's what he did?" I asked, imagining how appalled Paige would have been to know that she had unknowingly goaded him into the confrontation that got him killed that very day.

"I have no idea," Diane said. "Everyone who might have known is gone, or just as good as, in Zeph's case."

"If even George knew anymore, I never saw that knowledge in him," Simone put in, from the back seat. "Although I can tell you now that nearly all the pain we saw last night belonged to George at the pond. George at the house had no concerns about betraying Paige or anyone. He'd come back to her the instant he died, and thought they'd been living up there at the house together ever since. He'd felt almost no pain at all until she suddenly disappeared, which is likely why not even Paige had been aware of him before." She paused a moment. "She might have been aware of him unconsciously," she added, sounding thoughtful. "It would help explain why such a forceful, generally happy woman never seemed to care about finding that kind of love again. Maybe, deep in her heart, she too already had it, all along."

"Wow..." I thought again of poor Emile Fisher. *He was there between us the whole time...*

"But, that's why George divided himself up that way," Simone went on. "To keep all the pain there at the pond from poisoning the joy that could still be had by George up at the house."

As she said this, I remembered George shoving his arms into the air last night and whooping in victory. Had George at the pond experienced any of that happiness at all? Or had he just hidden there in silence the whole time, until Paige arrived, and set him free?

The thought gave me chills.

"You learned all this last night?" I asked in amazement.

Simone nodded. "So many things became *much* clearer once I tethered both of him to me—which, as I feared, was a dreadful moment for all three of us."

"I think Diane and Florence may have...heard some of that," I said.

"I wouldn't be surprised."

"How did you do that?" asked Diane. "I still haven't thought to ask! And I apologize for saying this, but it does seem like the sort of skill we might need again someday."

"I don't know that it will prove reproducible," Simone said. "The tether last night turned out to be Paige. Only the possibility of being reunited with her was enough to overcome George's horror of confronting himself. I feel fairly sure that we will never have another Paige to make that work again. Nor am I sad about that, honestly. Strapping that much pain to myself by making promises I had no sure idea how to keep was…not a thing I'm eager to do twice."

We all fell silent for a minute after that. But then another thing occurred to me, and for the sake of my own household harmony, I really had to know. "Last night after Florence…did what she did, you said something to her about Paige…talking even to the cats?"

"Hmmm. Yes, that," Simone said grimly. "It seems that Paige asked the cats to abandon me, in hopes of forcing Florence to do just what she did."

"*What?*" Diane and I said, together.

"Florence is apparently so afraid and ashamed of her gift that she's rarely dared to use it for anything that might really matter. Only in ways she thinks trivial, or of importance to no one but herself. I guess Paige wished to fix that."

"By throwing you across the tracks?" Diane asked, angrily.

"So, she told the cats to leave last night?" I asked, still unable to believe it.

Simone nodded. "They were at my little party too. Did you not see them there?"

"No, I didn't." There'd been a lot of other things to pay attention to, most of them larger, louder, and higher off the ground. "Did she at least warn you she was going to do that?"

"In a way, I guess." Simone wagged her head from side to side. "I did think that it was rather odd to be sharing her thoughts about Florence with me, especially at such a moment. But I am beginning to suspect that Paige has told us lots of things in ways we wouldn't have to hear unless we wanted to."

"But, what if it hadn't worked?" Diane demanded, still obviously angry.

Simone shrugged. "She's a citizen of the otherworld now. Who knows how such beings parse these things? But, of course, it did work, clearly. Florence stripped bare the thing she's most ashamed of right in front of all of you to try something that was definitely going to matter—to everyone, whether it had worked or not. A very painful moment for her, I suspect."

Diane shook her head. "I told her how grateful I was, this morning. But I had no idea…"

"And while we're on the topic of cats," Simone said, "it seems all those animals in the house were courtesy of them."

Once again, both my head and Diane's swiveled toward her in astonishment. I nearly missed a curve. "How?" I asked as Diane asked, "Why?"

"Paige had asked them to leave me tetherless, and even James had known her far too well to argue with her. But, as I may have mentioned, most animals live, to some extent, on both sides of the otherworld. So, forced to leave the house themselves, the cats apparently went out and convinced as many other animals as they could to come through the doors and windows you had all so conveniently left open, and…stand in for them, in hopes that I would be able to use all their dual presences as tethers instead. A kind of last-ditch, Hail Mary pass, I guess. But, sadly, even many other animals together aren't the equal of a cat."

"And how do you know all of *that?*" I asked in disbelief.

Simone gave me a slightly incredulous look. "The cats told me this morning, of course." She turned away and smiled. "They were quite apologetic."

I kept my eyes on the road, but my mouth was hanging open now. "I'm really going to miss you guys, you know. Life won't be the same. More restful, maybe. And less complicated. But…nowhere near as interesting."

"Well, if you have any further problems of this nature," said Diane, "feel free to call us. We'd be very happy to come back and enjoy your company again."

"Do you expect us to have further problems?" I asked, mildly alarmed.

"Oh, no dear," scoffed Simone. "George is nowhere in that house now. I checked very thoroughly this morning. I'm quite sure he's gone with Paige. I believe Diane was just trying to be polite."

"Which I've never been much good at," Diane said, seeming totally unbothered by Simone's remark. "But I wasn't just being polite, dear. I've had a very good time here."

Well…by some definition of "good time," I guessed. But all I said aloud was, "I'm glad to hear that. Thank you!"

"And you don't need to have a ghost to call us," Diane said. "I have no idea if it matters, but Paige did at times ask me for investment advice, which my particular skills often prove useful for. So, if you ever—"

"Yes!" I said, then bit my lip. "I'm sorry. I mean, *thank you*, but yes I would be very grateful for any help you might want to give me there. I am…so not very good at understanding all of that." Though *someone* sure was, I didn't add.

Diane smiled, and looked away. "Paige wasn't either, honestly. But that's what friends are for. No one can be good at everything."

☙

When Florence asked if we'd mind her staying a few more days, we assured her we would not. But we saw very little of her after that, except at breakfasts and dinners, which she still seemed to enjoy quite a bit, and praised very lavishly. The rest of her time with us was spent elsewhere, though she said nothing about where to either of us.

And then, one morning after breakfast, she thanked us for our outstanding hospitality, and said that she'd be settling up her bill now and leaving around lunchtime. When I asked if she'd want a ride back to the airport—I didn't even bother mentioning the ferry landing—she just smiled and shook her head. "I'll be having lunch with a friend. A car will come for me."

Of course it would. This sort of thing no longer dazzled me, or annoyed me either. It had become a kind of running gag now that only made me want to smile, though I didn't do that either. Not with her right there to see it.

When Jen and I had finished in the kitchen, I went back upstairs, intending to lie down in my room with a good book, and start trying to remember what that "peace and quiet" Simone had mentioned might feel like. But as I approached my bedroom, the Blue Heron Suite's door opened, and Florence waved me over. "Have you got a minute to talk?"

"Sure."

She stepped aside to let me enter, and sat on the bed as I came in. "Please, sit anywhere," she said, grinning at the vanity's chair, which was my only option—besides sitting next to her there on the bed, of course.

"So," I said, sitting at the vanity. "What's up?"

She looked down awkwardly—a very unusual thing for her to do. "First, I need… I *want* to thank you. This hasn't been just a lovely visit. And this isn't just a lovely inn you two are making here. The past week has been…an inflection point for me." She looked up, unsmiling, and met my eyes. "All this…has changed my life. And you've had everything to do with that, as I believe you know."

Talk about jumping right in at the deep end… I had no idea what to say. So, as one brilliant conversationalist to another, I came up with, "Can you be any more specific?"

For an instant, she merely stared at me. Then she threw back her head and laughed. It was a real laugh, though. Not one of those *charming* ones she'd used on me before. "You are…so unpredictable! But, yes, actually. I intend to be a great deal more specific. About a lot of things, which is why I asked you to come in."

I just nodded this time, having had my shot at snappy repartee.

"I've spent a lot of time the past few days out on my own, just walking. Thinking. And this morning, before breakfast, I had a remarkable phone call with Elle—who says hello, by the way."

"Oh! How is she?" I'd been planning to call her too, as soon as everything calmed down a little. Because it totally would, right?

"She is…*Elle*." Florence spread her hands with a helpless smile. "She also asked me to thank you again for the amazing party. But…I'm still not entirely sure which party she was referring to. You saw her there the other night, I assume?"

"Yes. Though I'm still not sure what she was doing there, or a lot of other people either."

Florence looked at me curiously. "Paige seemed to think you had brought most of them. Or that your gift had, somehow? She talked some about that, but didn't ever mention vanishing."

"Paige talked to you about *me?*" I thought about the giant conversation Paige and I had shared in that tiny instant at the end, and wondered why she would have wasted a second of her time with Florence on me. Then again, she'd wasted time with Simone on Florence; and Simone seemed to wish that she'd paid more attention. So…

"Actually," said Florence, "we talked *mostly* about you."

Now I felt my mouth fall open. "*Why?*"

"Well, Paige thinks you have important things to teach me," she said quietly.

I stared at her for a long moment. "Like what?" I asked at last.

"To begin with, Paige told me that you know something about fear of being seen?"

"Oh... That's kind of true, actually."

Florence nodded. "Well, I think it's time I started learning how to take that kind of risk as well. And so...there are some things I'd like to try letting you see now, if that's all right?"

"Of course it is," I said. "And one important lesson about learning to be seen that I can think of right away is that...you'll need to get past asking for other people's permission to do it. Eventually, I mean. Not now. Now, where you are is fine."

Florence smiled, even as her eyes grew pink with tears. "Well, there; you see? You've already proved her right." She drew a deep breath, took a quick swipe at the corner of one perfectly made up eye, and said, "I told you that night in the cottage on Lopez that our falling-out was not the worst wound I'd received that day. Do you remember?"

I nodded.

"So, now I'd like to tell you what I meant by that—mostly just because I've never wanted you or anyone to know."

"That sounds like a place to start being seen."

She looked down again, and bit her lip. "The wound I was...not telling you about that night didn't really happen that day either. It goes back over sixty years, actually. But that old blade *had* gotten twisted very badly at the pond that night."

Over sixty years... She had told us all about what great besties she and Paige had been here back when George had come along, but I'd still never put two and two together—until now. I think my brain just couldn't go there. But if they'd been pals way back then, then... this Hollywood temptress must be nearly Paige's age! I was looking at a ninety-year-old woman who could still blow Cher out of the water.

Fortunately, this revelation left me speechless.

"You see... I have always..." She paused again, clearly struggling with whatever was next. "I have always held myself responsible for... what happened." She looked back up at me, as if expecting that I'd see it now, and be appalled, I guess. But...I didn't. "To George and Paige," she clarified, as if that helped.

"What part did *you* have in any of that?"

She looked down again; not like she was thinking this time, but like she couldn't look me in the eyes. "I...think I caused their argument. Not just that morning, but...from the start."

"But, you told us they argued about his fear of conflict, and leaving

Paige responsible for all the scary work in their relationship while he kept playing nice. That wasn't true?"

She nodded. "Oh, yes, that much was true. But I'm quite sure they'd have worked all that out like lots of other people in love do, if not for me." She finally looked back up at me again, like someone who's decided just to go ahead and take a punch.

"And why would you think that?" I asked quietly, bracing myself to hear there'd been an affair between herself and George after all.

"I guess...I've started in the wrong part of this story." She looked over at the window. "I told you that my gift is actually a curse. Here's what I mean by that."

To my surprise, she started telling me about her life as a child: how endlessly delightful it had been for her to see nothing but charmed excitement and approval on the faces of literally everyone she met—even her parents—nearly all the time. She hadn't known that she was doing anything to cause that yet, except for being herself.

She went on about being the most celebrated paragon that anyone at her high school had ever known, either teachers or her fellow students. How she'd gotten pretty much straight A's in all her subjects, and any part she wanted in the school plays, had boys lined up to date her, and been chosen prom queen every year. And even then she'd just thought herself a very lucky, gifted girl—in the very normal sense.

But then, in college, where she was elected president of the most popular sorority on campus—in her sophomore year—pursued by all the M.E.B.s (Most Eligible Bachelors), and headed toward a grand career in liberal arts, which even now she couldn't quite explain, she had finally run into someone else who had "a gift," in the extra-natural sense, and knew it. A girl in her English class, who knew almost right away what Florence was as well, and did her the favor not just of explaining it, but proving it to her too.

"From that moment," said Florence, "my life went from Olympian dream to hellish nightmare. I was not—am not—a stupid person; and looking back, I realized that nothing I'd accomplished, nothing I'd been given, nothing I'd been celebrated for, had anything to do with me. It had all just been stolen with a great big, inescapable lie."

"No. Wait a minute," I broke in. "Did you cheat on all the homework and tests behind those A's in high school?"

"No, but that's not—"

"Were you cast in spite of being awful in those high school plays? Somehow, I doubt it. Did you do a crummy job as president of that sorority? Was your taste in clothes and all the rest actually dreadful? Because, I've got to say that, if that's true, I'm wondering what happened to that loser since then. Whatever brain-trick is involved in these magic spells you put on people, I was a damn good salon stylist back in Seattle, and I think your taste is phenomenal. And that merry chase you led Sheriff Clarke on in our room on Lopez took breathtaking brains to put together on the fly like that. Which you clearly knew, by the way. Oh! And as overblown as that miracle you worked down in the parlor may have been, Simone's continued existence seems like a very real achievement to me, and to them too. She and Diane are people like us, who recognize a gift when they see one as well as anybody can. So, who cares how you're doing those things, as long as they're really done? Where's this great big lie you're talking about? I just see you being what you were. What you *are*."

Now it was her turn to look startled, which was…reassuring, I supposed.

"You're still hiding quite a lot in there, I see," she said. "I haven't heard that kind of eloquence from you before. Why is that?"

Good question. That perfect two-fingered whistle I'd pulled off at Simone's party came to mind. But this was not a dream. Was it? It was harder to be sure now than it had been once. I thought of what Simone had said to me that night about my gift—how *it* knew the game, even if I didn't. *Just open it!* Was this another thing like that? My gift…using me? Even here?

Or had it just made me so angry to hear a self-shaming voice in Florence that was so like the one I still remembered hearing in my own head once that I'd…forgotten for a moment to hide some part of what *I* was? Perhaps the part of me that had wanted to be a playwright for a while? That had *been* a playwright for a while, I corrected myself.

"That's… I'll think about that question. It's a good one," I said. "But you were telling me about you when I went off and interrupted that. My bad. I'm sorry. Please go on."

She went on gazing at me for a moment before nodding. "And I will think about all you just said. But, even if you're right, there are still certain things to which your…*generous logic* does not apply—the most important of which is love. I guess that maybe, if I do a good, or even better job than others might have, it may not matter how I won the chance to do so. But would you agree that a man who says he loves you because *he* has decided that he does is fundamentally different than a man who truly believes he loves you because *you* decided that he should?"

Okay… I checked in with my gift, but it didn't seem to have any instant-eloquence answers to that one. Except… "What about a man you knew you hadn't done that to?"

"And how would I know that? I'd lived for nearly twenty years without knowing I was doing anything at all before that girl in English opened my eyes. What happened with Simone down in the parlor," her eyes skittered away from mine again, "isn't going to happen unless I will it to. But I told you the other night how hard a gift like this one is to control in less exaggerated situations, and why. How could I ever be sure the man who says he loves me, and believes it, can be any more certain than I am about whose idea his love really was?"

"I'll…get back to you on that one," I allowed. "But I'm still not seeing how this connects to George and Paige."

"Can't you? Really?" Florence gave a small, sad laugh. "But then you're not Diane, of course. So, from that moment in my sophomore year of college when—right or wrong—I'd come to see my life as a giant lie, I never could believe again that any man had ever really loved me, or ever really could. Love could be a very enjoyable game for someone like me, but must never be 'taken to heart.'

"I met Paige three years later, at the same party in Los Angeles where Simone did. The party parodied in her dream, actually. Simone's mother was also gifted, and understood her daughter's ordeal better than she'd ever let on to Simone, not wanting her to know too soon, before she'd matured enough to bring at least some perspective to deciding what to do with that knowledge. But, as Simone neared college age, her mother threw that party to acquaint other gifted friends with her daughter, and let Simone meet them as well—hoping that the rest would just come out later for her, in more natural ways. I lived in L.A. then, and was invited too.

"But the biggest beneficiaries of that gathering may well have been Paige and me. We bonded within minutes, because, of course, we were both people it was nearly impossible not to love! If in such different ways and for such different reasons, though it would be a while before we really understood that. At first, we were just the world's most beloved and unstoppable duo—everywhere we went. We 'brought the party,' as young people like to say these days.

"Soon after our friendship was cemented, I went to lead an even more glamorous life in San Francisco, while Paige came here, to this tiny, isolated island. Looking back, the real differences between us were visible right there.

"But the main reason our friendship hadn't just imploded right away was that Paige had understood what my gift was, and what it did, almost the minute we met, and had the strength and self-possession to call me on it every time, refusing to be compelled. She thought that who I was and what I did were a hoot, but she wasn't having any of it herself. Do you see what that did?"

"It…made you feel thwarted? Or second fiddle?" I asked.

"Heavens no!" said Florence. "It made me feel safe! Here at last was a person who knew exactly what I was, and had the power to refuse me, but still loved my company—and me—anyway! I never had to wonder if she was just another adoring slave. She made it oh so clear that that could never happen—which made Paige the single most important relationship of any kind in my whole life. That is who we were, when George Harper came along."

"Oh," I said. "You…were jealous."

"Yes," she said, watching me like I'd seen people watch butterflies or birds, wanting them to stay, but waiting for them to fly off and disappear. "I was jealous of both of them. George for having Paige's love in ways I never would. And Paige for being, and having, what I never could. Not that I understood any of that then as I do now. There was just a nameless tension that I kept sweeping under the carpet—not so much to hide it from them, as from myself."

"So…what happened?"

She looked at me in silence for a long time then. Or in my direction, anyway. I soon realized it wasn't me she saw. "I'm the one who first pointed out to Paige that dear, sweet, kind George, whom I adored almost as much as she did, was…really something of a coward, if a very well-disguised one. That his problems at work, and with Paige, might all have the same root. I…pretended to be helping her make it work, defining the problem so that it could be fixed."

Florence and I stared at each other as it all came into focus for me.

"I never meant to drive a wedge between them," she whispered. "Or I didn't think I meant to. And in time, it was the end of me and Paige as well, of course." She sighed and let her gaze fall to the floor. "You found the funny clock I'd given her...stuffed with everything she'd saved from the day she lost him. In a box together beneath her bed where she would never have to look at any of it again."

I had no idea what to say.

"Until last week," said Florence, "I thought that my *influence* had driven them apart, and made him leave." She went on staring at the floor. "But not until that night at the pond did I lose the ability to deny that my interference in their love had cost George his life—and worse things than that."

"Oh, no…" I said. "Don't do that. You can't be sure that it was really you."

"Have I really not explained it clearly enough? My relationship with being *sure*? I can't be sure it wasn't." My eyes moved to his ring, hanging from a chain around her neck. Seeing where my gaze had gone, she reached up and tucked the ring into her blouse. Then she drew another long, deep breath. "Which brings me to the second thing that Paige said I must ask you about."

Really? I thought. *After the bang-up job I just did with that first one?*

"The beginning of the end for Paige and me," said Florence, "was in the nature of our gifts to start with. For all their superficial similarity, hers drew love from those around her to her love of them, empowering her to understand them and help cultivate the best of what they needed to be and do. Mine drew people to nothing but what I wanted them to be or do for me. Or so I've always believed until Paige suggested that I ask you about letting our gifts use us, instead of using them." She found another smile somewhere. "Oddly, Elle brought up the very same topic again this morning—as if she and Paige are in league against me, somehow. I won't ask if you know what they mean, because I've seen you do it for myself already, I think—and not just in Simone's dream, or whatever that was. But…I still can't see what that has to do with me. Can you think of any helpful tips in that regard?"

"What time did you say that car is supposed to be here?" I asked.

Her smile widened. "There should be time to make a start, at least."

"Yes," I said. "And probably a finish too; because I'm not sure I have much to tell you. I'm still trying to figure out what Paige meant by that, myself. Or what to do about it, anyway. Because it always seemed like she was just telling me to do nothing with my gift at all."

"Well, that sounds like wonderful advice," Florence said wistfully. "I'd love nothing better than to follow it. But *my* gift seems to go on using itself no matter how I try to stop it."

"Oh! Then I'm afraid you already know as much as I can tell you."

"What?"

"Well, that's pretty much what Paige kept telling me. That gifts like ours weren't tools for us to pick up and use. She seemed to think they used us—that they have some plan of their own we can only get in the way of if we try to steer instead of just doing whatever the gift wants us to do." I gave her a helpless shrug. "Which sounds very nice until you try to follow her advice, right? I mean, if only my gift knows the plan, how am I even supposed to know what it wants me to do?"

I mistook the expression on her face for total confusion, which seemed about right. But I was mistaken.

"Oh my goodness!" she murmured in apparent surprise. "I never thought of it that way—but if it's true…"

"Wait, that makes some kind of sense to you?" I asked.

"If what she said is right, then it's not about using our gifts well, or learning not to use them at all, or even how to feel about whatever comes of them. It's just about…staying out of the way!" Her mouth remained open, as if she were absorbing some shock. *"Letting*…it all happen," she whispered, to herself it seemed. Then her eyes focused on me again. "We don't need to *know* the plan if…if all we have to do is let things happen…without getting in the way."

I was suddenly unsure which one of us Paige had meant to benefit from this conversation. "But, if we don't know what the plan is, how can we know whether we're getting in the way?"

"If the gift is running things—then whatever comes of that is not…" She shook her head in what looked like wonder. "I've spent my whole life…" She fell silent, seeming to struggle for emotional control. "I've spent my life either trying not to use my gift, or using it selfishly just to…vent my anger. At myself and all the rest of it. Always hating what I did. Or what my gift was doing. I never thought there was a difference. The gift was me, and I could be nothing but what it made me. But if I'm not the gift. If I was never in charge of what it does, or of making it stop…" She looked up at me again. "None of this is just my fault! None of it was ever *mine* to fix!" She finally lost control and burst into tears.

And for a moment, I was too lost in revelations of my own to do more than let her. *Without getting in the way...* That phrase had seized my attention, and wasn't letting go. Paige had known she was going to die, and hadn't given me a chance to say goodbye. She'd changed her will, and never let me know. She'd known others like herself and me, but never told me who they were or where to find them. She'd had such an amazing life before we met, and hardly ever mentioned it to me. And I'd been wondering why, ever since Jen had shown up at the A-frame to tell me she was gone. Wondering why she'd hidden all of that from *me*. But...had she just been staying out of the way?

If she'd told me any of those things ahead of time...it would have changed all sorts of things. Would that have gotten in the way? It was...a strangely terrifying question. For reasons I still didn't clearly understand. So much surrender. So much...risk. Was I supposed to...

"Thank you," Florence said, swiping at her eyes. "I...can hardly tell you..." She looked up—at the ceiling, or the sky, or Paige maybe, wherever she was now. I had no idea. "I'm so glad that I was here. That I stayed," she said, to who, exactly, I couldn't tell.

And we were likely out of time, I realized. "When is your lunch date expected?"

She looked at her lovely silver watch, as delicate as pea vines. "Any minute now. And I must look a wreck. Will you excuse me for a minute?" She grabbed her suitcase before I could answer, and rushed into the bathroom.

Ten minutes later, she emerged looking like a cover shot for the special AARP edition of *Cosmopolitan*.

As we started down the stairs together—Florence carrying her own suitcase again, in spite of my insistence that doing that for her was part of my job—she asked if I was sure I didn't want to keep the clock. "It's...kind of heavy. And I bet your guests would find it whimsical."

"Thanks, but no," I said. "Our lives here seem plenty whimsical already."

"Yes," she said. "You've had four gifted people in this house for almost two weeks now. I'm surprised that you're still standing."

"It wasn't *that* bad," I said, smiling to make sure she knew it was a joke.

"Still. Now you see why we live so secretly, and separately. Just one of us can barely move through the world without disrupting everything we pass. I see that now, as I never have before. Whether we mean to or not: we change things; bend or break them, elevate them sometimes, then deprive them of that elevation after we move on, and leave them worse off than before we came along. Put three or four of us together in one place for even a short time, and look at all the chaos it can cause!" She laughed. "And, if Paige was right, none of that is my fault after all! I don't know how to thank you, Cam."

"I don't think you need to. I didn't understand what I was telling you as well as you did, obviously. I'm still trying to make sense of it now."

At the bottom of the stairs, she set her suitcase down and turned to me. "But living secretly and separately doesn't have to mean living alone—or so Paige told me the other night. She claimed she'd never pushed me away. She said I'd painted our friendship with my own shame and pushed her away instead. Now I understand what she meant. And I'll try not to make that same mistake with you."

"No worries," I said. "I wouldn't let you."

I'd never seen such an unselfconscious smile blossom on her face before. "You sounded just like Paige then."

"Thank you. But I'm not, and never will be. Remember that, and maybe I won't disappoint you."

"I think it's too late for you to disappoint me. Let's stay in touch. And if you ever come through San Francisco, please don't be a stranger."

We both turned toward the crunch of gravel on the driveway, and the purr of a quiet but powerful engine. Florence blew me a kiss, picked up her suitcase, and let me get the door for her at least as she went out, waving at her ride with that Hollywood smile I knew so much better now than I had once.

I went to the window and watched her hand her suitcase to a well-put-together man in his mid-sixties, maybe, who went around to put it in the back of his big, shiny jeepish truck. I didn't recognize the brand, but it screamed *money*. As he returned to help Florence climb up into its cab, I wondered who *this* friend was, and what their secretive liaison might be about.

A week ago, I'd have assumed it would be just some new power play of Florence's, meant only to go on feathering her own vast nest, somehow. But I couldn't think of her that way anymore. How changed was she? I wondered. Would she go off to lunch with this latest mysterious tycoon, and convince him to fund an orphanage, or to back some bunch of climate change activists? I doubted I would ever know.

As they drove off, I headed for the kitchen to make lunch, wondering what it would mean for someone like Florence to let her gift use her. Probably pretty much the same as it would for the rest of us, I decided. She'd go out to lunch on someone's yacht without any plan at all, see what, if anything, came up, and follow as best she could. Plans were fine. They were necessary. There was really no way to make it through a day, much less a lifetime, without them. But in the end, what were plans really but placeholders filling unknown spaces until actual events came along to replace them? Illusions of control. Because, as anyone who's paying attention understands, it's just folly to imagine you can ever know what's really going to happen.

EPILOGUE

Suddenly, it was very, very quiet.

After six months of constant change and activity, Jen and I had nothing to cope with. No unexpected crises or life-changing surprises, no giant moves or all-absorbing renovations, no big gatherings or events, no guests. Even our ghost was gone, not that Jen was likely to notice that. But I did. My life was just a large, empty inn, some patches of garden gone nearly dormant, and a handful of animals to care for—which, don't get me wrong, was still a handful. But...such a small, quiet, unhurried handful compared to the relentless chaos I'd grown used to since the morning I'd learned Paige was gone. Florence had said that when gifted people show up, things change, and she was right. I had...no idea how to live quietly anymore.

So, when Jen set down her coffee cup one morning a few days after Florence's departure and said, "Well, I think our soft opening's gone pretty well. I feel like we've shown we know how to do this. You think we're ready to go live?" I said "Yes!" Though I had no clear idea what that actually meant—right now, exactly, in a practical sense. Because all this "peace and quiet" was just going to make me crazy.

"So what's the plan?" I asked my friend, the innkeeper.

"Well," said Jen, "we get Dylan to activate the open registration pages on our site, and send out another email to our mailing list about our winter availability and activities here."

"Do we have activities?"

"I meant activities on the island. Whatever those are. But you're right. We can't just say, *'Hey! We're open!'* on our website, and expect anyone to notice." Well, I was glad to have been right, though I didn't remember saying any of that. "Because, who's even looking?" Jen went on, clearly honing in on something. "What we need now is visibility. Something that draws attention and makes people not just say, 'Hey, they're open,' but *'Hey! They're cool! We have to go and check this out!'*"

"Okay," I said. "Like what?"

"Well… A party of some kind, maybe? I mean, look at all the guests we got just from that party after Paige's memorial."

"Your food got us those guests, not the party," I said, though of course, our ghost was what had really gotten us those particular guests. But Jen's food had definitely made them want to come back. "So let's make sure there's lots of food at this party."

"Well, that goes without saying," said Jen. "But it can't just be about the food. That's not called a party. That's called a restaurant, and if you thought setting up an inn was hard, you don't want to even think about us trying to be a restaurant!"

No, I sure didn't. Which was why I'd never suggested that either. "Okay, what then? Do we need a theme?"

"Yes!" Jen turned to me with those wide-open eyes and that fanatic look that meant she'd found what she'd been honing in on. "It's a couple weeks from Halloween! That's the best holiday for parties! We need to throw the mother of all Halloween parties! *Oh!* We need to turn the whole inn into a *haunted house!*"

I stared at her. Hadn't all of us just spent… But no, Jen hadn't. She'd only spent the last few weeks running an inn, and looking after three eccentric aunties. If there'd been any plausible way to shout *"NO!"*, believe me, I'd have done it. But there wasn't. So I didn't. Jen's owl-eyed look of glee made it very clear that we'd already passed that off-ramp.

☙❧

AND SHE WENT ALL OUT, because of course she did. An entire day spent ordering from online Halloween supply sites had resulted in skeletons and gravestones and spooky lighting in the front yard; glowing jack-o-lanterns, cobwebs and spiders on the porches; creepy music playing throughout the house. Tattered fabric draped everywhere, including over every lamp—and every light bulb in those lamps had been switched out for blood-red or zombie-green or black-light bulbs. Ghouls and goblins hid behind doors and ghosts peered out of eerily lit upstairs windows; an unsettlingly realistic corpse lay drowned in Jen's and my bathtub. And a disturbingly uncanny-valley black rubber cat sat at the base of a bubbling cauldron in our luridly lit foyer.

Not a single thing our real ghost would have been able to make heads or tails of.

I stood at the bottom of the stairs, admiring how just the change in lighting had turned everything here from elegant and inviting to macabre. And it made me laugh. What a fabulous cartoon we aquarium dwellers had made of death. Yet, wasn't that the best way to go out? Too happily to see it coming? I wondered if we might want to talk our guests into a Halloween Bunny Hop tonight. Because Jen was right. Everyone was going to love this—including our full house of paying guests. Excuse me, paying-*extra* inn guests! We'd advertised the haunted house party with a fifty-dollar-per-guest upcharge, and booked up at once.

"See?" Jen had mused, as she'd clicked "accept" on the final reservation, "people are happy to pay for experiences. And, baby, this is going to be an experience!"

All three couples had brought elaborate costumes; and not wanting to be outdone by our guests, Jen and I had gone all out too.

"Are you going to stand there admiring the scenery all night?" asked the wicked witch herself, a.k.a. Jen, appearing at the upstairs landing rail. "We've got food to plate, and punch to make, and just an hour to do it!" She adjusted her pointy hat over her long black wig and smoothed her ragged-hemmed black lace dress, showing off blood-red fingernails. Then she grinned down at me, showing a few black teeth.

"Oh, you look great!" We'd kept our costumes secret from each other, because we liked surprises. Or, at least, silly fun ones like this. Jen hurried down the stairs, pausing at the midway landing to show off her fabulous costume again with a little curtsy before coming the rest of the way down to join me.

"Okay…what in the world are you supposed to be?" she asked, looking me up and down.

"Do you like it?" I turned my back toward her and waggled my rolled-up green tail.

She stared at me. "I don't know. Are you…some kind of lizard?"

"Some kind, yes. No better guesses than that?" I turned again so she could see my front.

"Ew! Those bulgy eyes are particularly disturbing. And is that…dangly pink thing…supposed to be a *tongue*?"

I laughed. "I'm a chameleon!"

"Ohh….kay… At least there's no flies stuck on it." She leaned down to pat the rubber cat on its creepy little head. "Don't worry, Lucifer, the big scary lizard won't hurt you."

There was a knock at the front door, and I opened it to find Lisa Cannon with a big brown grocery bag in her arms, and all dressed up as… "Nurse Ratched?" I laughed.

"Hey, it was available in a hurry, and can you think of anybody scarier to be on Halloween?" She thrust her grocery bag at me. "The ginger ale you asked for."

"Come in, my pretty!" Jen cackled in her best witch voice. "And let's go put that poisoned elixir in the fridge." She took the bag from Lisa as she entered. "It's too soon to make the punch," Jen said, abandoning her witchy voice as she headed for the kitchen door. "It'll lose all its fizz before they get here."

As I closed the door behind her, Lisa walked around the foyer, gazing through the front parlor pocket doorway, and up the stairwell at all our spooky décor. "You two really don't do things halfway, do you," she said, clearly impressed.

"This is all Jen," I said. "I only held the tacks while she was on the ladder, and helped screw in all these light bulbs."

She turned around, and looked more carefully at me. "So, what are you, exactly?"

I rolled my eyes. "Big curled tail," I said, wiggling my butt to illustrate the point, "large bulgy eyes, long sticky tongue. What has all those things?"

She scrunched her lips in thought. "Jabba the Hutt?"

I made an exasperated noise. "I'm a chameleon!"

"Oh! Of course! You just look…so different on the cover of *National Geographic* magazine." She waved at the décor again. "Where are you going to keep all this stuff the rest of the year?"

"We have a barn for that," I reminded her. "Shall we go help Jen with the food?"

Lisa followed me into the kitchen, where Jen was already busy assembling a plate of green "severed finger" cookies. Her tiny ghost cupcakes and jack-o-lantern cookies were still on their cooling racks, and the room smelled heavenly.

"Oh, Jen!" said Lisa. "I wish I'd known about you back in the days when I was always hiring caterers. You really are a marvel!"

A skull draped with prosciutto (which looked even more disgusting than it sounds) was already on its platter surrounded by deviled eggs adorned with little black spiders made of olives, and the makings for our black magic margaritas were set out on a counter. Spaghetti for the eyeball pasta would need to go on soon. And about two dozen other dishes, in various stages of preparation, were crowded onto the other counters and the kitchen table.

"What I need, if you guys would be so kind," said Jen, "is help setting up the buffet table in the dining room, and then putting all this out there as it's ready. Okay?"

Lisa and I saluted, grabbed the plates and cups and napkins off the counter by the sink, and got started.

Forty minutes later, I was chatting in the dining room with our wildly attired paying guests, after plying them with black magic margaritas. They were suitably impressed with both the decorations and the snacks. And we'd just started sharing our best scary childhood Halloween stories when I heard Kip's voice in the kitchen, which meant he was back from Porter's house with the wine. I excused myself to go help him.

I walked in to find him already opening bottles, as Jen and Lisa worked frantically on final touches to all the rest.

"There you are!" I said, going up to him with a smile.

"I don't even know how to kiss you in that getup," he said, frowning down at me.

I pushed the hood of my costume back and leaned up to him. "There."

He planted a proper kiss on my lips.

"You look very cute," I told him.

"I'm supposed to look dashing and daring and manly," he said, brandishing his Indiana Jones whip, which caused his fedora to tip askew.

"You do," I assured him, setting the hat straight again. "And cute."

He kissed me again, and returned to opening wine bottles.

And then the doorbell rang. Our first non-paying guests had arrived! I hurried back out to the foyer to see who had beaten everybody else to the punch—very literally.

"Trick or treat!" Colin called from the doorway.

"Oh wow," said Priya. "That cat is just *wrong*."

Colin looked me up and down. "You a dragon?"

I sighed and shook my head. The only person who would really have gotten this private little joke of mine was somewhere in the otherworld, and—hopefully—not even going to be here. What had I been thinking?

"Come in, come in!" Jen sang, coming out to greet them. "Blood punch is in here, and you *must* try the severed fingers…"

❦

THE PARTY WAS ALMOST AS jumping as Simone's had been by the time Sheriff Clarke arrived—dressed as a Canadian Mountie, which seemed a little weird. Like…here I am as me but in a different country? I was surprised to see him, actually. We'd put up posters and taken out ads, like we had for Paige's memorial, because the whole idea was visibility, right? But Clarke had never seemed the party type to me. Though that may just have had to do with the nature of most of our previous encounters.

"Ms. Tate," he said, tipping his crisp Mountie hat.

"Sheriff Clarke." I nodded. "How great to see you! Come on back to the dining room and get some wine." I'd had a couple glasses now, and was feeling very relaxed.

"So," he said, staring down with a perplexed expression at the rubber cat beside our cauldron, then up and around the haunted foyer. "This is your inn!"

"Well, yes, and no. It doesn't usually look like this, of course."

"Oh!" His eyebrows shot up in surprise. "Is this a party? On Halloween?"

"Very shrewd observation," I said.

"I have done some detective work from time to time." He studied my costume. "Are you…a snake?"

"Really? Does nobody around here know what a chameleon looks like?"

"A chameleon! Well, no. I don't suppose anybody around here sees those too often." He looked at me with something trying not to be a smile, as if waiting for some response from me. But I didn't know what it could be. *"But,"* he said, rather broadly, "I guess nobody would *see* a chameleon around here, even if we had 'em, right?"

It was the wine, I'm sure. But for a second, I was afraid he'd figured out my secret, and this was his way of telling me. Then I got it. "Oh! It's a joke!"

He looked chagrined. "Okay. I didn't get your costume, and you didn't get my joke. So, now I guess we're even." He looked around. "You mentioned wine?"

"Right this way," I said, turning to lead him through the raucous, dancing crowd between us and the dining room. Jen's spooky sounds recordings had been replaced by now with "Werewolves of London," Michael Jackson's "Thriller," and the "One-eyed Purple People Eater" song, among many, many others in the all but endless playlist she and I had put together.

By that time, however, the big rush for food had largely died away, and nearly everyone had moved back out to dance and socialize in the parlors. There was a lot more space and quiet around us in the dining room now as the sheriff poured himself half a glass and picked up a cookie. "If you'd care to take a moment somewhere a little more private," he said to me, "I could fill you in on where things stand."

"Oh. Yes, thank you. Have you got everything you'd like here?"

He nodded. "These'll do."

"Come with me then."

I led him into the kitchen where there was no one now, though someone might still come in, and out the back door to the kitchen porch. After we'd both looked around to make sure we were actually alone, he told me about the admissions made by Anna Levine and her friend Rheena, and that, yes, at least most of George's remains had been found in the Hendersons' pond, with the rest still being searched for. For all intents and purposes, it seemed an open and shut case already. He thanked me for sending them the sample of George's hair, but told me not to hold my breath waiting for results, as the state lab where DNA tests were done was understaffed and continually backed up. Not that the results really mattered much, at this point. There seemed so little left to prove, and no one to hold accountable; it made no sense to relocate Zeph from his nursing home to some penitentiary for the year or less he likely had to live.

I must have forgotten to don my poker face, because when he had finished, he looked at me for a moment, then sighed. "And you already knew all that, didn't you. Even about Anna."

"Um... I was kind of in on the ground floor of this one," I said.

He nodded. "Well, I have a couple other cases on my desk right now. If you're ever in the mood to come over for an hour or two and solve them for me too, I'd be most appreciative."

I gave him an apologetic smile. "Is there really no faster way to test the DNA?"

"Well, there are private labs, but they can cost up to fifty thousand dollars per case, and no one's going to authorize that kind of cost for a sixty-year-old cold case like this one, with all the investigative questions already answered."

"Well then, let me know when it's done, please." I'd been thinking, and decided that Paige's and George's remains should be together somehow. "Have you found out if he has family anywhere?"

Clarke shook his head. "Without something more than just his name, I'm not sure how anybody's going to find them after all this time, or that anyone who would have cared is still alive. He was about Paige's age, right?"

I nodded. "He'd come from the Midwest somewhere. That's really all I know."

"Well then, unless there was a driver's license or some other actual documentation for him somewhere in Paige's things, we can't go looking for George Harper somewhere in the Midwest. And the DNA isn't going to help that. Forensic DNA wasn't even a thing before the nineteen-eighties. So…I think this is all we're going to find out—which is more than anybody would have hoped for, honestly. Good work, Detective Tate."

"It wasn't me," I told him. "It was all the aunties' doing."

"The aunties?"

I shook my head. "Never mind. Thank you for telling me all this. Is that why you came?"

"Oh no, Ms. Tate. I'd just heard so much about this costume of yours, I had to come and see it for myself." He winked at me. "And your inn, of course. From the crowd in there, I'd say you're off to a great start."

☙

Porter thought I was a fish. Katrina, Jen's boss at the Barnacle, had wondered if I was a parrot. Charles had even thought I was a *Pokémon* of some kind, whatever that was. By the time the party finally started winding down, I was just nodding every time, no matter what somebody guessed, and saying, "Yep! Got it in one!"

Finally, there were just a dozen of us left, including Lisa and the Wendergrasts, and our six paying guests, all gathered around the second parlor fireplace with a few last glasses of wine and the dregs of our buffet. Our mainland guests were endlessly curious about life on this peaceful little island, and Porter and Verna, at least, seemed just as interested in their stories about life back in the outside world these days. All of us had started yawning when, suddenly, a clattering sound raced across the ceiling above us—as if a child had just run across the upper landing.

"What was that?" Lisa asked, as we all stared up at the ceiling.

"I thought everybody else was gone," said Jen.

"We're all here," said one of our six guests, as they looked back and forth between themselves.

There was a thumping crash above us, accompanied by the yowling wail of several cats and more clattering footsteps racing first in one direction, then another, as if the child up there was just careening around in circles now.

"What the hell?" Kip murmured, standing up to head through the front parlor as the rest of us followed him toward the foyer.

"Were there children at this party?" asked one of the guests as we all approached the second pocket doorway.

"I didn't see any," said his wife.

"Then where did—" Verna started, but fell silent as Harry, Sam and James all came tearing down the stairs as if their tails were on fire, and kept racing right between our legs and back through the front parlor to the second one as we turned in astonishment to watch them go. Then a thump, thump, thumping coming down the stairs made all of us whirl around in time to see a skull bouncing down the last few steps to spin and wobble across the foyer floor, coming to a halt almost at our feet.

"Is this something you arranged?" asked Lisa.

"No!" said Jen.

Oh…please, please, please, I thought. *Don't tell me that Simone was wrong.* Was George back for some reason? Had we made him angry with this party?

A loud crack, like splintering wood, came from just out of sight above the stairwell, and a headless skeleton wrapped in tattered lace came hurtling over the railing and plummeted onto the bottom flight of stairs with a horrific clattering crash, as the childish little footsteps raced off again across the darkened upper landing. Several of our guests ran shrieking back into the parlor as Kip raced toward the stairwell, leaping over the fallen skeleton, and taking stairs two at a time from there. I started after him, wondering what I could even do to help if he ran straight into whatever angry apparition we were dealing with now. But before I'd even reached the stairs, we heard Kip shout, *"It's a goat!"*

ආ

Half an hour later, all of us but Porter and Verna, who'd thanked us for a very memorable evening and gone home to get some sleep, were back around the fire in the second parlor, laughing our heads off—not as literally as that skeleton this time—and still too pumped up with adrenaline to turn in yet.

"That was the best party of my life!" said the fellow staying in the Dragonfly Room. "Goats! I'm going to win *all* the vacation story contests now!"

"I just hope we can sleep in," said his wife. "Any chance we could push back breakfast just a little in the morning?"

"Absolutely," said Jen. "I'd love to have a little more wake-up time too."

Everyone agreed that was a super idea, and Lisa wished us a good night too.

Apparently, as the house had heated up during the party, someone had opened the large balcony window upstairs that overlooked the driveway. And some other party guest, after a bit too much wine presumably, had gone out to see Clara and her kids—maybe thinking they were in a petting zoo?—and not latched their gate behind them. It was actually very useful to know now that by jumping up onto our little innkeeper's kitchenette shed on the back kitchen porch, a goat could jump up next onto the house's wraparound porch roof, and from there to the narrow balcony outside that upper landing window.

Having been inside the house once before, and not all that long ago, Clara must have been intrigued by all the things she'd found to nibble on in here, and decided it was worth the climb to have a second shot at that. Kip had found her still chewing avidly at a tattered chunk of the lace robes from that ghost manikin she'd beheaded in her epicurean frenzy, before breaking off its wooden stand to send it plunging down the stairwell. I'd been careful not to give the secret of Clara's earlier visit away, of course; but we'd be watching for that hazard next time.

It had taken Kip and me a while to drag Clara back out, though she'd been more cooperative this time than she had the last, probably knowing how the drill went by now. And then a little more time to find and herd her kids back into their pen too. Happily, the guest room doors had all been closed for the party, and Jen had used more of our cleaning supplies to mop up the messes Clara had left behind her here and there—which had the upside of disguising any signs of her last visit that might still be detectable in the finish of our hardwood floors.

As our guests finally got up to make their goodnights and head up to their rooms, Jen, Kip and I walked, yawning, back into the kitchen to get as much cleanup done as we could before falling into bed as well.

When we were all in there with the doors closed and the water running, I said, "So, do you think we should give them discounts on this stay, or just refund their money for tonight?"

"Are you crazy?" asked Jen. "You heard them laughing out there. They think this just makes the whole thing a better story! And it'll get even more hilarious as they keep telling it. Ka-ching, ka-ching, hon!" She looked over at me with an avaricious grin. "We'll give them a coupon for twenty-five percent off their next visit. That's what we'll do. Because they will so be coming back now. These are the kind of happy accidents that we can build a business around!" She went back to her dishes with a dreamy look. "If only there were some way we could stage that sort of thing every Halloween. We'd have to expand the building!"

<<<>>>

RECIPES

Jen's Newest Cocktail with the Dumb Name

This can be scaled up or down depending on how many servings you need, so only proportions are given, not specific amounts. If you're making one drink, start with one ounce of gin, and calculate from there.

Ingredients:

1 gin
½ sage liquor
¼ lavender shrub
¼ St.-Germain
1 sparkling water
Heavy dash herbal bitters

To Prepare:

Combine all ingredients in a cocktail shaker with plenty of ice. Shake gently, then serve in a martini glass garnished with a fresh basil leaf wrapped around a juniper berry.

French Toast Casserole

A great "set and forget" breakfast option, for the busy innkeeper who needs dishes that can be prepared ahead, and that can take care of themselves in the oven while she's out taking care of the guests.

This is another dish without specific quantities or measurements, which seems to be a thing with Jen. It grew out of her desire to make French toast and sausage for a crowd, while having everything be ready at the same time, and with no need to stand over a hot griddle.

Ingredients:

1 loaf of nice sourdough-style bread (Jen likes a round salted rosemary loaf, from Island Market or Trader Joe's)
12-18 eggs (depending on how big the loaf of bread is)
Milk and/or half-and-half
Vanilla, and other seasonings you like in French toast (cinnamon, nutmeg, etc.)
Chopped fresh rosemary, if you didn't use rosemary bread
Pre-cooked sausages—Jen uses Aidell's chicken-apple, but any sausage should work, including vegetarian if that's your jam

To Prepare:

Cut the bread into cubes and place in a large baking dish, 9x13 or bigger. Cube the sausages as well and stir them in. Jen didn't give an amount here because it's up to you, but she likes them to feel like an ingredient and not just a seasoning.

Beat the eggs with enough milk and/or half-and-half to make it fairly milky, and add your vanilla and other seasonings. Pour this over the bread-sausage mixture, making sure all the bread cubes are coated. It is at this point in the preparation that Jen usually finds herself breaking four to six more eggs because she couldn't believe it was really going to use that many.

Cover the dish in foil and refrigerate overnight.

Remove the dish 30 or so minutes before baking, or it will take FOREVER and everyone will drink too much coffee and get hangry. Bake, uncovered, at least 45 minutes at 350 degrees F., maybe even an hour, until a knife inserted in the middle comes out clean, and the top and edges brown a bit. Serve with heated maple syrup at the table, along with fruit, grapefruit mimosas, and/or whatever else makes it feel like "fancy breakfast at a B&B" in your house.

Salmon-Rice-Miso Bowls

Nourishing, warming, and oh-so-delicious. Easy, too. This is for two servings, and can be scaled up.

Ingredients:
2 thin boneless salmon filets (about 8 ounces total)
Salt
Toasted sesame oil
3 cups water
5-6 small mushrooms (brown or white), thinly sliced
2 scallions, white and green parts separated from dark green, thinly sliced
1 tablespoon light miso, plus more to taste
Pinch or two of dried seaweed, such as Undaria pinnatifida
1 tablespoon soy sauce
1 teaspoon mirin
2 cups cooked white rice

For dressing the bowls: more toasted sesame oil; Japanese-style seasoning such as Katsuo Mirin Furikake and/or Nori Kimo Furikake

To Prepare:
Pat the salmon filets dry and season them lightly with salt.

In a medium saucepan, combine the water, mushrooms, and the white and light green scallion slices. Bring to a boil, then reduce the heat to low. Ladle about a cup of the broth into a small bowl and whisk in the miso, then stir this back into the pot. Taste, and add more miso if desired. Add the dried seaweed, stir, then cover and keep warm over very low heat while you cook the salmon.

Heat a nonstick skillet on high, add sesame oil when hot, then lay the fish fillets in the pan, skin side down. Cook about three minutes, then turn and cook about two minutes more. You don't want it overcooked, but it should be done enough inside to flake with a fork, because that's the next thing you're going to do: remove the salmon from the pan and break it into flakes.

Turn off the broth and add the soy sauce and mirin, giving it a good stir.

To serve, portion the rice into two bowls. Top each rice bowl with 1½ cups of broth, half of the flaked fish, a drizzle of sesame oil, a sprinkling of the Furikake seasoning(s), and the dark green scallion slices. Serve with soup spoons and chopsticks.

Rhubarb Compote with Earl Grey Tea, Cardamom, and Orange Zest

This stuff is so versatile. It's good with ice cream, whipped cream, or fresh ricotta; it can go over yogurt, shortcake, or pound cake; on pancakes or with scones—and that's just the sweet options. It's delicious with most any kind of meat; Jen serves it at breakfast over smoked pork chops, though it would be equally fine with most chicken dishes, or spread over roast pork tenderloin. Is there *anything* it can't do?

Jen thanks her buddy Jan Hersey for this amazing concoction!

Ingredients:

4 pounds rhubarb, cut into 1-inch pieces
2 pounds tart apples, peeled and cut into 1-inch chunks
2½ cups white sugar
5½ tablespoons lemon juice
Seeds only from 4 green cardamom pods, crushed well with mortar & pestle
6 Earl Grey teabags, steeped in 2½ cups of just-boiled water for three minutes, then cooled; tea should be dark and rich in color
Zest from 5-6 oranges

To Prepare:

Place chopped fruit into a large, heavy-bottomed pot. Add lemon juice, sugar, crushed cardamom seeds, and brewed tea; toss to mix. Stew gently on stovetop for 30-50 minutes, stirring regularly, until bubbling and thickened. Stir in orange zest.

Allow to cool; preserve in small containers in the freezer, or you could can it if you had the patience for such things.

ACKNOWLEDGMENTS

Quite a crowd helped Laura Gayle write this book! Starting, as ever, with the very real authors who comprise the still-imaginary Laura: Shannon Page and Karen G. Berry—who are now joined by Mark J. Ferrari. "Team Laura Gayle" has expanded, and we couldn't be happier about that fact.

The authors send out a *huge* thank-you to Holly King at the Orcas Island Library for her enthusiastic research assistance, and also to Meryl and her team at the Orcas Island Historical Museum, for the many, many documents, books, and newspapers they dug up for us and so generously shared.

Mandy Troxel and Amy Lum, at Lum Farm, cheerfully spent a delightful evening in their goat barn with us answering every goat-related question we had—and about a thousand other questions we hadn't known to ask. (Maybe the wine helped?) Any erroneous goat facts still in the book are the fault of the authors—either accidentally or intentionally, because we thought it made the story better.

Lisa Motherwell provided a wealth of inside information on the vagaries of life on Lopez Island. Bogdan and Carol Kulminski were yet again a font of information, this time about running a bed-and-breakfast. Jan Hersey provided the delicious rhubarb compote recipe. And we would like to thank San Juan County Sheriff Eric Peter, for stepping in to give us his advice and assistance, now that Sergeant Herb Crowe has (alas!) retired.

Tide Pool Coffeehouse provided a cozy place to write for our regular Friday morning crew—thank you for all the delicious drinks and pastries! And the memories, for in another "alas," Tide Pool is now no more.

Books are nothing without bookstores, and this time we would like to extend our deep and abiding gratitude to *four* stores: our beloved Darvill's here on Orcas Island, where Jenny, Kelly, Becky, and the rest of the team have been tireless promoters of our mysteries for years now; Watermark Book Company in Anacortes, for enthusiastically jumping at the chance to carry our books—and who keep asking for more of them; Griffin Bay Bookstore in Friday Harbor, our newest venue, who are already just as excited about the books as the other stores; and the Lopez Bookshop, where we found copies of our books already on the shelves the first time we stopped in!

The weekly "Sheriff's Report" in *theOrcasonian* online newspaper is a treasure, an amazing resource, and a constant delight. We are only sorry we couldn't find a way to work this gem into the story: "The deputy encouraged the sheep to go home by waving his arms around." (August 18, 2023)

Sherwood Smith provided invaluable feedback that helped to improve this book immensely—in the nick of time.

And a very special thank-you to Mark and Lori—who know why.

Photographs courtesy Mark J. Ferrari

ABOUT THE AUTHORS

Laura Gayle began life as the nom de plume of two friends who love to collaborate, **Shannon Page** and **Karen G. Berry**. In 2023, with *Orcas Afterlife*, **Mark J. Ferrari** joined the writing team, after editing the earlier volumes for some years before, while Karen is taking a break from the project.

Shannon Page was born on Halloween night and raised without television on a back-to-the-land commune in northern California. She writes fantasy, mystery, science fiction, and personal essays, and she also loves to edit anthologies. Shannon is a longtime yoga practitioner, has no tattoos, and lives on lovely, remote Orcas Island, Washington, with her husband, author and illustrator Mark Ferrari. Visit her at www.shannonpage.net.

Karen G. Berry has lived in or near Portland, Oregon, for forty years, but remains solidly Midwestern in outlook. She has one wonderful husband, three wonderful daughters, two wonderful grandsons, and several thousand books. A marketing writer by day, Karen is a prize-winning poet and has published seven novels and one nonfiction book, *Shopping at the Used Man Store*. As a committed underachiever, Karen finds all of this fairly amazing. Visit her at www.karengberry.mywriting.network/.

Mark J. Ferrari has been a commercial genre illustrator since 1987. His first fantasy novel, *The Book of Joby*, was published by Tor in 2007, honored as a Booksense Pick, made Booklist's "Top Ten" for science fiction/fantasy in 2008, and was chosen as a finalist for the Endeavour Award. He currently resides with his wife, Shannon Page, on Orcas Island, Washington, where he is a committed—one might even say obsessive—gardener. More info on his art and writing can be found at www.markferrari.com.

Made in the USA
Monee, IL
13 March 2025